The White Flag

By

Gene Stratton-Porter

The Echo Library 2019

Published by

The Echo Library

Echo Library
Unit 22
Horcott Industrial Estate
Horcott Road
Fairford
Glos. GL7 4BX

www.echo-library.com

Please report serious faults in the text to complaints@echo-library.com

ISBN   978-1-40682-243-4

THE WHITE FLAG

BY

GENE STRATTON-PORTER

FRONTISPIECE
BY
LESTER RALPH

S. B. GUNDY   TORONTO
DOUBLEDAY, PAGE & COMPANY
GARDEN CITY   NEW YORK

1923

First Edition

TO
THE BOYS AND GIRLS "GROWN TALL"
WITH WHOM, IN CHILDHOOD,
I PASSED UNDER
THE WHITE FLAG

BOOKS BY GENE STRATTON-PORTER

Nature

The Song of the Cardinal
Homing With the Birds
Birds of the Bible
Music of the Wild
Friends in Feathers
Moths of the Limberlost
Morning Face

Novels

Freckles
At the Foot of the Rainbow
A Girl of the Limberlost
The Harvester
Laddie
Michael O'Halloran
A Daughter of the Land
Her Father's Daughter
The White Flag

Poetry

The Fire Bird

"What does my heart know of the heart of a child beating beneath it?"

CONTENTS

LIST OF CHARACTERS

- MAHALA SPELLMAN, the Model Child
- MAHLON SPELLMAN, the Dry-goods Merchant
- ELIZABETH SPELLMAN, a Fine Lady
- MARTIN MORELAND, the Harvester of Riches
- MRS. MARTIN MORELAND, a Bewildered Wife
- MARTIN MORELAND, Junior, a Chip from the Paternal Block
- BECKY SAMPSON, Bearer of the White Flag
- EDITH WILLIAMS, the Child of Discontent
- MARCIA PETERS, the Bearer of Chains
- JASON PETERS, Walking the Road
- MEHITABLE ASHCROFT, Teacher of Room Five
- PETER POTTER, the Village Grocer
- ELLEN FORD, a Wild Rose
- JEMIMA DAVIS, a Friend in Need
- NANCY BODKIN, Who Believed in Face Values

Remainder of characters:

School children, villagers, a minister, a doctor, a lawyer, etc.

THE WHITE FLAG

CHAPTER I

"He That Was Cold and Hungry"

Elizabeth Spellman opened her eyes, turned on her pillow, and minutely studied the face of her sleeping husband. To her, Mahlon Spellman was not a vain, pompous, erratic little man of fifty. When she looked at him she saw the man who had courted her, of whose moral and mental attainments she had been so sure. She had visioned him as a future deacon of the Methodist Church, a prominent member of the School Board and the city council, and her vision had materialized; reality had been better than the Dream. He was Chairman of the County Republican Committee, frequently a delegate to state conventions, the Methodist Sunday School Superintendent, the richest dry-goods merchant of the town. As she studied his features that particular September morning, she choked down a rising flutter of satisfaction. Mahlon, as he lay there, represented success, influence, wealth. He slept as fastidiously as he walked abroad; he seemed conscious of his dignity and pride even as he lay unconscious.

Her home, of which she was inordinately proud, was his gift to her. The very satisfactory life she was living was possible because she was under the shelter of his sufficient hands. The child she mothered was the offspring of her love for him. She did not know that the elements in him which she mentally labelled "neat" and "thorough," were denominated "fussy" by his neighbours. She lauded the scrupulous cleanliness and precision which kept him constantly flicking invisible dust from his sleeve and straightening his tie. To her this only meant that personally he was as scrupulous as she was herself; to her these traits never revealed the truth that Mahlon was an egoist, who kept himself constantly foremost in his own mind, a man selfish to a degree that would have been unendurable had not his selfishness encompassed his pride in her, their child, and their home as the fulfilment of one branch of his personality. His craze for power she denominated laudable ambition. The position in which he was able to place her socially, she accepted as her due; she spent her days prettifying her really beautiful home, doing everything in her power to pamper Mahlon physically, to uphold and further his ambitions, because she was comfortably certain that there was no eminence to which she could boost him that she might not share in proud security with him. Among the demands of society, her position as a Colonial Dame, a pillar of the Church, leader of social activities, charities, and the excruciating exactions she bestowed upon the office of motherhood, she was a busy person.

At that minute she sighed with satisfaction, thinking of her wonderful achievement in marrying Mahlon Spellman; but with the thought came the memory of the duties that such a marvellous alliance entailed. At the present minute it was her duty to slip from their bed so quietly that Mahlon, the bread winner, the bearer of large gifts, the roof of the house, might have a few minutes more sleep. She slipped her feet into her bedroom shoes, tiptoed to the closet, and gathering up her clothing, stole softly to her one of the three bathrooms of the town, where, with exacting care, she made her toilet for the morning, aided by the magnificence of a tin tub and a marble bowl that absorbed stains with disconcerting ease.

She glanced from the window to watch the small town of Ashwater waking to the dawn of the first Monday of September. It lay among the hills and valleys of rolling country. A river wound around it following a leisurely course toward the sea. Ashwater was one of the oldest towns of the state, peopled by self-respecting merchants, professional men who took time to follow the ramifications of their business in a deliberate manner, and retired farmers who were enjoying, in late life, the luxury of being in close touch with social, political, and religious activities.

It was early morning. The sun was slanting across the hills, showing the country brilliant in autumnal foliage. A blood-red maple lifted like a flame in her line of vision, and close to it was the tapestry of buckeye and the rich brown of oak. The big white colonial house in which she, the wife of the wealthy dry-goods merchant, lived, was surrounded with gorgeous colour from every shrub, bush, and tree that would endure the rigours of winter. She looked approvingly on the white picket fence that shut off her small world from the worlds of her less fortunate neighbours. She approved of the screening evergreens that made homing places for the birds, and the gorgeous beds of chrysanthemums brocading the smooth turf of the lawn. Her view from the bathroom window was restricted, but mentally she envisaged her surroundings and knew that they made a picture which would indicate to any passer-by that here was a home of wealth and comfort. She was certain that any one going by would think it a home of happiness.

She stood a minute before the mirror, studying her pretty little face. She was nearly twenty years younger than her husband, an exacting woman, perfectly capable of muttering "prunes and prisms" by the hour for the shaping of her mouth as she moved about her occupation of being her husband's wife, her daughter's mother, her own social Influence. Elizabeth Spellman believed in Influence. It was her duty to set a shining example. She had no vision of a modest candle—when she let her light "so shine" she meant it to be a headlight, and of no mean proportions at that. As she patted her hair in place, set the bow at her throat with exact precision, she smiled with pleasure over the picture her mirror held facing her. But Elizabeth Spellman was a woman who firmly held duty above pleasure, or rather, who found her greatest pleasure in her personal conception of her duty; so she turned from the mirror, gathered up her belongings, and leaving everything in place, went hurriedly down the hall. She softly opened a white door and her eyes instantly sought a small bed, standing in a room made dainty with pale pinks and blues. She hurried to the bed, and bending, laid her hand upon the little girl sleeping there.

11

"Mahala," she said softly, "you must wake up now, dear. It's the first day of school, you know, and you mustn't spoil a year, that I hope will be extremely beneficial to you, by being late. And certainly you must not slight your other duties in order to be on time."

Elizabeth Spellman said this because she was the kind of woman who would say exactly this without the slightest regard as to whether her little daughter were sufficiently awake either to hear or to understand it. She said it in order to give herself the satisfaction of knowing that in case Mahala did hear any part of it she would have got the right impression. She believed in impressions quite as firmly as she believed in influence—possibly even more strongly—for if one did not make a good impression, she would lose her influence, or, fatal thing! have none to lose. Elizabeth Spellman was a firm believer in the fact that, if the twig is bent in the proper direction, the tree will be inclined in the right manner.

Mahala opened her eyes and looked at her mother. Then she shut them and tried to decide how long she might lie still before she made a move to get up. She discovered that there was no time to waste that morning. A firm hand turned back the covers and gripped her shoulder. So she mustered a smile, swung her feet to the floor, and still half asleep, stumbled down the hall before her mother.

Her bath thoroughly awakened her. She was old enough to have been of some help to herself, but helping herself with her toilet was not a point stressed by her mother, who took particular pride and pleasure in bathing the exquisitely shaped little body under her hands. She examined the ears particularly. She made sure there were no obtrusive "boos" disfiguring the small nose by the use of a handkerchief stretched over a hairpin. Mahala's hair curled naturally around her face. Her mother assisted the long heavy back hair occasionally. She now unwound the golden curls from their papers and brushed them into place with exquisite precision. Every small undergarment she put upon the child was of fine material, hand made, elaborately trimmed. A mirror was lifted from the closet and set upon the floor before which Mahala had to stand and see that her stocking seams were straight in the back. The ruffles of her pantalettes were carefully fluffed; her slippers were securely buttoned. Her petticoats and her wide-skirted dress were in the height of style and of expensive material. The finishing touch to her toilet was a white apron having a full skirt, and wide shoulder pieces meeting at the band, then curving to form deep pockets. From an open drawer a handkerchief was taken from a box and carefully scented.

"Please, Mother, put some on me," begged Mahala.

Elizabeth Spellman laughed softly. She tipped the contents of the bottle against the glass stopper which she touched in several spots on the golden curls and over the shoulders.

"My little girl likes to be sweet like a flower, doesn't she?" she asked.

And the child answered primly: "Yes, Mama, so that Papa will be pleased with me."

Whereupon her mother immediately kissed her and commended her for thinking of anything that would be a pleasure to her father.

As she gathered up Mahala's nightdress and turned the bed to air, she said to the child: "Now run, dear, and waken your father, but remember you must not muss yourself or spend too much time."

Mahala hurried down the hall, softly opened the door to her parents' bedroom, and poised on her tiptoes. Her heart was racing. Her eyes were big pools having dancing lights. Her muscles cried for exercise. She wanted to make a flying leap and land on the bed, but she knew what her reception would be if she did; so she crossed the room very primly and laid a soft hand on her father's face.

"Papa, dear," she said, "wake up! School begins this morning and you won't be in time to have breakfast with me unless you hurry."

She leaned over and kissed him and patted his face, but, when he reached up and drew her down in his arms, she was instantly on the defensive.

"Papa, be careful!" she cautioned. "Mother has my curls made and I am all dressed for school. She wouldn't like it if you were to muss me."

Instantly Mahlon's arms relaxed.

"No, she wouldn't like it," he said, "and neither would I. Give Papa another kiss and run to your music, like a little lady."

So Mahala hurried back to her room, where she took in her arms a beautiful wax doll, almost as large as herself, carefully carrying it down the stairs and into the living room. With her keen eyes she surveyed this familiar place, but the same stiffly starched lace curtains depended from the fringed lambrequins, the same gorgeous flowers spread among the scrolls of the Brussels carpet, the same mahogany chairs stood, each in its exact spot, each picture covered its size in the original freshness of the wall paper. She could not see a thing to arrest or interest her, so she proceeded to the parlour, where the big square piano stood among the real treasures of the house: rosewood sofa and chairs, a parlour table having leaves, cabinets for books and bric-a-brac, a loaded what-not, and the roses of the velvet carpet so big and so bright that it was a naughty trick of Mahala to pretend she stubbed her toes and stumbled over them. Here the lace curtains fell from velvet draperies and spread widely on the floor; a china dog guarded glass-encased hair flowers on the mantel, while the morning-glories climbing up the wall paper must have sprung from the same exuberant soil that furnished the originals of the carpet roses.

Mahala swept this room also with a bird-alert glance and seeing not the change of a fleck of dust anywhere, set Belinda on a chair beside the piano stool and surveyed her minutely.

"Belinda, can't you sit like a little lady?" she said reprovingly. "Two curls over each shoulder, the rest down your back; heels touching, toes out. If I got to wear a silk dress every day, let me tell you, I'd swish it properly."

She spread the silken skirts, fixed the curls, and placed a hymn book in the hands of the doll. Carefully spreading her own skirts, she climbed to the piano stool. Hearing her mother's step on the stairs, in a sweet little voice she began singing, to her own accompaniment: "I thank thee, Father, for the light." Then she slid from the stool, exchanged the hymn book in the doll's lap for a piece of sheet music, and climbing back, began practising her lesson. She worked with one eye on the door of the living room and the other on the keyboard. Every time her mother's back was turned, she stuck her feet straight out, and with propulsion attained by setting her hands against the piano, whirled in a circle on the stool, first to the left until the stool was too low, and then to the right until the stool was the required height. She was so dexterous at this that she could accomplish one revolution between the measures of the music in places where a rest occurred. Her face was sparkling with suppressed laughter whenever she feelingly struck a chord and then accomplished a revolution before catching the next note and continuing her exercise. But she was quite serious, seemingly intent upon her work, when her mother stepped to the door to announce: "Your time is up, Mahala. You have still a few minutes remaining that you might profitably spend with your needle."

Mahala slipped to the floor, put away her music and Belinda's, and going to the living room, took from a cupboard a small sewing basket. She sat down in a rocking chair beside the window, placing the doll in a chair near her. She put a piece of sewing into her hands and gravely reproved her for careless work. Her own fingers were weaving a needle in and out, executing a design in cross stitch in gaudy colours on a piece of cardboard. When her mother was within hearing she leaned toward the doll and said solicitously: "Now be careful, my dear child. You never will be a perfect lady unless you learn to take your stitches evenly. No lady makes a crooked seam."

But, when her mother stepped to the adjoining dining room, with her brows drawn together she said sternly to the doll: "Belinda, if you don't sit up straight and make your stitches even, I'll slap you to pieces. You needn't look as meek as a mouse. I shall do it for your own good; although, of course, it will hurt me more than it does you."

When the breakfast bell rang, Mahala folded her sewing neatly, returned to the basket the piece she had given Belinda, put the basket where it belonged, and the doll on the sofa, and then walked to the dining-room door. She held her apron wide at each side and made a low formal courtesy to each of her parents exactly as if she had not seen them before that morning.

Primly she said: "Good morning, Papa dear. Good morning, dear Mama. I hope you slept well during the night."

This drilling Elizabeth Spellman insisted upon because she considered it very pretty when there were guests in the house. When there were not, she thought it better to have it rehearsed in order that it should become habitual.

When they were seated at the table Mrs. Spellman and Mahala bowed their heads while Mr. Spellman addressed the Lord in a tone which was meant to contain a shade more deference than he would have tried to put into addressing the President or a Senator. He thanked the Lord for the food that was set before them, asked that it might be blessed to their good, prayed that all of them might execute the duties of the day faithfully, and returned all of their thanks for the blessing they were experiencing. Then they ate the food for which they had given thanks because it was very good food. They had every reason to be thankful for such cooking as Jemima Davis had accomplished in their kitchen during all the years of their wedded life.

It was just as Mr. Spellman was buttering his fourth pancake that the voice of Jemima Davis arose in the regions of the back porch in a shrill shriek. Mahala laid down her fork and stared with wide, expectant eyes. Mrs. Spellman started to rise from her chair. Mr. Spellman pushed back his own chair and looked at his wife.

"Now, now," he said admonishingly, "be calm. You are familiar with Jemima's divagations."

Another shriek, wilder than the first, broke upon them.

"I will attend to this myself," said Mr. Spellman.

Arising, he vanished in the direction of the kitchen. Finding that room empty, he proceeded to the back porch and there, at the corner of the house, he saw Jemima tugging at the rear anatomy of Jimmy Price. Jimmy Price was the village handy-man. His task that morning was to mow the Spellman lawn and trim the grass around the trees. Just why he should have been standing on his head in the rain barrel was a question Mahlon Spellman did not wait to ask until he had upset the barrel and allowed Jimmy the privilege of backing out. When Jimmy lifted his drenched tow head and sallow, freckled face, there was no need for explanation. In one hand he grasped a pair of sheep shears which he used to clip the grass around the snowball and lilac bushes. Exactly why or how he had lost them in the barrel was not a matter of concern to his employer. At the precise minute that Jimmy backed from the barrel, soaked and spluttering, Mahlon was felicitating himself upon the presence of mind which had kept his wife and daughter from witnessing a sight so ludicrous. At the same time he realized that he could not so easily control the neighbours and the street. Mahlon felt like a fool to be seen in proximity to such a ridiculous sight, and he hated feeling like a fool more than almost any other calamity that could possibly overtake him. In a voice highly touched with exasperation he cried: "James Price, is it quite impossible for you to perform your work without having some sort of fool accident or doing some ludicrous thing every fifteen minutes? Are you a man or a monkey? You don't seem happy unless you are making a back-alley spectacle of yourself,"—"and me," Mahlon added in his consciousness.

Jimmy wiped the muck of the barrel bottom and the water from his face, and looked at his employer.

"Yes, sir. Thank you, sir," he said humbly.

"I wonder what for," muttered Mahlon Spellman, and turning, marched back to the dining room where he resumed his place. As Mahlon went, Jimmy squared his shoulders, smoothed his dripping hair, set in place a tie he was not wearing, and flipped a very real bit of soil from his sleeve in Mr. Spellman's best manner.

Jemima launched the back porch broom at Jimmy's head and he dodged it expertly.

"You poor bumpkin, you," she cried. "Don't you dare be aping the master!"

"But I was merely following the natural impulses of a gentleman," said Jimmy, as he used the sheep shears to flirt slime from his sleeves, while Jemima suddenly retreated, but not before Jimmy in deep satisfaction noted her heaving shoulders.

Mrs. Spellman opened her lips and an inquisitive little "What——?" escaped therefrom.

"Nothing of the slightest importance, my dear," said Mr. Spellman, waving his hand to indicate that the matter was of such slight moment that it might be carried away in the wake of the gesture without consuming any of their valuable time for its consideration.

Mrs. Spellman bowed her head in acceptance of her husband's ultimatum. Mahala distinctly pouted. In the back of her small head she knew that her mother would leave the breakfast table and go immediately to the kitchen for information. She would be sent to school and might never learn why Jemima had screamed so wholeheartedly. It was not fair; but then, Mahala reflected, there were few things that were fair where young people were concerned. That being the case, she lingered at the table, watched her chance, and slipped to the kitchen.

"Jemima, what made you scream so?" she whispered as she watched the doorway behind her.

Jemima wiped the batter from the pancake spoon with expert finger: "That half-wit Jim Price laid the sheep shears on the rain barrel," she said scornfully. "Of course they fell in and of course he went in head first when he tried to get them out!"

Mahala clapped her hands over her mouth and danced until her curls flew.

"Careful, honey, careful," whispered Jemima.

Instantly Mahala became a demure little maiden again. Her glance swept the kitchen as it had the other rooms and rested on a basket of clothes standing ready for the washerwoman. She backed to the table, asking questions of Jemima, snatched up a fine big apple, and with a swallow-swift dip, tucked it under the sheet covering the basket at the handle, covered to be sure, yet visibly there to the experienced eye.

"Mahala, what are you doing?" asked her mother at the door.

Mahala's swift glance took in her nightdress in her mother's hands. She lifted her face to Jemima: "Thank you for my good breakfast," she said. "Allow me, Mama!" She took the nightdress from her mother's hands, tucked it under the sheet at the handle opposite the apple, and ran after her books.

"Jemima, did you ever see such a darling, thoughtful child?" asked Elizabeth Spellman, and Jemima answered wholeheartedly: "I never did! God bless her!"

Mahala watched the filling of her book satchel with an occasional anxious glance toward the kitchen, but nothing happened; the apple had not been discovered. With the satchel strap over her shoulder and a bottle of ink in her hand, accompanied by her mother, Mahala went down the front walk. Mrs. Spellman opened the gate for her, kissed her good-bye, and stood waiting until she should turn to look back and throw a last kiss from the corner, the rounding of which carried her from sight.

All the neighbours were familiar with this proceeding. They were familiar with the demure step and studied grace with which Mahala turned the corner and threw back the kiss; and those whose range of vision covered the corner were also familiar with the wild leap for freedom with which the child flew down the street, the corner having been accomplished with due decorum. She sped up the steps of an attractive home, rang the bell and waited for a dark, lean little girl of her own age, dressed quite as carefully as she, to join her on their way to school.

The contrast between the children was very marked. Edith Williams was a sallow little creature, badly spoiled in the home of the leading hardware merchant whose only brother had died and left his child to her uncle's care. She was not attractive. She was full of complaining and fault-finding. Her little heart bore a grudge against the world because she had not health and strength with which to enjoy the money left by her father, which her uncle would have allowed her to use had she not been naturally of a saving disposition.

It was a strange thing that children so different should have been friends. It is quite possible that their companionship was not due to natural selection, but to the fact that they lived near each other, that they constantly met going in the same direction to church, to school, and to entertainments, and that they had been sent to play together all their lives. This morning they kissed, and with their arms locked, started on their way to school.

Two blocks down the street they passed a big brick house surrounded by a thick hedge of evergreen trees inside a high iron fence having heavy, ornate gates. There were a few large trees scattered over the lawn and a few flowering bushes, while among them stood cast-iron dogs, deer, and lions. This was the home of Martin Moreland, the wealthiest man in the county, the president and the chief stockholder of the bank, a man whose real-estate and financial operations scattered over several adjoining counties.

While Mrs. Spellman had been dressing her little girl for school, Mrs. Moreland had been trying to accomplish the same feat with her only son; but her efforts had vastly different results. Junior was a handsome boy of eleven, with a good mind. His mother was trying to rear him properly. His father was ostensibly trying to do the same thing, but in his secret heart he wanted his son to be the successor not only to his business but also to his methods of doing business.

Mr. Moreland was a man of forty, tall and slender, having a fair complexion, light hair, and a fine, athletic figure. His eyes were small, deep-set, and penetrating, a baffling pair of eyes with which to deal. They looked straight in the face every one with whom he talked and reinforced a voice of persuasive import. But no man or woman ever had been able to see the depths of the eyes of Martin Moreland, and no man or woman ever had been perfectly sure that what his persuasive voice said was precisely the thing that he meant.

Mrs. Moreland was five years older than her husband, and it was understood in the town that he had married her because of her large inheritance from her father. She tried to be a good wife, a good mother, neighbour, and friend. She tried with all her might to love and to believe in her husband, and yet almost every day she noted some tendency in him that bred in her heart a vague fear and uncertainty, and years of this had made the big, raw-boned, dark-haired, dark-eyed woman into a creature of timid approaches, of hesitation. Sometimes there was almost fear in her eyes when she looked at Martin Moreland.

This morning she had tried repeatedly to awaken her son. Over and over she called to him: "Junior, you must get up and dress! Don't you remember that school begins to-day? You mustn't be late. It would be too bad to begin a new year by being tardy."

From a near-by room Martin Moreland listened with a slight sneer on his handsome face. When his wife left the boy's room in search of some article of clothing, he stepped to the side of the bed, shook Junior until he knew that the boy was awake, and then slid a shining dollar into his hand.

"Get up and put on your fine new suit," he said. "You'll cut a pretty figure being late for school. The son of the richest man in town should be first. He should show the other children that he is their natural leader. Come now, stir yourself."

Junior immediately slid out of bed and began putting on the clothing his mother had laid out for him, slipping the money into a pocket before she saw it. As he dressed, an expression of discontent settled on his handsome young face. Everything in his home was sombre, substantial, and very expensive, but he knew that it was not a happy home. At the last minute he entered the dining room, wearing a shirt of ruffled lawn, long trousers, and a blouse of dark blue velvet with a flowing tie of dark blue lined with red. His wavy black hair was like his mother's, so were his dark eyes, but his face was shaped very much on the lines of his father's. He dropped to his chair and looked at the table with eyes of disapproval.

"Why can't we ever have something fit to eat?" he asked.

"That is exactly what I am wondering," added his father.

Mrs. Moreland surveyed the table critically.

"Why, what is the trouble?" she asked anxiously. "Everything seems to be here. The food looks all right. How can you tell that it doesn't suit you, when you haven't even tasted it?"

"I am going on the supposition," said the elder Moreland, "that Hannah hasn't greatly changed since supper last night, which wasn't fit for a dog."

"Then I'd better discharge her at once, and try to find some one else," said Mrs. Moreland with unexpected spirit.

In his own way the banker retreated.

"What good would that do?" he asked shortly. "You would let the next woman you hire spoil things exactly the same way you have Hannah. We might as well go on eating the stuff she gives us as to have somebody else do the same thing."

Then he proceeded to eat heartily of the food that was set before him. But Junior fidgeted in his chair, pushed back his plate, and refused to eat anything until the clanging of the first bell on the school house reached his ears. Then he jumped up, and, running into the hall, snatched his cap from the rack and clapped it on the back of his head. He stood hesitating a second, then, returning to the dining room, caught up all the food he could carry in his hands, rushing from the house without taking the satchel of books his mother had ready for him.

A minute later Mrs. Moreland saw them and hurried after him. He turned at her call, but he would not stop. He went on down the street munching the food he carried, while she stood looking after him, unconsciously shaking her head. In her heart, depression and foreboding almost equalled any hope she had concerning him, yet it was on hope for him that she lived.

Earlier than any of these households, Marcia Peters opened a door that led to a garret of her small house and called: "Jason!" As she stood waiting to hear the sound of a voice that would indicate that the lad was awake, her hand rested against the door casing in a position of unconscious grace. She was unusually tall for a woman, her clothing so careless as completely to conceal her figure. Her hair was drawn straight back and wadded in a tight knot on the top of her head at the most disfiguring angle possible. She did expert laundry work and mending for a living. Her home was a tiny house, owned by the banker, on the outskirts of town. She made no friends and very seldom appeared on the streets.

"Jason!" she repeated sharply, and immediately thereafter she heard the boy's feet on the floor. A few minutes later he came hurrying down the stairway on the run. If he had stopped to think of it, he might have realized that most of his life he had been on the run. He ran all over town, collecting and delivering Marcia's work. Between times he ran errands for other people for the nickels and dimes that they paid him. Mostly he was late and ran to school. This continuous running on scant fare kept him pale and lean, but the exercise developed muscle, the strength of which was untried, save on work. There was a wistful flash across his thin, homely face at times, and continuous loneliness in his heart. Being the son of the village washerwoman he had always been snubbed and imposed upon by other children, while he never had experienced the slightest degree of mother love from Marcia. He milked the cow, watered and fed the chickens, and then hurried to the Spellman home to bring a big basket of clothes for his mother to wash. With these he stopped at the grocery of Peter Potter, on Market Street, for packages of food which he carried home on the top of his clothes basket, and in handling them his fingers struck the apple. How good of Jemima Davis! She had tucked in a teacake, a cooky, a piece of candy, or an apple for him before. Next time he must surely thank her. The apple was firm and juicy and tasted as if flavoured with flowers. He must surely muster courage the next time to thank her, but not if Mrs. Spellman was in the kitchen. She might not know that Jemima gave away her apples. He had heard her say in a sweetly inflected voice when money was being raised in church for foreign missions: "We will give fifty dollars"; but he had never known her to give an apple to a hungry boy. Then a thought as delicious as the apple struck him. Maybe——just maybe——He did not even dare think it. But she never had joined the other children in trying to shame him. Maybe——

His position in school always had been made difficult and bitter to him by cruel, thoughtless children. It did not help that he had an excellent mind and very nearly always stood at the head of his classes. In school he had a habit of setting his elbows on his desk, grasping his head with a hand on either side, and, leaning forward, he really concentrated. He knew that his only chance lay in thoroughly learning his lessons. He could not be clothed as were the other children, his mother's occupation shut him from social intercourse with them; he was not invited to their little parties and merry-makings. If he ever rose to a position of wealth and distinction like Mr. Moreland or Mr. Spellman, it must be through thorough application during school hours, because he had short time outside. The result was that his nervous fingers, straying through a heavy shock of silky reddish hair slightly wavy, kept it forever standing on end, and this, coupled with his lean, freckled face, made him just a trifle homelier than he would have been had his mother carefully dressed and brushed him as were most of the other children.

In school he allowed himself only one distraction. When he had pored over a book until his brain and body demanded relaxation, then he resorted to the pleasant diversion of studying the loveliest thing Number Five afforded. He studied Mahala Spellman. He was familiar with every flash of her eyes, every light on her face, each curl on her head. When she folded her hands and repeated: "Our Father Which art in Heaven," during morning exercises, she was like an angel straight down from the skies. When she hid behind her Geography and surreptitiously nibbled a bit of candy, or flipped a note to Edith Williams, the laughter on her face, the mischief in her eyes,—Heaven had nothing in the way of angels having eyes to begin to compare with the dancing blue of her eyes,—the varying rose of her cheeks, the adorable sweetness of her little pampered body were irresistible.

Jason hurried into the kitchen. Setting the basket on the floor he snatched off the groceries and laid them on the table and looked around to see if there was anything further he might do that would be of help before he left for school.

"That basket is about twice as heavy as usual," he said, "I am afraid it means a hard day for you."

Marcia Peters looked at the boy and in the deeps of her eyes there was a slight flicker that he did not catch. Neither did he notice that one of her hands slightly lifted and reached in his direction; the flicker was so impalpable, the hand controlled so instantly, that both escaped his notice.

"Elizabeth Spellman entertained the Mite Society last week," she said tersely, "and, of course, she used stacks of embroidered linen and napkins that I must send back in perfect condition. You had better take your books and march to school now, and be mighty careful that you keep at the head of your class. It's your only hope. Never forget that."

Jason crossed the room, and from a shelf in the living room took down a stack of books. He never forgot.

"I'll do my best," he said, "but it isn't as easy as you might think."

"I don't know what I ever did or said," retorted Marcia, "that would give you the impression that I thought anything about life was easy for either one of us. 'Easy' is a funny word to use in connection with this house."

Jason found himself standing straight, gripping his books, and looking into her eyes.

"I'm sorry you have to work so hard," he said.

His glance left the face of the woman before him and ran over the small mean kitchen, the plain, ugly living room. Without seeing it actually, he mentally saw the house outside, and the unprepossessing surroundings. There was a catch in his breath as he again faced Marcia.

"I'll try very hard," he told her, "and maybe it won't be long until I can be a lawyer or a doctor or rent a piece of land, and then I'll take care of you like a real lady."

And again a close observer could have seen a stifled impulse toward the boy on the part of the woman; but it was not of sufficient impetus that the boy caught it, for he hesitated a second longer, then turning on his heel, he ran from the room and made his way down the street, happy to discover that for once he had plenty of time.

So it happened that at the same hour these four children were on the different streets of Ashwater, all headed toward the village school house, a grade and high school combined in one brick building designed for the educational purposes of the town. The day labourers of the village had passed over those same streets earlier that morning. The people that the children met were doctors and lawyers going to their offices, and the housewives of the village, many of them with their baskets on their arms, going to do their morning shopping. Front walks were being swept and rugs shaken from verandas. Walking demurely arm in arm, chattering to each other, went

Mahala Spellman and Edith Williams. At the same time they saw an approaching figure and their arms tightened around each other.

Down the street toward them came a woman that all the village knew and spoke of as Crazy Becky. She wore the usual long, wide skirt of the period, with the neat, closely fitting waist. Her dress was of a delicately flowered white calico carefully made, her face and head covered by a deep sunbonnet well drawn forward. The children were accustomed to having only a peep of her face with its exquisite modelling, delicate colouring, and big, wide-open, blue-gray eyes with long, dark lashes. Sometimes a little person, passing her closely and peering up, caught a gleam of wavy golden hair surrounding her face. Over one shoulder, firmly gripped in her hand, was a long red osier cut from the cornels bordering the river. From it there waved behind her as she walked, a flag of snow-white muslin, neatly tacked to its holder and carefully fringed on the lower edge. In the other hand she carried an empty basket. On her face was a look of expectancy. Always her eyes were flashing everywhere in eager search for something.

Seeing the children coming in all directions, she stationed herself on the steps leading to the lawn of a residence that stood slightly above the street, and facing the passers-by, she began to offer them the privilege of walking under her white flag. In a mellow voice, sweet and pathetic, she began timidly: "Behold the White Flag! Mark the emblem of purity." Then, gathering courage, she cried to those approaching her: "If you know in your hearts that you are clean, pass under the flag with God's blessing. If you know that your hearts are filled with evil, bow your heads, pass under, and the flag will make you clean."

The people passing Rebecca acted in accordance with the dictates of common human nature. Those who knew her, humoured her, and gravely bowing their heads, passed under the flag to her intense delight. Several strangers in the village who had not seen her before and did not understand her pathetic history, stared at her in amazement and hurried past. It had been such a long stretch from the days when John had cried in the wilderness that he was forgotten. As always, there were the coarse and careless who sneered at Rebecca and said rough, provoking things to her. After these she hurled threats of a dreadful nature and the serene beauty of her face was marred with anger for a few moments.

Edith Williams walked slowly and gripped Mahala tighter.

"Let's run across the street," she whispered. "I'm afraid of her."

Mahala tightened her grip on her little friend: "I sha'n't run from her," she said. "I'm not afraid of her. She's never yet hurt anybody who treated her politely. She only fights with naughty boys who tease her. Smile at her and say: 'Good morning! Please, may I pass under your flag?' and she will do anything in the world for you. Mama always walks under Becky's flag. Watch me and do it as I do."

Then Mahala, who had been taught all her life that she was to set an example for the other children of Ashwater, dropped her arm from Edith's, and gripping her ink bottle and her books, bravely concealed the flutter of fear that was in her small heart. She marched up to Rebecca and made her a graceful bow.

"Good morning," she said with suave politeness. "Please, may I pass under your flag this morning?"

Encouraged by the pleased smile Rebecca gave her, she added: "I try very hard to be a good child."

"God has a blessing for all good children. Pass under the flag," said Rebecca. She drew up her form to full height, extended her arm and held the flag in the morning sunlight. There was beauty in her figure, there was beauty in the expression of her perfectly cut face, there was grace in her attitude, and the white banner, hanging from its red support, really appeared like an emblem of purity. A queer thrill surged through Mahala. She bowed her head and with precise steps passed under the flag reverently.

Then Edith Williams repeated her words and walked under the flag also, joining Mahala who was waiting for her. Close behind them came Junior Moreland surrounded by a crowd of boys of whom he was evidently the leader. He was a handsome lad in the morning light, and the beauty of his face and figure was emphasized by his rich suit of velveteen, his broad collar, and his tie of silk. The instant he saw Rebecca he whispered to the other boys: "Oh, look! There's Crazy Becky. Come on, let's have some sport with her."

Immediately the boys rushed in a crowd toward Rebecca, led by Junior. They made faces at her, they tried to snatch the flag which she held at arm's length high above their heads, they tweaked her skirts, and one of them, more daring than the others, slipped behind her and pulled the bonnet from her head by the crown, exposing her face and uncoiling a thick roll of waving gold hair. In an effort to be especially daring, to outdo all the others, Junior sprang high and snatched the flag from her hand in a flying leap. Then he trailed it in the dirt of the gutter. He pulled off his cap, and bowing from the waist before her, he offered the soiled emblem to her. To Rebecca this was the most horrible thing that could happen. Her deranged brain was firm in the conviction that it was her mission in life to keep that flag snow-white, to use it as the emblem of purity. Instantly, a paroxysm of anger shook her. Her face became distorted; she dropped the flag and started after the offender. Junior was afraid of Rebecca in a spasm of anger, because he knew that the strongest man in town could not hold her when she became violent. So he dodged from under her clutching fingers and ran toward the school house.

Mahala and Edith heard the cries and turned just in time to see the white flag polluted.

"Oh, the wicked, wicked boy!" cried Mahala. She dragged Edith out of the way of the oncoming rush, but as she did so, her eyes swiftly searched the board walk over which they had been passing. One of her feet moved forward from beneath the hem of her skirts and a toe tip was firmly set on the end of a loose board. As Junior approached, running swiftly, that board lifted slightly so that he tripped over it and fell sprawling, soiling his hands, his face, and sliding over the walk on his velvet suit. Unable to stop in her rush after him, Rebecca tripped and fell on him in a heap. Jason turned a corner and came in sight, reading one of his books as he walked.

Instantly he understood. He dropped his books on a strip of grass between the fence and the walk, and ran to Rebecca. He helped her to her feet, and knowing her aversion to having her head and face seen by the public, he flew to find and replace her bonnet. He found the white flag and did what he could to straighten and clean it, and, as he put it into her hand, he said to her: "Never mind, you can wash it, you know. You can make it white again in only a little while. If I were you, I'd go back home and wash it right away."

The fact that some one was sympathizing with her, was helping her, comforted Rebecca. She looked at Jason intently.

"You are a good boy," she said. "You have a white soul. I will go back and make the flag white again."

She turned and went back toward the small house where she lived alone on the outskirts of the village.

Junior stood scowling, beating the dust from his clothing. He was jarred and angry. He wanted to reinstate himself, to dominate some one. Jason was his legitimate prey. He advanced, blocking the other boy's way. Jason tried to extricate himself. He wanted to avoid trouble. He put out his hands to keep the boys from pulling at his clothing and tried to back from the crowd. As he did so he found Mahala Spellman by his side. She had been in the same room in school with him ever since they had begun going to school. To his amazement he heard her whisper at his elbow: "Out early and late like you are, I bet you ain't afraid of any boy in the whole world."

Jason stopped suddenly. His figure stiffened and straightened. A queer light passed over his face. At his elbow Mahala whispered: "Carrying those big, heavy baskets like you do, I bet your arms are strongest of any boy in this town."

Jason's fists clenched. His arms flexed involuntarily. At his elbow came the whisper: "Remember the bugs!"

Jason's mind flew to a poem in one of the school readers. Into his brain rushed the lines:

> Three little bugs in a basket,
> And hardly room for two—

and again, with the kaleidoscopic rush of memory:

> Then he that was cold and hungry,
> Strength from his weakness drew,

He pulled the rugs from the other bugs
And he killed them and ate them, too.

The son of the wealthiest man in town was standing before him, tweaking his coat, tormenting him. Suddenly Jason doubled his fists and struck his hardest blow. Junior fell back among the other boys. They started to close in around Jason, but they found a valiant figure blocking their way. With her arms stretched wide, stood Mahala. Her eyes were dark and her voice was high and shrill.

"Now you just keep back, you mean boys!" she screamed. "You just keep out of this! Junior started this, you just let him and Jason fight it out!"

Because there is a thing in spirit, and a power in right and fair play that a mob always feels, silent and acquiescing, the other children stepped back, and as they did so, the velvet-clad Junior glanced around him. On his face, it could be seen, that he was afraid. In his heart he knew that he was wrong. He was smarting from Jason's blow. He would have liked to run, but he had his position to maintain as the leader of the other boys; he had been their leader all his life. He was accustomed to the admiration and the praise of the girls. There was nothing to do but to prove that he was not a coward; so he drew up and rushed Jason. The two began to fight. Jason was taller, more slender, a few months older, and there was untested strength in his arms, in the back and the legs that had carried heavy baskets of clothing and delivered bundles; the body that had been scantily fed and thoroughly exercised was the tougher, the quicker. Only a few blows proved to Junior that he was soft and practically helpless in Jason's hands. In the delirium of victory, Jason seized the velvet coat at the neck and tore it off Junior. He snatched a ball bat from the hands of one of the boys, and hanging the coat on it, he waved it, crying: "Behold the black flag of riches! Pass under it and be damned!"

Then the children shouted with laughter, which so intoxicated Jason that he went to the further extent of dragging the coat through the gutter exactly as Junior had dragged the white flag. He threw the soiled, rumpled thing at Junior's feet. At the wildness of his daring, the children stood hushed and silent. Then, suddenly, they pretended to threaten Jason, but it was evident to him that they were delighted, that they were only trying to make Junior feel that they were sorry that he had been thrashed and soiled.

It was Mahala who picked up the coat, crying: "Oh, Junior, your beautiful new coat is ruined!"

She began brushing the dust from it with her hands. Jason stared at her in amazement, which changed to a slow daze when he saw that her swift fingers were enlarging an ugly tear across the front of the coat even while, with a face of compassion, she handed it back to Junior.

So Jason "learned about women from 'er."

Junior took the coat from her hands, smarting, crestfallen and soiled, and turned back toward his home, choking down gulping sobs that would rise in his throat, while the other children went to school. As they started, Mahala worked her way from among the others and dropped back beside Jason, who was left standing alone. "Did you find your apple?" she whispered. She slipped her hand into her pocket, took from it her dainty little handkerchief, and offered it to him to wipe the dirt and perspiration from his face. Jason refused to accept it, but when she insisted, he did take it; instead of using it for the purpose for which it had been offered he slipped it into the front of his blouse. Seeing this, Mahala suddenly ran to overtake the other children, but when she reached Edith Williams she found her crying and shaking with nervousness.

"I just hate you, Mahala Spellman," she said. "I am never going to play with you any more, not if you get down on your hands and knees and beg me till you are black and blue in the face! I just hate you!"

Mahala met this with the sweetest kind of a smile.

"I'd like to know what I've done to you, Edith Williams," she said innocently.

"You know what you have done to me, and I tell you I hate you, and I am going to tell your mother on you!"

Mahala looked at her reflectively.

"I wouldn't be a bit surprised if you did," she said. "It would be presackly like you. Doing things like that is why you haven't got a friend but me, and you have not got me any more. I'm done with you! You needn't hang around me any more."

Then Mahala turned a little back, very straight, with very square shoulders and a very high head, and marched down the street toward the school house, while the other girls crowded around her, delighted that she and Edith were having trouble.

Almost exploding with rage over his humiliation, hurt from his punishment, and thoroughly frightened at the condition of his new suit, Junior started back home, while with each step that he took in that direction his mental stress increased. In culmination he entered the room bellowing, while his father and mother were still at breakfast. His mother threw up her hands and cried out in horror over his condition. His father was not only shocked and angry over whatever it was that had returned to him in such a condition the boy who was the pride of his heart, the very light of his eyes, but he had a lively remembrance of what that velvet suit had cost him and the pride he had taken in purchasing it for Junior because he meant always that he should be the best-dressed boy in the town. He seized Junior, shook him violently, and raised his hand to strike, all other emotions submerged in the one impulse that made money his God even above love. Junior tore from his hands, and running to his mother, dodged behind her. His father pursued him. Mrs. Moreland arose, spreading her skirts and her arms to cover Junior.

"Wait, Martin! Wait!" she cried.

It was evident that her heart was bound up in the boy far above any financial considerations, and it was also evident that she was afraid of the angry man she was facing; but she was not so much afraid that she was not willing to interpose her own body, if by so doing she could screen the boy. At the same time she cried to him, "Junior! Tell your father what happened to you. Explain!"

Under the shelter of her protection, Junior stopped crying. He wiped his eyes and faced his father defiantly.

"If I was on the City Council like you are, I'd fix up the sidewalks of this nasty old town so the boards wouldn't fly up and throw folks down and ruin their clothes," he cried.

His father stared at him in amazement. Instantly Junior's mother agreed with him.

"That is quite true, Martin," she said. "Only last week Jenny Sherman tripped on a loose board on her way to church. She almost broke her knee and ripped the whole front out of a very expensive silk dress. Some of these days somebody's going to sue this town for damages and you will have the biggest part of them to pay. The only wonder is that Junior is not in worse shape than he is."

Reassured by her backing, Junior came from behind her, but he still held her arm. Martin Moreland surveyed the pair scornfully.

"Will you please explain," he said to his wife, "how merely tripping and falling could get Junior into his present condition?"

Realizing that this was impossible, and anger and humiliation surging up in him, Junior cried out: "Of course, just falling only started it. The minute I was down that mean old coward of a Jason Peters took his chance to jump on my back and start a fight when I couldn't help myself. I took off my coat and gave it to one of the boys to hold while I beat him up as he deserved, and when he couldn't do anything with me, before I saw what he intended, Jason snatched my coat and tore it and dragged it in the gutter on purpose."

This immediately transferred Martin Moreland's wrath and cupidity from Junior to Jason.

"Why didn't you tell your teacher?" he thundered.

"It happened on the street. I wasn't fit to go to school," Junior made explanation.

The elder Moreland lost control of himself. His power had been defied. The tangible proof of his wealth had been dragged in the gutter. The child of his heart had been hurt and shamed. Martin Moreland did not stop to remember that he had been at the point of hurting the boy himself; what he really was overpoweringly angry about was that he felt Junior's condition to be a blow aimed vicariously at his own person. In his heart he knew how many hands would be raised against him, if by chance a first hand were raised by a leader. He knew what would happen to any man attacking him; he would see to it that a blow struck at him through his boy, even by

27

another boy, should be so punished that another offence of the kind could never occur. He turned to his wife.

"You see how quick you can wash Junior and put him into his other suit," he said. "I will take him back to school in the carriage. I intend to have it understood by the Superintendent and the teachers that the son of the heaviest tax payer and the president of the School Board has some rights!"

An hour later the door of Room Five was suddenly flung wide and on the threshold stood the imposing figure of the banker, beside him his son, clothed in his second best suit, his composure quite recovered. The boy marched in and found a vacant seat among his classmates. Miss Mehitable Ashcroft dropped the book she was holding and stared at the banker. A whiteness slowly overspread her face. She had been teaching school so many years that she should have been fortified for anything; but she was not. As she grew older the nerve strain of each day of noise and confusion bit deeper into her physical strength. She lifted a bewildered hand to smooth down the graying hair that dipped over her ears and lifted to a meagre coil at the back, and then her hands fell and began fingering the folds of a black calico skirt liberally sprinkled with white huckleberries. Suddenly she found her voice and quaveringly she said: "Good morning, Mr. Moreland. We are so glad to see you. Won't you have a chair?"

Mr. Moreland was a tall man with a heavy frame. The lines in his face at that minute were not pleasant. He had eyes of intense vision; in anger they were ugly eyes. They went flashing over the room from pupil to pupil until they found and settled on the white face of Jason Peters. There was something of the look on Jason's face that was on the face of the banker as their eyes met and clashed; a hate of arrogant fearlessness. Martin Moreland lifted a shaking finger.

"I have come," he said, "to accompany Jason Peters to the office of the Superintendent. I will have it understood that while I am the president of the School Board and while I am the heaviest tax payer in this town, the sons of washerwomen, or the sons of any one else, will not undertake, in a cowardly and underhand manner, to abuse my son."

Martin Moreland was an imposing figure; he knew better than any one else exactly how imposing. He never saw himself in a mirror or reflected on a plate-glass window he was passing, without making sure that the imposing part of him was well in evidence. He was at his tallest, his coldest, his most arresting moment as he rolled out "my son" at the awed children, pausing to allow his words to sink deeply, and well gratified to note that they did.

The frightened children sat in silence in their seats. Mahala Spellman looked at Jason, studying his set white face; then she glanced at Junior, his head again lifted in prideful assurance; and then her gaze travelled to his father. She studied him intently, and slowly upon her little face there gathered a look of intense indignation. But on the faces of the other children there could be seen only the deep impression that had been made as to the power of riches.

"Jason," said the teacher, "you will accompany Mr. Moreland to the office of the Superintendent."

For one instant Jason sat very still; then he arose and left the room. It was a long time before he returned. When he came back his eyes were dry but he was white and shaken. It was evident to every one that he had been beaten until he was scarcely able to cross the room and reach his seat.

Facing the school, Mehitable Ashcroft studied the children. She hated herself as badly as she hated a number of them. She could see the brilliant spot on the cheek and the bright eyes of Mahala Spellman. She knew that if she asked her she would arise in her place and tell the truth about what must have happened on the way to school. She knew that she should have done this before she allowed Jason to leave the room. She knew, too, that he should not have been sent to be beaten and humiliated unless he deserved it. From what she knew of his character and his work in school, she was certain that he did not deserve it. On the faces of a part of the children she could read the message that they were trying to convey to her that an injustice had been committed; that she had countenanced an unfair thing. On the remainder of the faces she could read the fact that they, too, had this realizing sense but that they intended, the minute school was dismissed, to crowd around Junior and follow his leadership. She had no doubt in her heart that whatever had happened would be carried further and that Jason would again experience taunts and treatment that were unjust. She stood there—hating herself that she did nothing and said nothing. In looking back over the years during which she had held her position because of many occurrences of a similar nature, she might have found the answer as to why she was already nervous and prematurely ageing—as to why she hated her profession and herself. She had needed her position so badly, what she must do to hold it had been made so clear to her.

At the noon hour as the children left the school grounds, Junior was strutting proudly at the head of a group of boys, bragging about what his father could do to the old Superintendent, about what he had done to Jason, and about what was coming to any other boy who got smart with him. While this was occurring on a corner Mahala passed by, surrounded by a crowd of admiring little girl friends, who were followed by Edith Williams, darkly frowning, walking alone.

Mahala's quick eyes saw what was going on. Her heart was rebelling at injustice. She stopped on the sidewalk, pointed her finger at Junior, and began a sing-song chant:

> "Cowardy calf, cowardy calf!
> Teased a poor crazy woman
> And got the thrashing he deserved for it.
> Ran home bellowing to Papa

And told a lot of lies
To get a brave boy whipped.
Cowardy calf, cowardy calf!"

Then the other little girls and some of the boys, with the flexibility of childhood, pointed their fingers at Junior and began shrieking, "Cowardy calf!" until he was furious. But he was helpless among such numbers as were ranged against him, so, breaking from the group, he ran down the street with all his might. As far as he could hear, a shrill chorus followed him: "Cowardy calf! Cowardy calf!"

Jason lingered in the lower hallway until the other children had left the school grounds and were some distance ahead of him; then he followed. In passing down Market Street on his way home, he saw Peter Potter standing at the door of his grocery with a heaped basket in his hand, looking up the street and down the street, evidently wondering why his delivery wagon was not standing before his door as it should have been. Instantly, Jason changed his course and headed toward Peter, because he and Peter were friends. The time had been when Peter was the leading grocer of the village, but he had not been able to make his way against the new methods and the seductive advertising of an opponent who, in recent years, had been able to take a good deal of his trade. Peter was not suffering from either cold or hunger. His fifty years had left his British face round and jolly. He was not sufficiently energetic to exert himself to an extent that would bring him back his lost opportunities. Instead of trying to regain his position, he tried by closeness in all his dealings to recover his losses, but he only succeeded in narrowing his soul, which had been fashioned rather narrow in the making.

When he saw Jason coming toward him he began to smile. He had asked several boys passing to deliver the groceries and they had refused; but here was a boy who would not refuse. Here was a boy who frequently had helped him for very small pay. Peter explained that, for some reason, his wagon had not returned from the ten o'clock delivery and these later orders were wanted for the dinners of some of his customers. Jason immediately shouldered the heavy basket and started on a long trip across town. When he returned the delivery slips, Peter understood that Jason would not have time to go home for his dinner, so he cut him a very small piece of cheese and gave him a handful of crackers to pay for having delivered the orders. Jason started back to school munching as he went.

His body was stiff and sore, but his heart was crushed. The boys knew that he had tried to get away without trouble; several of the girls had seen Junior push and maltreat him; at his elbow there had been the whisper that nerved him—yet when his hour came he had stood alone. He had felt Mahala's eyes on him, but he would not let himself look at her, in the fear that he would seem to be asking her help, and so involve her in trouble. All of them, the teacher included, had kept still. He was to understand that Junior was to do with him exactly as he chose. He was a few months older, he was taller, he was stronger, but because he was poor and Junior was rich, he must endure taunt, insult, even submit to being pushed and pulled. A slow red rimmed Jason's ears. He lifted a hand to allay the pricking in his scalp. Would he follow alleys and back streets, and dodge and hide from Junior, or would he meet him unafraid? He had no reason to fear Junior, but he remembered strong men who deeply feared the power behind the boy. As Jason slowly walked toward the school house, his brain and blood were in tumult.

When the last companion left her, Mahala had two blocks for sober reflection. She was ashamed of herself. She had incited Jason to strike Junior; when his father came into the school room she should have faced him bravely and cried out the truth. Maybe she could have saved Jason a beating. Never having suffered a blow herself, Mahala did not fully realize just what had happened to Jason. She did know that she had not been brave or fair in school. At least she had shamed Junior on the street and let him see what she thought of him. That made her feel better, and Jason knew she felt sorry for him. He did know that; but what must he think of her? And what ailed Edith Williams? Would Edith start to school early and tell the other girls things that would make them desert Mahala and be friends with her?

A daring thought flashed in Mahala's brain. She knew how to hold her ascendancy. Dinner was not quite ready when she entered the house. She kissed her mother, and slipping to the living room, she snatched her charm string from its place in the little mahogany sewing-table pocket, and hid it in the folds of her dress. Her mother would attend the Mite Society, held on Monday so that ladies of wealth might feel their superiority through having freedom to attend, and those that worked might gauge their inferiority by the amount of extra work they would be compelled to do in order to find time for the meeting. Mahala felt wildly daring; but her position demanded some risk. She darted across the door yard, tucked the heavy glittering string in a grassy corner of the fence, and managed her return unobserved. Now if only her mother would not be so silly as to follow her to the gate—but she was! So Mahala was forced to walk to the corner demurely, throw back a farewell kiss, and disappear. Then she must wait a palpitant interval, fly back on guilty feet, thrust a small hand through the fence, draw out the precious charm string, carefully, and race headlong toward the corner again. Safely past it, she might pause and hang the glittering length around her neck in gleaming festoons to her knees. Edith Williams would turn the other girls against her, would she? Mahala proudly swung the string before her and made a tongue-exposing face at an invisible Edith. She knew what would happen, and she was secure in her knowledge. The first little girl who saw her ran straight to her side and remained; the others came as they appeared around diverse corners—and remained. Every one of them had a charm string, but what meagre little things compared with the magnificence of the string of the merchant's daughter who might have the sample button from every emptied box as it left his shelves, to whom wonderful buttons of brass and glass and bone and pearl came in handfuls at every trip to New York to buy goods. Mahala's eyes were shining, her heart was throbbing. She knew the history of every button on her string: "Post Commander Johnston cut that right from the vest of his soldier suit, and that's the top left-hand one from Papa's dress vest, and that is from the coat of Mama's best friend——" she told them over like a rosary as they slipped through her fingers—great, brass-rimmed circles of glass with gay flower faces showing through, carved insets of bird and animal, globes of every size, colour, and cutting that ever held fast a garment worn by man or woman—Edith Williams indeed!

Mahala could scarcely step for the eager crowd around her. She disposed of the rule that charm strings were not to be brought to school by leaving hers with the teacher with a polite little speech, and got it safely back in place before her mother's return from the Mite Society. Such is the reward of a slight degree of daring. Edith Williams! Indeed, twice over!

That night in her bedroom, when Mahala's mother was undressing her, she saw the empty pocket with eyes that nothing escaped, and exclaimed: "Oh, Mahala! You couldn't have lost your beautiful embroidered linen handkerchief. I purposely make your pockets so very deep."

Mahala hesitated. Her first impulse was to say that she had lost the handkerchief because she knew that her mother would disapprove of her even speaking to the son of their washerwoman. But her astute mother had cut off that avenue of escape by pointing out the depth of her pocket. So she assumed a look which she knew her mother considered angelic, she clasped her little hands before her and lifted her face, exclaiming: "Oh, Mama dear, please excuse me! I gave it to a poor boy to wipe his tears."

Instantly Mrs. Spellman gathered Mahala in her arms and kissed her passionately. She sat down in a chair, drawing the child to her lap. She was thoroughly delighted.

"Tell me, darling, tell me what happened," she said.

Mahala, in detail, told of the troubles of the morning. She told precisely the truth where it concerned Rebecca and the desecration of the white flag. She left untold her part in any occurrence where she knew her mother would disapprove. When the story was finished, Mrs. Spellman felt that Junior Moreland was not being properly reared; that Jason had been abused; and that her Mahala was growing into precisely the kind of a woman that she wanted her to be. She went on undressing the child with customary precision, hanging each of her garments upon a hook, having her set her shoes in a certain spot with the toes even, patiently and carefully brushing and stroking her hair and winding it upon the curlers for the morning. Then together they knelt beside Mahala's bed while she said her prayers. Then the mother prayed. She asked of the Lord that He would make of her little girl a good child, an obedient child, and one having a fair mind and a tender heart. She begged that Mahala might be given the courage always to set a good example before her playmates. Then she tucked her into bed, kissed her repeatedly, and turning out the lamp, she left her to go to sleep.

As soon as the door was closed Mahala threw back the covers and sat up in bed. She listened until she heard the door of the living room close, then she expertly scratched a match and relighted the lamp. She was so accustomed to doing this that she managed the hot chimney without burning her fingers. She took the big wax doll, a gift from her father after one of his trips to New York, made it kneel beside the bed and then, in exact imitation of her mother's voice and mannerisms, she prayed for the doll the same prayer that her mother had used for her, to all intent. But if Mrs. Spellman had been listening she would have heard her own tones and accents saying: "And Oh, our Heavenly Father, help my little girl to always show the other bad, naughty children exactly how they should behave, and how their hair should be curled, and how clean their aprons should be, and how nice they ought to keep their slippers, and how they should be polite to grown-up people, and slap each other good and hard when they need it, and look like I do, and behave like I do. Amen!"

Then she opened the door to the adjoining room, and slipping in, she returned with an armload of clothing which she laid upon the bed. She pressed down the wrapped-up curls and tied them with a handkerchief; over them she put the carefully curled front which her mother wore with her Sunday bonnet and then she put the bonnet on her head. She stripped up her nighty and slipped into her mother's hoop skirt, and pulling the nightdress down over the circling hoops of the skirt, she looked at herself in the mirror and clapped her little hands tight over her mouth to suppress a shriek at the ludicrous aspect she presented. She unfolded a Paisley shawl and arranged it over her shoulders; then she opened a fan and posturing with it, minced up and down before the glass, wearing on her face an expression of sanctified piety. She made a journey about the room exactly in imitation of her mother, touching things here and there and repeatedly making little speeches to the doll. Sometimes as she passed the glass, she stuck out her tongue at her reflection, and tilting her skirts, did daring improvisations, dancing to tunes she softly hummed to accompany her performance.

When she was thoroughly tired of every ludicrous thing she could think of to do, she proved how very efficient her mother's teaching had been by returning everything to its place in such an exact manner that the estimable lady never realized that her precious possessions had been touched.

In his home that night, Martin Moreland spent the supper hour telling his wife, in Junior's presence, what he had done at the school, how terribly he had had Jason punished, and ended by admonishing Junior always to let him know if he was imposed upon or any of the other children did not treat him with respectful deference. He gave Junior a piece of money, telling him to take his books and go to his room and study his lessons for the coming day.

Junior said good-night to his father, kissed his mother, took up his books, and obediently went upstairs to his room. There he promptly climbed from the back window, slid down the slanting roof to a shed, from which he jumped to the ground.

Following the alleys, he made his way down town where he spent the money for a deck of cards, a number of clay pipes, and a package of smoking tobacco. Then he whistled at the back gates of several of the boys who were his particular friends and all of them crept up the alley beside the bankers house, entered the barn loft, and made a deep nest in the hay so that the candle light they used would not show from the outside. There they smoked and played cards until it became so late that they dared not remain longer.

Jason hurried home from school, fed the chickens, which were pets of his that he had bought with his earnings, milked the cow, and worked in the garden until it was dark. Then he came to the house, carefully washed, combed his hair, and sat down to a very scant supper that was awaiting him. Marcia did not speak to him or pay the slightest attention to his movements. She busied herself about the house or with some needlework. It was her custom to mend all the lace and fine linen that needed repairing in the washing that was sent to her, adding an extra charge to her bill. When he had finished, Jason washed the dishes he had used, put away the food, took his book, and sat down to a diligent study of his lessons.

At an early hour Marcia ordered him to go to bed, so he climbed the narrow stairway to the garret and undressed by the light of the moon shining in the uncurtained window. He was so sore and stiff that he soon fell asleep.

Immediately after he had gone, Marcia unlocked the door to one room of the small house which was always closed. Jason had never even peeped inside it. This room she entered and threw aside her working clothes. She bathed, unloosed and combed out a coil of beautiful curling hair, looping it in loose waves over her head. She rouged her cheeks and lips and powdered her face, hands, and arms. She opened her closet door, and taking out an attractive dress, put it on, transforming herself into a startlingly beautiful woman. From a drawer she took a book and sat down to read, but occasionally she lifted her head and listened intently. Presently she arose and went through the living room and the kitchen in the dark, and standing at the door, softly inquired: "Who is there?"

On hearing a low-voiced reply she opened the door and admitted Martin Moreland, who led the way to her room. She followed, closing and locking the door behind her, and turned to him with a smiling face, which gradually changed to one of doubt and uncertainty when she saw that he was in a state of almost ungovernable anger. His voice was shaking as he gave her Junior's version of what had happened during the day and then she noticed that in his hand he carried a cruel whip. He told her that he was going upstairs and beat the life half out of Jason. He was going to teach him for once and all that he could not interfere with the son of a rich man. He made the matter infinitely worse than it had been. Then he started toward the door.

Marcia caught his arm.

"But, Martin," she cried, "how are you going to account to Jason for your presence here?"

And he retorted: "I don't have to account to that brat for anything. He may as well understand that I came to teach him a lesson. He may as well know that I am master of this house, and of anything else of which I choose to be master!"

As he started up the stairway Marcia followed him. Then, realizing that Jason must not see her as she was, she turned back. She stood at the foot of the stairs, her hands clenched, listening to the sounds that came down to her. Several times she started up the stairs, but each time she remembered, and white and shaking, kept from sight.

Finally, when the banker left Jason's room, she went to her own, closed her door and locked it on the inside. When he turned the knob she refused admission, but after repeated hammering and threats she finally yielded and unlocked the door. He entered, sat down in the best chair, and lighting a cigar, began to smoke.

He said to her sneeringly: "You can take your time to cool off. That boy has got to realize once and for all that it is quite impossible for him to interfere in any way with any of the pleasures or the inclinations of my son."

Later she served him with wine and cake and delicious buttered biscuits, and when he had made himself thoroughly at home, he took his leave. After he had gone, she again locked herself in her room, tore off the fine clothing she had worn, and throwing it aside, pasted down her hair, slipped into her old dress, and, softly climbing the stairs, entered Jason's room. He was stretched on the bed in a light sleep, breathing hard. His face was white and full of suffering. She stood over him, looking down at him for a long time. Then she straightened the covers and slipped from the room. She went back to her own room, locked the door, and threw herself on her knees beside the bed, her arms stretched out among the finery she had worn, her face buried in the silken covers.

In these homes and in this environment the four children advanced until they entered the first year of high school.

CHAPTER II

"The Gifts of Light and Song"

During the recess period of a brilliant October day, Mahala spent her time inviting those pupils of her school who were her particular friends to attend her birthday party. At fourteen in appearance Mahala was what she had been destined to be from birth. Fourteen years of unceasing drilling, of constant care, of daily admonition on the part of Elizabeth Spellman had made habitual with her daughter an exquisite daintiness of person. The only criticism Jemima Davis had ever been known to make concerning Mrs. Spellman was that she was "nasty nice." Mahala instinctively drew back from contact with anything that might soil her clothing or her person. While she was thus dainty concerning her exterior, she was equally cleanly and refined in the workings of her heart and her brain. Hers was an unusually active brain; her eyes were flashingly comprehensive. All her life she had been seeing and understanding a great many things that her father and mother never suspected that she had either seen or understood. But since her personal fastidiousness extended to her brain as well as to her body, the result made a composite that was wholly charming.

Mahala's keen sense of humour kept her lips slightly curled, a dancing light in her eyes. She was always whispering to the anæmic shadow at her elbow: "Oh, Edith, did you see?" "Did you hear?"

Almost always Edith did see and hear, but her interpretations and conclusions were scarcely ever the same as Mahala's. The sour discontent of her really beautiful dark face came almost as a shock in contrast with Mahala's person; while mentally the girls were even more unlike. Mahala always had a remedy, always had hope; Edith believed the worst of every one; so when she had leisure time she spent it looking for something worse that she might believe on the slightest pretext.

The result was that every one in the village thought they loved Mahala, and it was curious that this should have been a universal attitude because the particularly spiritual quality of the child's beauty always had been enhanced by the most tasteful and expensive clothing, so that no other girl of the town could bear comparison with her. Because she always had been generous, always considerate, always just, and always mirthful, she was sure that she was among friends. Every pupil who had gone through seven years of schooling with her knew that her word was secure. If she talked of an incident at all, she could be depended upon to tell the truth. If she criticised an offender, she cut deep, but she did it with fairness. She never wore offensively her dainty clothing, so carefully selected for her in the Eastern cities where her father went to buy goods. She was quite capable of pulling off her coat on the street and allowing any of her girl friends to carry it home that a pattern might be cut from it.

The most shocking occurrence the town had to record concerning Mahala was that one day, in bitter winter weather, she had surrounded herself on the street with a circle of her girl friends and in their shelter deftly removed her exquisitely embroidered petticoat for the benefit of a schoolmate who was visibly shivering with cold. When Mahala, with watery eyes and a red nose, faced her mother that night and confessed what she had done, Elizabeth Spellman began by being shocked and ended by becoming bewildered.

"It was all right," she said primly, "for you to give Susanna Bowers *a* petticoat, but you should have gone to the store to Papa and gotten one suitable for Susanna."

Mahala looked at her mother intently.

"But, Mama," she protested, "Susanna was chilling. She needed something that minute; my petticoat doesn't care who wears it. It just loves to keep Susanna warm."

A slow red suffused Elizabeth Spellman's face.

"And you didn't stop to consider," she said coldly, "that all the hours of work I put upon that petticoat went there for my very own little daughter, and not for a girl who will not know either how to appreciate or how to care for it, and who will have nothing else suitable to wear with it."

Mahala's brightest light swept across her forehead.

"That's exactly the truth, Mother," she said emphatically. "I'll tell Susanna about the borax and the rain water and how to wash her pretty new petticoat, and I'll ask Papa to give me some more clothes for her, so the petticoat won't feel so lonesome and ashamed of the things it's with."

When Elizabeth Spellman detailed this conversation to Mahlon that night, she had considerable difficulty in gaining either his comprehension or his credence. There are not many men in the world named "Mahlon," while it is a curious coincidence that all of them who are, seem very similar. Every fastidious fibre in Mahlon Spellman's being rebelled at the thought of the high grade of pressed flannel bearing the exquisite handwork that always had enfolded his child, being put on the person of any Susanna of the outskirts. Such a wonderful town as Ashwater had no business with outskirts; it had no business with men who were not successful; it had no business with women who were not thrifty and good housekeepers. It was possible for every human being to be comfortably housed, well dressed, and well fed, if they would exercise even a small degree of the personal efforts of which each one was capable. Mahlon felt outraged and he said so succinctly. He told his wife in very distinct terms that she had failed in her manifest duty. She should have sent Mahala to recover the garment at once.

Mrs. Spellman looked at Mahlon intently. She usually toadied to him because that was the well-considered attitude that as a bride she assumed to be the proper one;

ordinarily it was effective, but there were occasions when she told Mahlon the unvarnished truth. This appealed to her as very nearly, if not quite, an Occasion.

"I did not tell her to go and bring it back," she said very deliberately, "because I had grave doubts in my mind as to whether she would do it. I have never considered it the part of wisdom to begin anything with our child that I feared I should not be able to finish. There was something about the look in her eyes, the tones of her voice that told me that she had done what she thought was right. I did not feel equal to the task of convincing her that she was wrong."

Mahlon Spellman habitually increased his height by rising on his tiptoes; in extremes he increased it further by running his fingers through his hair to stand it on end. He metaphorically relegated the whole race of Susannas to limbo by flipping wholly imaginary particles from his sleeves and wiping imaginary taint from immaculate fingers with an equally immaculate handkerchief. From this elevation and mental attitude, Mahlon glared accusingly at his wife. This was rather unusual; but the thing had occurred with sufficient frequency for Elizabeth to recognize its portent.

"I am constrained to admit," she said deliberately, "that there are times, very rare times, when Mahala's mentality so resembles yours that I am forced to confess myself unequal to the strain of controlling her. At such times I always have made a practice of sending her to you. Your superior judgment, your poise, and strength, will stand your child in good stead at such a time as the present."

Thereupon Elizabeth courtesied low to her self-ordained lord and master and swept from the room, leaving him a defenseless, a flabbergasted man. In his soul Mahlon knew that he was no more capable of controlling Mahala when she was in that mental attitude which her mother sometimes described as "having her head set," than was his wife. With hurried steps he began pacing the room. By the time Mahala entered, he was walking in nervous, flatfooted indecision; he had lost all height obtained by any subterfuge. He faced Mahala, and if his wife had been there to observe the interview, she would have been rejoiced to realize that Mahala was tiptoeing, while her father was on his soles. All the lofty attitude he had assumed with Elizabeth, vanished like river mist before an hour of compelling sunshine. Mr. Spellman was so undone that he nearly stuttered.

"Wh—what's this your mother tells me about this disgusting Susanna business?" he asked as Mahala stood slim and straight before him.

Her lips were curved in their very sweetest smile, but far back in the depths of her eyes there was a cold gray light that Mahlon Spellman did not recall ever having seen there before. He realized with a severe mental shock exactly what his wife had meant when she said that there were times when she did not force matters with Mahala.

But it was the girl's lips that were speaking, and the lips were sweetly saying: "How right you are, Papa! Isn't it disgusting and absurd, in a town where there is as much money and as many comfortable people as there are in this town, that any child should be started to school so thinly clad that her teeth are chattering and her hands blue and stiff?"

Mahlon tried to recover some least degree of his lost attitude.

"That girl's father never did an honest day's work in his life."

He tried to thunder it; he did succeed in making it impressive.

"That's exactly the truth," agreed Mahala instantly. "He never did, he never will. That's the reason why every one should make a point of seeing that Susanna has warm and comfortable clothing until she can get enough education so that she will be able to teach or do something that will help out her mother and her little brothers and sisters. I was just coming to you about it when Mother came to my room to suggest that I talk it over with you. I want you to tell about Susanna at the next board meeting of the church. I want you to tell those people plainly how narrow-minded and how selfish they are and what a disgrace it is to the whole town to have a member of their church trying to go to high school so thinly clad that she is stiff and blue—and she is one of the very best scholars in our class, too. Mind, I have to study good and hard to keep ahead of her and once or twice, I wouldn't have had my problems if she had not held up her slate and let me see how to begin a solution. I owe her that petticoat all right, Father."

Mahlon Spellman stood very still. He wanted to say something scathing. He had intended to be extremely severe about his daughter doing such an unprecedented thing as to remove her petticoat on the street. He wanted to tell her that she should be ashamed to accept help from anything so low down in the social world as a Susanna. But some way, memory performed a kaleidoscopic jump, so that he saw himself in crucial moments looking anxiously toward the slate of some of his fellow pupils. Then it struck Mahlon like a blow that he never, in his life before, had admitted even to himself that he had done this; but Mahala was facing him with perfectly frank eyes, acknowledging her obligations.

What he said was not in the very least what he had contemplated saying.

"The next time you feel that you owe any one a petticoat, come and tell *me*," he said. "There are some suitable ones of heavy stamped felt in dark colours that many of the girls of Susanna's age and size are wearing. It is scarcely fair to your mother that hours of painstaking work she has spent upon you, in an effort to express her love for you, should be discarded by you without a thought of her."

Mahala's eager face showed deep concentration.

"If that's the way you and Mama feel about it, Papa," she said quietly, "I'll pay for one of the felt skirts from my monthly allowance, and I'll go to-morrow and ask Susanna to accept it instead of Mother's beautiful work. Certainly I didn't intend to hurt Mother's feelings or yours."

Now this was precisely the thing that Mahlon Spellman had determined that Mahala should do, yet when she, herself, proposed making that trip, it touched his egotism from an entirely different point of view. He felt soiled and contaminated, even at the thought of such a thing, when he really came to picture his daughter, bone of his bone, flesh of his flesh, as being placed in such a humiliating position.

"You will do nothing of the kind," he said grandiloquently.

The strain on his tiptoes was crucial, the gesture that ran through his flattened hair raised it beautifully.

"You must learn to think before you do a thing in this world," he admonished Mahala. "I should consider it distinctly humiliating to me, to have a daughter of mine go and ask to be given back a gift that she had seen fit to make. Since Susanna has the petticoat, she must keep it. Simply fix in your consciousness the idea that the next time my daughter is not to be like the foolish little grasshopper that refused to look before it leaped, and so found itself in trouble."

There was a bewildered look in Mahala's eyes. Her teeth were set rather hard on her under lip. The breath she drew was deep. She turned from her father and laid her hand upon the door.

Then she faced him again: "I think," she said quietly, "that it would save Susanna's pride as well as ours if you didn't take this matter up with the church board. She's as old as I am; she probably would feel as keenly as I should about it. She didn't want to take the petticoat; I made her do it. But she really needed it, Father, she truly needed it awfully. And she needs a great many other things just as badly. Don't bring me anything the next time you go to the city, but let me come after school to-morrow and give me the clothing that will make Susanna comfortable. Will you, dear?"

When Mahala said, "Will you, dear?" there was not a thing on earth that Mahlon Spellman would not have undertaken to do for her, because it would have broken his heart to admit to her that there was anything on earth that he could not do for her if he chose.

"Certainly," he said suavely. "Most certainly!"

That night, in the privacy of their bed chamber, Mahlon told Elizabeth that it was the easiest thing in the world to manage Mahala; when he had put the matter to her in the proper light, she had immediately *offered* to go and recover the petticoat, but he had felt that it was beneath their dignity to allow her to ask to be given back a gift. It might look as if they were in straitened circumstances, or as if they could not trust their daughter to do what was right and proper upon any given occasion. He told his wife, also, that he had arranged with Mahala to come to him after school the following day and he would secretly provide Susanna with comfortable clothing so that she night continue with her school work.

Elizabeth immediately fell upon his neck and kissed him. She told him that he was the most wonderful, the most generous of men. Mahlon expanded with her appreciation until he slept that night with a beatific smile illumining his face. He never felt more thoroughly that he had justified himself to himself and to Elizabeth than he did in the matter of Susanna and the Spellman petticoat, while he could trust the clerks in his store, through a few words he could drop, to let his townsmen know of his essential rightness and benevolence.

Because of many diverse ramifications in Mahala's life similar to the petticoat affair, she always had been made to feel that she had the devoted love of every boy and girl in each advancing grade of her school work. Her teachers always depended upon her to tell them the truth concerning any occasion in the schoolroom otherwise inexplainable.

Mahala's mother had told her that she might invite her particular friends for the celebration of her birthday, so Mahala was busy delivering the invitations. She was also extremely busy facing a very uncomfortable condition. There was no one in the room who was not her friend so far as she knew. There was no one to whom she had not been lovely and gracious. There was no one who did not think her beautiful, who was not proud to be seen in proximity to her. But Mahala very well understood that her father and mother would not want to entertain in their home the Susannas of the town and neither would they wish to entertain the Jasons. That, she knew, was an utter impossibility, and yet, in her heart, she distinctly rebelled.

Jason always had been the best scholar in any grade to which he had advanced but Mahala knew that she dared not ask him to be her guest. She watched his lean figure as he crossed the playground. He would go to the well, take a drink of water, stretch up his arms toward heaven as if he were imploring that the gift of equality with the other children should be dropped into his hands. He would cast a slow glance of longing at the boys playing ball and leap-frog, then he would reënter the building, go to his desk and spend ten minutes on his next lesson, while the other pupils were playing.

She never had known him to practise an evasion. She never had known him, no matter how hard pressed, to do an unkind thing or to tell a lie. Sometimes, when unobserved she looked at him between narrowed lids, there came a feeling that, as he grew older and his lean frame filled out and became better clothed and his face took on maturity, he would be a pleasing figure physically. She dared not invite him to come to her party. Yet that imp of perversity that had always lived in the back of Mahala's head and found dancing ground on the platform of her heart, possessed her strongly at that minute.

She managed to pass near him, while as she did so, she said in a low voice: "I am asking my friends to come to my birthday party this week and I wish that I might invite you."

Jason stood very still; his eyes were on the ground. He dared not trust himself to look at the girl beside him. He was only a boy, but Marcia's harsh tongue had taught him many things. He realized Mahala's position instantly.

"Thank you," he said in a voice as lifeless as if he were struggling with a contrary equation. "Of course, I couldn't come, but it's good of you to want me."

Then he passed her and went up to the schoolroom. Taking out his books, he studied with a deeper concentration than he ever before had used. He had a new incentive.

Mahala drew a breath of relief. She had made Jason feel that she had thought of him, that if she could do as she liked, she would ask him to her party. Having cleared her conscience by placing the burden upon it on her parents where she knew it belonged, she turned her attention to the handsomest face and figure on the playground. She studied Junior Moreland carefully. Every year his father saw to it that he wore better and more expensive clothing. Every year made him increasingly handsome in face and figure; and yet, as Mahala studied him intently, she could see faint signs of coarseness creeping into his boyish face. The hollows beneath his eyes were too dark for a schoolboy. He carried himself with too great surety. His air was that of complete sophistication. What was there worth knowing that he did not know? Mahala resented the fact that Junior never approached her without the assumption that every one else should get out of his way. Day after day, as she watched him, the leader of every sport and amusement, she recalled how he often evaded the truth, how he twisted everything to his own advantage, how cruelly ruthless he was concerning their classmates who were in moderate or poor circumstances. He always tried to give the impression that she was his property, that none of the other girls and boys must pass a certain point in their intercourse with her.

There were times when her bright eyes watched him above the top of her Ancient History or Physical Geography and then turned to the background, where, hollow chested, hollow eyed, beaten and defeated, Jason sat rumpling his hair and plunging into his books. And sometimes, when he lifted his eyes and she met his glance, he gave her the feeling that he was a hungry dog that knew he had the strength to capture the bone, but from bitter experience, also knew that it was not worth while to make the fight, because superior power would intervene and take it away from him.

On the day of Mahala's birthday party, in the midst of the bustle of cleaning, merely from force of habit, that which was clean, of decorating that which was already over-decorated, a dray stopped before the Spellman residence to deliver an expensive piano lamp, the attached card bearing birthday greetings from Martin Moreland, Jr., to Miss Mahala Spellman.

When Mahlon Spellman stepped into his parlour that night, the first thing that attracted his attention was this lamp. He went over and examined it critically; then he turned a face white with anger toward Elizabeth, who stood hesitant in the doorway. He was horrified at the extravagance of such a gift between children.

"Why did you allow this thing to be left here?" he demanded. "Why did you not return it immediately? You know that it is not suitable that a gift of such extravagance should be permitted between mere children. It must go back!"

"Yes, that is what I think," said Elizabeth.

"Of course, that is what you think," said Mr. Spellman. "That comes from being a sensible woman. There is nothing else you could think. I strenuously object to having Martin Moreland furnish my house for me. A piano lamp! A piano lamp! Why didn't *he* get the piano and let *me* get the lamp?"

He leaned toward Elizabeth and thrust out his right hand as if he expected her to make an answer that would materialize so that he could pick it up and kick it through the door on the toe of his boot.

"Have you any idea," he shouted, "what that thing cost?"

"Yes," said Elizabeth quietly. "I heard Mahala say that she would like a piano lamp, so I looked at this same one yesterday, but I thought the price was out of all reason. They were asking thirty-five dollars for it."

Mahlon arose to the height of the price. He paced the room, talking and gesticulating.

"I won't have it!" he cried. "I won't countenance it! Why, in order to keep even, the next time Junior has a birthday, I'll be expected to help furnish Martin Moreland's house. I am not in the furniture business."

Mahlon arranged his cuffs and took a firm stand on widely spread feet; rocking thereon, he glared at his wife.

"Of course, dear," she said soothingly, "it shall be exactly as you say. The Morelands are always obtrusive and vulgar; but I thought that perhaps, on account of your business relations with Mr. Moreland, he might be trying to express his appreciation of you, and your patronage of his bank, and your influence in helping him with other enterprises."

Slowly Mahlon's lower jaw dropped on its moorings. A look of astonishment crept into his eyes.

"You mean," he said, "that you think the banker is using this opportunity to pay *me* a handsome compliment?"

"Why, it looks that way to me," said Elizabeth. "It is the only feasible thing I could think of. There is no reason why the Morelands should spend such an appalling amount of money on Mahala. There must be some favour that Mr. Moreland wants of you, or some reason why he is anxious to keep your good will. You know, dear, that the one thing in all this world that Martin bitterly envies you is your popularity, the high regard in which you are held in this community. To make himself appreciated by his fellow citizens as they appreciate you, would please him far more than money."

"Uh-huh," said Mr. Spellman. "I see your point. I think, as usual, that you are quite right. I never complimented myself so highly as I did in the selection of a partner for life. Undoubtedly you have arrived at the correct solution. We shall be forced to keep the lamp; while the next time Junior Moreland has a birthday, we shall utilize the opportunity to show the Morelands something about proper giving."

"Naturally!" said Elizabeth Spellman. "Naturally, you would want to do that. Now go and dress yourself in order that you may be ready to help me receive and entertain the children."

There was a small spot of deep red glowing on each of Elizabeth Spellman's cheek bones. She loved to give parties for Mahala or for herself and Mahlon, but she was compelled to admit that they were a strain. With her a party began, weeks before the actual day of entertainment, in general house cleaning, fresh laundering of curtains, fine dressing for beds and snowy table linens and napkins. Lavish and delicious refreshments must be prepared; clothing was a matter of immediate and intense concern.

For Mahala's birthday each of them must have a new dress. No hands but those of Elizabeth were sufficiently dainty and painstaking to make them, so that weeks of hemming fine ruffles, of whipping on lace, of setting insertion, of placing bows and looping draperies were necessary. For this particular birthday Elizabeth had done an unprecedented thing. She had accidentally clothed her small daughter in a combination purely French. The gold of the girl's hair was nearly the same shade as the tarlatan she had selected for her party dress. She had ruffled and trimmed it to the crest of the prevailing mode. She had combined with it little running wreaths of leaves that were exactly the blue of Mahala's eyes, yet they turned to silver in oblique light rays. Finally, she had smashed on to it here and there, exactly as a French modiste would have done, big, soft bows of black velvet ribbon. A pair of black velvet shoes with the toes brightly embroidered with blue daisies, brought to Mahala by her father on his return from a recent trip to New York, had probably suggested the bows and had been saved for the party, while a wreath of the blue leaves had been kept to bind down the silky curls hanging free, so that Mahala, thus attired, was probably as beautiful a picture as could be made with a child of her age.

The night of her party she stood beside her father and mother, quite as composed, as much at ease, as they, till the last of her guests had arrived. She was watching her mother carefully as certain faces appeared in the doorway. When Mrs. Spellman's lips narrowed and Mr. Spellman's eyebrows arose, Mahala made a point of darting out of line and offering both hands. She doubled in warmth her welcome for every child that she knew would receive only half a welcome on the part of her father and mother. There was always a guilty feeling in her heart when she invited certain children she knew were not wanted, not welcome in her home. She realized that the day was going to come speedily when her mother would say: "You may invite so many guests and not one more." On that uncomfortable day she would be forced to make a decision. The decision she would make would not be pleasing to her father and mother. To-night she thought fleetingly, merely realizing that there was a day of conflict coming.

On the arrival of the last guest, the games began. First they played "Who's Got the Button?" Then they advanced to "London Bridge" and "Drop the Handkerchief." All her guests thought it the proper thing to honour Mahala, and she had sped around the circle until she was weary. Mahala was given to precedents. She established one. She dropped the handkerchief behind Edith Williams. Glad of an excuse to get into the game, Edith snatched it up and ran. Junior saw and had a presentiment. Edith raced past him with intentions, but two things frustrated her. In her excitement her aim was poor and Junior cunningly side-stepped, dragging Sammy Davis with him. When the children shouted: "Junior, run!" Junior turned a deliberate head and refused to budge. All could see that the kerchief was behind Sammy. Sammy, delighted at the favour of the little rich girl, caught up the handkerchief and sped after Edith, only to find her in tears of rage and to get a well-aimed slap when he caught and tried to kiss her. The boys shouted, the girls "Oh-ed"—Mrs. Spellman raised her brows and cautioned behind an archly shaken finger: "Now! now! Little ladies! Re-mem-ber!" What all of the children always remembered was that Edith had chosen Junior and that he had evaded her. Someway her discomfort consoled the others. She was rich; she was Mahala's best friend. She had lost her temper and been rude, and Mrs. Spellman had chided her. In their hearts most of them felt a little less unhappy than they had been; a trifle less constrained.

It is very probable that Mahala was the only child at her party who was completely happy. Every pleasure she ever had enjoyed in her life she had experienced under the watchful eyes of her father and mother. She was accustomed to their constant restrictions, their persistent precautions: "Be careful of your dress," "Don't shake out your curls," "Don't damage the furniture," "Don't touch the lace curtains."

Her heart was so full of spontaneous enthusiasm, her body was so healthy, her brain was such a blessing, that all these millions of "don'ts" had left no mark upon her. Spontaneously as breathing, she answered: "Yes, Mama," "I'll be careful, Papa," "Yes, thank you!"—and went straight ahead with her pleasure.

The other children followed her lead, but they were awkward, their movements were stilted and perfunctory. They were afraid of the lady of dainty precision whose quick eyes were following their every movement in the expectation that they would do some damage. They were afraid of the wealthy dry-goods merchant, who was so punctilious in his courtesies, so immaculate in his dress, so self-contained in his personality. To them, the party did not mean really to throw off restraint and to have a natural, healthful, childish evening; it meant to get through with whatever was to be done in such a creditable manner that they would not be subjected to constantly whispered admonitions of "don't" and "be careful."

With the handkerchief dropped behind Mahala and Junior Moreland speeding around the circle, the doorbell rang its shrill peal.

Mahlon looked inquiringly at Elizabeth; Elizabeth looked inquiringly at Mahala. Elizabeth's hospitality had been strained to the utmost extent. Half a dozen children she had not expected were present. She had meant to be lavish, but she was worried in the back of her head for fear the ice cream and cake and pressed chicken would not hold out.

Mahala smiled reassuringly at her mother.

"It's some one to see Papa on business," she said. "Every one I invited is here."

Mahlon immediately remembered all the offices that he was accustomed to perform when he was destined to become, for an instant, the impelling object in the retina of one of his fellow men. The ceremony began with his hair, over which he ran his hands; it proceeded to his tie, which he felt to learn if it had the proper set; and slid down his vest ending with a little jerk at the points; then each hand busied itself with the cuff encircling the other wrist; while his eyes travelled rapidly over his sleeves, down his trouser legs, to the toes of his boots, which might well have reflected his entire person had there been proper lighting. Then Mr. Spellman, conceiving that the Morelands might have called to see how their lamp appeared beside his piano, with Napoleonic air, advanced to his front door, throwing it wide open. His wife forgot herself sufficiently to follow the few steps that would give her anxiety the easement of an unobstructed view. Mahala, quaking in her small heart for fear she had asked some one more, so that the ring might presage another unwelcome Susanna, followed frankly.

From his elevation, Mr. Spellman saw the catalpa trees and the evergreens decorating the front yard on a level with his eyes. It was with an inarticulate cry of delight that Mahala darted past him to pick up a little gold cage on a perch of which a bird as yellow as sunshine burst into song when the light from the doorway streamed on him, giving the impression of sunrise. Holding the cage outstretched in both hands, Mahala advanced to her mother. The bird trilled and warbled exquisitely. The child was entranced.

"Read the card, Mother! See if it is for me," she cried excitedly.

The card read, "To Mahala on her birthday, from a friend."

Elizabeth stared at Mahala; Mahlon stared at Mahala, and then at Elizabeth, and again at Mahala. Mahala wrapped her arms around the cage and laid her head against it and danced a lively waltz around the room crooning: "Oh, you lovely little gold bird! You lovely little gold bird! You are mine! You are mine! Oh, I never had anything half so wonderful!"

She set the cage upon the piano, stretched her arms around it, laid her face against it, and looked up at her mother, her big, wide-open eyes demanding love, sympathy, comprehension.

Elizabeth Spellman's face was a study; but Mahlon's was a problem. He opened his lips, but his daughter forestalled him.

"I just know that this lovely surprise is from you, Papa," she said. "Nobody ever can think of the wonderful things that you do."

Then she stopped, because she realized that her father's face was blank, even forbidding. The gift was not from him. She turned to her mother, her lips still parted, and met a duplicate of her father's expression. Then her eyes ran around the room in quick question to which there was not even the hint of an answer. And then, in her bewilderment and with the swiftness of thought, for one instant her face turned full to the window beside the piano which opened on the side lawn, while her sharp eyes thought they saw a fleeting glimpse of a face among the branches of a tree. Deliberately, she placed a hand on each side of the cage and again laid her face against the wires as near to the little gold bird as possible. Then she smiled a smile that would have been very becoming to any conceivable kind of angel, and her lips began chanting happily: "Oh, you darling little bird! I love you. You are the most beautiful gift I ever have had in my whole life."

Junior Moreland began to sulk from the instant Mahala appeared with the bird. Every one of her guests had brought her a gift, some of them expensive and attractive, some of them clumsily made kerchiefs and pincushions. To all of them she had given warm welcome and appreciation; but all of them put together had not equalled the magnificence of Junior's lamp at which the other girls had looked enviously, and which the other boys had hated cordially. Now, out of the night, there had come a bird of gold and Mahala had said that it was the most beautiful gift she ever had received.

All his life Junior had considered himself first. He was considering himself now. He felt abused and defrauded. He sneered openly. He said to Mrs. Spellman: "Are you going to let her keep such a dirty, messy thing as a bird in this elegant house?"

Mrs. Spellman hesitated. She was repeating "elegant" in her heart. As words go, she thought it the most wonderful she had ever heard from a young person. It was the joy of her life to be a perfect wife to Mahlon, to be a perfect pattern to her neighbours, but every year of her life made her task more difficult. The most difficult thing of all was the third task, which tried her more than either of the others—to be a perfect mother to Mahala, Pride might soar to undue heights where it concerned her husband or prestige; but the love of her small daughter cut to the very depths of her heart. Mahala was delighted over the bird. That was easy to be seen. But Junior Moreland was the son of the rich banker. He was a handsome lad. He always had been devoted to Mahala, and while there were things about him of which Mrs. Spellman did not approve, she had the feeling that under her influence, in combination with life with Mahala, Junior might develop into a man greatly to be desired. How very seldom did it happen that such a face and figure as his were combined with great wealth. Junior was an only child. If the sinister kind of power that made his father the figure he was in the little town, extended to the boy, Junior also would have great power—the power of riches—and how clever he was in the selection of the right word!

Mrs. Spellman smiled at the lad. He *was* the son of the rich banker.

"You know," she said evenly, "I've no idea who has sent this little bird to Mahala. There are several women in the town who raise canaries for sale. It's an inexpensive gift. Maybe it comes from some one Mahala has helped. She is always trying to do kind things to people, as is very proper that a girl in her position should. Perhaps, by morning, we shall be able to think who sent the birdie, and then we shall decide what to do about it."

CHAPTER III

"An Inquisition According to Mahlon"

When the other children began making preparations to go home, Elizabeth Spellman whispered to Junior to wait. After the last one had disappeared, she went to the kitchen and returned with a plate piled high with remaining refreshments, a heaped dish of ice cream and a generous big piece of cake.

Junior was not particularly grateful. There had been set before him, all his life, more excellent food than his stomach could hold. The delicacies that would have been a great treat to any of the other boys, were no particular treat to Junior; while he was sufficiently his father's son to allow the Spellmans to see that he was not deeply impressed. He picked over the food in a listless manner and ate very little either of the cream or the cake. In truth, he was sorely surprised and disappointed over the intrusion of the little gold bird on an occasion when he had reckoned on carrying off the honours with greater ease than usual. He was slightly older than Mahala and his brain was working with undue rapidity. He knew every one in Ashwater whom he chose to know—where had he seen birds being raised? In those days linnet and canary culture was extremely common. Almost every one had the tiny domestic singers in their homes. Brooding about the bird made him cross and sullen as he always was when he was thwarted.

Watching her mother's efforts to placate Junior, Mahala did some rapid thinking on her own part. She decided that if he left the house feeling better, there would be fewer objections on the part of her parents to her keeping the bird. She followed Junior to the hall door, then stepped on the veranda with him, where she stood for an instant in the moonlight.

The night was October at its most luring period. Natural conditions, not Junior, were responsible for the fact that she went down the front steps beside him, swung open the gate herself, then stood back that he might step through. As she closed it, she paused a moment longer, looking around her. The lure of the night air, of gaudy foliage wonderful in the white light, was upon her.

She said to Junior: "Did you ever see a more entrancing night?"

But Junior leaned across the gate, caught her by the shoulders, and roughly demanded: "Which of the fellows sent that bird to you?"

Mahala's lithe body straightened under his fingers. She had been carefully bred all her life; she thoroughly understood that her parents expected her not to antagonize Junior.

So she said, very simply: "I don't know. Some friend of Father or Mother, maybe."

Junior's hands gripped tighter. Suddenly he was saying in a hoarse voice that sounded as if he were going to cry very shortly: "I want you to understand that you are my girl, and when we finish school, we are going to be married!"

Mahala attempted to draw back, crying: "No! No, Junior! What foolishness! We are nothing but children."

But Junior tightened his grasp, and drawing her toward him, he leaned over and kissed her.

At that instant Mahlon Spellman appeared in his doorway. He was in time to glimpse a flying missile that came hurtling through the air, striking Junior a hard blow on the side of the head, knocking him down. He heard Mahala's shrill scream and saw her throw open the gate to kneel beside the boy. He paused long enough to call his wife, then rushed to help Junior to his feet.

The boy was half dazed. His head was cut and bleeding. As he recovered from the shock of the blow, he grew wild with rage and excitement. Mahala hurried to the kitchen to summon Jemima Davis and for a few minutes all of them were rushing through the house for water, bandages, camphor, and first aids. Mahala, standing beside the couch upon which he was lying, watched her mother's deft fingers exploring his temple. A rush of colour stained her white face when the verdict came: "It is nothing but a very bad bruise."

Instantly her head lifted and tilted in one of the bird-like movements familiar with her from childhood. Her mother was fully occupied; her father was chafing Junior's hands, trying to quiet him. Jemima was holding the basin in which Mrs. Spellman was dipping cloths to staunch the blood and cleanse the wound. To all of them in general Mahala announced: "I will bring some dry towels," as she slipped from the room.

She ran to the kitchen where she made a quick survey of everything. Then she caught up a box standing on a table and hastily, with flying fingers, she packed into it biscuit, slices of pressed chicken, pieces of cake—everything she could snatch from the remains of the lunch that had been served her guests. Then she darted from the back door, down the steps, and made her way among the shrubbery screening the side parlour window.

"Jason!" she breathed softly. "Jason!"

At once the bushes parted and Jason stood by her side. She thrust the box into his hands.

Her face was very near to his in order that he might hear her breathless whisper: "Can they ever find out where that bird came from?"

Jason's voice was dry and breathless, too, as he answered: "They never can. It didn't come from this town."

"Run!" urged Mahala. "The minute Junior feels better Father will be searching the shrubbery and the neighbourhood. Run!"

Then she was gone.

Jason stood still, holding the box. His heart was pounding until he had to grip tight to keep from dropping his gift. He could still feel her breath on his cheek. He could hear the shaken voice. In his nostrils was the odour of her nearness, of food that she had thrust into his hands. All this was a miracle straight from heaven, but there was a greater far—an overwhelmingly greater. She had not said one word of condemnation; she had neither chided nor reproached him.

Jason raised his head and tested his shoulders. Gripping the box carefully, he went down the Spellman back walk, through the gate, and then he entered a gate opposite, and skirting a house, came out on the adjoining side of the block. From there on, with no particular haste, he made his way home.

It would be closer truth to state that his feet made their way home; his brain knew very little about where he was going or why. He had given Mahala a gift. He had seen it in her arms. He had heard her voice crying out before every one that she loved it. He had punished Junior Moreland's rudeness and roughness. She had known that he had done it, and she had not even mentioned the fact that she knew.

When he reached home, Jason sat on the back steps in the beneficence of the October moon, and with the box on his knees, stared up at the sky. He was trying, with all his might, to understand what had happened, and how it had happened, and why. There had been no time to think. From the branches of a maple tree he had watched the progress of Mahala's party, even as he had watched hundreds of other parties from trees and bushes, all his lonely, neglected childhood. He had seen Mahala's trip to the gate with Junior. He had heard what they said; had seen Junior's rude act. He had had no time to think; he had followed an animal impulse. Of all the town Mahala was the one creature in woman's form who had been truly kind to him, who had tried to make him feel that he was not an outcast, who had put into his heart the thought, that if he would culture himself and do what was right, he might have an equal chance with other men when he grew up. When she was offended and had cried out, Jason had bridged space with a piece of brick wrenched from the wall of a flower bed beside which he had landed as he slid from the tree. When he saw Junior fall, he had been paralysed. He had not known but that he must go in the house and admit that he had killed him, until Mahala stood near offering him food, urging his flight to safety.

Jason studied the moon critically. He had never before realized that it was so big, that it seemed so close, that with his unassisted eyes he could trace the conformations upon it. Then he told the moon his secret.

"When she has time to study this over, she will think I am a coward to have thrown the brick. I should have overtaken him and beaten him with my fists."

Sick with shame and humiliation, Jason pondered deeply on the subject and made his high resolve. Hereafter, he would not be afraid. Hereafter, he would not be ashamed. He would do the level best that was in his power and some day, in some way, there would be a turning. Things would come right for him.

Resolves are wonderful. They brace mentality and the physical being as well. The odour of tempting food persisted, and still watching the moon, listening to the sounds of night, surrounded by the silver silence lightly flecked by the softly dropping gold and red leaves, Jason had his first experience with really delicious food, delicately prepared.

When he had finished the last crumb, he carried the box to the small, ramshackle woodhouse beside the back walk and dropped it behind a pile of split wood. Then he softly opened the back door and started to climb the stairs. Marcia's voice stopped him.

"Jason," she called through the darkness, "what made you so late?"

Jason stood still an instant, then he answered her: "I helped Peter Potter in the grocery for a while. I've laid the money I earned on the kitchen table for you." He hesitated an instant longer before he added: "And then, for a little while, I watched a party through a window."

He stood still, waiting, but as there was no comment, he climbed the stairs and sat down on the side of his old bed. Through the open window he began another review of what had happened, thinking things out in clearer detail, reasoning, studying, planning, and in his heart—hoping. He tried to picture what was going on in the Spellman home at that minute. He had a vision of Junior, cleansed and bandaged, making his way home in the white heat of anger.

But his vision was not nearly adequate. Junior was so dizzy that he could not stand, even when he tried bravely. Preceded by Jemima carrying a lantern, Mahlon Spellman entered his barn and harnessed his horse. If Mahlon had been asked to describe his feelings, he would have announced that he was outraged. He hated blood; he had hated it all his life. It was one of the things that he had given the widest berth possible. To-night he had been forced to come into actual contact with it. He hated mystery as badly as he hated blood, and who had sent that wonderful little bird that sang its way across his threshold and won his daughter's affections so easily, was a mystery. Really, it probably had been the cause of the whole trouble, and certainly it was sufficient trouble that a man of his position, of his dignity, should be forced at ten o'clock at night, an ungodly hour, to enter his stable to harness a horse. He had not dared take the time to change his clothing, and if there was anything on earth Mahlon hated worse than any other thing that could happen to clothing, it was stepping into a stable in the shoes and suit that he wore upon the streets. But he was afraid to wait to make the change for fear that Junior would realize what he was doing, while he was almost sick with fear that the boy might be seriously hurt. Even if Elizabeth could feel no yielding bones, no ragged seam, that was no guarantee that there might not be ruptured blood vessels or a clot forming inside the skull.

With shaking fingers Mahlon got the abominable harness upon the abomination of a horse and led it to the front door; and there, helped in by Jemima and Mrs.

Spellman, Junior leaned against the carriage seat, which there was every probability he would stain and disfigure, and was driven home.

With shaking fingers Mahlon tied the horse at the Moreland hitching post. With wavering legs he travelled the length of the walk and rang the doorbell. He could see through the lighted windows that the Morelands had not yet retired. He wondered why they were up so late when they were not having a party; and he wondered what he was going to say, and he wondered how he was going to say it. He had no idea what Junior would tell his parents. He had a very clear idea that he wanted them told nothing that would be detrimental to his standing with them. Too frequently he needed the accommodations of the banker when he bought heavy consignments of dry goods in the East; often he needed ready money when he speculated on bits of delinquent land or town properties that he thought a bargain.

Martin Moreland opened his front door. He and Mahlon Spellman had been boys together in the same village. They knew each other thoroughly, but they were not particularly well acquainted. Mahlon Spellman had been a boy as fastidious as the man he became later, while Martin Moreland had been the same kind of boy that developed the man he now was. There always had been sufficient reason why neither of them swam in the same bend of the river or climbed the same trees to gather nuts. Mahlon had done precious little of either.

Each man in his own way thought himself the great man of Ashwater. Each in his own way would have been better pleased to have witnessed the downfall of the other than anything else that could have happened on earth. For this reason, they were always particularly courteous to each other, always giving the impression in public that they were friends.

Seeing Mr. Spellman standing, white and shaken at his door, produced a throb of primitive joy in the heart of Martin Moreland. Perhaps he needed money. Possibly this time he could be hopelessly involved. He thrust forth his hand and cried in his most genial voice: "Why, Mahlon, what brings you out at this time of night? I had thought respectable people like you would have been in bed!"

Mahlon opened his lips in the hope, that as a result of his exemplary life, something exemplary would issue therefrom of its own accord, because he had no idea what to say. There was nothing sharper in Ashwater County than the eyes of Martin Moreland; by this time they had looked past Mahlon, down the length of the walk, and visualized the conveyance at the gate and the bandaged head it contained.

"You don't mean to tell me," he cried roughly, "that you have brought Junior home with a broken head! I didn't know you were having a prize fight. I thought I was sending the boy to a civilized entertainment!"

Mrs. Moreland could not have been very far in the offing. At Junior's name she hurried down the hall and caught Mahlon's arm.

"Is Junior hurt?" she demanded.

Mahlon's soul was in rebellion. He never had thrown a brick in all his immaculate life. Why any one who had known him all his life should assume that he would, or that he might be held responsible for bricks thrown by any one else, was beyond his comprehension. It was such pure insanity that he lost all respect for any one who could harbour such a delusion. It gave him the proper mental ballast and spinal reinforcement. He straightened himself, removed his hat, and stroked his sleeve. In his most correct and elaborate manner he answered very quietly, and congratulated himself even as he heard the sound of his own voice that it was clear and even, without a tremor. He wondered how this could happen when his heart was pounding until he had instinctively covered it with his hat.

"I regret to inform you that some roustabout in the street threw a piece of brick as Junior was leaving my gate this evening. He is slightly cut on the temple, but nothing of any moment. Barring a sore head, he will be as usual in the morning, I am quite sure."

"But why should any one throw a brick at Junior?" demanded Mrs. Moreland, thrusting a strong arm to sweep Mahlon back in order to clear a passage for her trip across the veranda and down the walk in the direction of her offspring.

By that time, Junior, encircled by his father's arm, reached the steps. The ride in the cool evening air had refreshed him. Circulation was somewhat reëstablished in his bruised head. His senses were beginning to clear. The one thing he recognized was that any indignity shown Mr. Spellman would be instantly carried home and detailed to Mahala, and concerning Mahala his conscience was not clear. If he had dared, Mahlon Spellman would have leaned on Junior and wept tears of relief and joy, because Junior's first words were the sweetest of music upon his anxious ears.

"Now, look here, you two old fuss-grannies," the boy said half laughingly, "don't make monkeys of yourselves, mollycoddling me. Somebody threw something at something and hit something, and I'm the something they happened to hit, and it happened in the street at the Spellman gate where Mahala and I were talking for a minute. Mr. Spellman doesn't know a thing more about it than you do, or I do. It was mighty nice of Mrs. Spellman to bandage me up and of Mr. Spellman to bring me home. What you should do is to thank him politely for his kindness and will he come in and have a bracer from your best brand of port? I would be thankful for a little help to get up the stairway and to bed, because I really was hit a pretty solid jolt."

Mahlon Spellman at that minute would have been happy to remove Junior's shoes—what was that about latchets?—even to have cleaned them if cleaning were necessary. He promptly laid hold of Junior's arm on the side nearest him and propelled him forward. What a wonderful boy he was! With only a few words to settle everything so quickly, so decently! The one place in which Providence had dealt unduly with Mahlon had been in denying him the consolation of a son. He felt at that moment that if he had been the father of a boy who could handle a difficult situation as easily as Junior had handled the present one, his delight would reasonably have known no bounds. Gladly he assisted in helping Junior up the stairs, in stretching him on the bed. Then the men left him to his mother and went downstairs to try the wine.

Port did one thing to Mahlon Spellman. It did quite another to Martin Moreland. It made Mahlon happy and discursive; it put wings on his mentality and set him sailing. It made Martin Moreland keen and analytical. It nailed him to one point and set him delving concerning its various ramifications. One good whiff of his best brand brought him straight back to the affair in hand. Why should his son and heir, the light of his eyes, and the pride of his heart, be hit upon his precious head with a brick? Who threw the brick? At what were they aiming when they threw it? If Mahala had been with Junior when the brick made its impact on his head, why had she not seen who did the throwing? He was not a lawyer, but he had met constant legal dealings in handling the diverse branches of his peculiar brand of banking business. He was very well informed concerning legal proceedings. Realizing this, Mahlon got himself from the Moreland home as speedily as possible, although the port was fine. Arriving once more at his own hay mow and feed trough, he called Jemima to hold the horse until he removed his shoes and best clothing. Jemima offered to care for the horse herself, and despite the fact that she had undergone many days of tiresome preparation for the party, Mahlon was the kind of man who would allow any one to do any personal service that was proffered on his behalf. So Mahlon entered his doorway to find Mahala had gone to bed, carrying the little gold bird to her room with her, while his wife was walking the floor in a torment of doubt and uncertainty.

She simply couldn't understand; she said so repeatedly and emphatically. She said so until Mahlon's sensitive nature could endure no more. He mounted the stairs and without preliminaries, opened the fourteen-year-old door of his daughter's room. He found that young lady sitting dressed as she had been for the party, beside a small table with a hand on either side of the attractive cage containing the little bird.

Mahlon sat down and faced the situation squarely.

"Mahala, dear," he said gently, "Mama and I are very much perturbed—very much, indeed! In the first place, neither of us approves of the expensive gift the Morelands saw fit to send for this supposedly happy occasion."

"Nor do I," said Mahala promptly. "Send it back. I don't want it. I can see very nicely from the chandelier."

"I wish," said Mahlon, a slight petulance tincturing his voice, "that you would learn not to break in on me. Have you lived with me fourteen years and not yet learned how I detest being broken in on? The gift before you is quite as inappropriate and far from inexpensive."

Mahlon saw the wave of stillness that swept over Mahala. He sensed the fact that every nerve and muscle in her was tightening.

"I cannot see that, Papa," she said very deliberately. "Canaries are not expensive. Why isn't a singing bird a delightful gift to give any one, especially a girl who loves music and colour as I do?"

Mahlon decided to dispense with subtleties and preliminaries. He brushed them aside. He leaned forward.

"Mahala," he said, in the deepest bass that he could instill into his tones and his most authoritative manner, "where did that bird come from?"

Mahala blessed her stars that the question had not been: "Who gave you that bird?"

As it was, her alibi was perfect. She could look her father straightly in the eye and answer in her best adaptation of his tones and manner: "I have not the least idea. There are several women in town who raise birds for sale. If you think it is not beneath your dignity, you might make it your business to ask each of them to-morrow. Possibly they would tell you to whom they sold a bird to-day."

That was precisely what Mahlon had intended doing, or having his wife do, but that clever provision "beneath your dignity" cut him to the core, even as his daughter intended that it should. She knew when she injected that neat little phrase that she had forever stopped her father and her mother from opening their mouths concerning the origin of the bird, because with each of them their dignity was more important than their souls—and more tangible in their own conception.

To Mahlon it was a body blow. He ran his perturbed fingers through his perplexed hair and stared at the innocent young face before him. Had he been any other man, he would have said that he would "be damned;" being himself, and a truthful man, he was absolutely confident that he should not be damned, while it certainly was "beneath his dignity" to lie on any subject. So he compromised by using milder methods.

"It passes my comprehension," he said, and his bewilderment became tangible, shrouded him like a blanket.

Mahala instantly agreed with him.

"Yes, so it does mine," she said. "Mother is very wise, perhaps she can think it out, or I may get some hint at school to-morrow. But, anyway, after all, Papa, is one small brass cage and one teeny yellow canary a matter of such very great moment? I don't know what cages cost, but seems to me I've heard some one say that you could buy a nice singer for three dollars. I've even heard of them as cheap as two. Why is it such a terrible thing to be given a little bit of a gold bird with a miracle in its throat? Please go to bed, Papa, and don't bother about it."

Mahala arose and put her arms across her father's shoulder, and her father drew her down in his lap and held her very close.

In his most warmly sympathetic tones of adjuration he said: "My child, this is only the beginning of the things Papa is forced to say to you to-night. I never have known you to lie to me. Your fact is impressively candid, I must admit. I must accept your word that you know nothing concerning the giver of this bird; but I have a very strong idea that you do know something concerning Junior's injury which might have

56

been, and yet may be, a thing extremely serious for all of us. There is such a thing as concussion of the brain developing hours after a blow on the head, you know."

"I hardly think, Papa," said Mahala, carefully settling Mahlon's tie in his own best manner, "that a blow on the *temple* is going to produce concussion. It's usually the back of the head, isn't it, when there are bad results?"

Mahlon drew a breath of exasperation. He caught Mahala's hands from his hair and his tie and shoving her to the extreme limit of his knees, forced her eyes to meet his or deliberately avoid them.

"Now, look here, young woman, let's get down to brass tacks," he said authoritatively. "Just what did Junior Moreland say or do to you at the gate?"

With perfect equanimity Mahala met the eyes of her stern parent, and realized that the time had arrived when she was past subterfuge, that she was facing a stern parent. She might as well get it over with because she really was both tired and sleepy, while she greatly desired a space of uninterrupted quiet in which she might think.

"He said that I was his 'girl,' and that when we finished school I was going to marry him. He was provoked about the bird. That's what made him say it."

"Has he ever said things like that to you before?" demanded Mahlon.

"He's been saying that I was his girl ever since I can remember," said Mahala; "but I'm not."

"Oh, aren't you?" asked Mahlon, and suddenly, to his daughter's intense astonishment, he was playful, he was arch, there was a smile on his lips, a light in his eyes; and correspondingly, there was no smile on her lips and no trace of light in her eyes.

"Of course not, foolish!" she said immediately. "I am your girl, and Mother's girl. How could I possibly be the girl of any boy in this town?"

"Um-m-m-m," said Mahlon. "You will find, young lady, that you will be glad enough to be the girl of one of the boys of this town one of these days, when you have finished your education and the time comes to go to a home of your own. And I don't know who there is that you know, or that you would be likely to know, that is so handsome or so admirably situated as Junior. Let me tell you, he did a mighty fine thing to-night, a manly thing, a praiseworthy thing."

"Tell me," said Mahala, delighted to have averted her father's attention from the bird and herself.

And so, Mahlon told her how very praiseworthy had been Junior's conduct in what she was constrained to admit had been a most embarrassing and difficult situation for her father.

"All right," said Mahala, "that was fine of him. I do like him slightly better than I did before you told me that."

"And now then, we will proceed," said her father.

"What answer did you make when Junior said that you were his girl?"

"I told him I was not," said Mahala promptly.

"And then what did Junior do?"

"He pulled me across the gate and tried to kiss me."

"Ah!" said Mahlon Spellman. "Now we are getting at the meat of the matter. He tried to kiss you? And what did you do?"

"Pushed him away and wiped my face—what any one would do," said Mahala.

"And then," questioned Mahlon, "the brick?"

"Yes," admitted Mahala, "the brick."

"Now it happens," said Mahlon, "that I picked up that piece of brick. Do you know where it came from?"

"I do not," said Mahala.

"Well, I do," said Mahlon. "It came from the border of one of your mother's flower beds, just outside the parlour window. It was thrown from that direction. Some one who had not been invited to the party was watching it through the parlour window. Some one who doesn't like Junior Moreland to think that you are his girl, threw the brick. Now, Mahala, women, even little girls of fourteen, are not sufficiently sophisticated to be in the first year of high school and at the same time so ignorant that they do not know which boy of their acquaintance is enough interested in them to risk taking the life of another boy who is guilty of no very great indiscretion."

"That all depends on the boy," said Mahala. "If he is the son of the rich banker, it's 'no great indiscretion;' if it had been the son of—say the washerwoman, for example, right now you'd be out trying to kill him."

"And I very probably should succeed in so far as I cared to go in such a premise," said Mahlon promptly.

"That's exactly what I thought," said Mahala.

Slipping from his knee and walking to her dresser, she began very carefully unpinning the little wreath of silver-blue leaves that bound her hair.

"I am waiting," said Mahlon with all the dignity of which he was capable—and he was capable of a high degree of really impressive dignity. No one can practise anything hourly for fifty years and not attain a high degree of excellence.

Mahala turned to her father, both hands still occupied with the wreath.

"Papa," she said very quietly, "you just got through saying that I never told you a lie. Do you think it would be any great achievement on your part if you should force me to tell you one right now?"

"I am not asking for a lie!" thundered Mahlon. "I demand that you tell me the truth!"

"All right," said Mahala, "I will. As you recall, when you stepped to the door my back was turned. You had a better chance to see any one who might have been in the shrubbery than I had. You have not the faintest notion who made the attack on

Junior. Do you think it would be fair for me to answer your demand for the truth with merely a surmise on my part? I didn't see who threw that piece of brick, so I positively refuse to make any surmise!"

Mahala turned again to the mirror and loosened one end of the silver wreath with something very closely resembling a jerk; while Mahlon, studying her back and her shoulders and the set of her yellow head, and catching a flash of the blazing eyes that the mirror reflected, suddenly remembered the advice that had been given him by his wife concerning the petticoat: "Don't begin anything with Mahala that you can't finish."

He realized that he had undertaken something that he was not man enough to finish. Maybe there was a man in the world who could have laid rough hands upon Mahala and choked and beaten from her the information he wanted. Because of Mahlon's inherent refinement he was not the man who, by any possibility, could do this. As gracefully as he ever passed down the church aisle on Sabbath morning with the contribution box, Mahlon arose, and walking over to the mirror, he put his arm around the small emanation of his own self-esteem.

"Very well, Mahala," he said, "as always, Papa accepts your word. If you didn't see who made this unjustifiable attack on Junior, of course, you cannot tell me who did it. I shall make it my business to find out for myself in some other way."

"Thank you, Papa, that will be fine," said Mahala, freeing the other end of the wreath. She opened her lips and looked at her father and then she closed them. What she had wanted to say was: "If there is a boy in this world who has the courage to throw a brick when Junior Moreland tries to kiss me, I am very much obliged to him!" But what she desired above everything else at that minute was to stop the discussion, to be left alone. Faintly in the distance, she now visioned a period, and so she stood carefully straightening the wreath, wordless and waiting.

Realizing something of this, Mahlon took her in his arms and kissed her tenderly. He told her that he hoped she always would be a good girl, and if, at any time, anything worried her or she was in any way annoyed, she must come straight to Papa, who only wanted what was for her good and that she should grow up into such an exemplary and beautiful woman as her mother was.

The period came at last, so beautifully rounded and of such touching sentiment that Mahala emphasized it by putting her arms around her father's neck, kissing him and thanking him, and giving him a slight propulsion in the direction of the door, through which he got himself without further speech. At last Mahala was left alone to the night and the bird.

Her first thought was to wonder if there could be anything really serious resulting from the blow which Junior had so richly deserved. She decided that on account of Junior's youth and strength, he would speedily be all right. That burden eased from her mind, she went back to the window, and with her arms around the cage again, leaned her face against the wires and looked into the night of wonder and tried to think deep and straight.

This was difficult for it was a night of enchantment to the girl. The clouds floated across the moon and obscured it, then drifted away and left the night silvered in the high lights, deeply black in the shadows. Her heart ached over the lean face she had glimpsed through the window. Why should the best boy and the best scholar in her class be an outcast through no fault of his? Hers had been a lovely party from her mother's viewpoint—weeks of preparation, pretty clothes, gifts, and adulation. Of course, the brick incident, annoying, but nothing of any moment—a beautiful party——

Mahala choked back an aching sob. She softly slipped her hand into the cage, picked the canary from his perch, and kissed his bright head before she went to bed in the early gray of morning. And even then, she was too restless, filled with pity, to sleep. She told herself repeatedly that she should have been anxious about Junior; but all the trouble in her heart arose from fear as to what might be happening to Jason.

CHAPTER IV

"Strength from Weakness"

Under the stimulus of his glass of port, Martin Moreland was wondering about his son—his idolized son. He climbed the stairway and stood at the foot of Junior's bed until the lad's mother had finished fussing over him. Then he said to her roughly: "Now you go on to bed. Junior and I want a few minutes to talk this thing out."

When the door had closed after his wife, Martin Moreland drew a chair to the side of the bed, and sitting down, said with visible effort to be calm: "Exactly how badly are you hurt, Junior?"

Junior answered truthfully: "Like the devil so far as pain goes. I reckon I'll be all right to-morrow, but I don't *know* whether I will or not."

"Had I better get Doctor Grayson?" asked Mr. Moreland.

"I don't see what he could do that hasn't been done," said Junior. "You know how nice Mrs. Spellman is. She washed and washed; she put on camphor that just about raised the hair on my head; she bound me carefully with clean cloths. What more could old Grayson do? You better let me go to sleep now and see how I feel in the morning."

"All right," said Martin Moreland.

His tones were so very grim that Junior glanced at him apprehensively; he realized that matters were very far from "all right" with his father. He could see him gripping his shaking hands one over each knee in order to hold himself steady.

Then came what he had to say: "As a rule, Junior, I am rather easy with you because you are my son and I want you to get some fun out of life before you begin the work and worry that will come when you are a man; but I am not feeling particularly easy at this minute because I happen to realize that a blow aimed at you is really intended for me. It should be my head that's bleeding right now instead of yours. Out with it! Who threw that brick?"

Junior lay very still. He looked straight ahead of him for an instant and then he studied his father craftily.

"It came from the direction of a patch of thick shrubbery beside the house," he said. "I could not possibly see who threw it."

"Nevertheless, you know who there would be that would throw it," said Martin Moreland, his voice rough with emotion.

"As it happens, since you feel it really was aimed at you, I don't know," said Junior. "But I intend to make it my business to find out and when I do, I'll tell you. This minute I am going to sleep if I can."

Junior turned his back and lay still. So his father blew out the light and went down the stairs. In the hall he met his wife.

"I have just remembered that I forgot to sign some papers that must go out in the morning mail," he said. "I am going down to the bank and attend to them. Go to bed and go to sleep. The boy's all right. I'll take another look at him when I come back. If I find he's feverish, I'll go after Grayson. If he's all right, we'll wait till morning."

Then he took his hat and left the house.

He followed the alley beside his residence to where it met a side street and here he took up a familiar route through unlighted ways and deep shadows to the outskirts of the town. His feet led him on a familiar path to a familiar door, and when he tapped upon it, immediately it swung open. He followed Marcia to her room, and when she turned toward him with a smile, she was dumbfounded to see that he was in the most ungovernable rage that ever had possessed him in her presence.

"Martin!" she cried, starting toward him, "Martin! What has happened?"

Martin Moreland opened his lips to speak, but he was so disconcerted that he could only utter a hissing, stammering sound. Marcia hurried to a cabinet and brought him a glass of wine. With shaking hands he took the glass but his body remained rigid against her efforts to guide him to a chair. Marcia stood before him in white-lipped wonder.

"Martin, what have I done?" she entreated.

Steadied by the wine, Martin Moreland found his voice.

"Done!" he panted. "What have you done? You've raised that hell-hound of a Jason in such a way that to-night makes the second time that he has attacked my son! *My son!*"

Martin Moreland's clenched muscles shivered the fragile wine glass until when he opened his hand, the blood was dripping from it.

"Oh, Martin!" cried Marcia, "I did my best with the boy! Before God, I did! I never mentioned Junior's name to him. I almost never speak to him at all, only about the work. The thing I did was to try to get him to study hard. He is a good boy, and I thought that was his only chance."

"'A good boy!'" raved Martin Moreland. "'A good boy!' He's an insidious imp of the devil! To-night he tried to kill Junior, and it may be that by morning my boy will develop concussion of the brain. *Concussion of the brain!*" He shouted each word at the terrified Marcia, wildly gesticulating toward her with his dripping hand. "I thought that first lesson I gave him would be enough for him. To-night I'll not leave him till he's in the same shape my boy is."

He turned and started toward the door. Marcia threw herself before him.

"Wait, Martin! Wait!" she begged. "Don't go to him feeling that way, you might kill him!"

He thrust her roughly aside and the bleeding hand left its impress on the breast of a white dress that she was wearing for his allurement.

"I'll take devilish good care that I don't kill him," he said, "because I cannot afford the scandal. Maybe you think I don't know every hound of the pack that would be at my throat if they had the slightest encouragement. Maybe you think I don't know the man who would lead in running me down, if I gave him the least hint as to where he could find an opening."

He turned and started toward the stairway.

Jason had dropped on his pillow just as he was, and had fallen asleep, his brain busy with the events of the evening. He was deep in the midst of a wonderful dream. He had seen himself with flesh on his bones, hope in his eyes, and pride in his heart. He made a surprising vision. He was wearing clothing as beautiful as the suits that always had been worn by Junior Moreland. He had seen himself, with the step of independence, standing before the door of Mahlon Spellman. He had used the knocker and had stepped inside. The great merchant had shaken hands with him and with his most urbane gesture had indicated that he was to walk into the parlour. He had boldly walked in, and in the presence of Mrs. Spellman and his schoolmates, he had offered Mahala the bird. She had been in such transports of joy as he had seen with his actual eyes that evening. She had opened the cage door and the gold bird had left its perch and flown to her finger; as she held it up, suddenly frightened at the faces and the lights, it had darted swiftly above their heads and from the open doorway.

Her cries of distress awakened him. His feet came to the floor and he swung his body upright. Then he heard. He arose and took three steps to the head of the stairs. He was unconscious that he had reached out and picked up a small wooden stool that stood beside his bed to hold a candle or water. He looked down the stairway. At its foot stood, what, to the boy, seemed to be a monster fashioned from unyielding steel into the shape of an inexorable ogre.

The distortion of Martin Moreland's face seen from the angle at which the boy was standing, was hideous. His mouthing threats were terrifying. His uplifted hand was dripping blood. Something tightened in the breast of the boy and arose in his throat, creeping back to his brain. Even as he gazed, there mingled with the terror he knew a slow wonder, for he was on a line with the locked door—that door inside which he had never had a glimpse. It opened into a room full of light; he saw beautiful furniture, dainty things, and silken hangings. Beside Martin Moreland, trying to block his way, clinging to him, there was a woman, a stranger woman, a woman that the boy never before had seen. She was wearing an exquisite wrapper of snowy white, foaming with laces, falling to her feet and heaping there as if she stood in a drift of snow.

At this apparition, Jason stared in dull wonder. Through the paralysis of terror in his brain there filtered the thought that Marcia could be made to look like that when the day came that he could give her beautiful clothing and such a room. A white ray of moonlight from the open window beside him fell on the boy and lighted the stairway. He saw the banker's awful hand crash against the breast of the woman. He heard her cry of pain and pleading. He heard the thick, shaking voice shout: "Save your damned mouthing! The chances are that I *will* kill him before I get through with him this time!"

The woman, in her feathery laces, was thrown aside; Martin Moreland started up the stairway two steps at a time. When he was nearly two thirds of the way up, Jason moved, the wooden stool curved a circle around his head; then it crashed down with the combined strength of his two arms of desperation.

Martin Moreland uttered a guttural, rasping grunt. He clutched at the smooth sides of the walls but there was no supporting rail. Slowly his body curved backward and went crashing down, and into the arms that were stretched out, he fell, bearing the woman to the floor with him. Staring dully, Jason saw her struggle up; saw her stretch the form of the banker at the foot of the stairs; saw a hand reach across him to close the door.

Jason turned, every line of his terrified face etched clear in the moonlight. He went straight to the window and climbing through it, slid down the slanting roof of the lean-to, and dropping to the ground, turned his face toward the adjoining pasture and the woods back of it, and with all the strength he could summon, ran for cover, for the protection of the darkness that the big trees afforded.

Kneeling on the floor beside the banker, Marcia ran her hand across his temple and was horrified to find that it was covered with a sticky, warm red. She staggered to her feet, and hurrying to the kitchen, she brought back a basin of water. But before she used it she again put brandy to Moreland's lips. For a few minutes she worked over him frantically. Then she arose, and stepping across his body, she called up the stairway: "I'm afraid you've killed him. Run, Jason, run! Run to the end of the earth and never come back!"

She listened, but there was no sound and no answer. She glanced backward, and then with flying feet, she climbed the stairs until her head was level with the floor of the garret, and in the pale light she searched the empty room and the vacant bed. Then she hurried back and renewed her ministrations.

It was a long time before Martin Moreland opened his eyes. Another long time elapsed before he allowed her to assist him to her room, where he dropped upon the bed and lay struggling to attain self-control.

"Can you feel if my skull is cracked?" he asked Marcia.

"I was afraid to try," she answered. "I don't think that it is."

"Feel!" he said. "Push against the scalp hard. See if it gives any, if you can detect a seam."

With sick eyes and nauseated lips, Marcia knelt beside Martin Moreland and felt his temple, ran her fingers through the thick, light hair covering his head.

"I am quite sure it is only a surface cut," she said.

Strengthened by the brandy and recovering slightly from the shock, Martin Moreland stopped raving. In slow, deliberate pauses of finality he laid down the law: "I will not risk coming in contact with that hound pup again," he said. "After this he'll shift for himself. After this you are going to live where such a scene cannot be repeated. You can get ready what you want to take with you. You are going to leave this house inside of an hour, if my legs will carry me down town."

Despite her entreaties, he arose and staggered from the house. It was not an hour later until a dray stood before the door. The beautiful room was dismantled, and into the night, with her personal belongings heaped around her, Marcia was driven from the only home she had.

CHAPTER V

"The Verdict Goes Against Jezebel"

Jason, fleeing through the darkness of a thicket at the approach to the forest, was running in headlong terror. He was ripped by thorns, rasped by blackberry vines. He was in no condition to think. He was escaping an enormous, blood-dripping hand clutching at his back in a threat against his life. Staring ahead of him, he ran wildly; he did not realize where his flying feet were taking him until he fell into a mass of warm, living things. A shriek of terror broke from his lips. Then the odour of cattle, the heavy breathing, and the slow arisings around him told him, even in his frenzy of fear, that he was among harmless creatures. He looked back to see the meadow lying white behind him. He could be seen plainly across it, so again he ran with all his might for the shelter of the forest. Into the darkness of its outstretched arms he plunged for refuge. He could not see where he was going. Repeatedly he ran against trees until he was bruised, half stunned, and finally, when his strength was almost exhausted, he fell across a big log and allowed his body to slide to earth regardless of what might happen to him. Throwing up his arms, he pillowed his head upon them while a dry sob tore from his lips. He was only a boy. He was not quite sixteen. There was no one who loved him, and there was no one who cared if the banker did kill him. There was no help from heaven above or the earth upon which he lay. In his confused state, it appealed to him that very likely he had killed the rich and powerful banker. What would be done to him if he had, he could not imagine, but he knew that it would be done swiftly, it would be done cruelly. Twice he had heard the threat to kill him. The first sob bred others. His face dropped against the cold, damp mosses of the log and he cried until he was exhausted. Then his breath came more evenly; his eyes slowly closed, and presently, with the quick reactions of youth, he was resting.

He had only slept a few minutes when there came in contact with his face a nauseating odour and the touch of a furred creature from which he drew back with a terrified scream. In the darkness he could see a pair of big, gleaming green eyes. He could not know that it was only a coon carrying a chicken taken from his own hen house. He could not know that the mouthful of chicken prevented the coon from recognizing the man odour until it had stepped upon him.

Jason sprang to his feet and went plunging through the forest again. His next period of exhaustion found him at a thicket of spice brush and he sank down beside it and lay panting for breath. It was only a short respite until a great, horned owl, screaming with the panther scream of its species when food hunting, plunged into the bushes, its wings wide spread, to scare out small, sheltered birds. This owl cry was as blood-curdling as that of any animal. Jason was so terrified that once more he went lunging forward until he fell in utter exhaustion and lay unconscious.

That morning Junior Moreland and his father faced each other across the breakfast table each having a bandaged head. In his heart, each of them was furious over his condition. Junior expressed the opinion to his mother that some one had hit him accidentally when throwing at a prowling cat or a loose animal. Mr. Moreland explained that he had been compelled to work late at the bank. As he was locking the door on leaving, some one had struck him a terrible blow on the head—struck him so forcefully that he had fallen as if he were dead, which evidently frightened the burglar so that he ran away without taking his watch and the big diamond ring that he always wore on his left hand.

These explanations were offered for the satisfaction of Mrs. Moreland. She sat in a sort of stupefaction, looking from her husband to her son, her mind filled with slow wonder, with persistent questionings, with sickening forebodings. She kept asking for details, when in her heart she knew they were lying to her. She so fervently desired to accept their word that she asked for particulars in the hope that one or the other might afford her a small degree of heart-ease by telling her something so convincing that she could believe it and not feel like a fool in so doing.

As Mr. Moreland left the breakfast table, he said to Junior: "Come up to the bathroom a minute. I want to be sure your head is all right before you risk going to school."

Once inside the most elaborate of the three bathrooms of Ashwater, Moreland Senior closed the door and faced Moreland Junior.

"Now, out with it, young man," he said.

Moreland Junior looked at his father speculatively.

"I told you the truth last night, Dad," he said. "I didn't see who did it, but, of course, it was Jason. There isn't any one else who would have dared. He's had it in for me since that time he spoiled my suit, and you had him licked for it."

A slow grin broke over Junior's face. He looked at his father with an impudent leer. His eyes focussed on the surgical bandages decorating the Senior Moreland's head, and then slowly and deliberately, he said: "He's a darn good shot, ain't he?"

Taken unexpectedly and in a tender spot, Moreland Senior caught his breath sharply as he studied his son.

"Of course, that burglar stuff is all right to feed Mother," said Junior. "A woman will swallow anything, and Mother's a regular boa constrictor, if you tell it to her real impressively. But you needn't dish out that burglar dope to me. You didn't have luck to brag of manhandling Jason for busting my head, did you, Dad?"

Moreland Senior lifted his right hand, also in surgical bandages, and then with the tips of the injured member, he slowly felt across his damaged head. He leaned forward to look at his reflection in the mirror.

"For God's sake, don't come to the bank to-day," he said. "It's going to look damned funny to the people of this town to see both of us in bandages. Keep your mouth shut and leave this to me. I'll see to it that you don't come in contact with that scorpion in school again. He don't know it, but he's through going to a school that I run."

Moreland Senior lifted the hurt hand toward the blue of the bathroom ceiling and eased his soul of mighty oaths. He swore that he would yet punish Jason to within an inch of his life; that he never should enter the high school again; and that whatever he attempted in life should be a failure.

Junior reinforced his wavering legs by taking a seat on the broad wooden rim surrounding the tin bath tub, while he looked at his father speculatively.

"Dad," he asked slowly, "why the hell have you got it in so strong for Jason Peters? He can't help it because his mother is a washerwoman and he can't produce anything in the shape of a father. Every one's got to admit he has the best brains of any boy in my class. I hate the pasty-faced, mewling thing, but I'm forced to tell you that there's something in him when he can stand at the head of his classes, and when he can get away with you and me both the same night."

Then Junior squared his shoulders, threw up his handsome bandaged head, and laughed until he started a pain that stopped the laughter. The Senior Moreland hurriedly left the bathroom, closing the door behind him with undue emphasis.

Among the thick branches of the Ashwater forest there were a few small openings. A brilliant morning ray of October sunshine found one of these and shot its level beam straight into the pallid face of a sleeping boy curled on the damp, frosty ground. Stiff with cold in his physical frame, stiff with terror yet in his heart, Jason opened his eyes, deeply set in an attractive framework, a forehead of intelligence above, the remainder lean and intellectual. At first he was so numbed that it was difficult to realize where he was or how he had got there. Then slowly he arose and made his way to the sunlight of the meadow; there he sat on the stump of a felled tree and began an effort to command a continuous procession of thought. He began as far back as he could remember, and year by year, he came down the progression of his days. He tried to figure out why the woman with whom he had lived had not been to him as other mothers were to their sons. She had worked hard, they had been poor; but many women in the village had worked harder, had larger families and been less capable of taking care of them. He had seen all of them evince for their children some degree of solicitude and of love. He could recall neither of these things ever having been proffered him.

He tried to figure out why the fact that Martin Moreland owned the house in which they lived, should give him the right repeatedly to enter it late at night and attack him physically. Of course, Junior had lied to his father. He lied to every one when a lie suited his purpose better than the truth. He lied habitually to his mother, to his playmates, to his teachers; but even so, Jason could not understand why his teachers were not left to deal with him, as they were with other boys in case of wrong doing. By and by, he remembered the long walk he had made to Bluffport for the canary which he had bought with some of the money he had saved for his own use, earned by doing extra work on Saturdays and of nights and mornings and during summer vacations in the grocery of Peter Potter. He had understood why Mahala could not invite him to her party, and he understood as surely that she would have done it if she could; and that made everything concerning her all right with Jason. To his mind, the will to do was in no way related to the power of execution. Because Mahala wanted to invite him, he had thought deeply, and the loveliest thing he could think of in connection with her was a bird, as gold as her hair, that spent its life in spontaneous song,—the tiny, domestic creature that loved the bars of the only home its kind had known for generations and would have been terrified and lost outside them. He had been compelled to walk far and fast, to beg rides when he could, in order to cover the distance, and get Peter Potter's hand to frame the note for him that he tied upon the cage, in time for the party. He had left the bird at her door; he had seen Mahala love it. He had felt her hand on his arm, her gift thrust into his fingers; he had heard her voice urging him to protect himself; but not one word had she said to chide him for the impulse that had caused him to tear the piece of brick from the border of Mrs. Spellman's flower bed and send it smashing against the head of the boy who had dared to touch her roughly, to lay the hateful red of his full-lipped mouth on her delicate face.

The sunlight slowly warmed Jason and comforted him. He began to feel the gnawing of hunger. He remembered with a shock that almost toppled him off the stump, that all the honours of the previous evening had been his. He had watched the party from the vantage of a maple tree outside the parlour window, and it had been a long time before he had gained the courage to set his gift before the door, ring the bell, and rush back to his viewpoint. Now he recalled the fact, that while Junior's gift had been shown to the other children and examined and exclaimed upon, it was his gift that Mahala had taken into her arms. He did not even have to shut his eyes to see her face strained against the wires of the cage. He could hear her voice crying: "Oh, you dear little bird, I love you!" in Billings' cattle pasture quite as plainly as he had heard it the previous night.

Jason drew a deep breath and stood up and tested his strength. So far as Junior was concerned, he would undertake to handle him in the future, not from ambush, not with the help of a piece of brick. He would engage, by the strength of his arms and the tumult in his heart, to meet Junior as man met man upon any occasion.

Then he advanced a degree further in his progression, only to face the power of the banker. How was it that a beautiful woman in fine clothing appeared in his humble home; that she called the banker "Martin"; that she dared lay her hands upon him; that she tried to stop him from coming up the stairs mouthing his threats to kill; that she endured the blow from his blood-dripping hand? Who could the woman of foaming laces and arresting beauty have been save Marcia Peters? In his heart Jason always had called the woman with whom he lived "Marcia Peters." She never had taught him to call her "mother." He never had attempted the familiarity even when a small child. She had said to him: "Marcia will give you a glass of milk." He had said to her: "Marcia, please give me a piece of bread." How was it that in his life with her she was plain and homely, bending over a washtub, quietly mending laces and embroideries, while behind a locked door there was a room full of light, of delicate colour, of fashionable clothing, a room from which emanated flower perfumes and the tang of wine, a room with which the banker must have been familiar since he stepped from it laying down the law of outrage?

Jason's shoulders were square and his face was toward home now. But some way, as he took the first step in that direction, in his heart he felt that he was slightly taller, stronger, different from the boy he had been the night before. He might get no satisfactory answer, but there were questions he intended to ask. He had no idea what he would find at the other side of the meadow. Would Martin Moreland be lying dead at the foot of the stairs? Would Marcia have dragged him into the locked room? Would she tell him to go and dig a deep place in the forest? Would they carry Martin Moreland out the coming night and lay him in it, and must they walk the remainder of their lives with a horrible secret stiffening their mouths and taunting their brains?

As he mulled these problems over and over in his mind he reached his back door. He realized that something portentous had happened. There were many heavy footprints, deeply cut wagon tracks; the cow was not calling from the shed; his white chickens that he had earned through the medium of Peter Potter, were not walking in their yard calling for their breakfast. He laid his hand upon the kitchen door, and tried to open it, only to find that it was locked. Then he went to the front door which was locked, while across it there was nailed a board upon which was printed in big, black letters: "This property for sale." Through the window he could look into the house and see that it was empty. Then he knew that the woman he had always thought of as his mother had abandoned him. Marcia must have been the woman that he had seen the night before. He sat on the top step and began to remember again. He remembered many things—little things. The rubber gloves she wore when she was washing. She had said that they were to protect her fingers so that she could handle laces and fine mending. He remembered the jealously locked door and the glimpse he had had inside it the previous night. How could she have emptied the house and disappeared in that length of time without the aid of a powerful influence? He had seen the powerful influence in the grim figure with the uplifted hand. He had seen her dare to touch the banker. He had heard her call him "Martin," he had seen the mark of his bloody hand on her white breast. She had been roughly flung aside as if she were a creature worthy of no consideration.

Suddenly Jason found that his face was buried in his rough, lean hands, while his body was torn once more with deep, dry sobs that rasped his being until the soles of his feet twitched on the board walk. When he had cried until he was exhausted, he slowly arose, and going around the house, he pumped some water and bathed his face and hands, drying them with a forgotten towel hanging on the back porch. He combed his hair with his fingers and straightened his clothing as best he could. He turned his face in the direction of the only friend he had in the world to whom he could go.

On the way, he made a detour and passed the bank on the opposite side of the street. Then he lingered until he saw Martin Moreland cross from the wicket of the paying teller to the private office of the President. Jason knew him by his height, his form, his bandaged head. The face of the boy took on the look of a man as he went on his way.

There was a lull in the business of the morning when Jason walked into the grocery of Peter Potter. Peter was precisely what his name implied—British, English of birth, as all Potters have a right to be, stable of character as all Peters have a right to be; the rock that a discerning mother had discovered in his small face before she had decorated him with the Peter appellation. Unquestionably, Peter had not been as progressive as he might have been. He had been faithful in the grocery business, but he had lacked talent. There were a thousand things that he should have been doing in the morning lull; instead he was smoking a pipe and contentedly stroking a cat. His florid face was very round, his bright eyes were twinkly blue. A hint of shrewdness and penuriousness lay in the lines around them; more than a hint of stubbornness lay in the breadth of his chin. Conservatism was written all over his baggy breeches and his gingham shirt, but no one would have dared to look at Peter Potter and say that he was not immaculately clean in person, honest in disposition, while the discerning might have surmised that he was misinformed as to the size of his palpitator. Peter prided himself upon being close.

Jason felt sufficiently well acquainted with Peter to venture a familiarity. Now Jason was not given to familiarities, but he had spent a searing night in the woods, he had spent the morning in Billings' pasture and at his deserted home. He had reached a decision, and that decision was that he was utterly alone in the world, that he had his own way to make, and that he must begin by using his wits. And so, in desperation, he thrust his past behind him, and spiritually as naked as at the hour of his birth and equally as forsaken, he stood before Peter Potter. In a voice that sounded peculiar to himself and that caught Peter in an unaccustomed way, Jason said quietly: "Peter, I have decided that the time has come when you need a partner in your business."

Peter Potter lifted the cat by each of its fore legs and setting one of its hind feet upon either of his knees, carefully surveyed its white belly and the exquisitely lined tortoise shell of its back, and replied: "Who says I haven't had a partner for lo, these many years? Hasn't Jezebel performed signal service when she's kept this place free of rats and mice?"

"She surely has," answered Jason, "but your store isn't going to regain its position as the leading grocery of Ashwater merely by being free of rats and mice—keeping a cat in their stead. Many people don't like cats in groceries."

Peter considered this as he carefully set the cat upon the floor and with a shove of his foot told her to busy herself about her predestined occupation. Then he lifted his eyes to Jason and was rather surprised to notice how the boy had grown since the last time he had looked at him carefully. Maybe his height was due to the fact that Jason was standing. Peter got upon his feet in order to bring his bulk more nearly on a level with Jason, and when he reached a level with the boy, he noticed that height was not the only attainment since he had last looked at him searchingly. His face had so many things in it that Peter blinked and turned his eyes from it. It was almost as if he had looked into a holy of holies where the eyes of a human being had no right to intrude. He wondered what could have happened to the boy in twelve hours that had turned him into a man.

There was something so heart-stirring in Jason's face that Peter Potter's voice was husky as he asked: "Why do you think I need a partner?"

Jason replied: "You need a driver who won't race your delivery horse when he's out of your sight. You need a clerk who will weigh your goods carefully, charge what he should, and use sense about giving credit. You need a partner who will put all the money he is paid into your cash drawer, and who won't spend his spare time fishing from your raisin jar and your cracker barrel."

Peter Potter moistened his lips with an interested tongue and ventured a study of Jason's face.

"Meaning you?" he inquired tersely.

Jason took off his hat and tried to see how tall he could look. He bravely answered: "Yes, Peter, meaning me. I could do a lot of things that would be a big help to you, if you would give me a free hand here until I could show you what I could do."

Peter reflected. "I don't see how you're going to do so very much in what time you have mornings and evenings; really to perform a miracle you'd need more of the week than Saturday."

"You are right," said Jason. "All the time there is, I can give to you. I'm not going to school any more."

Peter shook his head.

"No, Jason," he said finally, "that won't do. Eddication is a blasted good thing for any boy or girl to have I've taken a good deal of pride in you, bein' top notch of your classes. I've figured that I'd buy you a purty nice present the night you gradiate with the honours of your class."

Then Jason looked Peter through and through. A big warm surge of comfort suffused his wiry body. How wonderful! Peter Potter was proud of him! He had been planning secretly to buy him a gift. Jason forgot about how tall he was trying to look.

"Peter," he said, "I'm in trouble this morning. If you keep your eyes on Hill Street, you'll notice that both the banker and his precious son are wearing bandaged heads. And, between us, I am proud to admit that the bandages are worn in deference to the accuracy of my aim: in the case of the son, with a piece of brick, in that of the

72

father, with a heavy stool. There wouldn't be the slightest use in my going to school this morning, Peter. I'd be expelled before noon. I am staving off that action by staying away. There isn't room in the same class any longer for the son of the Ashwater banker and the son of the Ashwater washerwoman."

Peter Potter lifted a plump hand and drew it across the lips of his wide-open mouth, and then his jaws came together with a snap and from between his teeth he said slowly: "So *that's* the lay of the land?"

Jason nodded.

"Yes, Peter," he said, "'that's the lay of the land.' You're the only friend I've got on earth. Will you let me come into your grocery and see if I can clean it up and get back some of your business, and help you as a boy ought to help his father? And will you let me have room among the barrels at the back, or upstairs, where I can set a trundle-bed?"

Peter studied Jason and reflected. Then he delivered himself of his conclusion in the speech of fifty years of association.

"It's a blasted shame," he said. "It hadn't oughter be. This town oughter riz up an' stand beside you and see that you get your schoolin'. But I guess the truth is that Martin Moreland has got so many men in his clutches that they don't hardly know their souls are their own. I could have been in better shape myself, if I'd 'a' borrowed from him when I needed money darn bad, but I'd said I wouldn't do it, and I didn't do it, and so I let my stock run down and I lost trade. But I figure that I'm one of about half a dozen men in town that he ain't got his shackles on. It appeals to me that the rest of 'em comes mighty close to being critters that will jump through most any kind of a hoop that he holds before 'em when he cracks his whip. If you got your mind fully made up to this, you bet your sweet life you can have a bed in the upstairs. We'll push the barrels back and straighten the boxes and run a partition across and fix you a nice place. Be a protection to the store to have you there. What was you figurin' on about terms?"

"I'll tell you," said Jason. "You give me enough food, enough milk and butter and dried beef and eggs and green stuff, to just barely keep my stomach from cramping and pinching all the time, and let me work a month. Then you figure yourself what I've been worth to you. And if you will, help me to buy the bed. The truth is, I spent every cent I had yesterday."

"All right," said Peter Potter. "Things are always pretty dead about now. Let's go right up and push back the clutter. Then I'll go over to Jefferson's furniture store and fix you up a bed."

So together they climbed the creaking stairs and piled back barrels and boxes until they cleared space in the front part of the storeroom above the grocery upon which to stand a small bed for Jason.

While Jason washed windows, swept the floors, and began to dust the boxes and bottles upon the shelves, Peter Potter went to the furniture store, and out of the bigness of his heart, instead of a trundle-bed he bought a neat oak bed with real springs, a mattress, and a pillow. He felt almost militant as he marched into Mahlon Spellman's dry-goods store to buy a pair of pillow cases, two pairs of sheets, a heavy blanket and a comfort. That night Jason looked at the stained, cobwebby ceiling above him, the battered walls surrounding him, and mentally visioned the partition promised to shut him off from the remainder of the storeroom.

When they were ready to lock up for the night, Peter Potter bolted the doors on the inside, went back to his personal chair near the big iron stove, and sitting down with the tortoise-shell cat in his lap, motioned Jason toward another chair.

"Now," he said, "go ahead. Tell me all about this. I ain't intending to go home tale bearin' to Mirandy; I just want to have the satisfaction of knowin' in my own soul where I stand regardin' the Morelands."

So Jason began with the time of the tormenting of Rebecca and detailed occurrences up to the previous night. Peter sat quietly stroking Jezebel. Sometimes through narrowed lids, he watched the boy; sometimes his attention seemed wholly taken up with the cat. But when Jason had finished the last word he had to say, not forgetting the first look inside the locked door, Peter Potter sat still and meditated. Then surreptitiously he scrutinized Jason. He studied in detail the set and colour of the hair on his head, the look from his eyes, the shape of his features, the build of his body, his hands as they hung idly before him. Then he dipped back into what he called the "ancient history" of Ashwater, and thought over reports and rumours that had been current in the town a good many years before.

When Jason had finished, Peter arose without any comment upon what he had been told. He set the cat carefully on the floor and lightly shoved her from him with his foot.

"Jezebel," he said, "you've been a queen of a cat and a fine mouser, but your reign is over. There are them as object to cats promenading on the counters and sleepin' in the cracker barrel. Go chase yourself! Vamoose! Try Thornton's drug store. More of the stuff there is bottled. Farewell, forever!"

Peter recovered the cat, and standing with her in his arms, he said to Jason: "I think that you've done about the only thing left for you. I believe after this you can't go back to school. I'll get the carpenter to put in that partition as quick as he can, and if you'd like the walls fresh, we'll cover 'em with a cheap paper, and you may get some blinds to put on the windows. You may go to Thornton's drug store and get you a hand lamp if so be you want to keep up your studies. You may get a little table to match your bed at Jefferson's, and a chair, and then I feel you'll be better fixed than you've ever been before."

He locked the store for the night and carried Jezebel across the street, where he formally presented her to the druggist.

The next morning Mahala entered Peter Potter's grocery with an order to give to Peter, but when she saw Jason behind the counter, she went to him with it instead. As she handed the slip to him she said: "You'll have to hurry, Jason, or you'll be late to school. I missed you yesterday."

Jason slowly shook his head. To have saved his life he could not have kept a couple of big tears from squeezing from his eyes and rolling down his white cheeks. He turned his back and swallowed hard. He fought with all his might to wink away the tears. Mahala looked at him in consternation. She could plainly see that he had suffered terribly since she last had seen him. All the rising tide of fair play, of compassion in her heart, surged up to her lips and she began to quiver.

"Oh, Jason!" she cried. "What happened to you? What did they do to you?"

Then Jason turned to her.

"Nothing," he said. "They didn't get me, but it's no use for me to go back to school. I'd be expelled before noon, you know I would."

Mahala stood still, thinking. She lifted her clear, steady eyes to the equally clear, steady eyes of the boy before her. "I'm afraid you would, Jason," she said softly. "You shouldn't have hit him."

Jason considered that a minute and then he said conclusively: "Yes, I should have hit him. What I did that was wrong was to throw something and hide among the bushes. If I had been a man I'd have beaten him as he deserved with my fists on the street. It was not because I was afraid of him; it was because I dared not be seen where I was. You understand, don't you?"

Mahala stood so still that it scarcely seemed as if she were breathing.

"Yes," she said in a hushed voice, "I understand."

At those words of comfort the look on Jason's face changed to one of tormented heart hunger. He said abruptly: "I can't tell you all that happened. Junior's father came to our house threatening to kill me. If you pass the bank to-day, you may notice that the Senior Moreland has had an accident. That other time he came to our house, up to my room, and beat me almost to death. This time I flung a stool at him half way up the stairs and jumped from the window. Whatever is the matter with him is what I did to him. But I got my punishment fast enough. I thought I'd be hanged for killing him. I stayed all night in the woods and it was cold and awful. I went back to find Marcia gone and the house empty, but I've got a chance to work here for Peter."

Then Jason stopped and shut his mouth and held it stiff and tense, and by sheer will power, he kept back the impending tears. A slow red had crept into his cheeks and there was colour in his lips. Mahala was hurt intensely. Without a thought for anything, she crowded close to Jason. She laid her hands on his sleeve.

Across the grocery Peter Potter had been watching them intently. The street was full of people. Two women were heading toward his door. He walked back and placed his body between Mahala and Jason and the line of the door. He laid one arm across Jason's shoulder and then he said to Mahala casually: "Now you had better step along to school, little lady. Jason's a good boy. I'm goin' to fix him a room above the grocery where he can study his books and keep up with his lessons at night. I'd be deeply obliged, and so would he, if you could manage to run in once a week and tell him how far his class has gone with the lessons."

Instantly Mahala stepped back. She would not venture another look at Jason, but she met the eyes of Peter frankly, while in her most gracious manner she held out her hand.

"Thank you very much, Peter," she said, "I think it's splendid of you to help Jason, because you and I know that when he is the smartest boy in the class, he shouldn't be forced to quit school."

She turned and started from the grocery. Half way down the aisle, and directly facing the women who were entering, she wheeled, with a graceful gesture of remembrance.

"Peter," she called in her clear voice, "Mother says that she hasn't had a bite of such delicious ham between her teeth in two or three years as those last ones you got from the country. She wants you to save another one for us."

Then she smiled on both the advancing women. "Good morning, Mrs. Sims. Good morning, Mrs. Jordan," she said in her very best manner. "I was telling Peter to save another one of his delicious hams for us. You really should try them."

Then Mahala went on her way to school, and she failed in her lessons all day because her mind was not on her work. She longed to ask her mother several important questions, but dared not on account of the bird and Junior's injury. She was afraid to ask the questions to which she wanted answers of Mrs. Williams, for fear she would mention to Mahala's mother what she had been asked. She dared not tell that Jason had been forced from school, lest he be connected in the minds of her parents with Junior. For many days she carried a head full of disquieting thought, a heart of aching protest.

Mrs. Sims bought one ham, Mrs. Jordan bought two. After they had gone, Peter Potter planted himself in front of Jason and shook his head sadly. Then he said: "Now look here, my lad, don't you get any silly notions into your noddle. You've got to understand that the richest and the prettiest girl in this town ain't in any way connected with you. She's sorry for you, same as I am, because she knows you ain't gettin' a square deal."

Jason answered quietly: "I know, Peter. You needn't worry."

He went into the back room and sat down on a pickle keg, and with a brush and a can of black paint, on a smooth piece of pine before him, he began to paint. After he had worked for half an hour, Peter Potter tiptoed up behind him and looked over his shoulder. He read upon one piece of pine: "I dare you to look at this and not want to eat it!" and on the other: "We have turned over a new leaf. Have you?" Peter slipped away and indulged in the unusual occupation of deep and concentrated thought. His eyes were following Jason while he cleaned out one of the show windows, set the new sign of challenge in it, and surrounded it with bread, cake, cookies, and every delicious food in the grocery that he could display in the open. Through the other freshly washed window, the passer-by might read the leaf sign and see an assortment of cheese and pickles, and half of a ham that looked as pink as a piece of coral framed in a broad white ring of sweet, sugar-cured fat. A freshly dusted coffee canister stood near it. A big box of lima beans flanked it on one side and the brown and gold of smoked herring was on the other; along the back, an open keg of whitefish and another of mackerel, with samples of their contents attractively displayed.

Peter Potter stepped outside to reconnoitre. As he went, he noticed that the grime of years had been removed from his doors, which revealed the fact that they seriously needed a coat of paint. He looked through the windows with the fresh signs surrounded by such food as he did not know that he possessed, because he never had seen it so displayed. He stood there in the morning sunlight intently studying each of the windows. Presently, he realized that he was not alone. Two women with their market baskets on their arms had been attracted by the new display. He heard one of them say to the other: "Why, do you know, we ain't had mackerel in a long time, and there's nothing I like better."

"And doesn't that ham look good?" said the other. "What about some of them limy beans with cream and butter on them? Let's go in."

Peter stepped forward and opened his door.

"Ladies," he said in his politest manner, "I've turned over that new leaf for sure and certain. I'm going to show this town what really good eating is. Walk right in and see for yourselves whether what I'm tellin' you isn't the truth."

Then a shadow fell across Peter Potter's shoulder. He looked up, quite a distance up, to find himself in what to most of the village of Ashwater was the portentous presence of the village banker—of less portent to Peter Potter than to many others, because while Peter had fallen into second place through lack of initiative, he was not in debt. He did have a balance in his favour, but for reasons of his own, his balance was not in the bank of Martin Moreland. Peter followed Martin Moreland through the door. He had difficulty in keeping the lines of his rotund face in order. His soul was bathed in a secret flood of pleasure. He could not remember having been so pleased in years and years as he was now pleased to see for himself the substantial surgical bandage swathing the headpiece of the suave banker, and in noticing that his right hand was thrust into the front of the double-breasted coat that he wore to reinforce the impression of authority and circumstance that he desired to convey to his fellow men.

And Peter knew, also, that it was time to set his feet very firmly upon his own floor and to unchain that bulldog credited to the possession of every Briton by birth, whether he be in his native land or the land of his adoption. Luckily, Peter had his fair share of canine inclinations in fine working order because of some years of disuse. He knew perfectly well that Martin Moreland was not interested in his new signs and his attractive display of food. He knew that he had entered his place of business in order to search his aisles with keen eyes and see for himself if Jason were working there. Peter's eyes were sharply watching Martin Moreland's face as Jason came down inside the counter on his way to the scales bearing a couple of dripping mackerel upon a sheet of wrapping paper. Peter's heart turned over in his body and then stood still when Jason, looking up from the scale of weights, encountered the glaring eyes of the banker fixed upon him, and said smoothly and evenly: "Good morning, Mr. Moreland. I'll take your order as soon as I finish with these ladies."

Now Peter knew that Martin Moreland was not accustomed to waiting till ladies had been served, especially if the "ladies" carried market baskets on their arms and wore white aprons and cheap shawls across their shoulders. To use Peter's own description of the situation to his wife that night, he "was havin' a bully time.—Had to turn away for a minute to keep from snortin' right in Moreland's face."

The banker followed Peter down the aisle and jostled him roughly with his elbow as he said to him: "Now you look here, Peter Potter. Answer me this. Who's running this town?"

A very devil of perversity possessed Peter, for he answered: "Well, if you really think you are, your head looks like you're makin' a bally mess of it."

It had been evident to the employees of the bank that the attempted hold-up that Martin Moreland reported had upset his temper to quite as great extent as it had disfigured his head and his influential right hand. There was nothing soothing to the ragged Moreland nerves in Peter's retort.

"I came in here," said Martin Moreland, "to give you just fifteen minutes to get that scum of the brothel out of your store."

Peter Potter cocked his head on one side and looked at Martin Moreland.

"Martin," he drawled slowly, "ain't you makin' a fine, large mistake? Didn't you forget to study your books before you came rampagin' into my place of business? As I recollect, I don't owe you a red cent. You ain't even one of my reg'lar and influential customers. They's only one bill on my books that I'm carryin' in your name and tain't anything I'm proud of. I could spare it without a mite of trouble. Before you undertake to run my business, go back and stick your nose well down in your own. I ain't goin' to turn Jason out, and if you undertake to bother him, I got this same private account, that I'm going to increase against you a little in about a minute, that'd look peculiar to the deacons of your church and to all and sundry. If it's the same to you, I wish you'd step out the way of my reg'lar customers!"

Peter Potter swung his front door wide and held it open.

In rage too deep for speech, Martin Moreland turned and started from the grocery, but he was forced to stand aside, for at that minute, Rebecca Sampson, with a smile of youthful innocence on her face, bearing her white flag over her shoulder, filled the doorway.

She looked straight at Peter Potter, and as an evidence of a custom between them, she held out her white flag and Peter Potter bowed his bald, pink head and stepped under it with the kindliest kind of a "Good morning!" The change in his voice and in his manner broke the nerve of Martin Moreland, already at the breaking point. The oath he uttered was shocking. Startled, Rebecca pushed back her bonnet and looked up at him. A flash of loathing, of anger, crossed her face. She caught the white symbol to her breast and edged to the farthest possible distance from him permitted by the width of the store. She made her way back to where she was accustomed to being served, muttering imprecations upon the head of Martin Moreland that were quite equal to Martin's best in strong provocation.

In the high tide of anger, he took one step toward her. The resistant force with which he came in arresting contact was nothing less than the sturdy frame of Peter Potter in defensive attitude. Peter looked up at Martin Moreland with fire in his eyes and a sneer on his lips.

"Get it through your pate," he said tersely. "I'm one man out of a few in this town that's not a mite afraid of you. If we come to a show down, I've got something to show that would interest the rest of the town, I vow! I've asked you once to leave my store; now I wish you'd do it!"

Martin Moreland rushed through the door and turned in the direction of the bank, where he collided with Jimmy Price. Jimmy, on his way to work, had been interested by the extremely arresting pictures presented by the windows of Peter Potter's grocery that morning. Jimmy had started to work with the feeling that he was comfortably fed, and had discovered, as he viewed the display windows, that he was hungry. He found his mouth watering for half a dozen different things. With his feet planted widely apart and either hand at his waist band, he was giving himself over to the gustatory delight of imagining which feature of the window display he would most rather have served him piping hot in his wife's best brand of cookery. With eyes of longing he was studying the pink ham, the blue-and-silver mackerel. He had almost decided that the mackerel, boiled free of salt, slightly browned in butter, with a baked potato and a cup of coffee, would be wholly satisfying, when he innocently resolved himself into the immovable force coming in contact with a movable body.

Jimmy stood the impact amazingly well. Martin Moreland glanced off him and reeled to one side. Jimmy was rather substantial; in that instant his person converted itself into a materialization of the last straw for Martin Moreland. Here was a creature, shaped like a man, wholly at his mercy. The banker doubled his disabled hand into a fist, with which he launched a crashing blow in the direction of the most substantial part of Jimmy's anatomy. Jimmy had recovered from the mackerel sufficiently to realize that it was the mighty banker who had collided with him, while the blow had careened him to one side. Through daily manipulations of hoe, rake, and sickle, Jimmy had become almost a boneless creature. He evaded the menace as lightly as he sank to work with sheep shears or trowel, so that the fist of opulence shot over him and struck the window casing instead with sufficient force to break open the slightly set wounds, wrenching from the lips of its owner a hyena-like howl of shredded anguish.

For one moment Martin Moreland was too badly hurt to think of his position or his dignity—matters of his most constant concern. He was almost reeling with nausea and spleen. He felt for his hat to see that it was set as straight as possible above his bandages, and arranged his coat. He thrust the hand, through which wiry slivers of pain were shooting, into his bosom. He started toward the bank in what he hoped was his most dignified manner.

Jimmy, completing the dive he had made to escape the arm of malevolence, came to an upright position at the middle of the step leading to the grocery. He did not in the least understand why, in the "land of the free and the home of the brave," he might not be permitted to stand on the sidewalk and contemplate the deliciousness on display in Peter Potter's window if he chose. He did not understand why the august banker should not have been paying sufficient attention to where he was going not to collide with inoffensive human beings wholly within their rights. He did not even try to understand why Martin Moreland had launched a blow at him with a heavily bandaged hand, but it had caused hatred to flare in his heart. He resolved, that if he ever got a chance, he would show Martin Moreland that he was just as good as any old banker. He wondered about the heavily bandaged head. As he looked after the retreating figure, Jimmy became aware, as he always was aware of any slight chance to be in the limelight, that a number of people on the street and at the doors and windows of the different stores, were watching the proceeding with intense interest. Immediately, Jimmy straightened his figure, felt for his hat, set his coat, and thrusting one hand into the front of it, strutted down the street in such exact imitation of the stride of the banker that a roar went up the length of the block; the louder people laughed the more exaggeratedly Jimmy kept up his imitation.

Martin Moreland was conscious of being the butt of that shout of laughter. He was certain that the creature he referred to as the "town monkey" was performing some absurd antic behind his back which was making him the one thing he loathed being above any other—a laughing stock. His inherent pride was too strong to allow him even to glance behind him. He would infringe on his dignity if he permitted himself to pay the slightest attention to what he mentally denominated "the rabble." Exactly why the Senior Moreland should have felt in his heart that the "boys grown tall" among whom he had been born and had lived all his life, were "rabble" would be very difficult to explain. He was perspiring freely with pain, with nervousness, while his heart was almost suffocating him with anger as he mounted the steps and made his way between the huge bronze dogs guarding the portal of the Ashwater First National Bank, Martin Moreland, President.

CHAPTER VI

"The Golden Egg"

By what she could see in the October moonlight of the open spaces, Marcia Peters, pounding over the highway, surrounded by her belongings, imagined that she was on the way to the second largest town of the county, Bluffport, a dozen or so miles from Ashwater. She recognized the village when she was driven into it. She saw that she was passing the business part of the town and the better residences, and at last, as in Ashwater, she found herself on the extreme outskirts.

The dray stopped before a small house. The drayman unlocked the door, carried in, and with small ceremony, dumped her clothing and furnishings on the floor. Then he climbed on his wagon and drove away without having spoken a word.

Marcia closed the door behind him, and from force of habit, turned the key. She had been riding through the night until her eyes were accustomed to the darkness. She had no provision for light, but through the uncurtained windows she could see enough to distinguish the mattress of her bed. As she was desperately tired, she pulled it to a bare spot upon the floor, hunted a pillow, and lying down in her clothing, covered her shoulders with her coat, and mental strain culminated in the blessed surcease of tears.

Marcia whimpered to the darkness: "What had I to do with it? What is fair or just about treating me like this?"

And again: "Where in the world can Jason have gone? I didn't think he'd have the spunk. He might have killed him."

And later: "After the wreck of my life, after all the lies he's told me—to be cast off among strangers like this—I might have known!"

Then a last sobbing breath: "I did know. It's been coming for a long time. This is only a poor excuse—I did know!"

She was awakened in the morning by a burning ray of sunlight falling on her face. At first she was too dazed to realize where she was or how she came to be there. Slowly she arose and went to a window. She saw that she was on a pretty street of a village, the outskirts of which gave promise of being more attractive than had been her corresponding location in Ashwater. Turning slowly, she went through the small house. There were only three rooms, but they were much more attractive than the rooms in which she had been living. Mechanically she began picking up the expensive furnishings of her private room that had been hurriedly bundled together and dumped roughly anywhere there was space to drop them. In working at this business a few minutes, she collected her thoughts and remembered that she had been through tense excitement and nerve strain. She was dreadfully hungry. Through no fault of her own that she could recall, she had been picked up in one place and set down in another as if she were a piece of furniture instead of a woman endowed with some degree of intelligence. She had not been asked whether she would go, or, if she must move, where she wanted to locate. She had not been given time to exercise any care with the really beautiful things which had furnished her personal room. She had only a small sum in her purse. There was no one in Bluffport with whom she was acquainted. For over fifteen years she had cared for Jason. She had become accustomed to him. One of the very greatest fights of her difficult life had been to keep herself from becoming fond of him. The threat that he would be taken from her any day had been constant. Dimly she had realized for a long time that this hour was coming; and now it had arrived. For a mistake of her youth, for the giving of her heart when only her body had been coveted, she had paid the price of menial position, of isolation, of spiritual degradation. She realized that speedily she must face the town asking work with which to keep up her long-time pretense of being self-supporting.

Her stomach reminded her that she must have food, or very speedily, torturing headache would ensue. Marcia sat down on the mattress, took her head between her hands, and for the first time in eighteen years thought about herself instead of Martin Moreland. Suddenly there came to her the sickening realization that she was no longer young. Looking her mental problem in the face, she admitted that she was thirty-six. As youth was reckoned in her day, a woman was considered reasonably aged at forty. No doubt this was Martin Moreland's first step in letting her know that her reign was over. In retrospect, what a sorry reign it had been!—veiled suspicion, mental humiliation, isolating employment, heart-hunger for freedom to lift up her head and walk abroad with pride. She felt reasonably certain that the problem facing her now was not one of further concealment, but the necessity of being equal to taking over the entire care of herself and making provision for hopeless old age.

Under the urge of hunger, she arose, found her hat, straightened her clothing as best she could, and hunted her mirror. Setting it up, she studied herself, not the self that Jason had known for nearly sixteen years, but the secret self which was her real self—Marcia Peters without the disfiguration of unbecomingly dressed hair and concealing clothing.

Every fibre of womanhood in her being rebelled against a return to the disguise in which she had faced Jason and Ashwater all her life with Martin Moreland. In starting a new life, in strange environment, whether as formerly or alone, why should she not appear before the people as she was? Why should she not seek occupation less humiliating than that of washing the dirty clothes of another village? Staring into the mirror and thinking, Marcia began pulling out drawers from her dresser, and when she emerged from the house presently and locked its door behind her, she was not a figure that Jason would have recognized before his night of illumination.

She followed the street to the heart of the village, and entering a restaurant, secured her breakfast. Then she decided, under the spiritual reinforcement that developed from nourishing food, that she would at least step into a few of the stores in Bluffport and look around her. Possibly she could summon courage to ask if any of them were in need of help. There, too, was her needle. She knew herself to be expert with that. With small practice in fitting, she could make dresses for other women as beautifully as she made them for herself. Why not a room over some of these down-town stores, a modest sign announcing herself as a dressmaker? Some attractive, progressive occupation, the stimulus of ever so small a degree of human association, some relation—no matter how remote—to the lives of other people. Never before had she allowed a cloud of doubt and protest to gather to a storm head. Now the culmination came quickly in a tempest that shook her being. She knew that she was facing men, walking straightly; she felt as if she were at the mercy of a tornado, half-blinded, feeling her way before her with protesting, outstretched hands. For the first time in her thwarted, unnatural life she needed friends so badly, that she felt the despair and the hunger of that need, and while she walked mechanically, as the storm in her heart grew in intensity, she realized that even more than she needed friends, she needed God. That need made her think of Rebecca, scorching under summer suns, struggling through winter snows, on her self-imposed task of urging her world to pass under an emblem of purity—poor Rebecca, demented, isolated, searching, ever searching, for what? Preaching—scourged by the whips of adversity into thrusting her timid self before the gaze of her world, preaching purity—why? Who sent her on those missions? Marcia said to herself: "At least, it is a mercy that her brain is dulled. Maybe she does not suffer mentally."

As she went slowly along the street, after a time she found herself interestedly studying the windows she passed. Her feet stopped in front of a small wooden building centrally located. In either window of it, flanking the entrance door, there were examples of exceedingly attractive fall millinery miserably displayed. Marcia gripped her purse tighter.

"A veil. I'll say I need a veil," she told herself.

Then she opened the door and stepped inside. Her quick eyes searched the length of the store on either hand. As she looked her fingers itched to use a dust cloth, to pick up the really beautiful hats and display them to advantage, to rearrange the ribbon counter so that clashing colours would not set her teeth in protest.

She glanced around her, and seeing no one, she slowly walked to the back of the store. Everywhere it was stamped with what Marcia in her soul denominated "skimpiness." Even the hats that had been conceived in beauty, fell short of culmination because of cheap material, too frugal use of trimming. Pausing near the door that opened into the back room, Marcia looked ahead, and there she saw the form of a small woman, sitting beside a table piled with a disorderly array of wire forms and linings, ribbon and velvet, and glaring autumnal flowers. Her arms were crossed upon the table, her head buried in them, her shoulders shaking with sobs. For one long minute Marcia surveyed the bowed head; then she slowly turned her back and started down the aisle.

"Hm-m-m-m," she said softly. "Two of us. I wonder what's the matter with her?"

She made her way to the front door and opened it; then she closed it with sufficient force to be heard the length of the building, and with firm steps she went toward the back room again. Half the length of the aisle, she leaned on a display case, drumming with her fingers. Without turning her head, from the corner of her eye, she saw the woman in the back room rise and dab frantically at her face with her handkerchief. Presently, she came toward Marcia and asked in a voice she was making visible effort to control: "Was there something?"

Marcia looked at her intently. "Drab" was the adjective that sprang to her mind. Hair lacking the lustre of life, skin needing manipulation and the concealments of pink powder, deep facial lines of anxiety, eyes red with futile tears, a disappointed flat chest, rounded shoulders; a woman bilious from improper food and lack of exercise. Marcia smiled brilliantly. The smile was child of the thought that had just occurred to her. Washing might be a disqualifying occupation socially, but the bent back, the rise and fall over the board, the muscular wringing, the stretch to the line in hanging out and taking in, the steaming open of the pores of the face and neck, the exercise on foot, the swing of the iron—washing had no social standing, but daily exercise the round of the year at its exactions never bred a Nancy Bodkin. Marcia could have wrung Nancy like a wet sheet and hung her in the fresh air and sunshine to her great benefit. Suddenly, she was thankful for the steaming and exercise of every muscle of her body that had made and kept her a creature of fresh face and perfect health.

"Yes," she said deliberately to Nancy, "there are a number of things. I wanted to see if I could find a veil. I'm a stranger in town. I came this morning. I intend staying here. I noticed what a good central location you've got and I wondered whether you'd like to rent me half of your space and let me do dressmaking—or, maybe, you'd like a partner in the millinery business?"

The woman behind the counter stared at Marcia with widely opened eyes while her lower lip drooped.

"You—you're a milliner?" she asked.

"No," said Marcia, "I'm not a milliner. I never made a hat in my life. But I can make stylish dresses. I do know how to keep a room clean, how to display goods in an attractive manner."

"Do you know anything," asked the woman, her hands gripping the inner edge of the showcase, "about keeping even—bills, and money, and things like that?"

For the first time, in she could not remember when, Marcia laughed aloud. Laughter was an unaccustomed sound on her lips. When she heard the tones of it, she was so shocked that she stopped abruptly as if she had committed an indiscretion.

"Yes," she said, "I do know enough about business to run a place like this without the least difficulty. To tell the truth, I've had a lot of schooling on how business should be done to be successful. What have you been doing? Letting your customers take away your goods without paying for them, and now the bills are due, and you've no money to meet them?"

The woman nodded.

"Hm-m-m," said Marcia. "Well, I could go out and collect all that I could pry out of people. I could clean up this place. Maybe I could convince your banker that he'd be safe in letting you have what you'd need to tide you over till we could get things started on a new and safe basis. Would you like to have me come in with you and try to help you into really prosperous business?"

Suddenly the little woman across the counter, clasping a pair of needle-roughened, shaking hands against her defrauded chest, looked with the beseeching eyes of a starving creature at the face of the woman opposite her.

"Oh, would you? Oh, would you, please?" she begged.

Marcia was taken unaware. She did not know that there was a soft place remaining in her heart capable of the response she felt herself making to that artless appeal.

"I certainly would," she answered. "I'd be mighty glad for the chance. I don't know a thing in the world about you. You don't know a thing in the world about me. Shall we agree to take each other on trust, to ask no questions, but start from now together and see what we can make out of life?"

"I'd be tickled to death!" said the little woman, recklessly toppling preconceptions and precautions of a lifetime.

"Is there room for me here?" inquired Marcia.

"Come and see what you think. And my name is Miss Nancy Bodkin," said the milliner, leading the way to the back room.

"Very well, Miss Nancy," said Marcia. "My name is Miss Marcia Peters. Let's explore your living arrangements."

Then she followed into the work room and found that there opened from it a bedroom sufficiently large for two people, and back of it was the combined dining room and kitchen in which Miss Nancy Bodkin had been existing for many years. Looking about her, the fingers of the capable Marcia tingled for order, cleanliness, fresh wall paper and paint, but she sensibly reasoned that these things could come later.

"You know the ropes here," she said. "Find me a drayman. I'll go and bring my things and we'll begin business right away."

That was how it happened that an hour later Marcia was back in the house in the suburbs with a stout drayman standing at her elbow. There was no possible way in which the drayman could know that Marcia was saying in her soul as she handed him an article, "Soapsuds," or that she was saying as she discarded a certain piece of furniture or attractive clothing, "Scarlet." All he realized was that the woman was making a division of the goods before them, and that the greater number and the better part of the things he saw, she was leaving.

When Marcia had satisfied herself, she found a sheet of paper and a pencil and she wrote: "I have bowed my head and passed under the White Flag. I have taken nothing that was purchased with your money, since you are far poorer than I." There was no beginning to the note and no signature.

When the drayman had carried the last load from the house, Marcia locked the doors on the inside. She propped the note in a conspicuous place on one of the pieces of furniture she was leaving and laid the key beside it. Then going to the kitchen, she raised a window and climbing from it, closed it behind her and followed down the street to the millinery shop.

There was such a fluttering in the breast of Nancy Bodkin that she could scarcely breathe. She was scared to death over what she had done. Why should a woman as attractive as this one, and having as fine clothing, want to live with her and to share her business? She felt that she had been wildly impractical. She should have consulted her minister and her banker and several of her best customers. She should have learned who the woman was and where she came from. And just when she was in a panic of uncertainty and nervous doubts, Marcia returned and lifted the hat from her head. She ran her fingers through her red-gold hair and drew a deep breath.

"Now, then, in about two shakes we'll get right down to the business of straightening you out," she said.

Nancy, a lean doubter, the victim of frustrated nature and business unsuccess, heard in golden wonder. Such assurance! So heartening! After all, whose business was this save her own? Why should she start any one to gabbling? Why not dignify herself and her affairs by reticence? Possibly the good God had seen fit to answer in this way the salt-tinctured appeal she had been clammily venturing in frank disbelief that He really would hear or answer when Marcia appeared. What if He were greater than she had thought? What if He had heard and cared? Such strength! Such energy! So capable! Some one to share the long, lonely hours—— Ask questions that might prove disastrous and spoil things when they were none of her real business? She guessed not! What was that about taking the gifts the gods provided? Who cared a whoop concerning the past of the gosling that had developed into the goose that laid the historical egg? It was the egg that really mattered—the egg!

Miss Nancy vibrated; she positively fluttered. Thinking of eggs made her want to cackle, but since it was the golden egg of a goose she craved—how did a goose voice rejoicings on such a momentous achievement? If she quacked, Miss Nancy was quite willing to quack. What she lacked was knowledge, not incentive.

All the time the drayman was carrying in furniture and bundles. Marcia opened a dresser drawer and took therefrom a dress, an apron of clean calico, and a pair of easy shoes. Standing in the back room, she stripped off the clothing she was wearing and put these on instead. Nancy was struggling to keep from asking Marcia where she came from, why she had brought furniture before she knew for certain that she would find work, but the lure of the Egg was upon her. She looked at the arms and shoulders and the curves of Marcia's bust with eyes of frank envy.

"My goodness, you are the prettiest thing!" she said. "And your clothes are so tasty."

Marcia smiled quietly, thinking of certain garments she had discarded.

"Now, the first thing to do is to arrange this bedroom and kitchen the best we can to accommodate my things," she said, "then we'll begin at the front and go straight through. When I've gotten everything clean, and in order, then you can tell me about who owes you and where they live and I'll see what I can collect. And then, we'll try to arrange the show windows more attractively, and since I can't make hats, maybe I'd better try them on and sell them, while you go on making them. You really do make beautiful hats, but be as speedy as you can, because I feel it in my bones that I am going to sell lots of them."

Then, with strong arms and assumed assurance, coupled with inborn abhorrence of dirt and disorder, Marcia Peters advanced to the rescue of the Bodkin Millinery.

The first visible sign of any change in that establishment came to the town of Bluffport when a good-looking woman emerged from the door with a bucket of foaming suds, a rag in her hand and a towel over her shoulder, and by standing on an empty packing case for necessary height, she polished the glass fronts and the glass of the door to iridescent sheen. After that it was evident from the outside that the activities of the newcomer included the vigorous use of a rag-covered broom on the ceiling and the side walls, the inner glass of the door and windows following. And then the shelves and the cases came in for their share of cleaning. The next day the front windows were filled with an appealing array of fall and winter hats judiciously and advantageously displayed. Between the stands that held the hats there wound lengths of ribbon of alluring colour and texture, while here and there were masses of colour from roses of velvet, the glitter of beads and bright leaves.

Straight back through the building went Marcia, every hour growing more interested, every hour given to intense thought as to what could be done, how it could best be done, and what the utmost financial return that could be extracted from it might be. One hard day's work consisted in emptying the bedroom, thoroughly cleaning it and rearranging it with such of Marcia's possessions as she had purchased herself. A small table that held a lamp was installed in the centre of the room, comfortable chairs placed on either side of it. The beds were attractively made and covered. Then the kitchen received attention.

The next Bluffport saw of the new venture was Marcia again mounted on her packing case with a bucket of white paint and a brush, energetically applying it to the window casings and the door. Pleased with results, Marcia recklessly painted as high as she could reach and then realized that the remainder of the false front, which reached two-story height with no backing in the dubious assumption that the building appealed to the eye of the beholder as what it was not, was out of her province. She had funds to hire a painter to complete the job, so she used them, although Nancy protested that she would pay half.

By that time, the change in appearance of the Bodkin Millinery was so great that parties interested in fall millinery and innovations, were beginning to come in. In the most attractive dress she possessed suitable for such use, with her really pretty hair drawn back loosely and coiled becomingly on her head, Marcia proved herself equal to the tongue of each newcomer. She had the advantage of not being taken unawares. She knew how the wolves of society harried the sheep of adventure; she had no intention of becoming their prey. Who she was, where she had come from, why she was there, she evaded, as slickly as the dews of night roll from the cabbage leaf of dawn. The qualities of satin and velvet, the colouring of ribbons and flowers, she found engrossing subjects. She had a way of picking up a wreath of artificial flowers and twisting the leaves into the most attractive shapes. Before she offered any hat for sale, she set it upon her own head and walked up and down behind the counter, turning and twisting to show the customer how it looked upon the head of a woman. When the customer had tried it upon her own head, if it did not fit or was not becoming, Marcia said so frankly. In these cases she ended by telling the purchaser that the shape of her head and her face were so individual that the only thing to do was to build a hat to suit her. She was capable of picking up a piece of buckram and with the shears deftly cutting therefrom a pattern for a hat, that with a little twist here and there, and trimming, would evolve into a shape that comfortably fitted and greatly enhanced the facial lines for which it was intended. Often she suggested a change in hair dressing, at times made a friend for life by deftly making the improvement herself.

It took Marcia six weeks to make Bodkin's Millinery the most attractive hat store in the flourishing town of Bluffport. With the first money that the firm could spare, the entire front of the building got a second coat of paint and the interior both paint and paper. The one thing that surprised Nancy Bodkin and caused the townspeople a minute of wonder, was the fact that when the freshly painted sign went up, it was an exact duplicate of the old one. Said Nancy: "Now that sign must have your name on it, too, and from the start we must share equally in the profits. It's a sure thing that all the work you are doing and the wonderful way you can sell things, is worth as much to me as the use of the building is to you."

But Marcia said authoritatively that she thought the best thing to do was merely to go on using the old sign, with which people were familiar. She had noticed that human nature was so perverse and contrary that it did not take kindly to changes. She thought the sign had much better be left merely "Bodkin Millinery."

Marcia had her surprise, equally as great, from an entirely different source. It had two ramifications. For days, at each opening of the door, her eyes had turned toward it, while fear gripped her heart, but as time went on and she neither saw nor heard from Martin Moreland, she concluded that she had been right in her surmise. He was as sick of his part of their bad bargain as she had become of hers; he was probably as glad to give freedom to her as she had been to accept it.

The other thing which amazed Marcia unspeakably was the fact that she was deriving intense enjoyment from the life she was living. There had been no sufficient reason why she should not go occasionally to the church services that Nancy attended. It seemed ungracious to refuse. It was good business to go. Adroitly Nancy adduced reasons as to why it would be better economy to run into a mite society or a church supper for a meal than to take of their time to prepare their own food, while they were benefiting the church and charity organizations as well. On these occasions she made a point of introducing Marcia to every man and woman with whom she was acquainted—and her years of business in the village had made her acquainted with every soul who homed there and hundreds from the country as well. Presently, Marcia found herself stopping for a minute at the bank to say a word about the weather or political conditions; occasionally business men dropped in to solicit a subscription to some enterprise the town had undertaken. In a short time, Marcia was feeling thoroughly at home. She was really enjoying the life she was living. She was interested in the people she was meeting; she was truly concerned about what they were doing. In her heart she knew that she was delighted to return to church as she had gone in her girlhood. One point she made definite in her mind and kept scrupulously. She never opened her lips to ask a question or to take the slightest interest in anything that might have been related to the life of Nancy Bodkin previous to their arrangement of their partnership. Naturally, she set the same seal upon Nancy's lips that she wore upon her own.

Nancy, frail in body and in parts of her brain, was surprisingly strong in others. In the back of her head she knew that when a woman of Marcia's appearance and ability walked into such a shop as she had been keeping, and regenerated it and straightened the business into a hopeful concern in a few weeks' time, she was not an ordinary woman; she had reasons of her own for being where she was and doing what she did. But the results were so gratifying to Nancy Bodkin that she shut her lips tight and drove her capable needle through flower stems, folded velvet, and buckram with precision and force. She said to her heart: "I don't care where she came from. I don't care who she is. I don't care what any one thinks about her. She's awful pretty. She's smart as a whip. She's clean as a ribbon, and what's it of my business, or any one else's except her own, as to why she's here? I am good and thankful to have her, and there had better not any one poke around and hurt her feelings or they'll get a piece of my mind. The present and the Golden Egg are good enough for me."

That night Marcia capped the climax that she had reached in Nancy Bodkin's heart by a masterly stroke. In the privacy of their mutual room, after the store was closed for the day, she washed Nancy's hair, dried and brushed it to silkiness. The following morning she curled it and laid it in becoming waves and braids upon her well-shaped head. She applied some of the powder that she used upon her own nose to the nose of Nancy Bodkin, and performed a sleight-of-hand miracle upon her lips and cheeks. When Nancy looked into her mirror, she did not know herself. She did not ever want to know herself again as she had been. She was so perfectly delighted with what she saw within her grasp by a few months of work, that she had no words in which to express her feeling. The next thing she knew, Marcia came into the store with a piece of goods that she cut up, and in spare time, fashioned into a most attractive dress for Nancy.

That did settle the matter. Marcia might talk if she wanted to talk; she might keep her mouth shut if she so desired. It was patent that she was perfectly capable, honest, and attractive in appearance. Very shortly Nancy Bodkin worshipped her as she never had worshipped any human being in all her life. These feelings broadened and deepened because she realized, whenever she walked abroad attractively clothed and with all of her best points pronouncedly intensified, that people showed her a deference and a kindliness that she never before had experienced. In a bewildered way, Nancy slowly figured out the situation. If she had spent a small share of the time on herself that she had been accustomed to spending on hats for her townspeople, a larger share of their respect would have been bestowed upon her. It was a new viewpoint for Nancy. She had been thinking that she might earn the highest esteem by spending herself upon her profession to the exclusion of everything else, and now she was forced to learn, by overwhelming evidence, that the degree of respect she received from the village was going to depend very largely upon the height of the degree to which she respected herself.

CHAPTER VII

"Field Mice Among the Wheat"

It is a truism that time is fleeting, while never does it flee on such rapid feet as during school days. When Mahala became convinced that it might be best for Jason's self-respect and for his chances in life not to attempt further attendance in a school subjected to the cruelties of Martin Moreland, she undertook, in her own way, to superintend his education.

While in her classes, Jason easily had stood foremost; it had not been in her power to surpass the grade of the work that he did. In his absence, she found it possible to attain higher marks than Susanna or the most ambitious of the boys. The thing that Mahala never realized was, that whether her work was the best in her class or not, so long as her father was on the board it was so graded by a line of teachers who were accustomed to seeing her in the lead in every other activity among the children of her own age in Ashwater.

What Mahala did for Jason was simple enough, possibly not vital to him. With a firm determination, candles, and kerosene, he might have equalled what the other pupils were accomplishing in school, working in the room over the grocery at night. Faithful to his promise, Peter walled off a room of generous dimensions for Jason, papered its walls and ceiling freshly, while the boy himself put a coat of new paint on the woodwork.

After the first month of experiment, and steadily following down the years, Peter Potter paid him monthly a fair share of the proceeds of the business which prospered remarkably with Jason's assistance. Peter never objected when he found one of Jason's school books lying on his account desk or Jason deep in the book when he had the store cleaned and arranged to such a state that he felt he might use a few minutes for himself. Both knew that Jason's spare time was secured through deliberate planning of his work. Peter never knew at what hour Jason arose, but he did know that each morning when he stood in front of his store, he would find a fresh and attractive display of provisions and a new and luring sign containing some quirk or jest that caught people's attention and turned their footsteps into his door.

Among this daily increasing fleet of footsteps attracted by the window displays, the catchy signs, and the quick and efficient services of Jason aided by a rejuvenated Peter, who had taken a reef in his trousers and consented to wear a washable coat, there came once a week the daughter of opulence. Usually she arrived with a slip in her hand, ostensibly to order groceries for her mother. At times she walked in frankly. It was at Peter's suggestion that her endeavours for Jason were made under cover of a screened space where the desk bearing Peter's ledgers and account books was ranged. Its bill-papered grating gave them privacy while Mahala each week marked in Jason's books the extent to which the lessons in his class had progressed. Then she remained a few minutes to give him a hint as to how a difficult equation worked out in algebra; to help him over a knotty place in physical geography or astronomy, where the class had used authorities other than their school books and had kept notes. These she loaned him, and she took pains as she set them down in school to use great precision and fully elaborate points she well understood, that they might be clear to Jason.

Exactly why she took the trouble to do this, Mahala did not concern herself. She did it persistently, in the full knowledge that neither her father nor her mother would have approved, had they known. Mostly Mahala was willing to work diligently to earn the approval of her parents; but there were times when Elizabeth and Mahlon Spellman were enigmas to their daughter. She heard her father talk daily about brotherly love and charity and saw him truly love no man, saw him give only in public and when the gift would be talked about and redound to his credit for the length of the county. She heard her mother delicately voice the sentiment: "Love thy neighbour as thyself," when the girl could not help knowing that in reality her mother would be deeply shocked at the thought of such a thing as loving her neighbour. The truth was that she had no use for her neighbours either on the right hand, or the left, or fore or aft. Her chosen friends in the village were progressive people of financial circumstance and social position. The admirable precepts laid down by Mahlon and Elizabeth had been familiar to Mahala from her cradle. She had believed in her youth that her father and mother were always right, always consistent, always kind; she accepted their doctrines as her own law of life. But with Mahala "love thy neighbour" and "all things whatsoever" were not mechanical mouthings to make a good impression. They were orders which she, as a small soldier of the Cross, undertook to obey.

So, as the years went by, in daily contact with her parents, Mahala learned to watch them, to study them, and finally, God help them!—to judge them. By and by, there were times when her eyes narrowed in concentration; at rare times her lips opened in protest that she speedily learned was utterly futile. She soon found out that they had laid out their course and were following it in a manner which they deemed consistent. She was not permitted to speak if her father raised his hand. That sign for silence she never had dared disobey. She learned also that she might better save her breath than to use it in speech when Elizabeth's lips set in a thin, narrow line and her eyes hardened to steel-gray. Because she knew that the uplifted hand and the tight lips would be inevitable should her father and mother learn that she was helping Jason with his lessons, she took good care that they did not find it out. She openly rejoiced to them over the changed conditions in Peter Potter's business. She carried home mouth-watering descriptions of the food displayed in his windows. Sometimes she repeated the wording of a placard that amused her. Once, in laughingly recounting at the supper table how in Peter Potter's window there stood a huge, golden cream cheese surmounted by a neat sign which read,

Good people, this cheese,

Begs that you sample it, please,

she said that people were standing on the street laughing about it when it really was so simple that there was nothing to laugh over.

"That's exactly the point," said Mahlon. "It is so everlastingly simple that it becomes clever. It puts the burden of the request on the cheese and then leaves the cheese to prove itself. I'll wager it's a good one. Did you get a slice?"

Then Elizabeth lifted up her voice and remarked: "'Clever' is a word I never would have thought of applying to Peter Potter."

Mahlon responded: "And I wouldn't have thought of attributing those lines to Peter Potter. You can rest assured that they emanated from the brain of that long-headed young Peters, who seems to be getting on better in the world since his mother deserted him than he ever did before."

"It's a pity," said Mrs. Spellman, "that he thought best to quit school."

Mahala was like a bird with an eye on each side of the head. With one she was watching her father, with the other her mother. When no comment came to her mother's last statement, her sense of justice forced speech.

"It's more than a pity," she said earnestly. "It's burning shame. Jason always had the highest grades in the class. He was a good boy, but because he couldn't be well dressed and have money to spend, because he was forced to carry our and other people's washings, he was picked on and his life made miserable. For some reason that I don't understand, Junior Moreland, backed by his father, always abused him shamefully."

She stopped suddenly, realizing that the next question would be: "Why?" She felt that she did not understand the secret workings of the "why" and did not dare repeat such parts of it as she had witnessed.

When the "Why?" came, as Mahala had feared it would, she answered quietly: "I *suppose* it's because Martin Moreland and Junior have no sympathy with unsuccess. It offends their eyes, and stinks in their noses. They strike at it as instinctively as they'd strike at a snake—even if the snake happened to be performing the commendable service of cleaning field mice from the wheat."

Then Elizabeth Spellman laid down her fork.

"Good gracious, Mahala!" she cried. "S-st!—I forbid you ever to use such a dreadful word again! Where did you absorb such disgusting ideas? Snakes and mice in the wheat! I sha'n't be able to eat another bite of bread this meal! In fact, my supper is spoiled now."

Then Mahala laid down her fork, dropped her hands in her lap, and judged her mother with such judgment as she never before had rendered against her.

The next time she delivered an order at Peter Potter's grocery, she went deliberately and without the slightest regard as to who might be in the store at the time, and standing before Jason at the desk bearing the big ledgers, she spent an extra fifteen minutes telling him in detail things that had come up in the classes that she thought would interest and help him. There was a tinge of red on her cheeks and a sliver of light in her eyes when she told him concerning non-venomous snakes and field mice among the wheat and cautioned him not to strike until he knew the identity of a species.

Jason looked at her with adoration in his heart, commendation in his brain. She was the daintiest thing. She was the prettiest thing. She was the fairest thing in her judgments.

He said to her laughingly: "You know, there aren't a large collection of snakes running up and down these aisles, and the ones I do come in contact with I am not supposed to hit, no matter how venomous I know they are."

Mahala smiled because she realized that Jason was making an effort to be amusing. This happened so very seldom that she felt he should have a reward when he tried. Usually, Jason's face was extremely grave. Few days passed in which, in some way, he was not forced to feel the secret power working against him. He did not tell Mahala that twice since he had been with Peter Potter the store had been broken into at night by some one who was interested in finding Peter's old account books, since the intruder took neither groceries nor robbed the cash drawer. The ledgers were safe because Jason had urged Peter to take them to his Bluffport bank where they would be secure. He did not tell her how frequently, at the post office, the express office, at the freight office, among the business men of the town, he received a rebuff the origin of which he understood. He avoided meeting either Mr. Moreland or Junior when it was possible. When it was not, he went straight on his way. Many times it had been demonstrated to him that he was working in the one store in Ashwater in which the power of the Morelands was not strong enough to throw him out. Had he been anywhere else, he would have lost his work, his earnings, and his room, speedily. The thing that filled Jason with surprise was the fact that while Mr. Moreland and Junior wanted him to be poor, without friends, without education, the father, at least, did not want him to leave the town; else he would have awaited his return and sent him away with Marcia when she made her mysterious disappearance.

During the four years of the high-school course, there was no week in which Mahala failed to enter Peter Potter's grocery under some pretext, if she could invent a pretext; if she could not, specifically for the purpose of keeping Jason posted as to what was going on in school. In this matter she reserved the right to use her own judgment because in her judgment, Jason was not fairly treated, and the impulse to be fair to every one was big in her heart. In her opinion, the town was full of things that were unjust and unfair. People were forever standing up in churches and in public places prating about the poor and the downtrodden, but there was no single person, not even the ministers, doing the things that Jesus Christ had said should be done in order to make all men brothers. Her life was filled with preaching concerning the spirit of the law. She knew of no one who was following the letter—not even herself—as she felt she should. In self-analysis, her scorn included herself.

Sometimes in talking of these things she had made bold to say that Rebecca, carrying her white symbol and urging all the people she met to cleanse their hearts, was the only consistent disciple of Christ in Ashwater. She was forced to say that laughingly, as a daring piece of impudence. It would have been too shocking for the nerves of Mahlon, Elizabeth, or any of their friends, had the girl allowed them to surmise that she truly felt that Rebecca, mentally innocent, physically clean, with the fibre of persistence so strong in her nature that, year after year, she undeviatingly followed her hard course, was the only Christ-like one among them. To Mahala, given from childhood to periods of reflection, to consecutive thought, Rebecca came closer to being truly an envoy of Jesus Christ than any minister or deacon or church member she knew. Yet she had been so trained since childhood by her father and mother that she found it impossible to defy them openly. Even at times when her lips parted and the words formed, she had not quite the moral courage to say what she thought and felt. The one thing that she did realize concerning them was that they really had persuaded themselves that they were sincere; they felt they were right. Their love for her was unquestionable. She could not cry at them: "You drug yourselves with narcotics that you brew for the purpose. You lie to yourselves almost every time you open your lips." In her heart she was hoping that a day would come speedily when she should be independent, when she might begin to try, by ways however devious, to show every one what she truly thought and felt.

During the high-school years she had never once lost her ascendancy among her classmates. She had been so consistently straightforward, so frank in her likes and dislikes, so clever when a controversy arose, that she had maintained the position in which her parents had intentionally placed her through giving her the best of everything and making her conspicuous from the hour in which a tiny ostrich feather had been attached to her quilted hood and she had ridden in state in the first baby carriage the town had ever seen—an arresting affair, ribbed top covered with black oilcloth sheltering the bed which was mounted on two large wheels having wooden spokes and hubs and a tiny third on the front to make it stand alone. The upcurving tongue ended in a cross piece by which Elizabeth, strong-armed with the strength of a prideful heart, dragged this contraption, shining with black paint, gay with gold lines and red and blue morning-glories, after her over the flag-stone and board walks of Ashwater. This was no easy work for a woman of Elizabeth's natural proportions, but come what might personally, Elizabeth made the daily and hourly task of her life that of seeing that her child came first, and had the best.

Mrs. Spellman's deft fingers had been busy in their spare time for two years at elaborate embroidery preparing against Mahala's day of graduation and her following advent to the best girls' school of the land. For the same length of time, she and

Mahala had discussed a subject for the valedictory which naturally should fall to Mahala. Her mother had been unable to select anything from the store sufficiently dainty and suitable for a graduation dress. Mahlon had been commissioned to bring something especially fine from the city for this purpose. The best sewing woman the village afforded had been in the house working on the foundations of this dress. When it reached a certain point, Mrs. Spellman expected to finish it herself, ably assisted by Mahala whose fingers had become so deft in time set apart each day for their especial training, that, as a needlewoman, she was expert in the extreme.

Even while absorbed with this delightful work, both of them could not help noticing that Mahlon was unduly nervous and excitable; that slight things irritated him; while they confided to each other that they were surprised over the fact that Papa was getting almost stingy. He was not generous as he used to be. He was constantly cautioning them against undue expense. Mother and daughter were considerably worried about a new dry-goods emporium that had located in the town almost immediately opposite Mr. Spellman's place of business. The Emporium was a brick building, aggressive with marble and paint; the stock of goods fresh and elaborate. Vaguely Mahlon Spellman's womenfolk began to feel that his business might possibly be undermined by these new competitors, who had no scruples of an old-fashioned kind in their dealings with the public. They represented modern methods. Gradually it became Mahlon's part to stand in his store and sadly watch many of his best customers going in and out of the opposite doors, and he had been more and more frequently compelled to seek Martin Moreland for larger loans to meet the payment on heavy orders of goods that he was not selling because the cheaper stock handled by his competitors looked equally as attractive, but could be sold for less money.

In the guest room, the graduation dress stood on a form on a sheet tacked on the floor, carefully covered with draperies to keep it fresh, awaiting the finishing touches that Mahala insisted upon adding herself. Standing before it one evening, contemplating the folds of its billowing skirt, the festoons and ruffles of lace, Mahala smiled with pride and delight. It was to be such a dress as Ashwater never before had seen. The only cloud that was on Mahala's sky twisted into the form and took the name of Edith Williams. Edith had more money at her disposal than Mahala. Her clothes were more expensive. The reasons why her appearance was never so pleasing as Mahala's were numerous. She remained out of school for long periods of time, partly because she really did not feel well, mostly because she was sour and dissatisfied and did not try to overcome any indisposition she felt by giving it the slightest aid of her mentality. The aunt who pampered and petted her kept the village doctors constantly dosing her with pills and tonics, and allowed her to do precisely as she pleased on all occasions. She went upon the theory that if she bought Edith the most expensive clothing, she was the best-dressed child. She followed this theory for years despite the fact that her friend, Elizabeth Spellman, was constantly proving to her that the best-dressed girl was the one whose clothing was in the best taste and most becoming to her.

Edith and her aunt loved heavy velvets, satins, and cloth of rich, dark colours. And these, piled upon Edith's anæmic little figure, served rather to disguise than to emphasize any glimmering of beauty that might have made its manifestation.

As she stood before her graduation dress, Mahala, with her alert brain and keen habit of thinking things out, figured that very likely the dress which Edith would not allow her to see and about which she refused to talk, would be white, since white had been decided upon for all the class, to Edith's intense disgust. She knew that white was not becoming to her dark face and hair. Mahala, in figuring on how to hold her long-time supremacy on the night of her graduation, depended upon Edith and her aunt to select heavy velvet or satin, and to have it made in a manner that would be suitable for a prosperous grandmother. She softly touched the veil-like fineness of the misty white in which she planned to envelop herself when she stood forth to deliver the valedictory.

Mahala was perfectly confident that she had figured out the situation as it would develop. When she and the girl who always had been supposed to be her best friend, faced each other on their great night, Mahala believed that she would appear mist enshrouded. She was fairly confident that Edith would be looking dark and sour, too heavily and richly dressed in expensive materials and the height of poor taste.

A shadow fell across her work and she turned to find her father watching her. With an impulsive gesture, she stuck her needle into the breast of the form and ran to him, throwing her arms around his neck, rumpling his hair, and drawing him into the room. She began lifting the skirt and turning the form on its pedestal that he might see her handiwork, how charming the gown she was evolving. He stood quietly beside her, assenting to her eager exclamations, worshipping her pretty demonstration of her pride in her art and her good taste.

"It's very lovely, little daughter, very lovely," he said, "but aren't you almost through with putting expense on it?"

Mahala faced him abruptly.

"Papa," she said, "is business going badly with you? Are those cheap-johnnies that have started up across the street taking your customers away from you? Are you only worried, or is there truly a reason why we should begin to economize?"

Mahlon Spellman suddenly turned from a thing of flesh and blood to a thing of steel and iron. He opened his lips. This was his chance to gain sympathy and love, even help—and to save his life, he could not speak. He had been the be-all and the do-all for Mahala throughout her life. It had been his crowning pride and his pleasure to give her practically everything she had ever wanted. To tell her that he was in financial straits, that her freedom might be curtailed, that her extravagances might be impossible, that he was in danger of failing just when her hour and her greatest need for the lovely things of life were upon her, was a thing that he found himself incapable of doing. As he stood in silence, he felt her warm, young body pressing up against his.

"You know, dearest dear," she said quite simply, "that if you're in hot water, I'll help you. I won't go to college. I'll stay at home and take care of you and Mother and myself, too."

Mahlon was perfectly delighted with this exhibition of love and sacrifice on Mahala's part. Instead of telling her the truth, he told her a good many deliberate lies, and when the glow of rejoicing over her words had died down somewhat, he realized that he had been a fool for not availing himself of the opportunity that she had offered him, and he sank back to intense dejection, which the girl dimly realized as he left the room.

That night she said to her mother: "Mama, do you realize that the front of our store is the only thing on Hill Street that hasn't changed during the past four years?"

"What do you mean?" asked Elizabeth Spellman, asperity in the tones of her voice, on the lines of her face.

"I mean," said Mahala, "that one of these new inset fronts with show windows that you look in as you walk back to the doors and a fresh coat of paint, and new sign lettering, would help a whole lot to make the front of our store look more like that new one across the street."

"You haven't thought of anything new or original," said Elizabeth. "Your father and I have realized this and we have talked it over several times. The high-class goods that he buys have got to be sold for a price that will make him a reasonable profit. He cannot lower rates like those cheap cut-throats that started up opposite him. He doesn't think that he can afford the changes he would like to make, much as you would like to see him make them."

"I don't know," said Mahala, "but that it would be a good thing to sacrifice something else and make those changes. You know how down and out Peter Potter was when Jason Peters quit school and went in with him and made things hum. He began with fresh paint and ended with a fine new store. Since they put up that new corner building, just look how everything has gone with them. I think they are doing twice the business of any other grocery in town right now, and I think it's Jason Peters's brain that's at the back of most of it. Every one has come to look for the signs that are posted fresh in their windows nearly every morning. This morning one window was full of food that no one could see without a watering mouth, and the other window was full of the most attractive lamps and a display of every kind of soap you ever imagined, with a big sign reading: 'Let us feed you, soap you, light you, and love you.' You needn't tell me Peter Potter did that."

"It would be a good deal better," said Mrs. Spellman, "if Peter Potter would put some check on that youngster. He's too cheeky. Imagine him sticking up a sign announcing that he'll 'love' us!"

Mahala giggled: "It isn't supposed to be Jason who's saying that. It's supposed to be Peter Potter's business. Isn't it conceivable that Peter might be trying to express his love for his fellow men by giving them clean, wholesome food and the conveniences of life at a reasonable price?"

"Oh, yes, it's conceivable," granted Elizabeth, "but it's unthinkable."

Mahala laughed outright.

"Mother," she said, "you are becoming absolutely profound."

"Well, what I am trying to point out," said Elizabeth, "is the fact that Peter Potter in his dirty grocery, with his run-down stock, and in his baggy breeches and his collarless gingham shirt, didn't put his business where it is right now. Look at that delivery wagon—red as a beet, with gold and black lines on it and a canvas top, and a horse like a circus parade! And look at Peter Potter in a wash coat and a new building, and the most attractive show windows this town has ever seen!"

"I've been looking at him," said Mahala. "He's been on the upgrade for four years, and I think that it's the result of Jason and the cleanliness his washerwoman mother instilled in him, and his willingness to work, combined with Peter's horse sense in giving him freedom to try new things. I think that if the same kind of cyclone should blow through Papa's store, it would be a good thing. I wish to goodness Jason was in Father's store and would freshen things up for us as he has for Potter's Grocery."

"Oh, my soul!" cried Elizabeth Spellman, aghast, "you don't truly mean that you wish that?"

"But that is precisely what I do mean that I wish," insisted Mahala. "I wish anything that would keep Papa from looking so worried and being so peevish as he is lately. And as for having Jason in his business, I can't see how Papa could be hurt, while Peter's new grocery proves what help did for him. Have you seen Jason lately?"

"No," said Mrs. Spellman, "I haven't seen him, and I shouldn't look at him if I did."

"It might be your loss at that," said Mahala deliberately. "In four years he's grown very tall and not having to be on the run constantly to deliver heavy baskets and be on time to school, he's gotten more meat on his bones and his face has filled out, and a sort of gloss has come on his hair. Because Peter has had the manhood to befriend him, he speaks and moves with a confidence he didn't have when every one was treating him a good deal like a strange dog that might develop hydrophobia."

"My soul and body!" said Elizabeth in tense exasperation. "Mahala, you do think of the most shocking things! Why in the world should you mention strange dogs and that loathsome disease in my presence?"

Mahala looked at her mother reflectively.

"Why, indeed?" she said earnestly. "Forgive me, Mother!" And then she turned and went from the room.

Elizabeth Spellman was pleased. She thought her daughter had apologized for her lack of delicacy.

CHAPTER VIII

"A Secret Among the Stars"

While the general appearance of improvement and progress was becoming distinctly visible and encouragingly permanent on the leading business street of Ashwater, precisely the same thing was happening in its nearest neighbouring village, Bluffport. The old board side walks had given way to flagging. The muddy streets had become paved with cobblestone. The new brick bank and the hardware store and two dry-goods stores radiated affluence. A fine, big high school stood near the centre of the town and the spires of three churches lifted their white fingers toward the sky as if to write thereon in letters large and plain: "This is not a Godless community."

Perhaps nothing new in all the village so became it as the proud brick structure that arose on the corner where Smithley's junk shop had sprawled its disfiguring presence to the mortification of the city that was beginning to lift its head and to take pride in demolishing fences and spreading abroad smooth lawns brocaded with beds of gaudy flowers. And this new building which had risen like magic on one of Bluffport's most prominent corners gave over its second story to Doctor Garvin, who really cured a large assortment of Bluffport's ills, and Squire Boardman, who really settled a large proportion of Bluffport's troubles. Their offices were across the dividing hall from each other. They were a pair of honest and respectable men, each of whom was trying, in his own way, to do his share for the improvement of Bluffport and to acquit his soul in a graceful manner of the obligation to love his neighbour as himself. Neither the doctor nor the lawyer felt that he was loving his neighbours in the degree in which he loved himself, but they did feel that they were making a sweeping gesture in that direction, which was infinitely better than apathy. Also, they regularly paid a reasonable rent, which contributed to the prosperity of the owners of the building.

The lower story was occupied by, and the entire building belonged to, Nancy Bodkin and Marcia Peters, and was so entered in the records of the office of the county clerk. The corner location gave them advantageous front-display windows and a large amount of side space. These windows proved that, to an exclusive and attractive line of millinery, there had been added fashionable neckwear for the ladies; scarfs of silk; breakfast shawls of Scotch plaid and flowered merino; fancy hosiery; pincushions and toilet articles, and a seemly collection of decorated china.

The window displays were attractively managed. Inside the millinery was kept in drawers and curtained cases. Several big mirrors and a number of chairs constituted the greater part of the furnishings. Any one stepping into this room had almost an impression of entering a well-ordered home.

The back part of the building was taken up with Nancy's work room; the living arrangements, which had increased to a separate room for each of the friends, a most attractive sitting room, a small dining room, and a tiny kitchen. For four years these two women had lived and worked together. They had engaged in small financial enterprises and taken part in the civic life of the town. They could be depended upon to superintend attractive and unusual decorations when the principal street needed to become festive upon some great occasion. They could be depended upon to do their fair share for the churches, for the schools, for the Grand Army, for their political party. Under the guiding hand of Marcia, Nancy had bloomed like the proverbial rose lifted from the hard clay soil of lingering existence and set where its roots could run in congenial earth, watered with affection, nourished in the sunshine of love. The change in Nancy had been so convincing that Bluffport only dimly remembered a time when she had been an anæmic, discouraged, overworked little woman. At the present minute, she was not overworked. She had her work so beautifully in hand that she could accomplish it and find time for rest and reasonable recreation. She had nourishing food, skilfully prepared, and these things wrought a great physical change. She was enjoying the companionship of a woman who was alert and eager, who felt that life owed her much and who was bent upon collecting the debt to the last degree, if it were a possible thing. When Marcia had finished exercising all the arts of the toilet she knew upon Nancy Bodkin, Nancy gradually developed into an extremely attractive woman. She evolved a healthy laugh and a contagious interest in the flowing of life around her.

As for Marcia herself, she was in truth blooming. Such a huge weight rolled from her shoulders when she began life in the daily living of which there was nothing secret, nothing questionable, nothing of which to be ashamed. She might look her world in the face and go on with her work in a healthful and prideful manner. Always an attractive woman, under the stimulus of self-assertion and prosperity she had become beautiful. Natural grace had developed until she had become gracious.

These two women were together every day and within speaking distance every night. They were making of life the level best thing that was possible for either of them through their united efforts. Nancy was born a designer. Marcia had been born with executive ability. The combination produced as a result the attractive store, exhaling prosperity, and a pair of women of whom Bluffport was distinctly proud. The whole town was proud of the Bodkin and Peters share of improvement on the business street, proud of the two good-looking, well-dressed women who managed their affairs so capably that they were able to meet their business obligations and were rapidly repaying the encumbrances they had shouldered in the erection of the building.

In this close contact, and in what the town supposed to be intimacy, these two women, rapidly approaching middle age, lived and worked together. The town would have been dumbfounded had it known that Nancy Bodkin never had asked her new partner one word concerning her life previous to her advent into the partnership. Conversely, Marcia had respected the little milliner. They had simply begun life with the hour of their meeting and gone forward to the best of their combined ability. Neither of them had seemed inclined to be communicative concerning herself, and each of them had too much inherent refinement to engage in a business that a popular poet of their day graphically described as the "picking open of old sores." If either of them had an old sore, she was depending wholeheartedly upon the other to help her in concealing it. In breaking away from the years of her life with Martin Moreland, Marcia had followed an impulse. In her heart she had always known that this thing would happen some day. She had steeled herself from the very beginning against Jason. She did not want to love him; she did not want him to love her. When the day of separation came, as she always had felt that it would, she figured upon reducing the pain of it to the minimum. Exactly what she felt concerning the boy was a secret locked in her heart. Freed of his presence and his influence, she found that the greatest feeling possessing her concerning Martin Moreland was a feeling of fear. Twice she had witnessed his brutality toward Jason when to her it was without sufficient reason. She realized that any day the same storm of wrath might break upon her head for as small cause.

When the sudden resolve had come to her, after the injustice of being picked up bodily and forcibly without her consent or approval and set down among strangers in a strange town, there had developed suddenly in her heart a storm of rebellion that had ended in her seeking refuge and independence with Nancy Bodkin. She had no idea what Martin Moreland would do when he went to the house to which he had sent her, with the expectation in his heart that he would find at least one room of it to his liking and warm with the reception to which he was accustomed. She had thought that he would come to the store, and in the daze of the early weeks of her transplantation, she had lifted a set face and a combative eye every time a hand was laid upon the latch.

One day she had seen Martin Moreland upon the opposite side of the street, and sick at heart, she had fled to her room and thrown herself upon her bed, complaining of a headache. For several hours she lay there in torment, expecting each minute that the door would open and Nancy Bodkin would level the finger of scorn at her, that the clear light of her gray eyes would pierce her covering and see burning upon her breast the loathsome scarlet brand. But night had come and Nancy Bodkin had brought her a cup of tea, had brushed her hair and unlaced her shoes.

In the days that followed, Marcia found herself still watching the street and the front door, but each day of her emancipation so fortified her that she began to develop a confidence and an assurance. She did not know Martin Moreland as well as she thought she did, when in the third year, she had definitely made up her mind that he would not come. She did not realize that he was the kind of a man who figured in his heart that every step higher she climbed in the community that was so graciously receiving her, would make harder the fall when the day came upon which he decided to turn the tongue of gossip and slander against her. Whenever he was passing through Bluffport on business, he made a point of stopping on the opposite side of the street and taking a detailed survey of the millinery store. He watched from the small beginnings of soaped glass and painted casings, through the four years to the new

102

brick building with its attractive windows. The first time he passed the new building, obtrusive in its newness, glowing with the dainty colours of its excuse for being, the smile on his face was a fearful thing to see. It was a thing shaded by such a degree of malevolence that his consciousness realized that no one must see it. It would be an outward manifestation of such an inward state as would shock a casual observer. Even as that smile gathered and broke, with the same instinct which prompted it, Martin Moreland clapped the palm of his deeply scarred right hand over his face and an instant later applied a handkerchief. As the smile died away, in its stead there came a look that was very like the expression on the face of a hungry panther ready to leap with certainty upon an unsuspecting victim.

Martin Moreland knew that, early in their separation, Marcia would expect him and be on the defensive. He figured that by waiting until the passage of time had given her assurance, his descent would be all the more crushing and spectacular.

So it happened that Marcia occasionally saw him passing upon the street and grew firm in her confidence that she was to go free. With the passing of the years, she succeeded in a large measure in forgetting her ugly past and allaying tremors for the future. It appealed to her that Martin Moreland could do nothing to hurt or humiliate her without humiliating himself; and that, she figured, he would not do. She became all the more certain of this because occasionally she saw Junior on the streets of Bluffport, and from the security of the store, she watched him as he walked the streets or stood talking with other men.

To the observer, Junior was an extremely handsome man. He had his father's height, his mother's dark hair and eyes. There was a dull flush of red in his cheeks and on his lips. He could not have helped knowing that he was a handsome and an attractive figure. He could scarcely have helped being unmoral through his father's training from his early childhood. Always he had been supplied with a liberal amount of money to use as he chose in the gambling rooms of Ashwater with the other men and boys. Occasionally he lost, but frequently he came into the bank with surprisingly large sums of money which he gave to his father to deposit on his account. A few times, lounging in the bank, even during his school days, he had listened to discussions between his father and other men concerning matters of business and he had made suggestions so ingenious, so simple in their outward manifestations, so astute, so deep in their inward import, that the Senior Moreland had been in transports. He always had been proud of his son. When to his fine figure and handsome face he added indications of shrewd business ability, he fulfilled his father's highest dream for him.

Whenever occurrences of this kind took place, Moreland Senior immediately supplied Moreland Junior with an unusually liberal allowance with which to cut a wide swath in the social life of the town. During the junior and senior years of high school, Junior made a practice of arming himself with large boxes of sweets and huge bouquets of expensive flowers and going to call upon Mahala.

Mahala always greeted him cordially, always accepted what he brought casually as a matter of course, but never with any particular show of pleasure. Having been accustomed to the admiring glances of women and the exaggeratedly lavish praise of an element of the town greedy for his father's money, Junior could not believe that this attitude on the part of Mahala was genuine. She must think him as handsome as his mirror proved to him that he was. She must see that he was tall and straight and shapely. Knowing the value of dry goods as she did, she could not fail to know that always he was expensively clothed in the very latest fashions sent out from the large cities of the East.

A few days before Commencement, armed with a particularly ornate box of candy and a bunch of long-stemmed roses by way of an ice box from Chicago, he made an evening call upon Mahala. The box of candy she set upon the piano, unopened. The roses she arranged in a large vase. She commented on their wonderful shape and velvet petals, the splendid stems and leaves faintly touched with the bloom of rankly growing things. She said that they were so perfect that it almost seemed that they were not real roses that would yellow and wither in a few days.

They talked of the coming Commencement and Junior jestingly asked Mahala if she were going to allow Edith Williams to be more handsomely gowned than she. Mahala was amused that he should think of such a thing. She looked at him with eyes so frank that to the boy they seemed almost friendly. She laughed the contagious laugh of happy youth.

"Now, Junior, you know without asking," she said, "that if anything like that happens, it won't be in the least little bit my fault. It will be because I haven't sized up the situation properly."

"And how," asked Junior, "have you sized up the situation?"

"I've depended," said Mahala, "upon Edith running true to form. In a given circumstance, she always has done a given thing. I can't imagine her changing. If she has, there's nothing to do but accept it gracefully."

Junior laughed.

"For a level head commend me to you, young woman," he said. "Now, here is a state secret. My mother and Mrs. Williams are great friends, and"—Junior lowered his voice and spoke through a trumpet made of his hollowed hands, giving himself an excuse to draw very near to Mahala—"my mother has seen the gown and she says it's a perfect humdinger."

Mahala's laugh was young and spontaneous and thoroughly genuine.

"Naturally," she said, "it would be. I figured on that."

"And I fancy you figured," said Junior, "on a dress that in some way will go just a little bit ahead of Edith's."

"'Naturally,'" mimicked Mahala, "being Edith's best friend and closest companion, I have figured on a dress that I hope and confidently believe will be the prettiest thing on the stage, Commencement night."

"And I haven't a doubt," said Junior, "but you've figured as correctly as you ever did in algebra or geometry. But just suppose for once in your fair young life that you've figured wrong."

"Well, now, just suppose," said Mahala. "Of course you have figured on being better dressed by far than any of the other boys. And at the last minute, if John Reynolds or Frederick Hilton should turn up with a later-cut and finer goods than you were wearing, what do you think you could do about it?"

"But the cases are not analogous," said Junior. "In the back of my head I am pretty well convinced that the clothing that Edith Williams always has worn has cost more money than has been spent on you. That has not been the case with any boy of Ashwater. Father always has seen to it that I had the best. Where you have consistently gotten away with Edith has been through being so much handsomer, through being lovely to every one, and through the exercise of a degree of taste and ingenuity on the part of your mother and yourself, that no other women of this flourishing burg can equal. I haven't a doubt but you'll be the loveliest thing in the building the night of Commencement, but I just thought I'd come around and give you a hint of what you're up against."

"Now that's nice of you," laughed Mahala, "but you haven't told me a thing that I didn't know and for which I was not prepared. Probably your mother didn't say, but I'd be willing to wager that Edith's gown will be either of velvet or heavy satin, and a crowded room in Ashwater grows distressingly warm in June."

Junior threw back his head and laughed heartily.

"Bully for you!" he said admiringly. "I'll back you for a winner in any undertaking in which you want to engage. It would be downright mean of me to go any further with what Mother told me after she had seen Edith's dress, but I'll say you are a winner in drawing nice deductions."

And then Junior realized that he had not had such an enjoyable and friendly talk with Mahala, that she had not been so cordial with him, in he could not remember when. So he ventured further.

"What can we plan for this summer that will be a lot of fun?" he said. "We ought to celebrate this getting through with school by picnics and parties and excursions. It's our time to have fun, and who's to object to our going ahead and having it?"

"Aren't you going to college, Junior?" asked Mahala.

"Going to college?" repeated Junior scornfully. "Why would I go to college? Which college does my father hold in the hollow of his hand? Where could he pull the strings and make the professors dance like a pack of marionettes?"

Mahala stared at him wide eyed, and at the same time she was amazed to find herself commending his candour.

"Well, you certainly have nerve," she said. "Of course everybody knows the influence your father always has had with the School Board, and from the time we've been little children we've had demonstrated to us what your combined efforts could do, but I didn't think you'd sit up and boast about it—openly admit it!"

"Why not?" said Junior. "What's calculus and radicals and Greek and Latin got to do with figuring on exactly how big a mortgage it would be safe to place on Timothy Hollenstein's farm? I've gone through the motions of this school thing. I've got the scum of it. Did you ever see me make a mistake in addition? I'm not interested in subtraction, and I'm not very particular about division, but have you ever noticed that I'm greased lightning on multiplication?"

And again Mahala laughed when she knew in her heart that she should do nothing of the kind. Coupled with Junior's physical attractions there was this daring, this carelessness of what any one might say or think, this disarming honesty concerning transactions that had been the width of the world from honesty or fairness.

"All right," she said, "don't go to college. You'd get nothing out of it but the fun of spoiling other boys who were really trying to make men of themselves. But I'm going. I think I shall go to Vassar, and as for picnics and parties, I must put in the greater share of my time this summer in making my own clothes. I figure that the new store has cut into Father pretty deeply and I think I ought to help all I can by doing my sewing."

Then Junior, reinforced by the most agreeable evening he had ever spent with Mahala, reached over and covered one of her hands with his. He grasped it lightly, giving it a little shake as he said to her: "I have to inform you, young lady, that it's written in the stars that you're not going to college."

Obliquely Junior watched the girl, and he was wondering what she would think if he told her reasons that he could have told her, as to why she would not go to college.

Mahala withdrew her hand under the pretext of rearranging her hair, and laughingly remarked: "That's very unkind of the stars to write things first to you concerning me. But, while we're on the subject, in the epistle did the stars tell you what it is that I'm going to do?"

"Certainly," said Junior. "I hope you noticed that I always came the nearest to making a decent grade in astronomy. I have to inform you that the swan went swimming down the Milky Way and he told a star lily floating there that you were going to preside over the finest house in Ashwater, furnished far more exquisitely than this place, that there was going to be a devoted lover at your feet and your door plate is going to read, 'Martin Moreland, Junior'."

For one minute Mahala stared at Junior with questioning eyes. Then she decided that to laugh was the thing, so she laughed as heartily as she possibly could. She laughed so heartily that it became an exaggeration and then she shook her head and said: "Put no belief in astronomical communications. They're too far-fetched. I think Vassar will suit me best and in about a week after Commencement I'm going to begin a trunk full of the nicest school clothing that has gone East in many a long day. And that reminds me that I've quite a bit of sewing to finish before Commencement, and I must be at it. So take yourself away, but for pity's sake, don't tell Edith that her aunt showed her dress. It's against the law and she'd be furious."

"She'd be so furious," interrupted Junior, "that she'd turn a darker green than the Lord made her."

"If you want to keep up your credit for a customary degree of observation," said Mahala, "you'll have to admit that Edith is rapidly shedding her greenness, that she is rounding out. She still insists that she's half an invalid, but if she'd take some exercise and forget herself as I try and try to make her, she'd soon be the prettiest girl you ever saw."

Which proves that Mahala was strictly feminine, not that Junior was not eager and willing to pick up the challenge.

"Yes, like hob she would!" he said instantly. "That sour green kicker would come within a long shot of being the prettiest girl that I ever saw while you're in Ashwater!"

"Well, I'm not going to be in Ashwater long," said Mahala, "and then you can watch Edith and see how fast she grows handsome. You can go and take a look for yourself right now, if you want to, because I really must get to work."

Junior arose and because he was accustomed always to think of himself and his own considerations, he forgot to veil the glance that he cast toward the big vase of rare flowers and the big box of unopened candy. A cursory glance, but Mahala caught it and she knew that he left with the idea that he had thrown away his money, and the merriest smile of the evening curved her lips behind his back, because that was precisely what she wanted him to think, and she hoped in her heart that he would follow down the street and spend the remainder of the evening with Edith Williams. Since they had been little girls, in the days of charm strings and rolling hoops, Mahala had known that the one boy whom Edith Williams preferred above all the other boys of the village was Junior Moreland. She could not recall that she ever in her life had seen Junior extend to Edith even decent courtesies. He made a point of being rough with her and saying annoying, irritating things to her, of flatly repulsing even the most timid advances that she might make in school or upon social occasions for his preferment. And Mahala pondered as she climbed the stairs with a bit of lettuce in her hand for the little gold bird, just how it happened that Edith should care so much for Junior Moreland and Junior Moreland should take malicious pleasure in hurting her feelings.

At the window of her room, she glanced down the street. If Junior turned the corner, there was a possibility that he might delight Edith by spending an hour with her. But Junior went straight on to Hill Street. He made his way for quite a distance along it, and then turned into a showy restaurant on a side street.

At his entrance two or three flashily dressed serving girls gathered around him. He led the way to a booth in the corner. Here he swung one of them to a table, took another on his lap, and kissing a third, he ordered her to go and get everything good to eat that the shop contained for a feast. Smilingly the owner of the restaurant encouraged the party. If Junior was pleased, his bill would be larger, and this was a thing that happened frequently.

When the food was brought, Junior unhesitatingly helped himself to the parts for which he cared, leaving the remainder for the girls to divide among themselves. He was familiar with them as a boy might be with his sisters, but he was not vulgar. He treated them lavishly, taking only a little of his first choice for himself.

When his bill was brought to him, he went over the figures carefully, and then he forced the manager to make several changes. He proved conclusively that while he was willing to spend money as he chose, he was possessed of a close streak, and did not intend to waste it.

His appetite appeased, he kissed all of the girls, assured them that he would be around again shortly, asked them how they would like to go to Bluffport for a ride some night in the near future, and going out, he rounded a corner, slipped up an alley, climbed a back stairway, and in answer to a certain number of measured rappings on a darkened door, was admitted to a room where a number of prominent men and boys of the village were playing games for money.

Junior sat down carelessly, and leaning back, watched the games casually until he decided that he would play poker. By midnight he had swept up most of the stakes, and when the other men insisted that he should give them a chance to retrieve their money, he laughingly explained: "I've got to get home early to-night. To-morrow's a final examination."

"What difference does that make to you?" exclaimed Anthony Jones, a schoolmate of Junior's. "You know perfectly well you can't pass in two or three branches unless you cheat."

Junior stood under a swinging lamp, lighting a cigar. He glanced at the boy, a smile on his handsome face.

"My father has given old Dobson his job for the past four years," he said, "and so far as I know, Dob wants it for four more. Why should I have to do anything but go through the motions? I ought to get something out of it, oughtn't I?"

"You ought to have to dig in and work for your grades like the rest of us do!" retorted Anthony.

Junior expertly ringed his first puff of smoke toward the ceiling.

"Oh, I'll work all right when the time comes. I do a whole lot of thinking and scheming and planning right now that nobody knows anything about. I'll work, all right. But the trouble with you will be that you won't know when I'm working and when I'm not, because when I work it does not always show on the surface."

"Well, there's one thing certain," said Anthony, "you'll work the Superintendent for a diploma; you'll work your father for all the money you want."

Junior stuck his hands in his well-filled pockets and sauntered to the door. Just as he passed through it, he leaned back so that the full light fell upon his face and figure, and he laughingly inquired: "How about working you fellows once in a while?"

CHAPTER IX

"Sometimes Your Soul Shows"

It was mid-June before the night of Commencement arrived. The Methodist Church, being the largest suitable edifice of the town, was used for the imposing occasion. The lower grades of the high school and friends of the graduates, as well as the alumni of preceding years, had all combined in decorating the building for the Commencement exercises. The big swinging chandeliers hanging from the ceiling were wreathed in greenery accentuated with flowers. The edge of the pulpit platform was outlined with gaily blooming plants. The space intervening between that and the altar railing was filled with showy plants in tubs and buckets, one end finishing with a white oleander in a mass of snowy bloom, the other exactly like it except that the flowers were peach-blow pink. The pulpit had been removed. Back of the chairs for the graduating class there was a second row for the principal, the teachers of the schools, the School Board, and several ministers, and lining the wall, a small forest of gay leaves and bright flowers. Every window was filled with the lovely roses of June, with flowering almond, japonica, iris, and gay streamers of striped grass.

It was the custom to hold the graduating exercises in the church, then to repair to Newberry's Hotel for a supper which was the last word in culinary effort on the part of the owners, helped out by table decorations provided by the alumni and the lower classes of the high school. The long tables for the graduates and their parents, for the singers and speakers, were lovely. They were laid with linen that was truly snowy, with silver provided by several of the wealthiest families of the town, with china that came from the same cabinets as the silver; and these tables were made beautiful beyond words with great bowls of yellow, white, and purple wild violets, starry campion, anemones, maidenhair fern, and every exquisite wilding that knew June in the Central States.

After the banquet, the class and its guests took up the line of march across the street and in the upstairs of the big building known as Franklin's Opera House, they danced until morning. Commencement was the one great social affair known to Ashwater. Nothing else in the history of the town called forth such an audience. It was the one occasion upon which the church people forgot that the lure of the dance would imperil the souls of their young. They went and drank lemonade and fanned themselves as they sat in double rows of chairs lining the walls, many of them joining the dance to the mellow notes of a harp brought all the way from Indianapolis.

Never was a gathering more cosmopolitan. The invited guests were relatives and friends of the graduates. So it happened that the august person of Martin Moreland, the banker, might come in very close contact with that of Jimmy Price, general handyman, in such case as to-night when one of Jimmy's lean daughters was a graduate. For once in his life Jimmy might don his wedding suit, accompanied by any remnants of dignity that forty years of playing the clown had left in his mental cosmos, and making an effort to be grave and correct, he might have this one peep at what the truly great of his town did when they entertained themselves.

June in the Central States is a hot month; mid-June the crucial time. The thermometer is likely, at that period, to hover persistently at anywhere from ninety-five to a hundred and ten. The dew of night closely following such a degree of heat was sure to breed a moist stickiness that washed the pink powder from the noses of the august, and in slow streams of discouragement, saw to it that artificially waved hair degenerated into little winding rivers of despair. It was very likely to emphasize mothy complexions and deeply cut wrinkles by washing into their cruel lines white or vivid pink powder, leaving high promontories lacking decoration in ghastly contrast. To appear cool and fresh and charming upon such a night, was the height of triumph. It was the thing that few people even remotely hoped to do. The men frankly mopped their streaming faces and the backs of their necks. They tried to look cheerful if they found that their high linen collars were even half way upstanding; mostly these were protected by a tucked-in handkerchief until the doors were reached. They were often seen wiping their hands and their wrists with these same moist handkerchiefs, and the ladies, in their billowing skirts containing yards upon yards of heavy goods, in their tightly fitting sleeves and waists, religiously wearing headgear, which they would have thought it absolutely indecent to remove, dabbled frantically at their complexions, the corners of their mouths sagged in despair as they felt the hair slowly drooping over their foreheads, while they fanned frantically in an effort to keep sufficiently cool to save their silk dresses.

It was the custom for the omnibus from Newberry's Hotel to drive to the residences gathering up the graduates and depositing them at the side door leading into the prayer-meeting room of the church, slightly before the time the organist began to play the entrance march.

Usually the four walls of the church heard nothing gayer than "Onward Christian Soldiers" or "Marching to Zion," but it was conceded to the youth of the city that on Commencement night the organist might tackle what was spoken of, in rather awed tones, as "sheet music." It was customary to hire, for these occasions, a graduate from the Fort Wayne Conservatory to sing several solos. This marked a high light in the exercises. These graduates from a musical school might do the daring thing of coming clothed in billowing silks of peach-blow pink. In one instance, the crowd had lost its breath over such a dress glaringly trimmed in blood-red. This, in conjunction with a bared breast and arms, a becurled head as yellow as the cowslips down by the Ashwater river, had been almost too much for the morality of the audience. The young lady had saved the situation by a sobbingly pathetic rendition of "When the Flowing Tide Comes In." When she had her audience audibly weeping over the "ships that came in clouds like flocks of evil birds," and then led them on to the salt-saturated ending of "remembering Donald's words," the weeping crowd so thoroughly enjoyed the performance that they forgave what they considered the extreme bad taste of the blood-decorated pink dress.

In gathering the graduates, it might have been instinct on the part of the driver, and it might have been suggestion on the part of authority, at any rate, it was customary to bring in the poor and the unimportant and give them this one ride of their lives in state, usually down Hill Street, past the bank, the main business buildings, and the Court House, ending at the side steps of the Methodist Church. After all the poor and the unimportant had been collected, then by degrees came the socially and financially prominent, it being generally conceded that the boy or girl having the salutatory came next to last, while the valedictorian held the place of honour.

In to-night's exercises every former custom had been religiously kept and religiously exaggerated to the last possible degree. In the annals of the town, such a distinguished class never before had been graduated. This class embodied the son of the banker, the handsome, carefree boy concerning whom every one prophesied evil, whose escapades were laughed at and glossed over as they would have been in the case of no other boy in the community. Men who should have known better, rather evinced pride when Junior Moreland stopped to say a few words to them. It was the common talk of the town that the Senior Moreland lay awake nights thinking up ways to indulge, to pamper, his only son. The influence of Junior's good looks and his brazen assurance was so pronounced that the whole town combined in helping to spoil him. Where he should have had a reprimand, where any other boy would have had it, Junior usually evoked a laugh. So he had grown to feel that he was a law unto himself; that he might do things which the other boys might not; that he was a natural leader upon any occasion on which he chose to lead.

This night's class embraced Edith Williams, grown thus far to womanhood with most of the ills and the discontent of her childhood clinging to her. It was very probable that Edith's first conscious thought was that she had been defrauded. Why didn't God make her with a strong, beautiful body? Why didn't He give her voice the power of song, her fingers facility for the harp or the piano that she could buy if she chose? Why did He take both her parents and leave her to live with an uncle whom she never could endure, and with an aunt, sycophant to such a degree, that the child shrewdly suspected, from a very early age, that the otherwise estimable lady was hoping that she would die and leave "all that money" to her only heir, who happened to be the husband of the lady in question. Edith had heard about "all that money" ever since she had been born. She had come to understand that it could buy her the most expensive clothing worn in the town. It could buy her entrance into any gaiety taking place in any home. It could buy the most expensive house in Ashwater and any furnishings her taste might dictate. It could, in fact, buy everything to which she had been accustomed all her life, but it could not buy her the two things which she craved almost above life itself—beauty and happiness. No one could convince her that at least a moderate degree of beauty lay within her own power. She had only contempt for a woman like Elizabeth Spellman, who tried to tell her that keeping irregular hours, practically living on cake and candy, that the wearing of stays which reduced her slender proportions to pipe-stem slenderness, were responsible for the things in life against which Edith most strongly rebelled. In vain Mrs. Spellman tried to point out that regular sleep, regular bathing, a diet consisting largely of fruits and vegetables, freedom of the body, and regular exercise, were responsible for Mahala's bright eyes, her rounded figure, her hard, smooth flesh. These things Edith coveted to an unholy degree, but not sufficiently to change one wrong habit or to shake off her natural indolence in order to attain them. Edith's happiest moment was, in all probability, the one in which, dressed in the extreme of the prevailing fashion, she lay upon a sofa with a box of rich candy and wickedly read a French novel that she was not supposed to have and that no one ever knew precisely where she secured.

Commencement time marked a thrilling epoch in Edith's life. A few days after the great event, she would attain the age at which her dying father had specified that she should come into full and uncontrolled possession of his large fortune. As the time approached, Edith spent hours dreaming of trips to New York and Chicago, of the beautiful clothing that she would purchase, and how these advantages would certainly add to her attractiveness to such a degree that finally she would succeed in completely overshadowing Mahala. She was so certain that this would be the case, that she had decided to make the first step the night of graduation. She had horrified both her uncle and her aunt by the extravagance of her outfit. She had persisted in making her own selections.

Commencement night found her in a nervous state bordering on a sick headache. She had been absent from school a great deal. She never had known what her lessons were about when they concerned mathematics, astronomy, or any difficult branch requiring real concentration and study. Her brain was almost wholly untrained; it kept flying off at queer tangents. With the help of her uncle and her aunt she had succeeded in getting together a creditable essay which she was supposed to read from memory. She had gotten through it on several occasions with slight promptings, but in the final class rehearsal, she had broken down completely and been forced to take refuge in the written pages held by the professor. After that, she had really studied, but it had been too late. She never had made public appearances as had many of the members of her class because she hated the mental work required to commit poems or orations to memory. She was too indolent really to work at anything because she never had been taught that in work alone lies the greatest panacea for discontent the world ever has known.

It was a general supposition in Ashwater that Commencement night should be the happiest period of a girl's life. To many of them it was a happy period. There was joy of a substantial kind in the honest breast of little Susanna, who had been helped in a surreptitious way with her lessons and her clothing all through her school course by Mahala, and who, in turn, had worshipped Mahala dumbly and had returned all the help she could give upon knotty problems when her brain had begun to develop to a commanding degree. Many of the boys and girls who were to graduate that night had worked hard and conscientiously. They were proud of the new clothes they were wearing; eager to begin the life they had planned for themselves.

This class included the daughter of the dry-goods merchant. No one was happier than Mahala. She had worked hard all her school life. She had been perfectly willing to receive the same help from others that she was accustomed to give when she was more fortunate in mastering a difficult problem or a perplexing proposition in any of her studies. Her facility in music and the superficial part of her education, her quickness in picking up hints and indirections, the clever way in which she made her recitations, made her vastly popular with all of her teachers to whom she always showed a polite deference never equalled by any of the other pupils.

The valedictory was hers because she had earned it, and for several other reasons. Her mother had kept her eye upon that especial honour for her only child from the day of her birth. She had not arisen from the sheets of accouchement without having decided upon a great many things concerning the career of her little daughter, and one of the essential things had been the valedictory upon the night of her graduation. She and Mahala engaged in a number of long talks concerning this momentous occasion, and in the seclusion of their room, she and Mahlon discussed these things interminably. They were both agreed that Mahala must have the valedictory, quite agreed that she must honestly earn it. This the girl felt she had done. They were agreed that she must be exquisitely clothed. This was their part. They were unanimous as to a compelling subject; also she must handle it in an interesting manner; she must deliver her valedictory without a flaw in composition, delivery, or deportment.

Long before the remainder of the class had even thought of subjects, in the secret conclaves of her family, Mahala's subject had been decided upon, outlined, and developed. Many things she had wanted to say had been ruled out for reasons paramount in the minds of Elizabeth and Mahlon. Once or twice a week, she had been put through her paces either by her father or her mother, occasionally before both. The thing had become so habitual with Mahala that she recited her valedictory every night before she went to sleep and snatches of it were in her mind many times during the day. In all this intensive study, she had dwelt upon pronunciations, upon phrasing, and inflection until she really had an extremely praiseworthy offering at the tip of her tongue, one which either Elizabeth or Mahlon could have delivered equally as well. All her life she had been making her bow and speaking her piece at mite societies and tea meetings, at Sunday School festivals, last days of school, and Grand Army celebrations.

To Mahala, Commencement night was not a thing of cold shivers, shaking knees, and throbbing heart. She had been trained from birth and was an adept at public appearances. She could recall no occasion in her life when she had come in contact with any of the other boys and girls in public in which she had not easily made the most attractive figure and carried off the honours.

At the noon hour, her father had said to her: "I'm going to stop at the Newberry House and tell the busman he needn't come for you to-night. I don't propose that you shall risk soiling your shoes and your dress by climbing into that dirty omnibus, even though there is a supposition that it is to be cleaned after the last load of drummers is taken to the train."

Mahala hesitated a second, then she looked at her father with speculative eyes. "Don't you think, Papa," she said, "that it would be better for me to go with the others?"

There were nerve strain and asperity in Elizabeth Spellman's voice that Mahala recognized. She gave Mahlon no chance.

"Mahala," she said, "when Papa tells you that he's going to do a thing that he has studied out and has decided will be the best thing for you, the proper answer for you to make is: 'Yes, Papa. Thank you very much for your loving consideration.'"

"I was only thinking," said Mahala, "that the other boys and girls might resent it; that it might make them feel that they were unfortunate not to have a father who had made such a success of life that he could do for them the lovely things that Papa daily does for me."

Mahala looked at her father to see what effect this would have, and her heart took one surging leap and then stopped for an instant and stood still, frightened by the whiteness of Mahlon Spellman's face. She noticed his grip upon the fork he was handling and that his hand was shaking so that he put back upon his plate the food he was intending to lift to his lips. For one long instant Mahala surveyed him and a little bit of the light went out of her eyes, the keenest edge of the colour washing in her cheeks faded. She saw the shaking hand, and in her heart she said: "Either Papa is dreadfully troubled, or he's getting old; and come to think of it, he is nearly twenty years older than Mama. He's been a darling papa, so I've got to begin taking extra good care of him." Her mind reverted to the variety of care that always had been taken of her, and while she rebelled against a great deal of it, even as she was now rebelling against this distinction to be made between her and her classmates, she was placed where all her life she had been placed, in such a position that she would look heartless and ungracious to refuse.

"I am going," said Elizabeth Spellman, "to spread a sheet all over the back seat of the surrey and on the floor. Jemima has wiped the seats very carefully and the steps, and swept the carpet until there isn't a particle of dust. You cannot crowd into that omnibus without crushing your skirts. I think we can lift them in such a manner when you enter the surrey, that by occupying the back seat alone, you won't need to sit upon them at all. It will enable you to head the procession down the church aisle with your frock as fresh and immaculate as when it is lifted from the form to be put upon you."

"Very well, Mama," said Mahala with a little sigh. "It's awfully good of you and Papa to take so much trouble and I do appreciate it, but I cannot help thinking it would be better——"

"There, there, Mahala!" said Mrs. Spellman.

A queer, ugly red with which Mahala was very familiar crept into her mother's cheeks. So nothing more was said on the subject until that night in the sweltering heat when the Newberry House omnibus had pounded up and down and across Ashwater, picking up a red-faced boy here, a perspiring girl there, pausing in state before the humble door of Susanna and shortly thereafter before the gate of the banker.

The surrey was waiting to take Mr. and Mrs. Moreland to the church. Junior's mother came on the veranda with him and stood looking him over. Her face was very pale and her hands were trembling.

"Do you think," she questioned eagerly, "that you won't get frightened, that you can remember your speech?"

"You bet your life I can remember my speech!" said Junior boastfully. "When did I ever forget a speech, if I wanted to make one? Never broke down in my life. Why should I now? I'm going to try the old bank a little and if I don't like it, I'm going to be a lawyer. I think it would be a lot of fun to be a lawyer, and you bet a lawyer doesn't forget a speech. You needn't sit and shake and worry, or Father either. Don't have cold feet and hot sweats."

The driver of the omnibus hallooed and called to Junior to hurry, that he was two minutes late. In order to show his authority and his position in the village, Junior deliberately stepped inside the door. He could not think of a thing on earth to use as an excuse for having done so. His handkerchief was in his pocket, the notes for his speech he had placed himself in order that he might refresh his memory if he felt a bit rattled as his turn came to speak. He had no need to look in the mirror to see that he was as handsome as a boy well could be. His mother hurried after him.

"Junior, what is it?" she cried in a panic.

"Oh, I just thought I'd wet my whistle once more," said Junior, starting toward the dining room. His mother hurried to bring him a drink of water, and when he was perfectly ready, Junior kissed her, telling her to get his father and hurry up because she should be in her place before the march down the aisle began. Mrs. Moreland, comfortable in the dignity of reserved seats, also took her time. She was to be separated from her lord who sat upon the platform as President of the School Board.

She left Mr. Moreland at the side door opening into the small room where the official board of the church transacted its business. He was the last one of the officials to arrive. His fellow townsmen and neighbours amused Martin Moreland that night. They stood so straight, their faces were so grave, they were gasping in the heat, they felt over their hair and held their heads at an angle calculated best to allow the perspiration to run down their necks without touching their stiffly starched high collars.

116

In casting his eyes over the gathering, he noted with satisfaction the absence of his old enemy, Mahlon Spellman. Not that Mahlon knew that he was the enemy of the banker. He did not. He thought that Martin thought that they were friends. There was no intuition which told him that Martin Moreland hated his precision of language, hated his taste in dressing, hated his poise and self-possession, hated to loathing scorn his fidelity to the paths of virtue, cordially hated any appearance in public that he ever had made. It certainly was unfortunate for Mahlon that only the spring preceding Mahala's graduation his period on the School Board had elapsed and a new man had taken his place.

As Mahlon made his way down the church aisle with Elizabeth on his arm, he was probably the only man in the room who was not perspiring. A sort of clammy indifference seemed to have settled upon him. It was purely from force of habit that he ran his fingers over his hair, felt of his tie, and went through the old familiar gestures of flecking his sleeve and straightening his vest as he stepped into the light of the chandeliers and marched to the strains of the organ down to their reservations.

The unconscious Elizabeth was in the height of her glory. She had waited for this, she had prayed for this; only God knew how she had worked for it. She had just accomplished the delivery of her offspring at the side door of the church without a fleck of dust having touched her shoes of white satin, without a fold or crease disfiguring the billowing skirts of her frock. She had done her share perfectly. Never a fear crossed her mind that Mahala would fail. When had Mahala ever failed? Why *should* she?

As Mahala stood a second to shake out her skirts after stepping down, her mother had deliberately gone to the door and looked in upon the assembled graduates. She had eyes for only one figure. She wanted to see Edith Williams. Standing in the centre of the room, Edith had given her a distinct shock.

All day the girl had been nervous, frantically trying to remember her speech. In the humid heat of the evening she had gotten herself into a closely fitting dress of heavy white velvet. It was a dress that a queen might have worn upon a state occasion. Pearl-white like the shell of an oyster, very plain both as to waist and skirt—a dress that trusted to the richness of its material to make up for any lack of the elaborate trimmings of the day. As Edith had stood before her mirror giving the finishing touches to her toilet she had seen above the tightly embracing waist her face flushed with the strain of fear that she might forget her speech, her figure tense with the nerve strain of her unaccustomed public appearance. That minute she was wildly envying even Susanna who could have been called upon and recited any one of a hundred poems from the readers that had been used in the school course or supplementary works on elocution. The doubt and uncertainty in her mind had given to the girl a flashing vividness she never before had possessed.

Lifting her skirts around her, she had entered the omnibus and glanced at its occupants. She had said nothing until the driver turned the corner and started in the direction of the church. Involuntarily she threw up her hand, crying: "Stop him! He has forgotten Mahala!"

Instantly, Junior Moreland arose in his place, and catching a swaying strap above his head, leaned to the opening beside the driver and spoke to him roughly, crying: "Here you! You've forgotten Mahala Spellman!"

Without stopping, the driver cracked his whip over his team and plunged ahead. There was rather a dazed look on Junior's face as he lurched back and dropped into his seat. Edith Williams leaned forward and with wide eyes looked at Junior.

"What did he say?" she cried.

"'Father's fetching her,'" answered Junior tartly, and it happened that he accompanied the information by a look at Edith. Unquestionably he saw the lunge of her angered heart. He saw the red blood surge up to her lips and paint her cheeks. He saw the black malice that stirred in the depths of her eyes. He caught the smothered exclamation, a shocking exclamation, that arose to her lips, and he knew, and every member of the class knew, that the bitter little "Damn!" which sprang past the lips of Edith Williams was unadulterated, forceful invective.

She was outdone in the first round. Mahala would not ride to the church with the remainder of the class. Why was she in that omnibus among the sons and daughters of blacksmiths, and cobblers, and lawn cleaners? Why had she not had the sense to think of having her uncle take her in their beautiful surrey? Why was she always letting Mahala Spellman get ahead of her? There rushed through her heart the conviction that when Mahala stepped through the door, in some way she would have managed, probably with half the money Edith had spent, to outdo her costume.

The velvet of her dress, rose-petal soft, shut her in like the walls of a furnace. The heat and anger in her eyes made her what she never before in her life had been— arrestingly beautiful. She bit her dry lips and clenched her gloved hands. What matter that she had bought herself what she felt would be said to be the handsomest basket of flowers that would be carried to the stage that night, with the imaginary name of an imaginary lover attached by her own hands to the handle? What matter that she had coached both her uncle and her aunt concerning the handsome offerings that they were to send up to her? In some way, Mahala would see to it that she would have finer. For one thing it was certain, after the expense of the piano lamp of four years ago, that Junior would stop at nothing. No doubt the basket he would send Mahala would far surpass hers.

When the omnibus stopped at the church door, with his usual lithe smoothness of movement, Junior was on his feet and out of it first. Instead of marching straight into the church in the lead, as all of them expected him to do, he had surprised them by turning, and with one white-gloved hand upon the door, he had looked into the eyes of Edith Williams. Instantly she arose, gathering her skirts around her, and made her way to the door. She laid her hand in Junior's outstretched one; she encountered the look in his eyes in a state of dumb bewilderment. She came carefully down the three steps leading from the eminence of the omnibus. Her ears heard the sweetest music this world ever had vouchsafed to them: "I say, Edith, you are a riproaring beauty tonight! Keep your head up, and show folks how it's done!"

In that instant Edith remembered that she knew her speech. A sort of cold self-possession washed in a big wave through her entire body. Her head tipped to a coquettish angle and she looked into the eyes of the boy she was passing so closely, with an alluring smile.

"Thank you, Junior," she said in dry breathlessness. "I'm so glad you like me."

Then she passed him and hurried across the sidewalk into the prayer-meeting room.

Junior stood his ground and gave his hand to the girls in turn as they alighted from the omnibus. In his heart he was saying to himself: "Oh, Hell! I didn't say I 'liked' her. I was trying to say that she was good-looking for the first time in her life, and maybe the last. But if she *could* keep that up, she'd be some punkins to look at, and that's the truth!"

Junior's words had been overheard by the class behind Edith. They stood back, carefully scrutinizing her, and realized that what he had said was the truth.

Edith worked her way to one side of the room and from her left hand let slide down among the folds of her dress the copy of her speech that she was carrying. With a deft foot she kicked it under the seats, confident that no one had observed the movement. In this confidence she retained her poise and her pose, and it was thus that Mrs. Spellman saw her.

At that instant the voice of the organ, rolling an unaccustomed march, came to their ears. Again involuntarily the thing that was deep in Edith's mind arose to her lips, "Mahala!" Mahala's mother was standing in the door, smiling and bowing and speaking in her gracious way to all of the boys and girls, cautioning them to keep cool, to keep in mind the opening phrases of their speeches and the rest must follow; then she made way for the Superintendent, who ordered them to "Come on!" and in mechanical obedience, Edith led the way from the room. In the darkness of the early June evening she could see a blur of white waiting on the sidewalk.

In the order in which they were to sit upon the platform, the class fell into line. The sidewalk cleared of a waiting crowd of unfortunates who had not the clothing or the invitation to enter the coveted portals, who yet had come to press back into the darkness and watch the spectacle.

As Mahala advanced up the broad walk that led to the front steps of the church, there came scuffling through the crowd, she could not have told from where, a figure in white, as white as the new-born thoughts of white that contributed to her own dress. She realized that there was a catching and a snatching, an effort to make some one pause, and then she saw, scurrying up the steps before her, standing in the broad light of the open doors of the church, her bonnet lost in the crowd, Rebecca, her white flag lifted above the path the graduating class must follow to enter the doors. The figures of two working men in their shirt sleeves, with rough jests on their lips and their hands outstretched, started forward.

Mahala looked up. Her first thought was that never in all her life had she seen a figure so appealingly beautiful. Probably no one in all that crowd, since the day of her self-imposed appearance with sheltered face as the bearer of the flag advocating purity, had seen Rebecca Sampson as she really was. The years untouched by mental strain had left her the lovely rounded face of girlhood. The deeply shadowing headpiece, always stiffly starched and filled in with sustaining slats of pasteboard, had kept Rebecca's complexion that of a little child. Her hands and arms were soft and white. Her throat, delicately rounded, was a miracle of whiteness. The plain white dress that she wore was as mistily white as the petals of a cherry bloom. The fringed flag that she held in Mahala's pathway was as white as her dress. Suddenly Mahala threw out her hands.

"Never mind!" she cried to the men. "Let her alone! I have been passing under her flag all my life."

She smiled on the crowds pressing forward on either side of her.

"You know," she said, "somehow this seems fitting. I rather like the idea of passing under Becky's emblem of purity on Commencement night." She half turned and called back to the other boys and girls: "Come on! Let's all pass under the white flag with Becky's blessing. Maybe it will help us to remember our speeches."

She raised her skirts and stepped into the full blaze of light falling from the church doors, and like a misty veil of purity, she shimmered and gleamed as she climbed the steps. Her head was as yellow as sunshine, her eyes were deep wells of blue-gray, and her long, dark lashes swept her pink cheeks, while the smile with which she went toward Rebecca seemed to Jason, crowded tightly against the wall of the church looking up at her, the loveliest thing that this world could possibly have to offer. To him the gold head and the billowing skirts of gauzy fineness made Mahala look like a gold-hearted white rose.

Immediately back of her, with her head tilted and a new light gleaming in her eyes, came Edith Williams. There was a smile on Jason's lips. It was lingering from the vision of Mahala as she had bent her head and lifted her hands to her breast for the blessing of "Crazy Becky." But the smile merged into an expression of aroused indignation. His thought had been that Edith Williams looked like a lily that needed a gold heart, but that thought quickly passed, for with uplifted hand, she struck aside the white flag and entered the church door. The crowd outside heard Rebecca's shrill curse: "To the devil, you velvet-clad jade! You have a black heart—as black as your head!"

Little Susanna, ever anxious to save any unpleasant occasion, came next, crying to Rebecca: "My turn now. I want to go under your flag, Rebecca!" Instantly Rebecca was all smiles again and the flag was back in place while her lips were murmuring a blessing.

120

Down the line, Junior had heartily sympathized with the uplifted hand. What mummery that a crazy woman should be allowed to stand there! She might even come into the church and spoil the graduating exercises. He said to the men standing nearest him: "Watch her! Don't let her get into the church. She'll spoil everything. She ought to be taken to the lock-up at a time like this."

But as he came up the steps, Junior had not quite the courage to subject himself to the black curse that had fallen upon Edith. With a shamefaced grin and a muttered, "Better avoid a fight," he ducked under the flag and hurried into the church. Following the example of the graduating class, the Principal, the Superintendent, the high-school teachers, and the School Board passed under the flag to Rebecca's intense delight. The last man in the procession was Martin Moreland. Since he could not be first, he had deliberately chosen to be last. He would be more conspicuous in the outside seat than he would be between two other men. As he came up the steps, Rebecca's eyes fastened on him. Instantly, she whirled the flag from over the head of the man before him and snatched it to her breast. She folded her hands over it and held it there tight, crying to the outraged banker as he advanced: "Woe upon you, Martin Moreland, despoiler of white flags, despoiler of white women! The blackest curse of the Almighty is waiting for your head!"

Martin Moreland's outstretched arm swept her off the steps and backward into the crowd.

"Take that crazy helion where she can't possibly get into the building," he said. "I'll hold you responsible if it happens."

Exactly who was to be held responsible, no man knew. It was Jason who made his way through the crowd, put a protecting arm around Rebecca, who whispered into her ear words that would calm and soothe her, who led her to the outskirts of the crowd and saw her safely started on her homeward way before he slipped up the stairs and found a seat in the suffocating balcony from which he meant to watch until he saw whether his gift gained any attention from Mahala.

It was not until they were seated that Edith Williams had an opportunity surreptitiously to take a full look at Mahala from behind the screen of her swaying fan. Mahala had been ahead of her. From the sidewalk, behind her mother's back, she had secured a full-length look at Edith, and she had been as distinctly shocked as had Junior. There was no gainsaying the fact that Edith was wearing an exquisite gown, and for that night at least she was lovely. Mahala suspected that the red lips and the pink cheeks were painted, and there she partially misjudged. Edith was painted, but Junior had been the artist. She decided that Edith's dress was probably the most expensive in the church, that it was wonderfully lovely, but it was not appropriate for the occasion. She felt that it was not in as good taste as was her own; but there was a pang of disappointment, because the verdict in her favour would not be so easy, or so unanimous, as it always had been. Many in the house that night would think Edith quite as beautiful as she and more handsomely gowned.

CHAPTER X

"A Trick of the Subconscious"

Mahala had been born at a period in the wedded lives of her parents when both of them were at the high tide of joy in their union, of pride in their hearts, of happiness without a cloud. She had made her advent fortified with a happy heart. The slight pang that shot through her as she looked at Edith was of short duration. As swiftly as it had come, it was gone. When she caught Edith's eye, the smile she sent her was charming; a widening of her eyes, a little pucker of her lips, was meant to convey to Edith that Mahala was saying: "How wonderful! You look perfectly stunning." This added one more degree to the joy that at that minute was welling and singing in the heart of Edith Williams.

Out in the audience a satisfied flutter was rolling in waves through the building. In her secret heart, each mother was thinking, that in some way, her child had slightly the best of the other children. There was almost a bewildered look on the face of Elizabeth Spellman. She was constrained to admit, if only to herself, that she never before had seen Edith Williams look like that, and she never had supposed it was possible that she could look like *that*. It dawned upon her that a few pounds of flesh, a few waves of happiness, judicious assistance in dressing that would come to Edith when she travelled, were going to make of her an extremely attractive young woman.

When she lifted the programme in her hands and glanced over it, her eyes fastened upon two lines thereon and her slight sense of humour came to the surface to such a degree that she nudged Mahlon and ran her finger under them. What Mahlon saw, when he looked where the finger indicated, read: "Sowing Seeds of Kindness" and beneath it, "Edith Williams." It was a poor place to catch Mahlon unprepared and unaware. The gurgle that arose to his lips made him look, for an instant, as human as Jimmy Price. Nothing could have mortified Mahlon more deeply.

The organ was rolling again. The imported soprano was warbling among high notes about the "tide coming up from Lynn," and a few seconds later John Reynolds was delivering the salutatory and then sailing into the bay he had left and prognosticating what was going to happen upon the ocean that lay before him.

While her aunt and uncle clutched cold hands and dared not look each other in the face, Edith Williams stood up and sowed her "seeds of kindness" without a falter and without a break. She went straight through as if she could not have lost a word if she had tried, and sat down in such a spasm of self-congratulation that she could scarcely keep from applauding her own performance. Never in all her life had she been quite so surprised: never had she been one half so deeply pleased.

Immediately after her, looking as handsome as it was possible for him to look, beautifully clothed, cool and utterly self-possessed, taking his time, a jesting light in his eyes, half a laugh on his lips, for a few minutes Martin Moreland Junior held forth on the Constitution of these United States. He gave the impression that the Constitution should feel much better since it had his approval.

Then, in a dress half way of Mahala's making, the goods of her giving, flushed and attractive, Susanna Bowers told the audience her conception of the full duty of woman. It was difficult for any one in the audience to imagine where Susanna had gotten her ideas as to what the full duty of a woman might be. The audience would persist in thinking about the place from which Susanna naturally would have been supposed to gain her conclusions, but Susanna had been forced to go by contraries. She had gotten her material where none of the other girls had secured theirs. Her conception was one half the fruit of a vivid imagination, and the other half Mahala Spellman. All Susanna needed to do in writing her paper was to look at Mahala, then shut her eyes and concentrate on the kind of a woman that she believed Mahala would be ten years hence. It made an attractive paper; Susanna delivered it well.

Then Frederick Hilton repeated very creditably an oration of Patrick Henry's, and Samantha Price read what she had copied from encyclopædias concerning Grace Darling. The women in the audience developed expressions of uncertainty and from them there emanated a wave of veiled protest when Amanda Nelson sailed into the subject of the peril of Susan B. Anthony. There were a few women in that audience who did not regard Susan B. as a peril. They looked upon her rather as an anchor, or a light. They were not particularly obliged to Amanda for her version of what Susan B. was attempting. Even those high-minded dames, who had neither the desire nor the intention of soiling themselves in the handling of a ballot at such a questionable place as the polls, felt in their secret hearts that they should have the right to do this if they chose. There were even those among them who resented the arrest of Mary Walker, for appearing on the streets of New York in trousers. Of course, they could neither be bribed nor forced so to appear themselves, but if Mary desired to wear trousers, they rather felt that she was within her rights. The wave of disapproval washed up to very nearly a murmur of protest when the speaker made her best bow and sat down amid the deafening applause of the men. No other speaker up to that time had had such an ovation. The nearer the doctor, the lawyer, the judge, the sheriff, the postmaster, the county chairman, the state senator, the banker, and the dry-goods merchant, came to blistering their palms, the more the women of the audience felt, that if they could have done exactly as they pleased in seclusion, they would have soundly boxed Amanda Nelson's ears.

Before the cheers concerning the peril of Susan B. had subsided, Henrick Schlotzensmelter plunged into his discussion of whether Might or Right should prevail. Exactly how Henrick's paper passed the Superintendent and the Principal was a matter that Melancthon Reynolds, the county prosecutor, could not figure out, because Henrick succeeded very admirably in proving that "might" and "right" were synonymous, and that "might" must and should prevail because it was "right" that it should. His oration was even less popular with the men than had been that concerning Susan B. with the ladies of the audience. Most of the applause that fell to Henrick's share came from his father and mother, who had been born and had spent their early married life in Bingen on the Rhine.

There was a movement of exasperation on the part of Elizabeth Spellman, upon which Mahlon placed the high sign of his approbation, when little pasty-faced Jane Jackson began a discussion as to whether Carrie Nation should be suppressed, and again an intangible wave swept the audience. There were two opinions concerning that subject, also. Evidently, neither thought this the proper place for a discussion of temperance. When the ushers, who had been busy all evening flitting up and down the aisles carrying baskets and bouquets of every shape and condition to heap at the feet of those who had triumphantly finished, were through, it was noticed that the advocate, who felt very strongly that Carrie Nation should not be suppressed, had reaped a very light harvest in the line of flowers. There was no wonderful basket with a vine-wreathed handle standing at her feet; only a few roughly bunched, home-grown posies fell to her lot, flowers that had not been cooled in cellars and refrigerators, and were not reinforced with stems packed in wet moss. But she happened to be sitting beside Edith Williams whose bounty rolled over and so encroached upon her that it was difficult for the audience to tell where Edith left off and Jane began.

At last Mahala Spellman arose and came to the front of the stage, smiling upon her parents, her friends, and neighbours with precisely the same brand of assurance that had been hers ever since she had stood on that same platform at four years of age and recited:

"Hush, hush!"
Said a little brown thrush.

It had been agreed upon that occasion that Mahala was a wonder. The verdict held over. In the first place, standing in the spotlight of the big chandelier that the Mite Society had cooked and sweated so patiently, with such dogged persistence over a long period to pay for, Mahala made a grand showing. She did the whole town credit. Hair that has been carefully brushed twice a day for eighteen years is bound to be silky. Mahala's hung like spun floss brushed into curls over her shoulders. The silvery wreath that held it in place looked as fragile and white as the silver whiteness of the mass of ruffles and lace that billowed around her. As she lifted her hands in a grave gesture, the women of the audience noticed that she had a new sleeve. Lace edged, it flowed from her elbows in fullness to the region of her knees; from the elbows down to her wrists there was an inner sleeve that was a mass of ruffling of fine lace. The dress was a work of art, and in it Mahala looked like nothing else in all the world so much as a gorgeous, big white rose with a heart of gold—a vivid heart, for her lips were red, her cheeks were pink, her blue eyes were shining, and her hair remained gold.

She loved her subject because she was talking about "Our Duty to Our Neighbours." Mahala felt that every one had a duty to his neighbours. She did not feel that Ashwater always performed this duty creditably, and to-night was her first chance to say to the ministers, the lawyers, the doctors, and the church deacons, precisely what she conceived to be the duty of any individual to his neighbour. As she talked, simply, convincingly, at times eloquently, Elizabeth Spellman could not keep from burrowing the hand next Mahlon down against his side where she took a tight grip upon his coat, and he knew that she was praying with every fibre of her being that Mahala might acquit herself in a manner that would be unquestionably above criticism and redound inevitably to their great credit.

Mahlon's heart was pounding till it jarred him. There had been a great deal to agitate it for a number of years past. At the present minute the load it was labouring under was almost more than it could bear and function properly. Mahlon's feet were cold; his hands were cold; and his head was hot—far too hot. He did not know why these things should be, for the simple reason that there was not the shadow of a fear in his heart that Mahala would fail. He knew Mahala well enough to know that if she forgot the set speech she had arisen to make, she was perfectly capable of improvisation that would fill the bill creditably. And he did not know why he spent time thinking of such a thing as that, because it was quite impossible that Mahala should fail. He was a bit irritated at the grip of Elizabeth's clutching hand at his side. He knew that it was his full duty, as the head of the house, to quiet the fears of his womenfolk. He should have covertly secured Elizabeth's hand and allowed the waves of certainty that were possessing his veins to be transmitted to her, and why in the world he was not giving her this satisfaction in mental support, he did not know. But the fact was that he would have given quite a bit to be able to shake off her clutching hand. Why need she be keyed up to such a point concerning his daughter that she must clutch and grab? Why should she not sit erect in calm certainty that his daughter would acquit herself perfectly in whatever she undertook? Look at the splendour of her dress, fashioned mostly by her own hands. Look at her cool forehead, her graceful gesture, her natural curls having the temerity to curl tighter with the humidity of the night that was spelling tragedy for products of the waving board and the curling iron. Listen to the sweetness of her voice. Notice that her hand discarded the fan that others worked assiduously.

Suddenly, Elizabeth's hand dug in compellingly. She might as well have clutched a stone, for Mahlon had very nearly accomplished that transformation. Mahala was off the track! Elizabeth opened her lips to prompt her child with the next word, but shut them in sudden daze. Calm as she conceivably could be, Mahala was going straight ahead; but what was that scandalizing rot she was talking? Elizabeth would have given worlds to have had her daughter across her knee and a hair brush convenient.

"Perhaps the highest duty any man owes his neighbour is to respect his mentality, to grant to him the same intellectual freedom that he reserves for himself," the girl's clear voice was saying.

"Too much contact with Schlotzensmelters and Nelsons!" Elizabeth commented mentally.

"Each man has his personal relation to God to consider," Mahala was saying. "He wishes other men to respect his religion—to that same degree let him consider and reverence the religion of his neighbours."

"Campbellites slopping in a tank! Popery and bigotism!" hissed Elizabeth in her seething brain.

"Each man gives his party affiliations deep study and believes wholeheartedly in his views," the girl was saying. "Why should he deem his neighbour less interested, less capable of deciding for himself?"

"Democrats and Populists!" sweated Elizabeth, unsparingly kneading Mahlon's defenceless side.

"There are even those among us not willing to allow our neighbours to choose which newspaper they will take, what books they will read, what clothing they shall wear——" smooth as oil Mahala flowed on, but each phrase was a blow, each idea revolutionary.

"Why should men be such bigots as to require that other men shall conform to their ideas before they will grant them intellectual freedom?" cried the girl.

"I'll show you, Miss!" said Elizabeth.

But, hark! What was that? The church in a storm of applause, in the midst of a speech! Unprecedented! It kept on and on. Suddenly, Elizabeth found herself blistering her palms against each other. She looked at Mahlon, to find him doing the same thing. Of all the world! How they did applaud that slip of a girl! And those were some of the very things Elizabeth had suppressed, or thought she had.

Mahala was back on the track now. Her excursion had been the triumph of the Spellmans' life, but limply wet, exhausted, and secretly outraged, Elizabeth weakly prayed that Mahala would attempt no further improvisation. That prayer was answered. The Defense having been granted a brain as well as a body, Mahala was constrained to close as she was expected. Mahlon drew a deep breath and used his handkerchief. To him, as Mahala took her seat, with the sacred edifice rocking in the gust of approval, she was a sacred thing. Whatever she did came out right. She was a perfect picture, a white flower. That recalled him to the fact that, shrouded in tissue paper between his knees, was a horribly expensive basket that his pride had compelled him to order for her from the nearest city. She had not had a peep of it. Through the tissue enfolding it, Mahlon could feel the coolness that it distilled around his feet, since the generous applause had warmed them. From the corner of his eye he was watching the approaching ushers as Mahala finished and the organ swelled triumphantly to proclaim that the first great public event in the lives of these youngsters had been passed with credit to each and every one of them.

As the ushers came nearer, Mahlon found, absurd as it might seem, that it was going to be impossible for him to release that tissue covering without at least the usher and Elizabeth seeing that his hands were shaking. He kept them tightly gripped, one over each knee, to steady himself. He had ordered that bouquet. It was the emanation of his taste. He meant that nothing on the stage should approach it in elegance. His hand should be the one to burst it forth, a wave of artistic beauty for the eyes of the watching audience. In his heart, Mahlon never was quite so thankful as when Elizabeth leaned across and with a little twitch loosened the wrappings and lifted them, leaving the basket ready for his hand. After all, Elizabeth was to be depended on; she was his complement, she was the best thing in life that he had ever done for himself. He was distinctly sorry that he had not taken her hand during its clutching appeal but a few moments before.

He did manage to swing his left knee out of the way and with the right foot slide the basket across to the attention of the approaching flower girl. Her arms were already filled but she smiled on him, gave the basket an appraising glance, and whispered: "I'll come for that specially, when I've delivered these."

Mahlon approved, because it was not suitable that his wonderful gift should be overshadowed or in any way brought in contact with anything else. So he sat waiting while the flower girl laid her offering at the feet of his smiling daughter and came back to bear aloft his triumph alone.

Then Mahlon's heart played him another queer trick. He had forgotten that young upstart of a Moreland. Why hadn't it occurred to him what the fellow would do? Mahlon's sick eyes saw Mrs. Moreland arise and step into the aisle in order that there might be lifted from before her a long, tray-shaped basket with an ornate handle that was outlined with purple violets, while the basket was heaped with pale roses of peach-blow pink, and walled in with the purple of a great roll of Parma violets, and silver tulle and pink satin ribbons were showering down from one side of the handle. Mahlon heard Elizabeth's little gasp beside him. They had seen the great armload of red roses that the Morelands had sent up to their son; they were not prepared for this exquisite demonstration that they were sending before the eyes of the assembled town, to Mahala. Elizabeth's hand was digging into Mahlon's side in spite and vexation until it hurt him, and this time he reached for it and clung to it hard.

It was abominable luck. He would have given anything to be in the secrecy of his bedchamber where he might have said all he thought to sympathetic ears. But ill luck for the Spellmans was only beginning. Down the opposite aisle came another flower girl, and those immediately concerned had not seen who had delivered to her a great, upstanding sheaf of enormous crinkly white roses with hearts of gold. Here and there through the sheaf were big waxen lilies with hearts of gold, and sharply etched leaves of tall fern, while through and around them there was a mist of lacy maidenhair, so fine that no one ever had seen its like. The sheaf was bound around the middle like a sheaf of wheat with a great broad ribbon of gold. Thrust through the knot there was a mass of the delicate fern leaves and daringly there glowed and flamed one smashing big, blood-red rose.

Under the eyes of Junior and Martin and Mrs. Moreland, and before the faces of the quivering Elizabeth and Mahlon Spellman, this triumph of the florist's art had been borne down the aisle and stood at the knees of the valedictorian.

"*My land!*" gasped Elizabeth Spellman, for Mahlon's private ear. "Who do you suppose?"

Mahlon's whole body was a tense note of protest. He did not suppose. He was too stunned to suppose. He was too outraged to suppose. Where had the damned thing come from? Elizabeth's hand was cutting into his. It required the reinforcement of Mahlon's left hand to keep his mouth shut.

Spontaneous as always, Mahala had picked up the *pièce de résistance* of the evening, an offering beside which all else paled into insignificance. She lifted it lightly, smiled on it, turned it a bit that she might see its full beauty, her head cocked on one side in a bird-like gesture habitual with her, lifted it level with her breast, buried her face among its waxen satin petals and gracefully ran her delicate finger-tips through the clinging maidenhair. Then the audience caught the fact that she was searching for a card. She was looking, and her fingers were feeling—and her search was not being rewarded. The handsomest floral tribute that the Ashwater Commencement knew that night had either been sent anonymously, or the card had been lost.

Mahala's curiosity was making her look over the length and breadth of the heap in front of her and at the two gorgeous baskets set before it. Then she gently set down the lilies and roses at her knees and lifting her head, she searched the audience with a long and deliberate look. There was only one person in the audience who knew when that look found its resting place. There was only one person, high up, far back, in the gallery who read to the depths of Mahala's eyes in that instant and through whose heart flowed the cool acquiescence of peace when he saw her fingers slip out and deliberately break from its stem the bud of a white rose that she thrust among the laces covering her bosom.

It was only a moment more before the music was pealing; the Superintendent had made his short speech, as president of the School Board, Martin Moreland was telling what increasingly wonderful work was done each year by the youth of the town, how well deserved were the sheepskins that he was now to bestow upon them. The boys were trying to figure out a problem none of them had remembered to concentrate upon—how they least awkwardly might accept and dispose of the beribboned roll thrust at them. They did not know whether to hold it like a ball bat or a fan. It took the daring of Junior Moreland to make of it a trumpet through which he sent a message to his shocked mother in the audience. It was only a few seconds later that

Jemima Davis was on her knees in front of Mahala gathering into the folds of a widely spread sheet every tribute, large and small, bearing the girl's name.

Guarding like a soldier the beautiful baskets and the sheaf, she whispered to Mahala: "Who sent you them lilies and roses, darlin'?"

Mahala leaned to Jemima's ear to respond: "Hunt through them carefully, Jemima. If you find a note, you will hide it for me, won't you, old dearest dear?"

Jemima answered convincingly: "You just bet your sweet life I will!"

So with a heart of contentment, Mahala led the procession down the aisle, climbed into the omnibus before her parents had a chance to object, and with the others was carried away to the banquet at the Newberry House.

The big dining room filled speedily. Ranged around the long centre table, having the graduates at one end, their parents at the other, were smaller tables for the alumni, the School Board, the teachers, and the invited guests of the graduates. The centre table was the pinnacle of fame that night. The flushed, happy graduates, free of a haunting fear of weeks' duration on the part of most of them, could now laugh and talk and be natural, the result of a whole school life of association. The other end of the table had its troubles. When the Morelands, the Spellmans, and the Williamses undertook to break bread and indulge in social intercourse with the Schlotzensmelters, the Bowers, and the Prices of the town, the situation soon became painful. The upper dog tried to be condescending; the under dog resented it, and speedily lost out by not knowing how to handle napkins, an array of cutlery, and a queer assortment of fancy food that belonged in strange places. Pa Schlotzensmelter, irritated beyond caution, audibly asked his wife: "Vere do I pud dose celery?" And Jimmy Price hastened to answer: "In your mouth." The Schlotzensmelters were outraged, but later their revenge was sweet when Jimmy took a drink from the rose-geranium scented finger bowl, whose use he had not observed by his neighbours, and passed it on to his wife, who followed his example!

The arising from the table was in the nature of a blessed release on the part of the elders. With the graduating class in the lead, the assemblage moved across the street to the dance hall.

Flushed and happy, Mahala stood on the floor, one little qualm of dread in her heart. In that slight interval of waiting for the music to begin, Elizabeth and Mahlon had their first chance at their offspring. Mahala saw them coming and knew that her hour of explanation was upon her. They never would understand how simple it had been. She smiled on them without guile and took the initiative in self-protection.

"I was just hoping for a word with you," she cried. "Were you badly frightened? You see, it was this way——"

"A very charming way," said Mahlon, gallantly kissing his daughter's hand. "Very charming! Your audience was with you. What more need be said?"

"You certainly acquitted yourself nobly," broke in Elizabeth, "and yet, little daughter, didn't you serve Papa and Mama rather a naughty trick?"

"'Trick?'" Mahala's eyes widened. "'Trick?' Pardon me, Mama, it was like this: When I wrote the first draft of my speech I said what I thought and felt. You and Papa argued so strongly that I cut it at your suggestion, but every time I rehearsed it, those cut parts would flash through my brain. I couldn't stop them. I give you my word of honour, I never intended to say them. I didn't know I was saying them until I heard them, and then I couldn't stop until I had reached a place where I could get back smoothly. After that, I was very careful. It was the lights, the big crowd, the urge to express what I truly thought—you believe me, don't you?"

"Certainly, my child!" said Mahlon. "Don't give the matter another thought. I've never hoped to be so proud of you. It was a triumph!"

"Yes," conceded Elizabeth, "there is no better word for it; it was a triumph."

Mahala studied the pair of them. She said slowly, reflectively: "If you feel that over one little argument that pushed itself in, I wonder what would have happened if I had been permitted to deliver my whole speech as I wrote it."

"A hint was all right," said Elizabeth; "more would have ruined it."

She turned to Professor James, who was passing, to inquire: "Professor, did you notice Mahala's bit of impromptu work?"

The Professor looked at them and then at Mahala searchingly.

"I'd hardly call that impromptu," he said. "It so fitted with what had gone before, so rounded out our neighbour's side of the argument, that I can only say that it is a great pity Mahala did not pursue her conclusions a little further. It would have done all of us good."

Elizabeth was a Tartar.

"I scarcely agree with you," she said primly. "A touch might do, but more smacked too loudly of masculinity. Ladies should allow their men to say those things for them."

Mahala knew, having settled this point to her satisfaction, what would be coming next. She excused herself and hurried to join Edith who was waiting for her, the glamour of her triumph still illuminating her. Her programme was in very plain sight; as Junior came toward them, he could sense it blocking his path. He had been constrained to admit to himself that Edith looked that night as he had not dreamed that it was possible that she could. But he never had liked her. He did not care for her now, and every fibre of his being was in irritated protest against that sheaf of lilies and roses that had been given Mahala. It might have been from her father or mother, possibly she had out-of-town relatives, but if she had, why had she never mentioned them? Who was there who could have shown the taste and spent the money, and who had dared to set one blood-red rose in a sheaf of virgin white?

He brushed roughly past Edith, paying not the slightest attention to her. He seized Mahala's programme, and against her protests, began writing his name all over it. Her father and mother were standing directly behind her; beside them, his own parents. Edith glanced toward them in a vain effort to hide the quiver of her lips, and saw that all of them were laughingly acquiescing. Junior, looking over Mahala's head, saw them, also.

Carried away by their approval, he caught Mahala into his arms and swept her into the first dance. Then, guiding her to a flower-screened corner, in the scarcely adequate shelter of the foliage, he deliberately crushed her in his arms and kissed her on the mouth.

She pushed him away, protesting angrily. With a bit of lace supposed to be a handkerchief, she roughly scoured the curve of her lips to a brighter red than the freely flowing blood of the evening had tinted them.

That provoked Junior so that he said to her: "You might as well stop that! You're the only girl I love, or ever intend to love, and I'm going to marry you. I've got a lot selected and I'm working on the plans for our house right now."

Mahala drew back and looked at Junior intently for a few seconds, looked as deep into his eyes as any one ever saw into the eyes of either Moreland, father or son. She said slowly and deliberately: "If that's the truth, Junior, you're wasting time. I'm not going to marry any one until I've finished college, and I have not the slightest intention of marrying you at any time."

A slow red mounted into Junior's cheeks, a queer spark of white light snapped in the back of his eyes.

"You don't mean that," he said tensely. "You only say it to get me going. You want me down on my knees before you. You want me to whine and beg for you like a hungry puppy dog."

Mahala reached out a hand and deliberately laid it upon Junior's.

"Junior," she said, "listen to me. You know that isn't the truth. To save your life, you can't name one time when I ever said a word or did a thing to encourage you in the belief that I liked you better than any of the other boys. Think a minute. You *know* I never did. I'm not going to marry you. You might as well not set your heart on it. I don't want you to cringe and beg; I'm not asking anything of you but to leave me alone. Can't you get it into your head that I mean what I say?"

She brushed past him and started in the direction of her father and mother. Junior saw that the fingers of the hand that had lain upon his were now lightly touching the petals of a white rose that was homing on her breast.

He stood in a sort of stupor for a minute; finally he lifted his head and went swiftly from a side door. Without a deviating step, he took the shortest cut to the nearest saloon and there he drank until he became wild, so that he began throwing glasses and abusing the furniture. He was venting the insane anger that swelled up in his breast on anything that came in his way. Chairs and tables flew before him. Heavy bottles and glasses went crashing. It was an accident that a poorly aimed decanter smashed through the frosted glass of the front door, allowing the passers-by to see what was going on inside.

Martin Moreland, who never lost sight of Junior for long, had seen him draw Mahala into the flowery enclosure. In an ambling way he had sauntered to the front side of the flowers and taken up a position where he could hear what was being said while he was pretending smilingly to watch the dancers with great interest. With that smile on his lips, his clenched hands were aching to strike. The savage anger that many times in his life had overtaken and swayed him, was swelling up in such a tide as his tried heart never before had known. He wanted to take Mahala in her flowerlike whiteness, and twist his fingers around her delicate neck until the very eyes would pop from her head. He wanted to do anything that was savage and cruel and merciless to the girl who would thrust aside and repulse his son.

He realized, with that craft which forever walked hand in hand with love in his heart, that he must take care of Junior. He must avoid scandal. He hurried from the side door, knowing where he would find his boy. He had reached the saloon and had his hand upon the door when the glass came crashing into his face. Through the opening he saw Junior flushed and dishevelled, his clothing already stained and ruined in a wild debauch. Shaking off the splintered glass, he entered. He ordered the proprietor to nail a piece of carpet, anything, over the opening immediately; then he took his place beside Junior and made a deceiving pretense of helping him to demolish the saloon.

Surprised at this, Junior stood watching his father who was really doing no very great damage. He began to laugh and applaud; then he consented to sit down at a table and drink with his father, and very speedily his condition became helpless. Then Martin Moreland sent for his carriage and took his boy home and with his own hands undressed him and put him into his bed, a horrible contrast with the lad who had left the room a few hours earlier.

Mrs. Moreland, becoming disquieted by the absence of both her husband and her son, went in search of them. She thought possibly they had gone back to the bar of the Newberry House, but an inquiry there told her that they had not returned. So she hurried the few intervening blocks, and seeing the light in Junior's room, entered her home and climbed the stairs to find him helpless, stretched on his bed, his father kneeling beside him removing his shoes.

As a rule Mrs. Moreland let no word pass her lips that would irritate her husband. She had learned through the years that she had lived with him, to know what lay in the depths of his eyes. She had no desire to plumb the depths of cruelty of which she vaguely felt him capable. She stood one long instant studying the picture before her and then she turned to him and said deliberately: "How do you like your work, Martin? Are you pleased with what you are succeeding in making of your son?"

The Senior Moreland threw up his head and favoured his wife with a full glance. In her eyes there was written large the love with which she yearned over her boy. Something about her expression made more nearly an appeal than anything she could have said to him. There was not much mirth in the laugh he forced to his lips.

"Don't be an everlasting killjoy," he said to her banteringly. "It's all right for youth to have its fling. I followed him because I expected the strain of the night to end like this. He'll be all right in the morning."

Arising, he offered her his arm with extreme politeness and escorted her from the sight of the boy. Once the door was closed after them, he gripped her arm until his fingers cut into it cruelly. He rushed her down the hall faster than she could comfortably walk and thrust her into her room so roughly and forcibly that she fell upon her bed. Standing over her, he said to her: "If you can't manage to be anything better than a sickly idiot, you keep out of men's affairs altogether." And then, on a wave evoked by the nausea on her face, he added: "He'll be all right in the morning, I tell you!"

In the morning, when Mrs. Moreland lifted strained and sleepless eyes to the doorway, she was shocked until she shrank back in her chair. Junior was standing there, laughing at her. She could not see any trace of the dissipation of the night before upon his face or person. He had bathed and carefully dressed. He came across to her laughingly, and standing behind her chair, he tipped her head back against him and kissed her. He scolded her for the loss of sleep evident on her face. He assured her that he was perfectly capable of taking care of himself and that she never again was to worry in case he drank a little more than he should. He didn't care anything about the stuff; he simply drank it with the other boys when they wanted to have a celebration. He pointed out the fact that his father never had become intoxicated to a degree that in the slightest interfered with his business or with his social position in the community, yet he always had a drink whenever he wanted it. He really succeeded in reassuring her to such an extent that she went to her room and lay down to secure the sleep that she had lost.

CHAPTER XI

"The Driver of the Chariot"

When Mahala left Junior, she immediately hurried to her mother, forgetful of everything except that she wanted to be where she would not be subjected to further annoyance. She had forgotten, for the minute, what was in store for her the first time her mother found her alone. She was not allowed to forget very long. Instantly Mrs. Spellman had whispered in Mahala's ear: "Where did those lilies and roses come from?"

Mahala had taken time for mental preparation.

"I hunted all I dared on the platform," she said, "and I couldn't find the card. I told Jemima, when she took my flowers home, to watch especially for it and to save it if she found one."

"Do you mean to tell me that you don't know where such a thing as that came from?" demanded Elizabeth Spellman abruptly. She was trying to face Mahala down with deeply penetrant eyes. Mahala objected to having her good time spoiled by the ordeal she had known she was destined to undergo when the exquisite sheaf had been stood at her knees. She showed not the slightest inclination to avoid her mother's eyes. She seemed capable of looking into them with the utmost frankness.

"No, Mama," she said quietly, "I haven't any intention of telling you anything. If there's a card that belongs to the flowers, Jemima will have found it by the time we reach home. If there isn't, we will just have to make up our minds that somebody cares enough about me to make me a lovely gift, won't we?"

It was Elizabeth Spellman's proud boast that she had never struck her daughter. The chances are very large, that for the second time that evening, if she had been in seclusion, she might have been provoked to what her fingers were itching to do, but the one thing Elizabeth was forced to remember above everything else in time of crisis was that she was a lady. She could not very well slap her daughter's face at a Commencement dance.

"Am I to understand," said Elizabeth, "that we're once more facing a contribution from the mysterious source of your treasured canary bird?"

Her quick eyes saw a stiffening in Mahala with which she had been familiar from her childhood. It seemed to be a faint tensing of muscles, a bracing of the spine. It was with real relief that Elizabeth saw so offensive a personality as Henrick Schlotzensmelter approaching her daughter with a smile of invitation. She hated the whole Schlotzensmelter tribe with their sauerkraut and their sausage and their pumpernickel and their arrogant talk of might. Ordinarily, she would have done almost anything to keep the Schlotzensmelter fingers from even remotely touching the hand of Mahala. In the circumstances she made her way to Mahlon's side, sat down, and looked into his eyes. There she read that he was baffled, perplexed, and thwarted even as she, and she decided that it was not the time to whisper to him, no matter how surreptitiously, concerning any matter that would cause him the least disturbance. Her very deep annoyance over the Moreland flower basket and the anonymous white sheaf faded into insignificance when compared with the expression on Mahlon's face, the look in his eyes.

Behind a busily waving palm leaf she had picked up, she kept murmuring in her heart: "Hunted! Why Mahlon positively has a *hunted* look on his face. There's no reason why he should take his disappointment over Junior's flower basket and that nasty white sheaf as seriously as that."

To the last number Mahala danced out the party. She was wide eyed and laughing, and her contagion spread to other members of the class, some of whom would never again have the opportunity of a public appearance with the high lights turned on, in the social life of Ashwater. She was dancing with every one who asked her to dance—young or old—and all of the others were following her example. Even Edith Williams had danced with her uncle and with Mr. Spellman and with all the boys of the graduating class. Mahala had been surprised when she saw her on Henrick's arm, but she had been constrained to admit to herself that the evening had been filled with surprises. She had been surprised at Edith several times. Not more so than when Edith had whispered at her elbow: "Do you know where Junior Moreland is?"

She had replied: "I do not."

The surprise lay in Edith's comment: "I suppose he's in some of the saloons making a beast of himself. I should think he'd be ashamed."

Meditating on this, Mahala remembered that it was the first criticism of Junior she ever had heard Edith make. She wondered that Edith had remained and gone on dancing when she felt reasonably certain that she was not very greatly interested in what was taking place after Junior disappeared.

When, at last, the harp was carried away, the weary musicians left the orchestra pit, the lights were turned out, and the Spellman carriage stopped at the gate, Mahala ran into the house, straight into the waiting arms of Jemima, where a little wisp of paper was thrust deep into the front of her dress. She knew that her mother was immediately behind her, so she cried: "My flowers, Jemima, what did you do with my lovely flowers?"

Jemima answered: "I carried all of 'em to the cellar. I put what I could in water and I sprinkled the rest and put wet tissue paper over them. Your Ma said she wanted to have a picture made of them to-morrow with you in the midst."

Mrs. Spellman untied her bonnet strings and swung that small article from her head by one of them.

"Well, I don't know," she said in exasperation, "what made me think anything so silly. It would look more like a funeral than a celebration."

Facing the possibility of having to look at a framed copy of such a picture with the Moreland basket predominant in beauty above her own, and with the mysterious roses and lilies in evidence, Elizabeth had speedily decided that such a picture would be suggestive of a funeral to her.

Across Mahala's head she said to Jemima: "Was there any loose card or anything you found to tell where those white roses and lilies came from?"

Jemima very truthfully answered: "No, ma'am, there wasn't."

Her own curiosity had been sufficient to prompt her to read the little twisted wisp of note paper she had found tucked under the confining bow of gold that held the flowers, completely screened by the sheltering maidenhair. On that scrap there had been written: "With undying devotion," and there wasn't even an initial, back or front. So Jemima had returned it to its original twist and thrust it where she very rightly considered that it belonged, and at that minute it was pressing into the flesh of Mahala's breast, a vivid reminder that it was there.

She was thankful for the crunch of the wheels on the gravel of the driveway which indicated that her father would tie up the horse at the barn before he came to slip off his evening clothes preparatory to putting the animal away. Mahala went straight to her mother and slipping her arms around her, kissed her tenderly.

"Thank you very much, Mother dear," she said, "for every lovely thing you have done to make this night so wonderful for me. I'll slip in and kiss Papa good-night before I go to bed."

She was half way up the stairs before she heard her mother calling: "Wait, Mahala, wait!"

Because she had been all her life an obedient child, she paused with one hand on the railing and leaned down. There was a distinct note of exasperation in her voice as she asked: "What is it, Mama?"

Mrs. Spellman found herself equally unable to ask the question she wanted to ask, and to the same degree unable not to ask it. She wavered. Mahala could see the workings of her brain as plainly as she could see her lips. Taking the bull by the horns was an old habit of hers. She took hold now courageously as ever.

"If you're bothering your head about those flowers," she said very distinctly, "I'd advise you not to. It's wearing. They are very lovely. Whoever sent them had only the kindest intentions. Jemima told you that she didn't find anything to show where they had come from. What's the use to speculate when all of us are worn out?"

Mahala went to her room, closed the door, and standing before the mirror, surveyed her reflection from head to heels. She was not looking quite so fresh as she had the last time she had looked in that mirror, but she decided, that after delivering a valedictory and dancing for hours, she was still extremely presentable. She slipped from her dress and returned it to the form in the guest room from which it had been taken to serve its great purpose. As she shook out the skirts she said to it laughingly: "Let me tell you, you very nice dress, Edith gave me the hardest run to-night she ever did. But I still think that you're the prettiest dress and the most appropriate that was worn at Commencement to-night."

She leaned forward and for an instant buried her face in the laces on the breast of the dress covering the wire form. Going back to her room, she put out the light. As speedily as possible, she slipped into her nightrobe and then she went to the window where for four years the little gold bird had sung to her daily from its shining house of brass, and standing beside it in the moonlight, she smoothed out the twist of paper and upon it she read three words. She stood a long time in the moonlight looking across the roofs of neighbouring houses and down the moon-whitened street; then she turned and walked back to her dressing table. Among the bottles and brushes on top of it there lay a white rosebud. She looked at it a few minutes; finally she picked it up, twisted the wisp of paper around the stem of it, and went to her closet. From a top shelf she took down a beautiful lacquered box that represented one of the handsomest of her father's gifts from the city. It was shining in black and gold while across it flew white storks with touches of red above a silver lake bordered by gold reeds.

She lifted the lining of her workbasket and from beneath it she took out a tiny gold key. With this she unlocked the box and laid the white rose and the three words inside it, relocked and replaced the box, and returned the key to its hiding place beneath the lining of her workbasket.

Then Mahala laid her head upon her pillow and tried to go to sleep, but sleep was a long time coming. Never in her life had she found so many things of which to think. She knew that her mother would not give over her pursuit of the sender of the wonderful gift in the morning. She was reasonably certain that Junior would not be thwarted in his desires without putting up a fight that might very possibly, according to his methods of soldiering, become disagreeable. And there remained in her consciousness the memory of a look that she had seen in her father's eyes that night, a look that had been gradually disquieting her for a long time. She had tried to evade it, to forget it, to make herself think it was not there. From to-night on she knew that it was not a thing to be longer evaded. It was something to be faced and to be dealt with.

When she awakened in the morning, the house was so filled with sunshine, and there were so many people coming to see her wealth of beautiful gifts, to examine minutely the wonderful baskets and the sheaf of flowers that had been bestowed upon her, to try to fix in their consciousness, on the part of many filled with envy, just what amount of expense had been lavished upon Mahala's graduation, that her fears were forgotten. Many of these callers were making the rounds. They had already been to the Williams' residence and a few of them had felt sufficiently familiar with Mrs. Moreland to call there, also. By the time they reached the Spellmans', they were able to draw a convincing conclusion as to which young person of Ashwater had received the largest number of the most expensive gifts, the most flowers, and worn the costliest clothing.

Serena Moulton, who was responsible for the foundations of Mahala's dress, stopped in for a view of the finished product. As she stood before it, she clasped her hands and looked at Mahala laughingly.

"The first thing I know," she said, "you'll be taking my business from me. It just ain't in my skin to do all this little fine ruffly business and all the handwork that you do. I'm terrible beholden to a sewing machine. I do like a long straight seam that I can set down to and just make my old Singer sing."

Mahala knew that this was intended to be funny, and so she laughed as heartily as she could over it.

"Well, Serena," she said, "there's no telling which way the cat's going to jump in this world. It may happen that very way."

She almost started at hearing the words on her own lips, while a fleeting shadow swept across her heart.

But Serena was saying: "I've worked for Mrs. Moreland ever since Junior was a baby and I run in there. He's only got a few things—mostly from his Pa and Ma—but they certainly are wonderful expensive. I never saw the beat of the watch his father give him for just a boy like him. About all the rest he had come from his mother. If the Morelands only knew it, they're not any too popular with the folks of this town. Nobody's going to reward 'em for their overbearing ways by heaping presents and flowers on 'em. And I had a good deal the same feeling at Mrs. Williams'. There's an awful display of flowers and there's a lot of fine presents, but a body don't see such a flock of cards as there is tied to your stuff, and I think, if the truth was told, it would be that most that sour Edith got she bought for herself."

"Oh, Serena, don't!" said Mahala. "Mrs. Williams is a friend of yours. She'd be awfully hurt if she thought you were going about town saying things like that. Of course, I won't repeat them, but if you said them anywhere else, some one might."

"Well, it strikes me," said Serena calmly as her eyes roved over the array of books and pictures, of glass and china and dainty feminine trifles of all sorts spread on the top of the big, square piano, "it strikes me that the really popular person of this town is standing before me."

Mahala made Serena an exaggerated courtesy, and in her prettiest manner said: "I thank you, Serena. I think that's a very nice compliment."

Serena, looking at her clear eyes and the sweetness of her face, decided that she might venture, and so she said: "I saw Morelands sending up that awful elaborate basket, and I saw the nice one your Pa and Ma sent up, but I didn't see where that great wheat sheaf of lilies an' roses come from. It was terrible affecting. There wasn't nothing in the church to begin to compare with it. I never saw grander at any funeral. Who give you that, Mahala?"

138

The question was point blank. Mahala had faced it for a nasty half hour against the combined forces of her father and mother slightly earlier in the day. She was steeled for it, expecting it at Serena's entrance. She looked Serena in the eyes and laughed, a laugh altogether free of confusion and secretiveness.

"Now maybe that's a secret I'm not telling. Maybe the card was lost, and I don't know. Maybe any one of fifty things, whichever suits you best. I think, myself, that sheaf was the prettiest thing in the church last night."

Serena had the wit to know that she had all the answer she was ever going to get. A quiver of confusion ran through her heart. She knew she had had no business to ask the question. She had merely ventured depending upon Mahala's good humour, and Mahala had refused to answer, so that meant that very likely some out-of-town person, maybe some of the Bluffport boys, or some one that none of them knew anything concerning, admired Mahala.

Serena arose. She was not accustomed to giving up that easily.

"And while we're talking about the best-looking things in the church last night," she said, "what about you just pulling the wool over all of 'em?"

Again Mahala faced her with eyes of candour.

"I really don't think I did," she said. "Edith was as handsome as a girl well could be last night, and I suspect her dress cost almost twice as much as mine."

"Not if you count all the hours and hours of dainty handwork you put on it," said Serena. "I'm going through the kitchen and say 'Howdy' to Jemima."

"Oh, certainly," answered Mahala. She turned and preceded Serena to the kitchen. She opened the door, and meeting Jemima's glance, she gave her a sharp little frown and pulled down the corners of her mouth. There was a negative in the tilt of her head that Jemima well understood. As she stepped aside to let Serena pass, Mahala said to Jemima: "Here's your friend come to have a visit with you. She'll be wanting you to tell her everything about Commencement that I didn't."

"Because it happened to be a secret," put in Serena.

"Exactly," said Mahala, her eyes hard on Jemima's face.

Jemima shot back the answer for which she was waiting. With peace in her heart so far as Serena was concerned, Mahala closed the door and sought refuge in her room to avoid another unpleasant séance with her mother.

At ten o'clock that morning Junior Moreland went into the bank, stopping a moment to chat with the bookkeeper and the cashier.

He said jestingly: "I believe I'll just step back and suggest to the President that I've left the bay and the presidential chair is floating on the ocean before me."

He lifted the latest model in straw hats from his handsome dark head and laughed with the employees of the bank.

"Don't you think," he said, "that I'd better get on the job and give Father a rest? I have a feeling that I'd make a dandy bank president."

With the laugh that went up pleasant on his ears, Junior opened the door of the back office and stepped in.

He said to his father: "Dad, forget figures for a minute. I want to ask you something."

Moreland Senior indicated a chair.

"All right," he said, "I am interested in anything you are. Out with it."

Junior hesitated. He was studying as to the best way of approaching his father. Should he begin with what had occurred the night before, or should he go back to the very beginning and explain that ever since he could remember, Mahala had been the one girl with whom he wanted to play, for whom he cared, that from the hour of earliest preconceptions, he had selected for his very own? As he stood hesitating, he felt his father's eyes on his face and realizing that they were full of sympathy and encouragement, he smiled. It was a brave attempt at a smile, but it happened that the quiver of a disappointed four-year-old ran across his lips. The elder Moreland saw, and instantly a wave of rage surged through him. How would any one, any one at all, least of all a slip of a girl, dare to hurt Junior?

"I don't know," he said in a deliberate voice, in which Junior instantly detected the strain of effort at self-control, "that you've anything to tell me, Junior. I've known that you liked Mahala Spellman all your life. I even made it my business to get on the other side of that oleander screen last night and hear what the young lady had to say. I'm right here to tell you that if you want her, you needn't pay the slightest attention to what she says. She'll find before she gets through with it, she hasn't got the say."

Junior studied his father in amazement.

"I don't understand," he said.

Martin Moreland leaned back in his chair. With each word he uttered he brought the point of a pencil he was holding, down on the sheet of paper before him with a deliberate little tap that accented and clipped off each word with a finality and a certainty that were most reassuring.

"I don't know," said the elder Moreland deliberately, "that I've made such a very good job of being your father. Your mother thinks not; but I have tried, Junior, with all my might. You should give me credit for that. Ten years ago I began to figure that to-day would come. At the same time, I began to plan how to get the whip hand. Let me tell you without any frills that I've got it. You can stake your sweet life that I've *got* it!"

Junior crossed the room and sat down upon the arm of his father's chair. He ran his hands through his hair, and bending over, kissed him.

"I haven't a notion what you mean, Dad," he said, "but you're the greatest man in all the world. You've always been away too good to me, but some of these days I'm going to show you that it hasn't been wasted. You may go and travel clear around the world, if you want to, and I'll run this business, and you'll find when you get back that you haven't lost a dollar and you've made a good many. I've been watching the way you play the game all my life. You bet I can play up to you! But this girl matter is another question. I don't see how you're going to make Mahala change her mind if she doesn't like me and doesn't want me."

"You poor ninny!" said Martin Moreland scornfully. "Can you look in your glass and tell yourself truthfully that there is such a thing as a girl that doesn't want as handsome a young fellow as you are? Of course she wants you. But you've heard of chariot wheels, haven't you? They're an obsession that all women get in the backs of their heads. About Mahala's period in their career every one of them wants to think of herself as riding in a chariot at the wheels of which she is dragging—the more supine lovers the better. There's no such thing as getting the number too large. At the present minute, according to Miss Mahala, she has got you under her chariot wheels; she wants you to kneel and to cringe and to beg and to let her feel her power."

"I wonder now," said Junior. "Of course, if that is what she wants——"

"Well, you needn't wonder," said Moreland Senior. "Your Dad's had some experience with women, let me tell you. He knows. And whenever a real he-man meets a woman who's stressing this chariot idea to an uncomfortable degree, it's time for him to take the reins and do the driving for a while himself."

"But I don't fancy driving Mahala would be such an easy job, even for a strong man," said Junior, once more on his feet and pacing back and forth across the room. "I've spent the greater part of the day, ever since we were six years old, nine months out of the year, in the company of that young lady, and you don't know her very well, Father, or you wouldn't use the term 'drive' in connection with her."

"Don't I?" sneered Martin Moreland. "Don't I, Son? Well, let me tell you something. For the past ten years I've been loaning Mahlon Spellman every dollar I could get him to take, at the highest rate of interest the law would allow me to extract. I've got him tied up financially until he can't move hand or foot. I've got notes with his signature that will cover every dollar he's worth in the world, store and house, and furnishings as well. I'm not right sure but that if I made a clean sweep, I'd stand to lose, I've gone so damn far getting the finnicky little pickaninny exactly where I want him. All you've got to do is to say the word and Miss Mahala will get down on her knees to you and ask you very humbly to please lift her up and keep her in the position she has always been accustomed to occupying."

During the first part of this speech, Junior stood still in open-mouthed wonder. As his father progressed, he began to pace the floor again. As he finished, he was laughing and rubbing his hands.

He cried out: "You are the greatest old Dad any man ever possessed! What's the use to wait? Put on the clamps to-day! Let Mr. Spellman see right now whether he can influence Mahala to marry me and to do it soon!"

"Any time you say," said Martin Moreland, and the pencil came down with a vindictive tap.

"You know," said Junior, "she's got this going-to-college bug in her bonnet. There's no sense to it. She's got all the education she's ever going to have any use for. She can get the rest out of books she reads. I've come in here this morning to tell you that *I'm* ready to go to work. So should she. While I'm getting my hand in—and I've got a notion of what my job should be and how I could help you to the best advantage—she can go into the kitchen and have Jemima and her mother teach her enough about housekeeping so that she can manage a house as her mother does. I'm dead stuck on the way the Spellmans live. You can't start the wheels, Dad, too soon to suit me. Let's try this chariot you're talking about and see who's going to be the driver."

"Very well," said Martin Moreland. "Tell the bookkeeper to step across the street and say to Mahlon Spellman that I want to see him for a few minutes in my office."

Mahlon Spellman sat at his desk facing a sheaf of bills—heavy ones from the East for spring dry goods, smaller ones from town connected with Mahala's graduation. He lifted his head, a harassed look upon his face, when the bookkeeper from the bank delivered Mr. Moreland's message. Instinctively, his hands reached for his hair, and then paused in arrested motion. How did it come that Martin Moreland was sending for him as if he were a servant? What right had he to undertake to dictate? Nervously glancing at the row of ledgers facing him, and the overflowing pigeonholes before him, a wave of nausea swept his middle.

He got up, and for the first time in years, he put on his hat and left the store without looking in the mirror. He found that his hands were trembling as he climbed the broad stone steps, flanked on either side by huge dogs—big bronze creatures of exaggerated proportions, with distended nostrils that seemed to be scenting dollars instead of any living thing, their chests broad, their abdomens drawn in, their tails stiffly pointing. Cordially Mahlon Spellman hated them. He remembered the day upon which they had stood crated on the sidewalk before the bank and he had said to the banker: "Why dogs, Martin?"

There had been the hint of a snarl in Martin's voice as he had answered: "You'd prefer the conventional lion, would you, Mahlon? Well, give me a dog of about that size and build every clip. Especially a dog that I've trained myself. Watch dogs of the Treasury. Instinct may be all right, but I prefer training when it comes to guarding the finances of the community!"

There was nothing he could do to them with his hands. As Mahlon Spellman passed between the unyielding metal moulded in the form of powerful hunters, he felt as if he were a creature at bay, in danger of being torn and rended by their merciless jaws. He could not remember ever before in his life having wanted to kick anything. He would have considered such a manifestation as extremely distasteful on the part of any gentleman; and he almost recoiled from himself as he stepped over the threshold with the realization strong upon him that he would have given a fine large sum, if he had had it to give, in order to have been able to kick both of those menacing big bronze animals off their pedestals and into the farthest regions of limbo.

In a minute more he was sitting in an easy chair fingering a fragrant cigar and listening to the voice of Martin Moreland speaking so casually that he was quite disarmed. He was talking about the Commencement of the night before—how finely their young people had acquitted themselves; complimenting their schools and their teachers and the ability of the town to get together and handle an occasion like that in such a creditable manner to every one concerned. He was so suave, so extremely casual, so unlike the bronze dogs guarding his doorway, that Mahlon Spellman began watching him narrowly with the impression that there was something back of all this, and when Mr. Moreland looked him straight in the eye with the friendliest kind of a smile and inquired: "Does it impress you, Spellman, that my son and your daughter made the handsomest couple on the floor last night?" Mr. Spellman knew that the crux of the matter had been reached.

He kept fingering the cigar in the hope that the motion might cover the trembling of his hands. His eyes narrowed and he tried to look far into the future. It was with some hesitation that he finally said: "I quite agree with you, Martin."

"Have you ever thought, Mahlon," inquired Martin Moreland, "how very suitable a union between those two young people would be?"

Again Mahlon Spellman hesitated. A ghastly sickness was gathering inside him. He had thought of that very thing, and he had hoped for it. But he never had the slightest intention of coercion. He did not like the look of this way of going about a betrothal. He had to say something. He said it hesitantly: "Yes, I've thought about it. I have imagined that you were thinking about it. As soon as my daughter finishes college and becomes thoroughly settled in her own mind, I should like to join with you in the hope that they will think seriously concerning each other."

Martin Moreland had been decent almost as long as he was capable of self-control. Outstanding in his memory was a vision of Mahala, gowned like a princess, crowned with youth and beauty, scouring the touch of his boy's lips from hers as if he had been a thing of contamination. There was an edge to his voice and a touch of authority as he cried: "Nonsense! Sending a girl to college is the quickest way to ruin her! Send her to the kitchen and teach her how to be an excellent housewife like her mother! My boy is wild about her. He always has been. There's not a reason in the world why they shouldn't get married this fall and settle down to business."

During this speech there rushed through Mahlon Spellman's mind, first of all because he was Mahlon, his own estimate of what had just been said to him and the man who had said it. Then he thought of what his wife would say, and then he thought of his daughter.

Before he realized exactly what he was doing, he found his voice crying: "Impossible, Martin! Quite impossible! Mahala and her mother have their hearts set on the girl's going to college. They have prepared for it for years. They have her clothing very well in hand, and in any event, I don't think Mahala has ever given marriage a thought, and in that matter, of course, I couldn't attempt to coerce her."

All the cordiality dropped from Martin Moreland's voice; all congeniality faded from his face. The lean lines into which it fell gave Mahlon Spellman a start, for he found they suggested to him the long head and the set face of the bronze dogs watching outside. There was something so casual that it was almost an insult in the way Martin Moreland reached into a pigeonhole he had previously prepared in his desk and pulled out an imposing packet of papers. Slowly he began to open them and to spread them out on his desk. Mahlon Spellman, quivering like a moth impaled on a setting board, surmised what those papers were. His surmise was of no help to the internal disturbances at that minute racking him.

As Moreland spoke, Mahlon Spellman forgot the bronze dogs, and there was something in the slick smoothness of the banker's voice that made him think of a cat instead—a cat proportioned with the same exaggeration in comparison with the remainder of its species as were the dogs; a cat big enough to take a man and roll him under its paws, and toss him up and set sharp teeth into him until he cried out, and let him think he was escaping, and draw him back with velvet paws the claws of which flashed out occasionally.

"Your business is not very flourishing since the coming of the new store, is it, Mahlon?" asked Martin Moreland.

Mahlon Spellman's lips were dry, his throat was dry, his stomach was congested, his bowels were in spasms. He could do little more than tightly grip the arms of his chair and shake his head.

"Is there any chance of your being able to pay even the interest on what you owe me?" asked Martin Moreland, now a man of business, staring penetrantly at Mr. Spellman.

Mahlon sank in his chair. He literally cowered. As he collapsed, it seemed to his tortured brain that Martin Moreland was increasing in size and consequence. He looked to Mahlon, in his hour of extremity, as much bigger and colder and harder than an ordinary man as were those damned dogs at his doorway bigger than an ordinary dog. There was insult, positive insult, in the way he gathered up the big sheaf of notes. How, in all God's world, did there come to be so many? There seemed to be dozens and dozens of them. How did he dare to flip them through his fingers and leaf them over and beat them on the edge of his desk as if they were not the very heart and the blood and the brain, not only of himself but of his wife—his delicate, beautiful wife—and his daughter? And what was it that this fiend in human form was saying?

"These cancelled notes would make Mahala a fine wedding present from me, now wouldn't they, Mahlon?"

Terrified, Mr. Spellman started to protest. Then the smile vanished from the banker's face. He ceased to be like a cat and became like the bronze dogs again. He straightened up in his chair. He slipped a rubber around the notes with a snap, put them back in the drawer which he locked with great deliberation; then, in a dry, hard voice, he said: "Mahlon, between men, business is business. I'm not overlooking the advantage to me of this union between your daughter and my son. Mahala is a smart girl and a pretty girl, and capable of being the kind of wife that her mother is, and I'd prefer her about ten thousand times to some girl that Junior might pick up in a minute of pique and marry, without giving consequences due consideration. That's where the shoe pinches me. I don't hesitate to admit it. This bunch of notes is where the same shoe pinches you. You go home and talk this over with your wife, then your daughter—with your wife especially. Elizabeth's got the sense to see the point to things; especially if you explain to her the present condition of your business. As for the girl, no chit of Mahala's age is supposed to know her own mind."

For the rest of that day Mahlon Spellman walked in a daze. In order to escape being seen by his clerks, he carried home an armload of books and papers, and going to his library, he plunged into them only to realize that by evading unpleasant things and putting them aside and living for the moment, he had also evaded the knowledge of how deeply he had been putting himself in the power of the Senior Moreland.

At his moment of deepest despair, Mahala came into the room, her arms heaped with catalogues from girls' schools. She pushed the ledgers and business papers aside, and spreading the catalogues out in front of him, made a place for herself on the table facing him. After kissing him, she began holding the catalogues before him.

"Forget your bothersome old bookkeeping, Father!" she cried. "Come help me to decide which is the very nicest college for me to attend. I must make my reservations as soon as possible."

Then she had a comprehensive look at her father's face and knew fear herself.

With the candour constantly controlling her, she cried: "Father, dear, forgive me! I didn't know you were at important business. We can select my college some other time."

Mahala was on her feet, staring in wide-eyed terror, for her father's head dropped on his arms on the table before him, and the nerve strain of many months, and of the day in particular, broke into great, shuddering sobs. Mahala, at a very few times in her life, had seen her father's eyes moist with compassion, but she never in her life had seen any man cry as men do cry when their backs are against the wall and horrifying extremities yawn at their feet, when there comes to them the realization that they are not living for themselves, but for those that they truly love.

In a minute, Mahala was on her father's knees beside the table; her arms were around his neck; and by and by, when he had grown calmer and forced himself into quietness, she began asking comprehensive questions. With the memory of many months past culminating vividly before her, she was not long in realizing the difficulty. With quick intuition and the clear insight that had always characterized her, she knew the situation. When her father assented to her question as to whether Mr.

Moreland was pressing him about money matters, she knew the essential thing that was necessary for her to know.

"What a fool I've been," she cried. "I've always wondered why Martin Moreland was so friendly to you, why he was constantly urging you to accept his offers of loans and trying to induce you to spend more money than you really should for subscriptions and things. I've wondered and now I understand. Junior has sent me word that he's coming here to-night, and he's exactly like his father. He thinks that if he has enough money, he can buy anything in the world that he wants. Well, he is destined to learn that he hasn't got enough money to buy me!"

In a panic, Mr. Spellman grasped her arm. He implored her to think of her mother; to think of him; to think of herself. He tried to put into cold words that would make very clear to her understanding, the exact result of the ruin that would face them unless she prevented it. She laughed at him and told him it was lucky that her mother had forced her to learn to perform miracles with her needle.

"Only think, Papa," she cried, "how very capable I am! I can earn enough money with fancy embroidering and with sewing or millinery, to keep us all three in comfort. Lift up your head. Go tell Martin Moreland to take what belongs to him. Thank God that I don't belong to him. He can't buy either my body or my soul!"

In the midst of this Mrs. Spellman opened the door. Her husband and her daughter were so engrossed that they did not notice her. She stepped back and stood listening, first in amazement, then in sickening fear, at the end in rising defiance. At Mahala's last words, she came into the room. She took a stand beside her. She put her arm around her and told her that she was right.

She said to her husband: "No, Mahlon, Martin Moreland shall not force Mahala to marry Junior unless she has given him her love. Much as I should like to see her Junior's wife and presiding in the lovely home that he would provide for her, I say that she shall not be forced to take the step in order to insure comfort for us."

Mahlon Spellman held up a shaking hand.

"For God's sake, Elizabeth, be quiet!" he panted. "You don't know. You don't understand. Are you contemplating what being forced from the store, from this house, of being stripped of the greater part of its furnishings, is going to mean? How am I to face the world bankrupt, ruined, with not a penny for your care?"

Hopefully his eyes clung to the face of his wife; and in slow bewilderment, he saw her desert him. She only tightened her grip on Mahala. She only lifted her delicate head higher, and looked at him with calm deliberation.

"Don't feel so badly, my dear," she said. "All our lives together you have taken beautiful care of me and we've done our best for Mahala. If you have allowed yourself to fall into the clutches of a man like Martin Moreland, it's nothing more than hundreds, yes, thousands of other men in this village and this county, and many adjoining, have done. It is very possible that some other man in exactly your position is represented by nearly every transfer of real estate to the name of Martin Moreland that the county recorder makes. Let him take the store, let him take this house, let him take these furnishings, if we owe him that amount of money. He cannot take Mahala unless she is willing, unless she loves and hopefully desires to marry Junior."

Deserted by his wife, Mahlon Spellman's head dropped once more on the table before him. Sick, afraid, defeated, he groaned in anguish. He allowed his wife and Mahala to help him to the sofa where they put a pillow under his head and covered him warmly. They brought him a cup of strong tea; and after a time, when he lay quiet as they tiptoed from the room, they decided that he had gone to sleep, so they went upstairs to talk the situation over.

During this talk, Mahala began slowly to discern that the valiant stand her mother had taken had been one of impulse, because Elizabeth Spellman was impulsive, and her first impulse on matters concerning Mahala was to be natural. When she took time to think things over, to reason, to elaborate, she was very likely to be swayed by custom, by public opinion, by financial advantage. It was plain to the girl that in a short time she would be forced to combat the feelings of her mother as well as those of her father.

Youth is undaunted, full of hope, full of confidence. Ever since she could remember, Mahala had been in close contact with Junior much of the time. She was thoroughly familiar with the domineering traits of his disposition, his selfishness, his evasions, his cruelty, so like his father's, to those in social or financial position that he deemed beneath him. In a few minutes alone, before his arrival that evening, she had tried to face the situation fairly; and in those minutes she had realized that all during the past year there had been a feeling of unrest and disquiet, and a vague wondering if trouble might not be coming her way. She found that she had been fortifying herself against it; that she had been planning for it; that she had been wondering what she would do if it came. Now that it was here, there was only one thing that she could do. If her father was in Martin Moreland's debt to the extent of the store, of the valuable lands in which he had speculated, of their home even, then those things must be turned over to Martin Moreland even as the homes and the lands and the businesses of other men had been turned over to him. She realized now, as she never had before, that instead of being a tower of strength, her father had been a tower of weakness. In order to give her and her mother all the comfort and the joy to be gotten from life, he had brought this upon them. He had not had the strength of will to refuse them anything. He had wanted them to think that he was such a wonderful business man, so very successful, that he could pamper them and give them pleasure to any extent. At his elbow for years there had stood the man who had understood his disposition and preyed upon his weakness, and who would now reap a rich harvest.

Mahala was sufficiently practical to know that, in a foreclosure, property would go for half of its real value. She tried to think if there was some one to whom her father could turn for a loan that would give them time to dispose of the store and of lands and even of the house, at something like a fair valuation. Resolutely she went down to the library. She peeped in and saw her father still lying in a stupor that she supposed was natural sleep. She tiptoed to the desk, and sitting down, she began going over the long columns of his account book. At the foot of every page of entries a wave of indignation and scorn swept her being. But all of her anger was not directed against Martin Moreland; all of her pity was not expended upon the man lying in collapse in that same room. She was a woman now, and her mother had been a woman ever since she had married Mahlon Spellman—a woman with a good brain and a keen mind. She should have made it her affair to know something of her husband's business; she should have refused instead of placing her name upon mortgages and papers that imperilled their home and their living. Instead of laughing and dancing and studying her way through school, at least after she knew that her father was troubled, Mahala felt that she should have inquired into his affairs, herself. She should have tried to help him. She should not have spent the large sums that she had upon clothing and things she might have done without.

Since recrimination did no good, since she could think of no one who might help them in their hour of extremity, she was forced back to the original proposition of trying to determine what there was that she could do herself. Once she had a fleeting thought of Edith Williams. She knew that her uncle held large sums in trust for her. For a moment she wondered if Edith could secure for her a sum that would stay matters until they could be fairly adjusted. She remembered that even in personal expenses Edith always had been extremely close; that she would only spend money where she had a definite object in view, and in thinking deeply, there came to her the realization that it was barely possible that what Edith Williams would rather see than any other one thing was Mahala's downfall instead of her salvation. Dimly there crept into Mahala's mind the confused thought that not only Edith but many others might be glad to see her broken and humiliated. That, she resolved, they should not see. If what she had considered theirs was truly Martin Moreland's, he must have it. She had enjoyed her good time, now she would work.

She made herself as beautiful as possible and she was perfectly controlled when Jemima called her that evening. She found that on account of the humidity, or possibly in order that he might speak with her alone, Junior had taken a chair on the front veranda. When she went to him, she saw that he had brought her a huge bouquet of delicate flowers and an extravagantly large box of candy. All day the house had been sickening with the damp odour of the dozens of bouquets crowded everywhere. The piano was still loaded with pounds of candy that she must speedily give away or see it wasted in the heat. The very sight of the flowers faintly sickened her. She dropped them on the porch table and left Junior to relieve himself of the candy. Then she sat on a long bench running the length of the porch, sheltered by vines. Junior came over and seated himself beside her.

His first words were extremely unfortunate for he asked: "What has aroused the temper of my fair lady?"

148

Mahala felt that "temper" was not the correct word to describe the state of mind which Junior must know possessed her. Certainly she resented the assumption that she belonged to him. A sneer flashed across her face. At sight of it Junior lost his head. He threw his arms around her and tried again to kiss her. She roughly repulsed him, and there flew from her lips words she was sorry for the moment she had said them.

"Junior Moreland, if you had any sense, you would leave me alone! I know a girl who is crazy about you. Why don't you pay your attentions to her?"

Then Junior was possessed with anger. He had been encouraged by both his father and his mother to believe that he really had some rights where Mahala was concerned.

In a voice tense with emotion, he said to her: "Ever since you've known anything, you've known that I intended to marry you when we grew up, and you've always been nice and friendly with me. What is the matter with you now?"

Mahala drew back.

She waited until she could speak smoothly, and then she said deliberately: "I don't see how you can hold me responsible for what you've intended. If your father and mother were not stone blind with pride and conceit, they would know, and you would know, what this whole town thinks about the Morelands."

Angered further by this, Junior retorted: "And what's the whole town going to think when it finds out that the Spellmans will be in the poorhouse if my father chooses to foreclose the mortgages and demand payments on the notes that he holds on everything you've got on earth?"

In his anger and excitement, he had forgotten even to lower his voice. Inside the window, Mahlon Spellman, roused by his tones and the import of what he was saying, struggled to his feet and stood listening, one hand on a chair back steadying him, the other clutching his heart.

Under the nerve strain, big tears began slowly to slip down Mahala's cheeks. That word "poorhouse" brought something menacing and gravely real to her vision. She knew where the county poorhouse was and what it was. She had gone there with her mother at Thanksgiving and Easter and Christmas times to try to carry a degree of cheer. Could it be possible that such a place threatened her father and her mother?

The tears softened Junior. He commenced to plead with her.

He said to her: "There's no sense in a girl wasting time to go to college. You know how to sew and to keep a house beautifully. If you need a little help with the cooking, you can soon learn. You would only have to superintend. I could afford servants for you from the very start. Dad's crazy about you. He'd do anything in the world I wanted for you. Forget this college business. I can't eat calculus and radicals or drink syntax and prosody. You're all right for me and for Ashwater, exactly the way you are!"

He started to seize her roughly, but divining his intentions, she swiftly evaded him and swung a heavy porch chair between them, and then, anger surging up to a degree overcoming fear, she spat at him her real thoughts.

"You coward! You always have been a coward! You always will be! You never picked on a boy in school unless you were twice his size. You never passed an examination without cheating. You even made the Principal fix up the grades that allowed you to graduate. You've never cared what happened to any other girl or boy so long as you were the leader and had what you wanted."

At that Junior turned ugly. He stepped back and began to sneer.

"What about the leader you have been, dressed in your fine clothes from your father's bankrupt store?"

Mahala lifted her head and dried her eyes.

"I never cheated any one out of their property," she said. "My father is only one out of dozens of men whose fortunes have been deliberately wrecked by your father. If I can't afford the clothing I'm wearing, I'll take it off and put on what I can, and I'll earn with my own hands what I need to take care of myself and my father, too!"

Then Junior shouted with rough laughter. He pointed to her hands, and at sight of them, and at the thought of them being forced to work for a living, he tried to catch hold of them.

"And what is it you propose to do with those mighty hands of yours?" he asked.

Mahala held them up and looked at them speculatively.

"I'll admit that they're small, and that they're white," she said, "but they're strong as steel, and if you'll be pleased to observe closely, you'll notice further that they're clean."

Then Junior tried another tack.

"What about your mother?" he said. "Haven't you got the sense to realize that it will kill your father to lose his business standing, to be stamped a failure before the community? Don't you know that it will kill your mother to be driven from this house and to try to live in skimpy, ugly poverty? Don't be a silly fool!"

Then Mahala stepped back.

She said quietly: "I've always tried to treat you kindly, Junior. I've always hoped that you might see what it was in your power to become, and change your ways. But you never have. You don't see even now where you're wrong. You don't understand now why I'd die, and let my father and mother die with me, before I'd marry you and bring little children, who would be like you, into the world. I loathe the kind of man your father has deliberately made of you. I'd rather see all of us dead than to see us forced into the power of your horrible father!"

Inside the window that verdict struck Mahlon Spellman straight to the heart. Both of his hands were clutched into his aching breast as he slid forward across the chair beside which he was standing.

150

CHAPTER XII

"Those Who Serve"

Outside, Junior Moreland's inherent cruelty asserted itself. His face was transformed by anger and astonishment. His fists were clenched and his face distorted as he cried to Mahala: "All right! If you refuse to marry me, it won't be many days before you'll be kneeling to my father imploring him for mercy!"

Possessed of spirit far above his own, Mahala laughed at him tauntingly.

"How perfectly true you are to your teachings and environment!" she said. "Why put the dirty work on your father? Why don't you say that you'll force me to kneel to you and implore your mercy? Your words and the look on your face this minute prove conclusively the thing I've always, deep down in my heart, known about you. Won't you have the decency to go?"

Mahala stood still, watching Junior down the walk and through the gate, and as he went, dimly she visioned beside him the wraith of the girl she always had been. She lifted her hands and looked at them questioningly. She had made her boasts as to what she could do with them. She thoroughly understood that by the time Junior could reach his father and confide in him, her hour would have come. Again she looked back at her hands, small, delicately shaped, soft and white as a child's. Unconsciously, she opened and closed them and stretched out her arms to test her strength; then she turned to the door.

On entering the living room, she saw her father, whom she had forgotten in the excitement of her meeting with Junior. Rushing to him, she tried to lift his head, to change his position. One glance at the window told her that he had awakened and had heard. She ran her hands over his set face, then slipped them under his vest to the region of his heart, and to her horror, found that it was still. Then she lost self-control and screamed wildly, and this brought her mother and Jemima, who rushed about summoning help and sending for a doctor.

Leaving the Spellman home, Junior hurried to the bank. He went to his father's room and told him in detail what had happened. He said that he was convinced that Mahala really disliked him; that she had possessed the courage to tell him what it was in him that she hated; that she had defied him; that she had said she would prefer seeing her father and mother give up their lives with her, rather than to contract a marriage with him. He repeated her use of the expression "your horrible father." The face of Martin Moreland so reflected the ugly elements in his heart that Junior, staring at him, drew back, half afraid. Suddenly he dimly realized what it might have been that Mahala had seen and which she feared and loathed. But Junior was so like his father that this realization was a momentary thing and it passed, because watching him, Martin Moreland, the astute reader of the faces and hearts of his fellow men, saw that he was allowing too much of his personality to be mirrored by his face. So he covered it for a moment with his hands and made a physical effort to control himself.

There never had been sweeter music to his ears than the voice of his son asking him to start immediately the legal forms of attaching all the Spellman property that they could find. With any other man Martin Moreland might have gone through a pretence of dreading to do this. With his son it was not necessary. He drew his lean hands across each other and moistened his lips. The malevolence of his smile he made no effort to conceal.

"Ten years is a long time," he said in his cold, incisive voice, "to put into the building up of a structure, and it's twice as long when it must be put into the tearing down. The care used in building is not necessary in demolition. We will now pull the underpinnings from Mahlon Spellman, his sweet wife, Elizabeth, and the precious darling, and we'll watch them topple and fall."

That afternoon father and son, ostentatiously accompanied by the sheriff, went to the dry-goods store. As they approached the door upon which the official was to nail the notice of attachment, they were amazed to see heavy streamers of black crêpe fluttering from it, and they learned for the first time, that while they had been closeted with their lawyer working out details of the business, Mahlon Spellman had escaped them. They would never have the pleasure of seeing him with his heart broken and his proud body bowed. If they ever saw him again, it would be when the dignity of death had set its ennobling mask upon his features.

The groan that broke from the lips of Martin Moreland was taken by the sheriff to be the product of compassion. He looked at him curiously. He had thought he was a man who would enjoy the business with which he was occupied.

His voice was softened to sympathy as he said: "I supposed you knew. They say it was heart trouble, that he'd been bad with it for a year, but he was too proud to let any one know."

It was the elder Moreland who reached a detaining hand, saying: "We'd better defer this business till after the funeral."

It was Junior, his handsome face sharpened to wolf-like lines, who said tersely: "Brace up, Dad. You've always told me that business was business. It's too bad about the old man, but what's it got to do with us? If this doesn't turn the trick, nothing will. Nail it up!"

The sheriff was shocked. He protested. Martin Moreland ordered him to tack the notice above the crêpe on the store door, but to delay placing the one upon the residence until after the funeral.

As they turned away, Junior remarked: "I didn't think you were so chicken-hearted, Dad. Why don't you go through with it? Why don't you give them all that's coming to them at once?"

152

Martin Moreland walked in silence for a minute. Then he said quietly: "Junior, did you ever hear of a boomerang? It's supposed to be a weapon that you throw at some one else with the knowledge that it may miss its mark and return and bury itself in your own heart. There are plenty of people in this town who would be overjoyed at an opportunity to get their arrows into my heart. A wrong move in the present situation would in my judgment be risking the boomerang. It's better to go slow, to make a pretence of sympathy and let the law, which happens to be inevitable once it starts, and inexorable under headway, do the remainder for us."

This was why, during the days when Mahlon Spellman lay stretched upon the sofa, an expression of noble dignity on his face and forehead, that his front door bore only a wreath of myrtle and roses with floating ribbons of purple.

For the remainder of the day and during the first night following Mahlon's passing, Mahala had faced the prospect of meeting life alone. Elizabeth Spellman had been so deeply shocked, so terrified and hurt, that she had succumbed and had gone down to the verge of ultimate collapse. It required the utmost efforts of Jemima, of Doctor Grayson, and friends of the Spellmans who came in flocks, to keep the proud and dainty woman alive. When her inherent strength triumphed over the blow that had been dealt her heart, her brain, and her body, she lay stretched upon her bed, one hand gripping into the coverlet that had been accustomed to covering Mahlon's heart, the other clutching her own. The friends who attended her were compelled to watch closely in order to discover that she was breathing at all.

By the arrival of the third day the town had talked the matter over. Men had carried home news of the attachment upon the Spellman store. Women in passing had stopped and read it with horrified eyes. It was the talk of the streets and through the homes, that, but for the banker's decency in the matter, the same attachment would now be decorating the Spellman front door. No one ever had thought of or voiced such a thing before. Mahlon Spellman's dealings in real estate, the outward and visible sign of prosperity displayed by the Spellman home, the wife and the daughter, the constant attitude of Mahlon himself, had thoroughly convinced the citizens of his town that he was quite as prosperous as he desired every one to think that he was. Now it required the three days, and in some instances, longer, for people to adjust themselves to the idea that what they had thought was a pillar of stone was really one of papier-mâché—a thing that could be picked up, crushed, and broken within an hour. Strictly in accordance with the old manifestations of human nature, the snake tongues of envy and jealousy and greed broke loose. The unconscious Mahlon, lying in inarticulate dignity, became a target. First people exclaimed in horror. They shed tears of sympathy. Very speedily they reached the point where they dissected Mahlon as an expert surgeon would use a knife. They laughed at his weaknesses. They felt for their ties; they flecked their sleeves; they looked at their shoes with exaggerated care. Women who only a week before had supposed themselves to be the dearest friends of Elizabeth Spellman, suddenly discovered that she had been too proud, and that "pride always goes before a fall." Like a pack of hungry wolves they tore and worried every manifest characteristic of the dainty little woman who lay unconscious on the borderland. They blamed her every extravagance in the furnishing of her home. They pointed out the number of mantles, of shawls, and new gowns, of shoes and of bonnets, that she wore during a year. They sneered at the weakness which had made her spend her time and strength upon dressing and rearing Mahala as she had done. The air was thick with cold-blooded old maxims. Upon each lip there was heard the terse, sneering comment: "The higher you climb, the harder you fall." Through curiosity they rallied around Mahala with some show of sympathy until her father had been borne to the church, down the aisle of which he had loved to walk in his pride, and then to his final resting place in the Ashwater cemetery out on the River Road, where the birds sang among the maples and the river, in a monotone, accompanied them all day; where in spring the cradle swung through the golden wheat and in fall the lowing of cattle was heard on the hills.

The next day the sheriff decorated the Spellman front door with a copy of the writ of attachment that appeared upon the store. Mahala was told by Albert Rich, the lawyer who knew more of her father's affairs than any one else, and who had offered his help in her extremity, that there was very little if anything that could be saved, the Moreland claims were so heavy, so numerous. He would search the records diligently, and any possible thing that could be salvaged he would try to secure for her. He told her that the law would allow her to take for her use six hundred dollars' worth of the household furniture, and looking at him with sick eyes, Mahala had said almost to space instead of to Attorney Rich: "My piano cost fifteen hundred."

"Yes, I know," said Albert Rich. "You mustn't think of pianos to-day, my dear. You must think of a cook stove, a couple of beds, some bedding, dishes, and those things which you absolutely must have."

From this interview Mahala went to the kitchen and laid her head on the breast of Jemima.

"Jemima," she said, "now that you've had time to think things over, where do you stand? Do you feel toward us as you always did, or have you discovered that we are examples of monumental extravagance, whitened sepulchres who intentionally deceived our friends and neighbours?"

Jemima lifted a stove lid and poked the fire expertly. Then she carefully wiped her hands upon the corner of her apron, and took Mahala into her arms.

"You poor little lamb," she said. "If I could get at the necks of some of these old hens that have let you hear what they're saying, I'd wring 'em good and proper! The other day Serena Moulton came nosin' into my kitchen with her whitened-sepulchre sentiments droolin' from her lips, and I told her pretty quick to cheese it and get where she belonged among the other cats that was given over to clawin'!"

Mahala gripped her arms around Jemima's broad shoulders and buried her face in her warm breast and cried until she was exhausted. Jemima sat down in the one easy chair conceded to her idle moments in the kitchen and held the girl closely.

"Don't you think I don't understand, honey," she said, "and don't you mind. You just cry till you get through, then you wipe up your eyes and pick out what it is that you want to take with you that the law will let you have. I been thinkin' for you in these days when you haven't had the time to think for yourself. I've had Jimmy Price and his wife clean the stuff out of my house and haul it over to my sister's in Bluffport. She's got plenty of room to pack it away. Talkin' with Jason Peters when he brought in the groceries, I've found out that Peter Potter will let him use his delivery wagon to move things for us. Mrs. Price and Jimmy have got the house all clean, and while it's nothing to compare with here, it's shelter till you can look around and see what you can do. Fast as you make up enough bundles for a wagonload, Jason will stop and haul 'em over for you free and for nothing."

Mahala sat up and wiped her eyes.

"Jemima," she said, "only a week ago I thought I was possessed of what's commonly spoken of as a 'host of friends.' To-day that host has dwindled to you, Albert Rich, Peter Potter, Jason Peters, and possibly Susanna Bowers. Do you realize that Edith Williams has not been here since the day after Papa went? Mrs. Williams hasn't been but once, and since that writ of attachment is nailed on our front door, you'd think that it read 'Leprosy' instead of anything connected merely with dollars and cents."

"Never mind, honey," said Jemima. "Put this in your pipe and smoke it. Fair-weather friends ain't no good anyway. Them as sticks when the storm comes is the only ones that's worth having. Now you go pick out the things you want Jason to move. I'm goin' to stay right with you and take care of your Ma and cook for you, and you needn't bother about payin' me anything. I've been paid too much already. I bought my place with money I earned here. Whatever you do, you've got to do with your fingers. It's all you know. You write out the kind of a sign you want to use and I'll have Jason paint it like he paints them nice, stylish signs he sticks up fresh every day in Peter Potter's windows. He's real expert at it. He'll fix you a nice one and trim it up fancy, and he'll put it in the front yard, and then you'll soon find out whether there's goin' to be anything in this town you can do that will furnish us bread and maybe a slatherin' of butter once in a while."

Mahala arose, wiped her eyes, and for the first time in her life, she used her hands at work that was essential and not for the beautification of her person or her home. With Jemima's help she tried conscientiously to make a selection of what would be a fair six hundred dollars' worth of the things that would be essential in the furnishing of Jemima's little house that she had rented since her husband's death and her only son had married and moved to Chicago. Whenever Jason delivered a load of groceries, he drove a few blocks out of his way, and stopping at the Spellman residence, carefully swept out the wagon, spread newspapers over the bottom, and piled in as much furniture and household goods as the horse could draw comfortably, and moved them to Jemima's house.

Peter Potter had suggested that he should do this.

Coming in after the delivery of a load, Jason said to Peter: "Those women are being too honest. They're not taking enough to make them comfortable. It's a crime!"

"It's worse than a crime," said Peter. "It's an outrage. I'll tell you what let's do. Let's take this matter into our own hands. Let's fix up a plan between us and the night the folks move out, let's go and get what's right and fair they should have. We can store it in the upstairs here, or in your room, till they get to the place where they've a bigger house and use for it again."

That plan Jason endorsed with enthusiasm. The evening of a hard day, Jemima hitched up the Spellman horse and she and Mahala helped Elizabeth into the surrey and drove her to her new home, and then gave the keys to Jason. He was to return the horse and in the morning turn over the property to the sheriff. That night was the busiest in the life of Jason and Peter. The tongue of the exhausted delivery horse was almost hanging from its mouth. There were narrow streaks of red in the east when the conspirators sneaked into the alley behind the grocery with the last load that they felt they dared take. Jason spent the day carrying these things to the rooms which Peter Potter had made for him over the grocery.

When the returns from the public auction of the Spellman furnishings were brought to the Moreland bank, Martin Moreland was dumbfounded that they should have been so small. He talked about going to the new Spellman home and taking an inventory of what had been kept, but when he mentioned it at home, Mrs. Moreland said quietly: "Martin, for your own sake and for the boy's sake, don't push that matter any further. There's a reaction against the Spellmans right now because people can begin to see what big fools they were to do such a lot of things they couldn't afford, but there's never a wave breaks on the shore but some of the water runs back to the sea. There's going to be a considerable backwash in this affair. From what I can see and hear, Mahala's holding up her head and going at this thing so bravely, that by and by there's bound to be a reaction. If you press things too hard and cut too close, it'll be worse for you, for the boy, and for me, too, in the long run. Besides that, from the list of property you've attached that I read in the papers, it looks to me like you've got about three times what you should have had anyway."

A slow grin overspread the face of Martin Moreland.

"Three times?" he said. "Well, maybe. But in interest I usually aim to get about ten per cent. I don't know why you'd think in a deal like this that I'd be satisfied merely to triple things."

Mrs. Moreland stood very still. Then she looked at her husband reflectively.

"Would it be any use for me to ask you," she said quietly, "to go as light as you can? I don't often interfere in business. I don't recall that I ever have before, but I like Mrs. Spellman. I liked Mr. Spellman. I liked all of them. I thought they were fine people, and so did every one else. I can see from the aggregate that you've been piling—I mean, Mahlon Spellman's been piling—up heaps of indebtedness all these years. You shouldn't have let him do it. His affairs *could* have been managed——"

"Now right here is where you stop," said Martin Moreland tersely. "You don't know a damned thing that you're talking about. You're only indulging in guess work. If you feel that you have a conscience that must be satisfied in this matter, you come down to the bank and take a look at the notes, the mortgages, and the loans that I've made that poor fool, carrying him along, trying in every way to save his property and to help him out, till it got to the place where I just good naturedly had to get the money out of it or run the risk of smashing myself."

Mrs. Moreland closed her lips and stood in meditation.

At last she remarked: "They tell me that, stuck up big and white and all painted up fancy as if it were a thing to be proud of, Mahala has got a sign in the front dooryard asking to make over hats and remodel dresses."

"She has," said Martin Moreland. "I took the pains to see it myself. It's very big and the letters are most artistic; there's a glitter about it and it reads: 'Miss Mahala Spellman will remodel your last year's gown and hat in the latest Parisian mode. Let her show you how fashionable an expert needle can make you appear.'"

"For mercy sake!" said Mrs. Moreland, and then a glint came into her eyes and a look of determination to her face. "Well, I call that pretty nervy," she said, "for a girl that's been raised as she has, and has been expecting all her life to go to one of the best colleges in the land this fall, for four years more of pampering, I must say I like her pluck!"

Martin Moreland grinned.

"I wonder what you'd think," he said, "if I should tell you what the young lady you admire so much has to say about your son and about me." And then he told her what had occurred. But he did not tell her that because it had occurred, the writs of attachment had been issued at that time. He finished by saying: "Since you so greatly admire the young lady, by all means be her first patron. I've never seen you when either your gown or your hat wouldn't have been better for an application of Spellman taste."

Mrs. Moreland thought the matter over.

"Martin, I wonder at you," she said slowly. "Of course, it makes me mad to have her treat Junior the lovely way she always has, and then suddenly turn on him like this. I can't imagine why she did it. I can't believe she really meant it."

"Junior believes that she meant it," he said tersely.

"Anyway," said Mrs. Moreland, "I couldn't possibly follow your suggestion since you issued those attachments and made the foreclosure. It wouldn't look right for me to be the first, or among the first, to go and offer Mahala work."

Martin Moreland's laugh was so genuine that he almost convinced his wife of its spontaneity.

"Well, it would look good to me," he said. "It would look like just exactly the right and proper thing."

At the new Spellman home, with Jemima and Mahala at the task of ministering to the stricken woman and arranging the house, matters progressed speedily. In a day or two things were in a reasonable state of order. Lying in her own bed in the tiny, dingy room, Elizabeth Spellman kept her eyes shut, because every time she opened them her surroundings struck her dainty, beauty-loving soul a blow that brought into full realization the height and the depth of her loss. It was these shocking, ugly things obtruding themselves that threw her back constantly upon the greater proposition which constituted the loss of Mahlon. She had believed in him; she had loved him; she had waited upon him; she had well nigh worshipped him. He had completely satisfied her every desire and ambition. She had no conception of life that would not allow them to go hand in hand, as they had gone every day since their marriage, down a peaceful path that was supposed to end at the pearly gates. Elizabeth had no vision of Mahlon that did not encompass him marching in full pride, head erect and unchallenged, through these same pearly gates, and even the desire to be with and to help Mahala, could not keep her from wishing that hand in hand with him, she was marching beside him now. She could conceive of no reason in her orderly life as to why she should be challenged entrance. "Sweeping through the gates" with her was a literal proposition. She was sorry in her soul that when Mahlon swept through, she had not been with him, and her deepest wish at the moment was that she might join him as speedily as possible. She felt in her heart that it was impossible for her to survive ugliness and poverty and pity, not to mention the contempt, of her former friends and neighbours. She did not want to see any of them. She was thankful when they remained away. The few who came in order to inventory and report what had been saved, had not been able to control either their eyes or their lips.

Elizabeth Spellman was not mentally brilliant, but she was far from a fool. She could translate what was said to her with accuracy. No matter what was said, so long as she looked into eyes, she saw what the lips would say were they really honest. She asked to see no one and refused whoever called if it were a possible thing. She was not interested in anything. She made no effort. She simply lay still, and what time was not devoted to a dazed summary of her calamity and a struggle to think how and why it had befallen her, she spent upon Mahala.

She decided that she had not known Mahala; that she was not the delicate, sensitive creature she had thought her. She admitted that she had failed miserably in rearing her. How could the girl come into her presence with her curls twisted into a rough knot on the top of her head, her body tied up in one of Jemima's big kitchen aprons, her hands and arms visibly soiled, at times even her face? She would have had more respect for Mahala if the girl had lain down upon her bed, folded her hands, and announced that the blow was too severe for her. It is quite possible that, in such an event, Elizabeth might have arisen and gone to work herself. She felt in her heart that she would die from the horrible shock she had received; she also felt in her heart that her daughter obviously should be enough of a lady to do the same thing. And obviously, Mahala was not that kind of lady; some days her mother doubted if she were a lady at all.

With the elasticity of youth, Mahala accepted her troubles, faced front, and began striking with all her might in self-defence. She had done what she could to make Jemima's house as attractive as possible. What they were going to live upon she had not discussed with her mother. She wondered, sometimes, what her mother thought. She decided at last that she must feel that there was some income from some property which would furnish them food, and, in the future, the clothing that would be required when the present supply was exhausted. Mrs. Spellman knew nothing of the glittering sign in the small front dooryard, flanked on one side by lilacs and on the other by snowballs, its feet firmly set in the midst of a great bed of flowing striped grass, its outlines softened by an overhanging mist of asparagus. She did not pay enough attention to know that every minute of spare time in the kitchen, Jemima was ripping up old hats and dresses, pressing material, steaming velvet, putting a fresh edge upon artificial leaves and flowers, and that in the living room Mahala, from early morning till far in the night, was bending over frames and patterns, and with her deft fingers putting a touch upon the dresses and the millinery of the few people who came to them that set a distinctive mark destined to arouse envy in other hearts.

Mahala felt that eventually Ashwater would make its path to her door. She was already talking with Jemima of the time when they would freshly paper the walls and paint the house, and forecasting a time when there would be a bigger and a better house.

Every time Jason, hurt and anxious eyed, delivered a basket of groceries at the back door, he used the opportunity to offer to Jemima to hang pictures or curtains, or do any heavy work entailed by moving. One day, in Jemima's absence, Mahala unpacked a basket Jason had brought and she found in it several things that she had not ordered. These she returned to the basket.

She said quietly to Jason: "You have made a mistake. I didn't order those things."

Jason answered with hardihood: "No, but those things go into the baskets of all of our customers these days. They are samples that are sent to us by factories. They're new kinds of food that Peter Potter wants all of his customers to try."

In the face of this Mahala thanked Jason and kept the samples that he had brought. She may have had a doubt that every grocery basket in Ashwater contained the lavish number of samples that came in hers, but she realized that Jason and Peter were two persons out of the whole town who were trying to be generous, to be kind, to conceal their heartfelt pity for the thing that had happened to her and to her mother.

With the empty basket in his hand, Jason stood watching Mahala. He was trying to think of some excuse for remaining. To him she shone like a star in her dark, ugly environment. The boy who never had known a real home or mother love, worshipped her as he would have worshipped an angel. But in the close contact that he had reached with her in the days of her adversity, he had learned that her needs were strictly human. He could not help seeing that even her closest friends of a short time previous were beginning quietly but definitely to desert her. Through the assistance he had been able to give her in moving and settling, he could not keep from observing that none of Mrs. Spellman's former friends and none of Mahala's were on the spot to offer either sympathy or help. In his heart the old bitterness and the rebellion against the power of the banker surged up to white heat. Here was another manifestation of what riches could do.

He had watched every day to learn whether Junior was still Mahala's friend, and he had decided that Junior had deserted her when he discovered that she was not the creature of wealth and influence that she always had been. His heart almost broken for her, he impulsively started toward her.

"Mahala," he cried, "I wish——"

Mahala turned toward him. The detailed picture of her beauty struck him forcibly. He remembered the culture of her home life, her careful rearing, her mental and physical fineness.

She was smiling on him quietly as she said, in a subdued voice: "You wish what, Jason?"

Realizing the immeasurable distance between them, he found himself unable to say what it was that he wished, so he temporized: "I wish," he said, "that everything in this world was different."

Mahala knew that he, too, had been stripped of even the little that he had; that he had lost his mother. She wholly misunderstood.

She asked sympathetically: "Do you never hear anything concerning your mother, Jason?" and this, more than anything else, brought him to quick realization of the distance between them.

Slowly he shook his head.

At last he said: "She never in all her life acted toward me as I have seen other mothers act toward their boys, and since she went away and left me without a word as she did, I am beginning to believe that she was not my real mother."

When his own ears heard this shameful admission from his lips, he was overwhelmed. He wheeled and hurried from the house precipitately. Mahala followed a step or two to the door and stood looking after him thoughtfully. Then she heard her mother calling and hurried to attend to her wants.

CHAPTER XIII

"Only Three Words"

As the weeks went by and Mahala settled down to real work, she found that she had not boasted in vain. She was capable of doing as much work in a day as any other woman. She was capable of doing tasteful work, becoming to her customers to such a degree, that no one else in the town ever had even approached. With Jemima's help she was slowly beginning the foundation of a sum of savings that meant for them a better home in the future; and then one day she was called to the office of Albert Rich and told that in the settlement of her father's estate he had found a small, abandoned farm, with a ramshackle house standing upon it, wholly unencumbered. He had kept this find a secret until Martin Moreland had filed his last claim and taken over property sufficient to discharge all indebtedness, at a very low appraisement.

Mahala hurried back to Jemima and to her mother with the glad news that they really had a small inheritance.

The following Sunday, her mother feeling unusually well and being able to sit propped in her bed for an hour, Mahala took the lunch Jemima had prepared for her and started to the country on foot to see if she could find the property from the descriptions given her by Albert Rich. She wanted to see whether, by any possibility, the house could be utilized for a home, or whether it could be sold for enough to buy a small town house for them. She felt that if she owned a roof, the question of clothing and food would be easy. Those were the days when more goods could be bought for less money than ever before in the history of the world. They were the days when the country was cleared and developed to such a degree that gardens, orchards, vineyards, and farm lands were pouring out a wealth of fruitfulness. They were the days before the forests had been cut and land had been cleared to such a degree that the heat and drought that attacked a following generation were unknown. Factories all over the country were turning out lavish quantities of a high grade of goods. People were rapidly advancing to a degree of luxury and comfort that the country had never known.

With the furnishings from their former home, with the amount of fresh food that could be secured in the days when milk was four cents a quart, cream six, and a substantial pair of shoes could be had for a dollar and a half, while the finest silk and satin dress material might be purchased for from seventy-five cents to a dollar and a half a yard, if she but owned a roof, the remainder of her problem would be easy.

She had learned to her surprise that she liked to work; that she took pride in ripping up the old hats that were brought to her and making of them something so fresh, so dainty, constructed so becomingly to the face and figure of the wearer, that it was joy to do the work. She was learning that lesson which all the world was later to learn—that the greatest happiness that was possible to be experienced by any mortal came through the performance of work which was loved and which was beneficial to one's fellow man.

She had been careful from the start not to overwork. When she had sat for a certain length of time with her needle, she laid it down, squared her shoulders, and went for a few minutes to walk over the grasses of the front yard, through the garden where Jemima worked when she had no other employment.

This morning she went down the road, her head erect, her nostrils distended, hearing the bird songs above her, sensing the waves of sound sweeping through the air around her, absorbing with her eyes and her ears the rhythms of life that flowed in streams as she passed. She was trying to gauge the quality and the value of the land through which she had been accustomed to driving all her life in her father's surrey.

She was following what was known as the River Road. She paused on the bridge, looking up and down the length of the Ashwater, her heart and soul alive to the beauty of the lazily flowing water, the great sycamores, the big maples and elms which bordered it, to the gold shoots of the willows with their long, graceful leaves and the red of the cornels. She smiled down at the big, delicate pink mallows blushing at the beauty of their own reflections in the clear water. Her heart was weighted with grief over the loss of her father, with pity and regret for her mother. It was filled with anger against Martin Moreland and Junior.

She conceded her father's weakness in having gone on keeping up a business he could not afford and allowing himself to become so heavily involved. At the same time, she was certain that Martin Moreland had deceived him, had deliberately enmeshed him, had not mentioned notes that were overdue, had conducted business in a loose and unbusiness-like manner for the express purpose of accomplishing the downfall of a man whose popularity and place in the community had always been an offence to him.

That morning she tried to put these things out of her mind. She tried to think that in some way, whatever happened to her might work out for the best. She tried deliberately to fill her mind with the ripple of water, with the flush of the mallow, with the lark song over the adjacent clover fields.

When, finally, she aroused herself and went forward hunting for the inheritance that was vastly welcome no matter how small, she was almost shocked with the realization for the first time that ultimately peace would return to her heart; never would she relinquish her old pride in blood and breeding. Her father had been foolish, but he had not been wicked. He had misplaced his confidence. He had lost his money; but he had not involved other men. His name was clear. He might be blamed with the tongue of envy or of jealousy, but he never could be defamed with the tongue of slander.

As she chose her path beside the dusty highway, lifting her skirts and taking care of her shoes as best she might, she found that she was fervently thanking God for these things. Friends who did not stand by in such a case were not friends. She would forget them and gradually life would bring to her friends that were worth while.

When finally she reached the place that she had set out to find, she realized why her father never had mentioned it. He had not considered it worth mentioning. It probably had come into his hands with some other deal and had remained there because he was unable to dispose of it.

Mahala did not know how to measure land by sight. She did not know where the forty acres surrounding the house began or ended. The house itself stood close to the road. It was so old that the roof was falling in. The front door stood slightly ajar. Surveying the place from the road, Mahala slowly shook her head. No one had lived there for years. The rank grass falling over the board laid from the gate to the stoop for a walk, proved it. The tangle of flowers and weeds growing across the front of the house and on either hand, proved it. The myriad sprouts springing up around the cherry and pear trees surrounding the house bespoke years of negligence.

Mahala tested the broad front stoop and the veranda carefully before she bore her full weight upon them. She pushed open the front door and used the same care with the floors. There were places where she trembled lest she should break through. In many spots the plastering had fallen and the bare laths grinned at her. Wind-blown limbs had broken in the windows and pieces of brick and stone testified that wanton children had deliberately smashed the glass in many places.

She looked at the littered hearth of flagging and wondered who had warmed their hearts before the fireplace. She counted the rooms and was dejected over their smallness—a living room, two bedrooms, a dining room, a lean-to kitchen, no upstairs, the roof and floors useless. The framework seemed sound. The chimney stood straight.

She walked around the house and found at the back a neglected old orchard of apple and other fruit trees and a stable slowly inclining southward with the burden of years and its own dejection. On a trip around the outside of the house, she found a wild sweet briar clambering up and covering one whole end, and looking closer she could see the siding boards that had outlined the dimensions of three-foot flower beds surrounding the building. Peering among the dry leaves and weeds, she saw that earlier in the season tulips, hyacinths, and star flowers had bloomed there. There were seed pods ripening on the spindling peonies and purple and white phlox were in bloom.

Instinctively, Mahala dropped to her knees and began to pull the weeds from among the flowers. Suddenly she sat back on her heels and looking up at the old building she smiled to it. Then she said to it: "So you were once a home. Some one loved living in you. Some one grew a wreath of flowers around you to make you pretty. Never you mind, you're my home now and as soon as I earn some money I'll come here to live—that's a promise—and I'll make you blooming and beautiful again."

When Mahala heard her own voice saying these words, she realized the pull on her heart of possession. This was a wretchedly poor thing, but it was her own, her all. Every weed seemed to point an accusing finger at her. The old apple trees reached pitiful arms, begging to be denuded of suckers, to have their feet freed of encumbering growth, for their soil to be fertilized. The old house needed a new roof, floors, and plaster. The greater its needs, the stronger the appeal it made to Mahala in the day of her own need. Here was something to fight for. Here was something tangible to love and to live for, for after all, soil is soil, and forty acres of it is not to be discarded because of neglect, when it lies in a fertile valley near a river.

Finally Mahala arose. She returned to the back of the house and managed to raise some water at the old pump. She washed her hands, and then going back to the front, she sat down on the stoop, lightly screened by sun-flecked shadows, and spread beside her the lunch Jemima had prepared. She sat and ate her food very slowly, because her ears were busy with the birds, her eyes were on the sky, among the bushes outlining the indolent old fence sliding down of sheer inanition. She noticed a distant figure trudging down the road, a figure that moved toward her with a tired step actuated by unwavering purpose, a figure that one could recognize as far as it could be seen as the plodding form of a human following a hard road under the lash of duty. Mahala's perceptions were quickened in this case by the fact that the oncoming figure was accentuated by a shimmering gleam of snowy white bobbing in the rear. She looked intently, and then slowly one hand reached out beside her and began dividing in halves the lunch that she had brought.

As Rebecca approached the gate, Mahala could see that she was covered with dust, that she looked more worn and tired than she ever had seen her. Whatever the thing might have been that inspired Rebecca's endless search, it had this time led her to far counties over rough roads. There were times when she had been reported as having been seen beyond the confines of the state.

Mahala, with the help of her foot, pushed wide the sagging gate, and with the best smile she could summon, held her hand to Rebecca. The lonely pilgrim on the long road paused and looked at her intently. She strode toward her and began her customary speech: "Behold the White Flag." Mahala listened respectfully, the smile fading from her face. In her heart there was a passion of painful emotion. There were reasons as to why she folded her hands tightly over her aching heart and passed under the flag in a spirit of deep reverence.

Then she pointed to the food on the stoop and asked Rebecca to come in, to sit down and rest, to share with her. Rebecca asked for water. They went back to the old well where the traveller manipulated the pump handle and Mahala, holding her cupped hands tightly together, caught the water and Rebecca drank from them. When she had quenched her thirst, Rebecca's hands—slender, delicate hands—closed together over Mahala's. Suddenly she bent her head and kissed the wet fingers she was holding.

"'Cold water in His name,'" she murmured.

Mahala was deeply moved. She took one of Rebecca's hands and started toward the front of the house. She noticed that Rebecca's footsteps lagged, her eyes were searching everywhere. She withdrew her hand, and going to the back door, pushed it open and peered inside.

After the words were spoken, Mahala was almost terrified to realize that she had asked: "Becky, what is it that you spend your life hunting?"

Instantly, Rebecca's figure grew rigid. Her face became a grayish white. The dark lights that Mahala feared gathered in her eyes; her lips began to tremble and her hands to shake. Terrified, Mahala again laid her hand on Rebecca's arm.

"Come," she said soothingly, "come, and eat your food and then I'll help you. We'll search together."

Rebecca stood still. Now she was looking intently at Mahala. Then she leaned her head and whispered: "No one ever offered to help me before. It's a secret. It's a dreadful secret. Terrible things will happen if I tell. My soul will be eternally damned."

Mahala returned Rebecca's steady look with eyes of frank honesty. "I wouldn't tell your secret, Becky," she said.

"You will swear it?" cried Rebecca.

"I will swear it," repeated Mahala.

Rebecca brought her lips close to Mahala's ear and whispered three words. Mahala drew back, staring at her with pitiful eyes.

"Oh, Becky!" she cried, "is *that* what you search for? I will help you! Truly I will! Come, now, and have something to eat. You're so tired."

They went back to the front stoop together. Because Mahala untied and slipped it back with gentle hands, Rebecca spared her bonnet, and for the first time, Mahala had the chance really to study her features, her hair, the set of her head upon the column of her throat, and the figure concealed by the unbecoming dress. She could see that in her youth Rebecca must have been a beautiful girl. Under the grime of travel and the nerve strain of fatigue, she was still beautiful.

Mahala made a pretence of eating after that. Surreptitiously, she pushed all of the food she had under Rebecca's fingers. When they had finished, Mahala discovered that Rebecca was studying her intently. Then she looked over the neglected dooryard, at the old house, and back to Mahala.

"Little angel lady," she said, "you are kind to me in Ashwater. Why are you here?"

A sudden tremor quivered across Mahala's face.

"Becky, dear," she said, "this is my *home* now. It's the only place to live, that I have left. You know that my father went to Heaven and I lost my beautiful home, so now this is the only home I have. I'm coming here to live, to see if I can cure my mother's broken heart."

Rebecca listened, her face full of intelligence.

Suddenly she leaned again and in a low voice she whispered: "Who broke your mother's heart?"

Mahala, to ease her own fear and because she credited Rebecca with little more mentality than a child, answered truly: "Martin Moreland broke her heart, Becky; broke it recklessly and deliberately; broke it with malice and through long-pursued purpose."

At the mention of that name, Rebecca stiffened. A look of deep concentration came into her eyes. Again she seemed on the verge of going into a violent attack. Her brow began to cloud, to draw down in threatening darkness.

She muttered ominously: "Martin Moreland, Martin Moreland, breaker of women's hearts, and the hearts that he breaks never can be mended!"

Afraid of her in violent moments, Mahala began patting her arm. In an effort to try to distract her attention, she begged her to listen to a bird of black and gold singing on a knotty old cherry tree, to watch big butterflies hovering over white phlox, to see the little growing things being choked by weeds.

After they had finished their lunch and rested for a long time, they started back toward Ashwater. They made a notable pair, Rebecca with her round, childish face, the white flag waving with her every step; Mahala, thinned and whitened with suffering and hard work, her arms filled with white and purple phlox. Beside the road, whenever they passed Canadian anemones, cone flowers, or any beautiful wilding, Mahala paused to gather a few; and when they reached the cemetery, she divided her fragrant burden in halves, and going in, she knelt beside her father's grave and scattered one portion over it, and burying her face above the spot where she imagined Mahlon Spellman's heart was resting, she sobbed as if her own would break.

After a long time, Rebecca's hand lifted her; she stood up and their eyes met. Rebecca's were clear and bright. She smiled at Mahala and then she said a strange thing: "Oh, the blessing, the beautiful blessing of tears! Mine all dried up long ago when I was young and pretty like you. But when you say your prayers to-night, remember to thank God for the surcease of tears."

Mahala stood very still. She resolved that when she went home, for the first time she would probe Jemima's memory to the depths. These were the thoughts and the words of a cultured woman. She remembered at that minute that she never had heard any one say who Rebecca Sampson was, or where she came from, or why she had no relatives. For herself she decided in that minute that there were two things that she knew. Rebecca had been a girl of radiant beauty; she had been cultured and was accustomed to proper forms of speech and carefully selected, meaningful words, and it seemed to Mahala, as they went down the road together, that from things she could recall, sharply accentuated by what she had been told occurred after her passing into the church the night of Commencement, that she might be able to point a finger very straightly toward the source that had wrecked the life of so fair a woman as Rebecca Sampson.

When Mahala reached home she was hungry and tired. With inborn fastidiousness she bathed and changed her clothing. She sat beside her mother's bed and told her of the day. She tried to paint the desperate old house and stable as they were, but she found herself saying that the beams and the partitions were of substantial wood, that the foundations were solid. When she came to the orchard, she realized that she was talking more of the bluebirds that twittered through the branches than she was of the cavities in which they were nesting. She was more concerned with the hair-like grass carpeting its floor than she was with the borers burrowing in its branches. She realized, too, that she was talking more of the many kinds of dear home flowers that marched in procession, hugging closely to the old house, than she was of the building itself. She deliberately embedded in her mother's brain the thought that here was a refuge, that here was a home that might be made into a sanctuary for them; that she might end her days among the bluebirds in the shelter of the pink boughs of the old orchard. For the first time since disaster had laid violent hands upon her, Elizabeth Spellman remembered that she was not an old woman. She was scarcely middle aged. She had been much younger than the husband upon whom she had leaned so confidently. The thought that there was something in the world that was really theirs, to which they had a right, was the first heartening thing that had happened. The hope that she might once again preside in a home of her own, provided by Mahlon, beautified by even a few of her former possessions, was such a tonic as nothing else in the world could have been short of resurrection and complete repossession.

When at last she had composed herself for sleep, Mahala slipped from her mother's room and going to her own, threw herself upon her bed, and without knowing exactly why, for the second time that day, she indulged in the luxury of unrestrained tears, tears that made her realize that Rebecca's words had been true. Tears were a blessing; they were a relief; they did wash the ache from the heart, ease brain strain, and encourage the soul. They were a soothing balm devised by a Great Healer for the comfort of earth's creatures.

Exhausted, she arose and began undressing, when she heard some one knocking at the side door. She remembered that Jemima had gone to attend the evening church services and probably was late visiting with some of her friends. She tried to think who it might be that was knocking at her door at that hour. The thought came to her that possibly some of the friends who had deserted her in her extremity might have regretted it. Maybe Edith Williams had remembered her and slipped to the side door to avoid disturbing the invalid. Maybe Susanna had come to extend to her a few words of love and loyalty.

The knock grew louder, and thinking of her mother, she dried her eyes, whisked a powdery bit of chamois skin across them, ran a comb through the waves of her hair, and hastening to the door, she opened it to be confronted by Junior Moreland.

When she saw who it was, Mahala planted her figure stiffly in front of the doorway. Emphatically she shook her head. She said tartly and with stiff lips: "No Moreland is welcome in this house," and started to close the door.

Junior caught it, pushed it open and stepping inside, leaned against it. He had dressed himself with unusual care. Looking at him with searching eyes of wonder, Mahala saw that never in her life had he appeared to her so unusually handsome, so attractive. But when he opened his lips, he said to her sneeringly: "Had enough yet?"

She stepped back, looking at him in amazement, and then she said deliberately: "You Morelands tortured my father, for how many years I do not know, and then murdered him deliberately. You are now engaged in the process of killing my mother by slow degrees. For all I know you may be able to do the same thing to me, but you sha'n't do it under the pretence of loving me. If you have determined to do it, if you are strong enough to do it, every one shall know that it is cold blooded."

This made Junior furious, but he did try to control himself. He said to her in a voice meant to be conciliatory: "Your father was naturally a bookworm. He never should have tried to run a business. Every one who knew him knows that he had no business ability whatever."

To his surprise Mahala nodded in acquiescence. She said slowly: "I think you are quite right, else your father would not have been able to complicate his business matters as he did. But my father was not the only man to suffer, since the name of Martin Moreland stands for more distress in Ashwater, and throughout the county, than the names of all of the remainder of the wicked men put together."

Before she knew what was coming, Junior had seized her in his arms. He gathered her to him roughly, repeatedly kissing her, her hair, her shoulders, the hands she thrust out to push him from her. Finally she broke from his hold. She stood before him, looking at him in scorn.

"I wish you could realize," she said at last, "that your touch is hateful. I feel positively soiled."

Then Junior lost his self-control. He said to her: "If you won't marry me, I'll teach you what it means to be soiled in reality. I'll put you where the dogs won't bark at you when you pass."

Terrified at his strength and so dire a threat, Mahala stepped back and pushed a chair between them. Under cover of this, she lightly ran through the house, opened the front door, and stepped upon the walk where she was in full view of the street, so that Junior was forced to leave the house.

He came near her in passing and said: "Aren't you afraid to refuse me?"

Mahala studied him intently for several seconds and then she said deliberately: "What you threatened is consistent with Moreland character. As I understand it, I realize that, if it is in your power, you will break me, even as your father broke the heart and the brain of Becky Sampson when she was young and helpless."

168

At that Junior became furious. He advanced upon Mahala threateningly, his fists doubled, his eyes blazing. "I won't take that even from you," he cried. "You lie! My father never knew Becky Sampson!"

Goaded beyond endurance, Mahala laughed at him.

"I dare you to ask Becky!" she cried.

Forgetting everything else in his rage, Junior once more hurried to his old refuge. He told his father what had occurred. The elder Moreland scorned the accusation.

He said to Junior: "I hope that at last you are thoroughly cured, that hereafter you'll devote your time to the winning of a girl worth while. Why spend any more time hanging around an evil-tempered little pauper?"

Junior thought this over; then he agreed; but as he turned from the room he said to his father: "Pauper? Yes. But the prettiest girl God ever made, and the prettiest pauper Martin Moreland ever made!"

Martin Moreland was pleased. He rubbed his hands together and laughed in high glee. Junior stood a few minutes thinking deeply. Then he disappeared.

The next morning Junior asked his father for the use of their best carriage for the day and upon its being granted, he took it and disappeared. In the middle of the afternoon he presented himself at the Moreland front door having Edith Williams in his arms, and to his astonished mother he introduced her as his wife. She had consented to go to Bluffport with him and to marry him while her aunt thought that she had gone into the country for a drive.

Exactly what had been in the heart of Edith Williams, who had adored Junior from childhood, when he suddenly appeared in her home and asked her to marry him, no one ever knew. The nerve strain had been so great that Edith was in a state of collapse when Junior brought her into his home. Mrs. Moreland immediately sent for Doctor Grayson and for her husband.

When Martin Moreland reached home and was made to understand what had happened, he was delighted. He did not share his wife's terror that Edith might die on their hands. He laughed when she suggested the possibility and shocked her soul into a fuller realization than it ever before had known concerning the inner workings of his mind when he said scornfully: "Whatever she does, the marriage is perfectly legal. He is now her husband, her only heir. Let her die if she wants to!"

While his wife was judging him with the severest judgment she had ever measured out to him, she came to an abrupt stop as she observed that he was lavishing every attention upon Edith. He was doing everything in his power to quiet her, to humour her, to ingratiate himself. Then Mrs. Moreland thought that possibly he had been unfortunate in expressing himself. He really did have a tender heart; he really was delighted to have Junior safely married to a girl they knew. She immediately set herself to follow her husband's example. She began doing things to humour and conciliate Edith, while Edith proved herself to have been wholly spoiled.

She hated the dark, forbidding house. The home in which she always had lived had been filled with light and sunshine and beautiful things of attractive colouring. She thoroughly disliked the sombre Mrs. Moreland with her sad face, her deep-set eyes, her sallow complexion. Beyond words, she hated Mr. Moreland. She could not endure his touch. The only thing in her surroundings she did not dislike was Junior. She had no hesitation about finding fault and complaining. Nothing pleased her; nothing was right; but she had no complaint to make concerning Junior. Both his father and his mother realized that to the furthest extent of her nature she was in love with Junior. She insisted that he should carry her to his room in his arms, and this he did. He helped his mother to put her to bed; he waited upon her like a servant. Junior, who never had performed for himself even the slightest service he could avoid, dumbfounded his parents by accepting the rôle Edith laid down for him. Instantly, he did exactly what she asked until his father remonstrated.

His face bore a look of shock and then of gratification when Junior said to him: "Can't you see that I've got to? She hates this house. She hates you and Mother. She's worth all that stack of money her father left. If I don't keep her in a good humour with me, she's got just three blocks to walk to go back to her uncle. Until I get her money in my hands, haven't I got to keep her pleased with me?"

This was the point at which the elder Moreland smiled—a sardonic smile, a smile that set upon his face the most agreeable look of which it was capable. He nodded in confirmation. He rubbed his slender hands in high glee. He told Junior that he was exactly right, to spare neither money nor pains to pamper and to please Edith. He set about spending money upon her himself. He brought her more expensive gifts than either her father or her uncle ever had given her. Very shortly after the marriage, he carried to her a book of plans. He told her to look over them at her leisure and select the kind of house that she would enjoy living in. He suggested that Junior take her in the carriage, drive slowly over the town and the immediate surroundings, and let her choose any location she pleased upon which she would like to live.

This diverted Edith's attention from herself. She delighted in taking these drives with Junior. She studied the residential locations of Ashwater with careful scrutiny, also attractive locations in the outskirts. Since the elder Moreland was complacent, since he had promised her a home for her wedding gift from him, she meant to see to it that she had such a home as would completely overshadow any other residence in the county. She was looking for an eminence, some place to set a house carefully planned and built, from which she could look down upon the remainder of the town. She meant to show every one that she had the finest, the most attractively furnished and located home among them. She was never so happy as when she rode beside Junior, or walked with him upon the streets, and when it was possible, before the eyes of even the most lowly, her face flamed with gratified pride if she could drop a handkerchief or a pair of gloves and let people see Junior snatch them up and return them to her. Her vanity was fed by his solicitude in public. She pretended to be more helpless than she was because she adored having the strong, handsome young man

170

wait upon her. Up and down the length of Ashwater, she metaphorically trailed Junior at her chariot wheels.

Junior kept his body straight, his head high, and with a prideful flourish, introduced Edith as his wife everywhere that she was not known. There were two things of which he could be reasonably proud. The one was the amount of her fortune which she began transferring to his hands as speedily as she could get it into her possession, while the other was her appearance. She was still the frail, delicate girl she always had been, but having hypnotized herself into the belief that Junior had been overpowered by her beauty Commencement night, that he had truly been so attracted by her that he had forgotten Mahala, when he had asked Edith to become his wife, she had blossomed into the wide-open rose of love. She was a handsome woman whom any man might have been proud to be seen with, while Junior was a man to whom anything that he possessed multiplied immensely in value, merely because it was his possession.

CHAPTER XIV

"The Cloud That Grew"

In the room over Peter Potter's grocery, Jason, every day growing taller, stronger, and developing in mentality, planned for spare time that he might spend at his books and in taking care of the things that he and Peter had salvaged for Mahala without her knowledge. As he had advanced in his work in the grocery, and his benefit to Peter in his business had become pronounced, Peter had generously recompensed him. In the new building, the front room over the grocery had been designed for Jason's needs. He now had a living room and a small separate bedroom. He had good lights, a table at which to work, a carpet upon his floor. This room was a private place, a personal possession of his. With the exception of Peter Potter and his wife, no one ever had entered it. Jason had no intention that any one should. There were many things in it which most of the people in Ashwater would have recognized.

Here Jason found his refuge; this was his place for meditation, for rest, for study. In the grocery below he worked indefatigably. Every few days fresh signs of the most attractive nature appeared in the windows. These signs, surrounded by attractively displayed goods, had been the means of reinstating Peter Potter. Two other clerks were busy behind his counters. Jason had drilled them according to his own ideas. They were not only efficient, but they were also honest. Peter found himself doing more business than both the other groceries of the town. When he reached this point he made Jason a partner in truth. Aside from a sufficient salary, he recompensed his good work with a third of the profits of the business. He realized that either of the other firms in town would be delighted to add Jason's ability, his untiring labour, and his personal magnetism to its stock in trade. He knew that he could keep Jason only by making it well worth his while to remain with him.

One day he said admiringly to Jason: "They tell me that young Junior Moreland is pretty keen on a deal, but I'll wager that he can't beat you."

Jason laughed as he replied: "Junior will cut circles around me when it comes to accumulating money because I am forced to be honest and he is forced to be crooked."

Peter had a way of opening his mouth wide, and then setting the thumb and forefinger of his right hand immediately under his nose, he outlined the orifice. Slowly he indulged in this familiar practice. Finally, when his lips came together, he was looking at Jason, his head tilted to intensify his vision, speculation rampant in his eyes.

"Jason," he asked suddenly, "who taught you to be honest?"

Jason considered his reply and then he said: "Outside of your grocery and what I learned at school, I can't remember that any one ever taught me anything. Marcia

172

never did, and when she let Martin Moreland beat me when I did not deserve beating, I began to feel that she was not even my mother."

Once again Peter outlined a circle back of which his tongue worked, and then he asked another leading question. "By what right did Martin Moreland come to your house and beat you?"

Jason's laugh was bitter, while his reply was: "By the right of riches; by superior strength, with the consent of the woman with whom I lived."

Peter thought this over.

"I've known a few men in my time," he said, "who were just naturally cruel; but Martin Moreland is just naturally a devil."

Jason assented, and then he asked his leading question of Peter.

"I've been told," he said, "that Becky Sampson goes into George Sand's grocery, picks up whatever suits her fancy, and walks away, and that Martin Moreland foots her bills. Do you know whether that's the truth?"

"Come here a minute," said Peter.

Jason followed him to the back of the store. Out of a safe which was a part of the new building designed to do away with some of his trips to Bluffport, since Peter had no use for the village banker, he took one of the old ledgers he had brought back. He leafed over its pages until he came to one at the head of which was written, "Becky Sampson." He showed Jason an account extending over years. He pointed to the foot of each page where the account was totalled and the total was carried over and added to the account of Martin Moreland.

As Peter closed the ledger and returned it to the safety of the vault he said: "I lost a good deal of his business when my store got to its lowest point. I lost the rest of it when I took you in; but I've made so much more with your help that I don't care. Martin Moreland always put my back up like a mad cat's whenever he came near me, anyway."

Jason went through his work the remainder of that day without giving much thought to what he was doing. In the back of his head he was thinking of the woman, who, from childhood, had been supposed to be his mother. While she never had treated him as he saw other women treating their children, she never had been aggressively unkind to him. He had been plainly fed on the simplest fare; he had been scantily clothed; but he was comfortable. He never had been forced to go to school with icy feet and a purple nose. He had always had a warm coat with mittens in his pocket. From earliest remembrance he had worked all day and in a manner that produced results. He realized that his deepest thanks were due to Marcia; that she had taught him to do this, and that, had he not known how to work efficiently and speedily when he was left alone, he would have been deserted indeed. If he had not been quick and neat and efficient, it would not have been in his soul to perform the near miracle that he had performed in the transformation of Peter's grocery from the third in the town to the first. He would not have been able to draw patronage in spite of the things that repeatedly came to his ear that the powerful banker was doing secretly to prevent Peter's business from flourishing.

There were many things that Martin Moreland could do to any man he had in his power financially. The one place in which Peter Potter always had shown deep wisdom was in keeping out of Moreland's hands financially. In his worst days, if he had a small surplus to bank, he had left the store in charge of Jason, climbed into his delivery wagon, and jogged to Bluffport. So long as he was not under financial obligations at the First National, so long as his store was fresh and shining, his windows filled with attractive signs encircled by attractive food in the way of corroboration, Martin Moreland had not been able either to say or to do anything that would injure him.

Reviewing all these things, and studying them over, Jason was slowly beginning to arrive at conclusions. As he grew older and watched the ramifications of life unfold everywhere around him, he began to see and to understand and to place his own interpretation upon things that had happened to him ever since his childhood. Because Marcia had never been actively unkind to him, because life with her was the only life he had known up to the time that she had vanished in one black night of horror, Jason's thoughts of her were not wholly unkind. As he studied the situation in Ashwater, as he realized what financial power like that of Martin Moreland meant in the hands of an unscrupulous man, he found himself thinking more frequently, and even in a kindlier way, concerning Marcia. If Martin Moreland were a man sufficiently bright mentally, sufficiently unscrupulous to encompass the downfall of one after another of the financial men of Ashwater and adjoining counties, it was not so very much of a marvel that he might also have in his power a woman who was standing alone.

Jason began to wonder where Marcia was; what life was doing to her; whether she really was his mother, and if she was, whether she would be pleased to see him, to know that he was prospering, to know that very frequently he made the journey to Bluffport for Peter Potter, and that in the bank there stood an account to his credit from which nothing ever had been deducted except for his barest necessities—food, clothing, and books. With the stigma of his mother's occupation removed from him, with the changed appearance through years of growth, sufficient food, and not too strenuous work, Jason was slowly developing into an attractive figure. Always he had kept in mind, that if he did make a noteworthy success of life, he must remember his books. He found that during the years when he had fixed his lessons in his mind, repeating formulas, tables, and equations at the same time he was selling tomatoes and raisins and tobacco, he had acquired what might be denominated the "habit" of study. He liked to study; he liked to carry a problem in his head, thrash it out to a certain point, and to experience the feeling of power he experienced when sudden interruptions diverted his mind, and yet, with the return of leisure, came the ability to return to his problem, take it up where he had left off, and carry it to a successful

174

conclusion. This argued well for the fact that he was able to attain for himself, by himself, a degree of culture that might possibly surpass that which others were acquiring in their school work. When Commencement was over and Mahala no longer entered the store to show him how far the classes had advanced, Jason had procured for himself higher books and gone on with what really were the beginnings of a college education.

Somewhere, inherent in his nature, there was a love of the soil. He was particularly interested in the wagons of the farmers who stopped at the back door of the grocery with great loads of crisp cabbages, golden tomatoes, purple beets, silvery-skinned onions, long white radishes with blue tops, and turnips of the same colour, spreading into great, juicy circles of crisp tartness. He liked to slice the top from one of these, peel it, and stand biting into it like an apple, as he negotiated the purchase of the load and its transfer to the back of the grocery. Sometimes he went and stood beside the teams and slipped his slender fingers under the harness, easing it about the horses' ears, straightening out the mane, talking to them as if they had been people. The one thing upon which he had determined was that he would not remain much longer with Peter Potter, and the other thing about which he had not determined, but concerning which in his heart he admitted the lure, was land. He would like to grow such wagonloads of fruits and vegetables as he constantly handled in Peter Potter's grocery. He would like to own a stable filled with cows and calves and sheep and horses. He would like to have around his feet once more a flock of chickens such as he had lost upon the night when he lost everything else on earth that belonged to him except his life and the clothing he wore.

He understood what it meant when boys who had scorned and taunted him at school began dropping into the grocery and asking him to the backs of certain buildings after working hours were over. Now that they knew he had money, they were willing to gamble with him. As he increased in stature and it became known that he really was a partner in Peter Potter's business, there were boys, and girls as well, who began to be friendly and occasionally he was asked to a party or some social gathering; but not in one instance had Jason ever accepted any of these invitations. Firmly fixed in his mind were his days of privation, the days when he would have been so delighted to be included at the merry makings devised for other children, the days when his heart and brain were hungry. Now that he was mentally occupied and physically satisfied, he could not quite control the feeling of repulsion that crept up in his heart when he met with an advance on the part of any boy or girl who, once upon a time, had seared his brain and repulsed his body with the taunt: "Washerwoman's son!"

Jason knew, in the depths of his heart, that as the years passed, the same hunger for love, for companionship, for the diversions of the young around him, were even stronger than they had been as a child. He realized that there was something for which he was waiting, something that he wanted with an intensity that at times seared his body like a fever, but what it was that he wanted was not a thing that could be supplied by tardy kindness on the part of his former tormentors.

For four years the bright spots in Jason's life had been the few minutes each Friday evening of the school week when Mahala, usually armed with a list of groceries, had slipped into the store, come straight to him and put in his fingers the neat slip giving the pages of advance over the previous week; and sometimes there had been written out the start of a difficult equation, a hint that read: "You will find a catch in the fifteenth problem on the sixty-seventh page. You divide by nine and multiply by fifty-four," and sometimes she had carried to him for a few weeks of his use, a volume of supplementary reading that helped him.

With Commencement these things stopped. Almost immediately thereafter, Mahala's troubles had begun, and then, to Jason's bewilderment, there had speedily come the time when there were things that he could do for her, things that saved her work, that saved her money, that helped her to keep her head high and her face pridefully lifted and fronting the world that so soon had forgotten her. There was beginning in his heart a yeasty ferment, a boiling up of many things, a wandering and a questioning, and above everything else, each day more deeply rooted, the conviction that the same hand that had so much to do with his destiny was the hand that deliberately had brought ruin into the life of the girl who, alone of the whole town, had gone out of her way to show him compassion and human kindness. He was beginning to wonder what there was that he could do to free Mahala from this sinister power under which so many others had fallen. He was beginning to study, occasionally to ask questions, and in his heart there grew a slow wonder as to just what money was, how it had originated, and why it gave to any man the power to ride in a carriage, to mingle in the best society, to hold up his head in the churches, to control for years in the schools and the town council, in every enterprise in which money or business welfare was concerned, and at the same time to be the unseen cause of financial wreck, of physical downfall for other men.

Definitely Jason was beginning to settle in his own mind as to what such power also entailed in the lives of women. Sometimes, when his thoughts were skipping over the surface, or delving deep, he thought of Mrs. Moreland. He remembered her dark face, the pathetic lines around her mouth. He remembered the story of how she had come to the village upon a visit in the days when she was young and good looking and richly dressed. He had been told of the whirlwind courtship of Martin Moreland and how she had married him, believing that he loved her, and how she had put her fortune into his hands and was now so dependent upon him that she might only spend of her own money by charging an account at the stores which would be paid by a check from the bank. Certainly, she was not a happy woman. Certainly, she could not be, if she knew anything concerning the financial transactions in which her husband indulged. Because she remained the larger part of her time at home and busied herself about her household affairs, it was generally conceded that she did not know many of the things that were known concerning her husband. There was a tendency to speak of her in a whisper as "the poor thing."

Then one day Jason's brain found a new subject for consideration. He had gone to the Bluffport bank, carrying an unusually heavy deposit for Peter Potter and himself. Standing at a small side desk, occupied with pen and blotter, going over his account, he caught an oblique glimpse of a woman entering the door, a woman in the very prime of life, having a frank face of alluring beauty. He noticed the attractive way in which her hair was dressed; he noticed the neatness, the dignity, the style of her clothing. The fact that she was bareheaded told him that she must be from one of the near-by stores. With the sure step of one accustomed by a long-formed habit, she took her place at the window of the paying teller and transacted her business. Jason slid around the corner of the desk, pulled his hat a bit lower over his face, and gripping the pen firmly, watched in almost stupefying bewilderment.

It could not be possible; but it was possible. There was no mistaking the tones of the quick, incisive voice. It was the same voice that had told him, almost every day of his youth, that his only chance lay through books. It was the same frame now fashionably, even expensively, clothed, that had bent above the washtub in the dingy kitchen of his childhood. It was the same face, with the accompanying miracle of elaborate and attractive hair dressing and a chamois skin dusted with pink powder. When Jason's lips met, he realized that they had been hanging open until they were dry. Above the marvel of seeing Marcia standing so confidently at the wicket of the bank, transacting a financial matter that appeared to be of considerable importance, came the marvel of the deference with which she was treated by the cashier. For her the wicket was swung open; for her there were polite greetings and a few words concerning the weather and outside matters; for her there was a laughing jest as she turned away and went swiftly as she had come.

Jason laid down the pen and followed at a distance. One block down the street she crossed and went into an interesting building on the corner. From across the street, he looked at the front window, at the side, at the entrance, and read, in letters of white china placed upon the glass, "Millinery and Ladies' Furnishings. Nancy Bodkin and Company."

Jason repeated it over and over—"'and Company.'" Did that mean that Martin Moreland had given liberty to his slave, that she was no longer a creature of dingy kitchens and the subterfuge of washtubs in order that for a few night hours she might be the creature Jason once had seen in the rose-pink environment and the dress of snow? Was Marcia the woman who could carry such an alliance further, and at the same time look and move and speak as he had just seen her?

Jason found himself entering the store behind him. It proved to be a drug store. He bought a glass of milk shake, and sitting down at the counter, he began a conversation with the clerk as he drank. He started by remarking upon the wonderful growth of Bluffport—how many new buildings and how attractive they were. Then he came to the point which concerned him.

"In all the tidying up you've done here in the past four or five years, I don't see anything to beat this establishment or the one just across the street. I'd call that the kind of an enterprise that wouldn't look so bad in Indianapolis or Chicago," he said.

"And that's a funny thing," said the clerk. "Ever since I was a little shaver running around town, Nancy Bodkin has been in the millinery business here. Good years she managed to make ends meet and bad years she didn't. And I've heard here lately that she was just at the point of going bankrupt and giving up in despair when along comes a stranger in town and they get to work together."

"Oh," said Jason, "then the stranger represents the 'and Company'?"

"Yeh," said the clerk, "represents the 'and Company.'"

"And the 'and Company' had money to pull the concern up to a corner building and all that foxy millinery and ladies' fixings?"

"No," said the clerk. "That's the funny part of it. The 'and Company' came in and went to work as she stood. There's been quite a bit of talk among the womenfolks off and on, but nobody has ever discovered, either from the 'and Company' or from Nancy, where she came from or how she happened to come. She didn't have anything but herself, but she knew how to wash windows and how to clean up. I can remember that I saw her myself the day she climbed on a store box and started painting the front of Nancy Bodkin's store with a bucket of paint and a brush. When she got it painted on the outside as far as she could reach, she painted it on the inside. She had such a knack of selling goods and she was so keen about buying, that in no time at all they pulled right out, and now look where they are!"

"You think they did it all by themselves?" persisted Jason.

"Sure of it," said the clerk. "So's every one else. They didn't get a cent of help from any one; the banker says so. This 'and Company,' whose name happens to be Marcia Peters, marched into the bank and told the banker what she was going to do and she told it so convincingly that he believed her. He loaned her what she needed for her first order of millinery, on the strength of her face and her convincing talk. It shows what a couple of women can do if they put their heads together and decide that they'll do it."

Without realizing precisely what he was doing, Jason reached up and took off his hat. He hung it over one of his knees and sipping at the milk shake, he sat looking across the street. He could see Marcia moving back and forth behind the counters. Once she followed a customer to the door and stood talking a minute, her face full of interest and animation. She looked the proud, competent, confident woman of business. He was possessed of an impulse to cross the street and say to her: "Mother, I am glad that you are getting along so finely. I'm gladder than I've any words to tell you that you are capable of taking care of yourself."

When the impulse was quite the strongest, there came to Jason the realization that the woman he was watching could not, by any possibility, have been his mother. If his head ever had lain under her heart through the long journey from conception to birth, if his lips ever had mouthed at her breast and his babyhands slid over her face, it would have been impossible for the woman he knew Marcia to be, to have vanished in the night as she had, five long years ago. It was because she had not known these experiences, that even the boy sensed as the life, the heart, and the soul of the experience of women who are mothers, that she could stand there with her head erect and her eyes clear, meeting the world openly and unafraid.

She must know that he was in Ashwater. She must know what he was doing. If she wanted him, she knew where to find him. Since she did not seek him, since she sent no word, why should he thrust himself upon her? He could see that she was happy. He could see that she was respected and prosperous. And he found as he watched her, that there was a feeling of satisfaction growing in his heart concerning her. She was more of a woman than he had thought her. She was one human being who had escaped the power of Martin Moreland and who seemed to have come out unscathed.

As he drove back to Ashwater he was debating in his mind as to whether he would tell Peter Potter about her and he was finding that he was consoled concerning her by the knowledge that she was comfortable and happy.

Jason was right in his conjecture. Marcia was happy. She was happy to such a degree as she never had hoped to experience. Prosperity was written large all over the millinery store on the corner. It was written on Marcia, which made small difference to Bluffport as it had no realization that Marcia might not always have been reasonably prosperous. The concern of Bluffport centred upon Nancy Bodkin, who, following Marcia's example, had lifted up her head, dressed her hair becomingly, powdered her nose, and exercised her art upon her dry goods as well as her head piece.

These two women, each with her own secret in her own heart, so far as the world knew, formed a combination that was the subject of prideful commendation in Bluffport. There was not an enterprise in the town in which they were not interested. When the Grand Army needed help for an entertainment, they were first class at decorations and resourceful in suggesting programmes. When a campaign was in full blast, they were of great help to their party in the decoration of wagons and the management of parades, and on one occasion, Marcia had stood in the full blaze of the sunlight of late October upon one of these wagons, in streaming robes of white, her gold hair unbound and falling almost to her knees, and shown all Bluffport and the surrounding country what a living, breathing Goddess of Liberty should look like. When an epidemic of diphtheria struck the town and the Presbyterian minister lost his wife and baby, leaving him helpless with another motherless little daughter, Marcia was sent by the church with lace and veiling to prepare the bodies for burial. Moving through the house at her work, she definitely caught the attention of the minister. He noticed her grace and her beauty. His heart was touched with her kindness to his terrified little daughter and her ability to soothe and quiet the frightened child. He carried the thought of her in the back of his head, and when time had healed his wounds and necessity had driven him to think of replacing his wife, the memory of Marcia came first to his thoughts and he began quietly and persistently to seek her company.

Marcia tried to evade him, to escape his attention, but he soon made it apparent to every one that he was deliberately seeking her. One day he entered the millinery store carrying an armful of beautiful flowers that one of his parishioners had given to him. He explained to Marcia that he thought that she might like to have them, and so he had brought them to her.

Peering from behind a case of hats, the little milliner watched with intense interest. If any male person ever had courted her, she never had mentioned the matter to any one. In her heart there was the interest which any woman feels in watching another woman whom she loves being courted by an attractive man. Nancy Bodkin's lips were parted and her eyes shining as she saw Marcia's hand reach out to take the flowers, as she heard her graciously thank the minister for his thoughtfulness. Behind them, through the open doorway, she saw the figure of a tall, slender man whom she knew. He had been pointed out to her years before on the streets of Bluffport as Martin Moreland, the richest man of the county seat, the banker, a land holder who had so many farms covered with mortgages that he was not supposed to know the exact number himself.

The minister was acquainted with Martin Moreland and at once introduced him to Marcia. Moreland explained his presence by saying that he wished to be shown a gray hat displayed in the window which he thought might possibly make a suitable gift for his daughter Edith. He spent some time telling the minister in detail what a charming woman his son had married, the delight he found in spending his hard-earned money for her pleasure. Then he began playing with Marcia.

At his first entrance he had merely bowed to her and devoted himself to the minister. After his explanation concerning the hat, he took it in his hands and examined it critically; he asked her personal opinion of it; he described the woman who was to wear it; then he asked Marcia to put it on in order that he could get its effect when worn.

Frightened almost to paralysis, tortured beyond endurance, afraid to refuse, Marcia put on the hat. It was one that had been built in particular reference to the lines of her face and head. As she settled it and turned, her beauty was strikingly enhanced. She was forced to stand before the two men, turning that they might get the full effect of it. Moreland admired the hat extravagantly and ended by purchasing it.

While Marcia was packing the hat in a box that he might carry it away, he said to her very casually: "You have displayed such wonderful art in the making of hats that evidently the good Lord designed you to be a milliner. I scarcely think you would be successful should you ever attempt to be anything else."

Marcia understood. She mustered the courage to look him in the face as she replied: "I have not the slightest intention ever to attempt to be anything except a milliner."

Moreland laughed; the old crafty look that Marcia so well knew was gleaming in his eyes. Then he took the hat and left the store with the remark that since he had discovered a place where such charming hats could be secured so reasonably, he thought that he would call again frequently. Swept by sickening waves throughout her being, Marcia had great difficulty in standing erect and keeping her facial muscles under control.

The first thing she knew the minister had reached across the counter and caught her hands. He was telling her that it was his opinion that the good Lord had designed her to be the helpmate in his clerical work, the love of his heart, and a mother to his lonely little daughter.

Marcia drew away, telling him that it was quite impossible that this should ever be. Disappointed, but unconvinced, the minister left the store, saying that he would give her time to think it over. He would come again and he would continue to plead his cause until he won.

He had not reached the front door before Marcia rushed to the seclusion of the back room. She dropped beside a table, covered with gay flowers and ribbons, and sobbed out her heart to Nancy who had become her friend in deed and in truth.

Since Martin Moreland had reëntered her life, Marcia contemplated herself in astonishment. How had she ever dared to hope that he would drop out of it so easily? Why had she ever thought that there was any possibility other than that he was merely biding his time, waiting to crush her, until he could make his triumph over her the greater? All the sunshine had vanished from her day; all joy was dead in her heart. The life she must face she visioned as a dreary thing of suspense and fear. In agony she slid to her knees on the floor, laid her head in the lap of Nancy Bodkin, and with her arms around her, purged her soul. A few terse sentences were all that were necessary.

Then in torture she cried to Nancy: "I am tempted to walk into the church and stand up before the minister and all the people, and proclaim myself!"

Horrified, Nancy began to protest. She told Marcia what she already knew: that the public never forgives a woman; that she would be driven from the town; that she would be forced to start life again among strangers; and that no matter where she went, Moreland would pursue her and try to exert his evil influence over her. Marcia stretched out her hands.

"Nancy," she cried, "when you say people never forgive, does that include you?"

Nancy began to cry. She threw her arms around Marcia's shoulders and drew her head against her breast, and there she stroked it with shaking hands.

"No!" she protested. "No! it doesn't include me. I have not one word to say. I know nothing about your beginning. I know nothing about your temptation. I know nothing of the forces—they must have been something underhand and terrible to drive so fine a woman as you into years of the life you say you have lived."

From that day forward it seemed to Marcia that she must never be out of the thoughts of Nancy Bodkin. Everything that she could do to protect her, to shield her, she did instinctively. When Nancy realized that Marcia was beginning to be afraid of the front door, she moved her work table to a point where she could command a view of it. She began the practice, whenever there were footsteps and the door opened, of sending a hasty glance in that direction and then nodding her head or calling to Marcia, and Marcia understood that in case Martin Moreland entered again, it was the intention of the little milliner to face him in her stead.

Because of these things there developed in Marcia's heart a feeling for Nancy Bodkin's breadth of mind, her largeness of soul, and her clear-eyed judgment, that was pitiful. There was nothing that she would not gladly have done for Nancy. When she saw the light beginning to fade from Nancy's eyes, the colour to pale on her cheeks, she was heart broken.

And Nancy, in watching Marcia, was hurt infinitely worse. So hand in hand, the two of them went stumbling forward, making their bravest effort to meet life having the appearance of being upright and unafraid, when in reality each of them was filled with dreadful forebodings.

CHAPTER XV

"The Last Straw"

As Mahala went intently and industriously about her work, she was doing a great deal of thinking. She was forced to the conviction that she had no real friends in the whole of the town who would pursue her with friendship, who would thrust themselves upon her and make an effort to force her to feel that all of the years of her life when she had tried to be reasonably considerate of the people with whom she came in contact, had not been wasted. Out of the wreck, she was left with her mother's servant, whose roof now afforded shelter. There were times when she tried to think in a sort of dull daze what would have become of them had not that shelter been forthcoming. She looked at Jemima and found that she was loving her and clinging to her, giving to her at least a degree of the gratitude and the affection that should have gone to her mother.

As she bent to stitch linings and wrestled with contrary wirings, Mahala was forever busy at her problem, because she had a problem to face. She realized from the manner in which her mother had listened that she would be interested in repairing the house and moving to the bit of land that had fallen to them. But if she did this, she must either keep a working place in the village and go back and forth, or she must undertake to handle the land in such a way as to make a living from it. On this part of her problem Mahala was helpless. She knew nothing whatever of sowing and reaping, the rotation of crops; of gardening, of chickens, and of the raising of stock. The only thing she did know that she could turn to dollars and cents was the thing that she was doing. The only way in which she could procure even a small degree of comfort for her mother was to keep on with the work she really could do with assurance and with extremely profitable results.

With a sharp eye upon every detail of expense, she began deliberately to see how much she could save that might be laid away toward the repairing of the farm house. If she had a few minutes to read, she found that she was reading about land. If there was spare time in which Jemima came and sat beside her and tried to help her with the coarser part of her work, she constantly questioned her to learn what she knew about soil, poultry, and gardening.

One day she said to Jemima: "Old dear, how much of your life are you going to give to me? I want to know definitely how long I can depend on you."

Jemima smiled at her.

"Now, my dear," she said, "don't be botherin' your head about that. There's only one thing on earth that could happen that would take me away from you."

"You mean your son?" questioned Mahala.

"Yes," said Jemima. "I mean my boy. He's a fine, upstanding lad. From the time his father died till he could look out for himself, I took care of him. He's a good boy; he's got a good wife. He's got a houseful of fine babies. As long as everything goes all right with them, I'm free to stay with you and do all I can for you, and if it's goin' to be any comfort to you, I want you to understand that's what I mean to do."

Mahala laid aside her work, and sitting on Jemima's knee, she kissed her and smoothed her hair and told her how deeply she loved her, how sure she was of her friendship and sympathy. Then she went back to thinking who else there was that had proved a friend in her hour of need. After Jemima, Jason loomed large on her horizon. She had no positive knowledge, but she felt a certainty that he must be amplifying the baskets he delivered to her. She could hear him in the kitchen offering his services for any hard work requiring a man about the premises. Any new food that was sent to the grocery, she was comfortably certain would be advertised with sufficient samples for a meal for the three of them in her basket. Any errand she could delegate to him he seemed delighted to do for her. So Mahala was forced to realize, that outside of her home, the best friend she had in Ashwater was the son of her mother's washerwoman.

Edith Williams had not been to see Mahala on a real, friendly, old-time visit since the day of her catastrophe. She had not been in her home upon any excuse for even a short period since the day of her marriage. Mahala had understood a great deal concerning that marriage. She had realized how hard it would be for Edith to come. She had scarcely expected that she would, and yet, when one is utterly stranded, altogether bereft, one will cling even to straws, and if there was a girl in the town who should have stood staunchly by Mahala, it was Edith Williams. Many times in a day there was a click of the latch of the gate at which Mahala lifted a busy head, and in the beginning, there frequently had been a rush of colour to her cheeks, a light in her eyes. As the weeks went by, very frequently she did not even take the trouble to raise her head. Life had reduced things to the certainty that any one entering her gate came to have a dress remodelled, a hat made over. The last straw was the desertion of Susanna of the outskirts, Susanna who had kept the embroidered petticoat. Thinking on this subject, Mahala fell into a mental habit of saying: "Even Susanna!"

In the beginning, Mahala forced her customers to realize quite all that she was worth to them. She did her work conscientiously and honestly. She could not be forced, in remodelling a dress, to make an extremely wide skirt and panniers for a fat woman; she would not put a narrow skirt and a long polonaise on a thin woman. She frequently required changes in hair dressing before she would make a hat for a customer. She flatly refused either to make a hat or to remodel a dress unless she were allowed to use her own taste. When her customers really learned what had happened to them under Mahala's skilful fingers, they were compelled to admit that she had made such a great improvement in their appearance that they were in her debt.

When she had fully forced this realization upon them, Mahala began quietly but persistently to raise her prices. She did nothing but good work. She made her charge

184

commensurate with the time and the labour she had expended. Gradually she began to teach the whole town how to make the most of their looks, of the material that they could afford to use. So it was only a few months until she was making a comfortable living for herself and for her mother, till she was slipping away small sums destined for the restoration of the old house.

One morning, one of her customers stopping for a word of gossip, told Mahala that Edith Moreland was a very sick woman. She was having great difficulty in breathing and was being frequently attacked with fainting spells, and the doctors had ordered an immediate change of climate. After the woman had gone, Mahala sat thinking. Some undiscovered malady always had preyed upon Edith. During the past year Mahala had hoped that she was better. This report seemed to indicate that she was not. As she bent above her work, Mahala was wondering what would constitute a change of climate. Where would they take Edith in the hope that she might escape a severe illness? She thought of Junior. She could picture his dismay at being bound to a woman who was ill. He had no stomach for people who were in pain and trouble; that Mahala thoroughly understood.

It was while she was pondering on these things that the grinding of wheels before her door caused her to look up, and to her deep surprise, she saw Mrs. Moreland alighting from her carriage and coming in. Mahala always had been sorry for Mrs. Moreland. She had recognized in her a woman who was trying to do what was right, to live an exemplary life before her community. Through her own distaste for the methods of Martin Moreland and Junior, she had arrived at a realizing sense of how frequently this same distaste must be in the mouth of a right-thinking woman who was trying to live with them daily.

She opened her door and admitted Mrs. Moreland quietly and with the self-possession which always had characterized her. It was evident that her visitor was very much perturbed. She refused to be seated.

Without preliminaries she said: "Mahala, Edith is very sick this morning. She can scarcely breathe. The doctor has said that her only chance depends upon getting her to another climate as promptly as possible. We have planned to start her South and she should go at once, but she positively refuses until she has at least a dress to travel in and a hat of the latest mode. Right away I thought of you. I want you to come and help me get her off as soon as possible."

Mahala stood very still for a second, then she said quietly: "Thank you very much, Mrs. Moreland. For your sake I should like to do what you ask, but it is quite impossible. Mother is still confined to her bed and I never go from the sound of her voice. I'm always here in case she wants me. Surely there is some one else who can help you with Edith."

"Oh, yes," said Mrs. Moreland, "there are a number of people who could, but you know as well as I do that Edith wouldn't touch what they did. She's always sent away for her things and had her dresses made by that woman in Covington who works on a form from her measurements. There isn't time to wait for her. It's a matter of life and death, I tell you!"

"I'm sorry," said Mahala, "but I can't possibly come to your house to work. As I told you before, I don't want to leave Mother, and in the next place, I can't afford to miss the work that I might lose by being away."

"So far as that is concerned," said Mrs. Moreland, "of course, I'm willing to pay you for anything you might possibly lose through helping us to get Edith off. I can't understand your refusal when you and Edith always have been the dearest friends."

Mahala opened her lips and then she closed them. She looked at Mrs. Moreland intently.

"I had supposed," she said gently, "that every one in Ashwater knew that I haven't been overburdened with friends of late. When I was in a position where I could not go to my friends and they failed to come to me, I had not the feeling that it was my right to seek them afterward. I took their failure to appear as conclusive evidence that they were not my friends."

"I scarcely think," said Mrs. Moreland, "that such a criticism applies to me."

"No," said Mahala, "it does not. You did come, and you were kindness itself. But you happen to be the one woman in town from whose hands I could not accept kindness."

"It seems to me," said Mrs. Moreland, "that you're not quite as big and as fine as I always have thought you if you allow anything that has happened to keep you from doing what you can to save a life. I'm sorry if you feel you have reason to blame Mr. Moreland or me for anything that happened concerning your father's loss of his property. Certainly, you can't feel that Edith had anything to do with it. She was your friend, and you were hers; and now she is ill and asking for you—such a little favour that you could so well grant—and you refuse. Mahala, I am surprised at you!"

It was on Mahala's lips to tell Mrs. Moreland that she was quite welcome to be surprised or the reverse. That pride that had caused her father's downfall was a lively part of her inheritance from him. It touched her pride that she should be accused of failing a friend when she was ill. Possibly it was her part to teach Edith the better way.

"If you put it in that light," she said, "I'll ask Mother. If she thinks she can spare me, I will come."

She stepped to the bedroom and found her mother soundly sleeping. Upon her relaxed face there was a look of quiet and peace that was not present when her mental processes were working. Mahala imagined that she was better. She went out and explained the situation to Jemima.

"You go straight ahead," said Jemima. "Go and do what they want, and then soak it to them good and proper. Make 'em pay fully three times what you would anybody else."

Mahala gathered up her workbag, the implements she was accustomed to handling in her trade, and climbing into the carriage, was driven to the Moreland residence.

Her first day's work progressed finely. She was given exquisite material that had been clumsily made to alter. With touches here and there Mahala could transform a dress into a garment expressing the height of the prevailing mode. The instincts of the artist awoke in her and she began her work with enthusiasm and growing confidence. Junior and his father did not appear. Edith was so ill that she only spoke to her when it was necessary to find out what she wanted done, and how she wanted it. When she left at night she took several hats with her to remodel. Until past midnight she was bending over them, changing, altering, then adding touches to heighten their attractiveness. When Edith sat up long enough to try them on in the morning, she was effusive in her gratitude.

An effort was being made to have her ready to leave on the noon train. She sat on a chair before the mirror where she could study the effect of the hats she tried on. Mahala was standing beside her fitting one upon which she was working, when Junior entered the room. He brought himself into immediate proximity with Mahala. He kissed Edith and made a great display of affection for her. He told her that his mother had finished packing her trunks and that everything would be ready for them to start on the noon train. He dropped into her lap, for safekeeping, a pocket book which he told her contained the money for their journey and also the money to pay Mahala when she had completed her work. He explained that he would be forced to return to the bank on some business matters that he must finish before they started.

Edith picked up the pocket book and returned it to him. She said: "Put it on the table in the parlour beside the coat that is laid out for me to wear."

Junior took the pocket book and stood an instant holding it, and then he said to her: "Is there any one else in the house?"

Edith replied: "No, there is not."

"All right," said Junior, "I guess it will be safe then, but I'll warn you to keep an eye on it. Father wants you to have every luxury while we're away, and he nearly broke the bank when he filled that pocket book."

He stepped into the parlour and laid the long bill book on the table where he had been told; returning immediately, he left by passing through the dining room and kitchen, stopping a minute to speak to the gardener who was at work in the back yard. He went out of the side gate, which opened into an alley used by the Morelands as a short cut to the bank, and there he encountered Rebecca Sampson.

Rebecca was coming down the alley, her well-filled market basket on her arm, her white flag flashing in the sunlight. When Junior saw her, he stopped short, seeming to be possessed with an idea. He paused in deep thought for a minute, and when Rebecca lowered the flag, crowded to the farthest width of the alley and started to pass him with forbidding countenance, he took off his hat and smiled at her in a friendly manner.

In an aggrieved voice he said to her: "Becky, I am surprised at you! How can such a beautiful woman as you are let other people see that you think I have a bad heart? How can you have a clean heart yourself, unless you forgive other people? I know I was wild when I was a boy, but I'm a married man now, a staid business man. I'll never tease you again or allow the other boys to, if you'll let me pass under your flag."

Instantly, Rebecca relented. She held up the flag, since one of the greatest objects of her wrecked brain was to see any one, whosoever would, bow his head and reverently pass under it. That her old-time enemy and tormentor had promised never to tease her again, had asked the privilege of passing under the flag, delighted Rebecca so that she held the white emblem high and said an unusually long blessing as Junior Moreland bowed his head and passed under. Then he talked to her for a minute longer and hurried up the alley to the bank. Before he left the alley, he turned and watched Rebecca's movements. When finally he saw her go from sight, he smiled to himself and hurried on his way.

Mahala put the finishing touches on the hat, and carrying it into the parlour, laid it beside the coat as Edith had told her to do. Returning to the living room, she closed the parlour door enough to conceal Edith from the view of any one who might enter the room, and began work on the front of the waist she was altering. When the waist was finished, her work was done. She gathered up her measures, her scissors, and began packing her workbag.

Edith watched her and into her selfish, indifferent heart there crept a pang of remembrance of the many happy times that they had enjoyed together as children.

She said to Mahala: "I can't tell you how much I thank you for helping me out. I really am awfully sick. I suppose I shouldn't have stopped a minute for anything, but I'm going to be better in a few days and I couldn't endure the thought of being packed off where I might look like a rag to Junior."

"You're quite welcome," said Mahala quietly. "I was glad to do anything I could for you."

Edith hesitated. She opened her lips. She knew what she should say, but she had not quite the moral courage to say it. Seeing Mahala, with the joy of youth wiped from her face, with the dancing sparkle lost from her eyes, her delicate hands roughened through handling contrary material and the constant plying of her needle, hurt her. She wanted to open her arms and cry: "Mahala, forgive me! Let's be friends again. When I come back, let's be friends!"

Lacking moral courage, as she always had lacked it, what she did say was: "Junior said the money to pay you was in the pocket book he laid beside my coat. Will you hand it to me?"

Mahala swung open the door and stepped toward the table. Then she paused and said over her shoulder: "Why, Edith, the pocket book isn't here. Mrs. Moreland must have taken charge of it."

At that minute Mrs. Moreland entered from the dining room.

Edith said to her: "Mother, have you been in the parlour?"

Mrs. Moreland shook her head. "No," she said, "I'm trying to help get a decent dinner on the table for you before you leave."

"That's strange," said Edith. "There's nobody else in the house, is there?"

"Not that I know of," said Mrs. Moreland.

Immediately turmoil began. Edith asked Mahala if she had seen the pocket book when she entered the parlour with her hat, and Mahala replied that she had. It was lying in plain sight on the table beside the coat. No one else had been in the room. There was a hush; and then both the Moreland women focussed amazed, questioning eyes upon Mahala. Suddenly it occurred to her that as she was the only one known to have entered the room, they were looking accusingly at her. A gush of red from her outraged heart stained her face and then sank back and left it, by contrast, all the whiter.

Both hands clutched her workbag tightly and she cried to Edith: "It is not possible that you think I touched that pocket book?"

Edith replied slowly: "I don't want to think that, Mahala. But since you're the only person who's been in the room, and since every one knows that you've been needing money so badly, I should say that, at least, it's up to you to find it."

Mahala lifted her head. All the pride of a long race of proud people was in her blood. Her voice was smooth and even as she said: "You're quite mistaken, Edith. It is not 'up to me' to do anything except to receive the pay for the work I have done for you and then to go home."

Edith's smile was the most disfiguring her face had ever known. Seeing it, Mahala spoke further.

"We were not in a position to see who might have entered the room while I was working on your waist. If you want to search me, I am perfectly willing that you should satisfy yourself that I have not the pocket book before I leave the house."

At this unfortunate juncture, Martin Moreland entered the room. Instantly, he sensed the tense situation and began asking questions. Edith reached out her hands to him and began to cry. Immediately, he rushed to Mahala, seized her roughly by the arm, and cried: "You'll stay right here, my lady, till you're searched from head to heels. You'll not leave this house till that pocket book is discovered. It was crammed as full as it would hold with money for this journey."

Edith immediately chimed in to explain that Junior had said that the purse contained a large amount of money when she had told him to put it with her coat. She had not been sitting where she could see in the other room, but there had been no sound, no one had opened or closed a door, no one had entered the parlour or passed down the hall. The pocket book must be in the room.

During the ensuing discussion, Junior came hurrying in to tell them that time was flying and that they had none to waste. His father and mother and Edith joined in excitedly explaining the situation to him.

Instantly, he went to Mahala, put his arm across her shoulders, and said to her in a voice filled with pity: "My poor little schoolmate, have death and misfortune driven you to this? If you needed money so badly, why didn't you ask me? You know I would gladly have given it to you."

Mahala sprang away from him, staring at him with tense, wide eyes.

Mr. Moreland straightened up.

"Junior," he said sharply, "we haven't time for any nonsense of that sort! Get yourself down town by the shortest cut and bring a policeman to search her."

At this Mahala lifted her head. She said to Mr. Moreland: "No officer shall touch me. If it is your wish that I be searched, you may leave the room and Mrs. Moreland may satisfy herself and Edith that neither the pocket book nor the money is on my person."

At this juncture Edith began to gasp for breath; then she collapsed on the sofa, declaring that she was dying. Mrs. Moreland spoke authoritatively for the first time: "No one is going to lay a finger on Mahala Spellman in this house," she said. "Every one of you very well knows that she's quite incapable of touching anything that doesn't belong to her. If she says she did not touch that pocket book, she didn't!"

Then she turned to Mahala and said to her: "Put on your hat, child, take your workbag, and go home."

"Thank you, Mrs. Moreland," said Mahala, and she started toward the door.

The elder Moreland stepped in front of her. He had worked himself into a rage. He declared that she should not leave the house carrying three thousand dollars with her. Junior agreed with him.

He said to his father: "This breaks my heart. What a dreadful thing that the loss of her money should have so undermined the principles of such a girl as we always have supposed Mahala to be!"

And then he turned to Mahala in direct appeal. "Mahala," he begged, "please tell me where the pocket book is and you shall go free. All of us will agree never to mention it. You couldn't possibly get away with stealing that amount of money."

He extended his hands to her and pleaded with her to save herself while there was yet time.

"Mahala, you can't do it! What are you thinking of?" he cried.

Mahala replied quietly: "I'm thinking of a threat you made only a few weeks ago to degrade me till even the dogs of Ashwater would not bark at me. I'm thinking that this is your first move in fulfilling that threat."

Edith immediately recovered her breath. She sat erect and demanded: "Why should Junior have made such a horrible threat as that against you?"

Mahala answered: "Well, if Junior were like other men, I should advise you to ask him."

Edith instantly turned to Junior. He went to her, forcing her to lie down, and begging her to calm herself. He turned to his father and said to him: "Take Mother and Mahala into the parlour. Shut the door. If this thing's carried much further, it may kill Edith."

The elder Moreland immediately obeyed.

As soon as they were left alone, Junior said to Edith: "You very well know how Mahala always hung around me and bothered me with her attentions, and there were times when she had me fooled into thinking she was the one I really cared for. But when I learned Commencement night how beautiful you really were, superior in every way to Mahala, and when I let you see it, right away she got ugly. She threatened to ruin our happiness when I told her that I meant to ask you to marry me."

Instantly Edith put her arms around him and kissed him and comforted him. She turned against Mahala, saying: "She's so plausible she could deceive St. Peter with her innocent face and her snaky airs. Go, and call a policeman. I don't care if you do. Make her shell out all that money and then put her out of this house!"

The horrible scene ended on the entrance of the gardener with the policeman, who forcibly conducted a search of Mahala and her bag, and announced that neither the pocket book nor the money was on her. When Junior was told that the bill book could not be found, he said slowly: "She must have managed to hand it out of the front door to some one to take to her house for her. Cheer up, Dad, if it isn't here, it's there. You'll find it all right!"

Martin Moreland then told the policeman to take Mahala to the station and detain her until he had time to swear out a warrant for her arrest and a permit to search her house. The policeman knew he had no right to detain Mahala without a warrant, but she did not, so he took her by the arm and started down the street with her toward the station.

As they reached the gate she said to him: "Will you kindly remove your hand from my arm? I've not the slightest intention of trying to escape."

It was the officer's first chance to display the depths of his nature to the girl against whom the venom of unsuccess in his heart had secretly been directed all her life. He deliberately tightened his grip until he felt her wince; he started walking so rapidly that every one was forced to notice that Mahala was in his custody, as he intended that they should. So the main street of the town stood gaping at the sight of Mahala being forcibly propelled in the direction of the station house by the village policeman.

In passing Peter Potter's grocery they met Jason arranging a display of baskets outside the window. In despair Mahala caught his arm.

In a low voice she cried to him: "Jason! Jason! Junior has managed to make trouble for me! Run quick to Albert Rich's office and ask him to hurry to the police station!"

A few minutes after her arrival, Martin Moreland entered. He was shaking with anger, white with emotion. Unhesitatingly he swore out a warrant charging Mahala with the theft of three thousand dollars, and also a search warrant for her home. He asked that she be required to furnish bail to cover the amount she was accused of having taken. Mahala was terrified; she was nauseated; but she tried to keep her head erect, tried to think.

She replied: "You very well know that I cannot."

A few minutes later she was behind the bars of a cell allotted to the vagrants and the common drunks of the town. She stood erect in the middle of it, holding her skirts that they might not be contaminated. Then Albert Rich and Jason entered the building. The lawyer immediately began to arrange details for her release.

With his first understanding of the situation, Jason said: "I will furnish the money for her bail, but if it has to be cash, I'll have to drive to Bluffport. I must draw it from the bank."

He begged that Mahala be allowed to go home, even if the policeman must accompany her, till he could secure the money. This was refused, and Mahala was forced to remain in the cell until Jason could make the drive to Bluffport and return with the amount needed taken from his years of savings. During all that time Mahala stood waiting. She never spoke save to ask repeatedly for water; thirst seemed to be consuming her. It was three hours later that the cell door was unlocked. Mahala stepped out, and between her lawyer and Jason, entered a carriage and was driven home.

There she found the Senior Moreland and the police officer searching the house in detail; her mother again lying unconscious, having been brutally told of the trouble. Moreland's complaint was formally lodged against Mahala and her trial was set, at her own request, almost immediately. In a daze she worked over her mother.

Jason and Albert Rich made frantic efforts. They exhausted every means possible to them to find whether any one had been seen around the Moreland house at that time. Most of the women in the town did their own work. It was near the noon hour that the pocket book had disappeared. All of the neighbours had been in their kitchens at the time. No one could be found who had seen any one upon the streets that was not a resident going about his business.

A few days later, in a dull daze, Mahala stood in the town court house and heard herself arraigned upon the charge of having stolen three thousand dollars from the residence of Martin Moreland. She listened to the readings of the depositions of Junior Moreland and his wife, who had left on the noon train as arranged on the day of the trouble. She listened to the harsh testimony of Martin Moreland. She saw him glare at his wife. She saw the cruel grip with which he clutched her arm as he pretended carefully to lead her to the witness stand. She saw the shrinking, cowering woman lift a blanched face to the judge, and having been sworn, she heard her testify to having seen her son enter the living room with the pocket book in his hand, to having been told by him what sum it contained as he passed through the kitchen where she was hurriedly preparing dinner. He had explained that the money to pay Mahala was to be taken from it and the remainder was for the expenses of his trip with Edith. She told of hearing his voice as he talked to the two women and of having spoken with him again as he passed back through the dining room and kitchen on the way out. She told of having seen him stand a minute in conversation with the gardener at the back door and then start on his way toward the alley gate to go back to the bank. She could testify to nothing else except entering the room when she had been called after the loss of the pocket book had been discovered.

Pressed by Albert Rich with the question: "Have you any theory, Mrs. Moreland, can you offer any explanation as to how that pocket book might have disappeared?" she hesitated, evidently suffering cruelly, then with dry lips she said: "I have not."

And again Albert Rich asked her: "Is it your belief that Mahala Spellman, the daughter of Mahlon and Elizabeth Spellman, stole that money?"

She answered promptly: "It is not."

Pressed again to explain how else it could have disappeared, she answered: "I do not know, but there must have been some other way."

Then Mahala was asked if there was anything she wished to say. She took the stand and clearly and unwaveringly, she made her testimony. She detailed every occurrence simply and explicitly. She admitted having seen the pocket book, which she described, in Junior's hands and again in the parlour lying where Edith had told him to place it, when she had been sent to lay the hat she had finished beside the coat. She stoutly denied having touched it.

Under skilful questioning by Albert Rich the facts were developed that it would have been possible for any one who knew that the money was there to have entered the hall quietly, either at the front or side door, and taken it away. In rebuttal the Morelands were prompt with the evidence that no one knew that the money was in the house except Junior and his father, both of whom were occupied at the bank at the time of its disappearance, and the people who had been in the Moreland home, each of whom could be accounted for. Mahala's lawyer made much of the fact that the money could not be found upon her or in her home, and that she had not been from the sight of the Junior Mrs. Moreland except for the minute when she had laid the finished hat beside the coat.

Anticipating this testimony, Martin Moreland had packed the front seats of the courtroom with his followers. At this statement all of them laughed immoderately. There was confusion in the court. Mahala turned deliberately, and so standing, she slowly searched the room filled with faces on not one of which could she find real sympathy, compassion, or comfort save on the agonized white face of Jason gazing up at her. Then she studied the jury, man by man, and as she did so, she realized that the power and the wealth of Martin Moreland had been lavished upon it.

She turned to the judge, who had been a friend of her father, with whose children she had played, and who had known her all her life.

Unexpectedly, she flashed at him the question: "Judge Staples, do you truly believe that I stole that money?"

The judge leaned toward her with tears in his eyes.

He answered: "What I truly believe, Mahala, can be of no earthly value to you now. The only thing that can help you here with this accusation against you, is for the prosecutor to fail in proving that you took it."

Mahala cried to him: "You know I cannot prove that I did not take it; but you know equally as well that he cannot prove that I did."

Sorrowfully the old judge said: "In order to be cleared of this charge, Mahala, the prosecutor *must* fail to prove that you took the money."

Her head bowed, Mahala stood thinking.

Finally she said to the judge and to the jury: "So far as I know, I am quite helpless. I have no proof to offer other than my own word. If you will not accept that I seem to be at your mercy. I beg that you will get through with this in the speediest manner possible."

The judge closed the case by instructing the jury on the subject of "reasonable doubt" and sent them to agree on a verdict. After a day's deliberation a verdict of disagreement was rendered. That jury had contained one man whom Martin Moreland dared not approach, a man who had convictions, and was above a price. He had obstinately refused to agree to finding Mahala guilty. He roundly scored the other men for their lack of penetration, of mercy, of honesty.

When Mahala heard the verdict, she quietly slid down in her seat and was taken home unconscious by her lawyer and Jason. When reason returned, many days later, she had to be told that the shock of the trial had driven her mother, in agony and doubt, to her long rest. There awaited Mahala this alleviation: Her case had been dismissed by the sympathetic judge. It was his feeling that the evidence was not sufficient to merit punishment on Mahala's part. He told the lawyer for the prosecution that he must produce something more tangible than the mere fact that Mahala had been in the house at the time the purse was taken.

This knowledge came too late to be of material help to Mahala. When Jemima tried to tell her, she discovered from her bright eyes, her burning cheeks, and a quivering of her lips that she had developed a fever, and for weeks she lay scorching and babbling while Jemima and Doctor Grayson, with Jason in the background, worked over her.

In leaving the courtroom, Jason made an attempt to attack Martin Moreland. The banker was half expecting that something of the kind might happen. He had so surrounded himself with people craving his favour that the boy was not able even to reach him.

Then Jason felt the hand of Albert Rich on his arm and he heard his voice saying: "Don't be a fool, Jason. You can't get at him that way. You can't help her that way. We must make a clean job of this even if it's a long one. We've got to trace this thing out and find exactly how it happened. Every one knows there's been some underhand work somewhere."

When Jason became more controlled, he said to Albert Rich: "Isn't it like Junior Moreland to make this horrible trouble and then disappear and leave his father to get through with the dirty work?"

"Yes," said Albert Rich, "it's exactly like Junior to do that very thing."

"The day is coming," said Jason, "and it's coming very speedily, when I shall be forced to kill both of those slippery snakes."

"Hush!" cautioned Albert Rich, "I tell you that when you say such things you make a fool of yourself. You must not let people hear you. If they did, and anything happened to either one of them, those who heard would remember and your day of trouble would come. In that case, you would cease to be of any help to Mahala."

With scarcely a thought of food or sleep, completely neglecting his work, Jason got through the first days of Mahala's illness. When he learned that it would be a thing of long duration, that it was an hourly fight that would stretch out for weeks, he saw that the best thing he could do was to find another woman to help Jemima and himself, to be on hand as frequently as possible in order that their every need might be quickly supplied. In this extremity Jason was so obsessed in helping with the fight for Mahala's life that he had no time to pay any attention to any one else. If he had been paying attention, he might have seen that there was something of a turning in the tide of feeling concerning Mahala. There had been many people who, in the beginning, had accepted the thought that because of her father's disaster and her need for money, she might have done this thing, even as Junior had pityingly suggested to every one he could before leaving.

But there were a number of people in the town, who, when they stopped to think for a few days, realized the fact that Mahala was not in financial extremity. Albert Rich had discovered a piece of land belonging to her, that with cleaning up and cultivation, might become valuable. Jemima was furnishing her a roof. With her own efforts she was earning a comfortable living for herself and her mother. It was these people who began saying, at first tentatively and later with confidence, that the whole thing was another piece of dirty work on the part of the Morelands; that it was quite impossible that the daughter of Mahlon and Elizabeth Spellman should be a common thief; that it was unthinkable that the little girl who had been reared among them with such fastidious care should have developed a moral nature that could so easily be broken down.

In the days that passed while Mahala lay muttering on her pillow, there were many people who began making the journey to her door, and the door was as far as any of them ever travelled. Right there the face of Jemima, as coldly graven as any face of stone, met them, and Jemima did not mince words.

She said to Mrs. Williams flatly: "You're about three weeks too late. The time you ought to have come and made a stand and done something was before that damned trial. You let things go on and let her be tortured to the breakin' point and now you want to know if there's anything you can do! Let me tell you pretty flat that there ain't! What Mahala needs right now is cold baths and any nourishment she can take, and the loving care of people who understand her and sympathize with her, and that she's gettin' from me. If any of the rest of the folks is meditatin' comin', at this time of the day, you can tell 'em from me that I wish they'd stay away. They're takin' up time and they're usin' strength that Mahala needs!"

She shut the door with all the emphasis she dared—but her consideration was solely for the girl lying in the room in which her mother had lain for such a long time before her. Her heavy hair was unbound and spread over the pillow. Her body lay quiet; her head kept rolling back and forth; her hands picked at the covers or twisted together, and from her lips there came constantly a plaintive murmur: Where were all her friends? Had she no friends anywhere in the world? Sometimes she spent hours trying to convince her father or her mother that she was not a thief. Sometimes she cried pitifully and begged the whole town to believe that it was impossible that she could have done the thing of which she was accused.

Presently, the greater part of the town began to believe this. Martin Moreland found he was meeting a look of cold questioning on the faces of men who always had been friendly. The pastor of the Presbyterian Church, of which he was a deacon, had entered his room at the bank and no one knew what took place behind the closed doors, but as he left the room, several customers in the bank had heard his voice distinctly as he said to Martin Moreland: "I have the feeling that the life of this girl is endangered. If it is to be saved, it is upon your head to discover the necessary evidence to save it." That was repeated over the town, and there were many who came to feel the same way.

For once in her life Mahala was being the perfect lady that her mother had always exhorted her to be. She was lying still, having the typhoid fever, undoubtedly from germs she had accumulated in the county jail where she had drunk avidly to quench a consuming thirst while she waited for Jason—having it quietly, in a way that her mother would have highly approved had she been there to dictate exactly the manner in which a lady should have a fever.

Sitting on the back steps waiting to see if the opportunity to be of any service might arise, Jason said to Jemima early in Mahala's illness: "I've been thinking. The money I put up for Mahala's bail has been returned to me. I've a notion to take some of it and fix up her house in the country so that it will be ready for her to go to when she gets over this. There's nobody here she'll be interested in seeing. The change might give her something to think of, it might help her. How do you feel about it?"

"I think," said Jemima, "that it would be the very thing. I'll go with her and we'll live together. We'll raise chickens and calves and pigs and she'll feel better, be stronger, than she would at what she's been doin'."

So the two conspirators began a plot that ended in Jason's finding a new interest in life. He told Peter Potter what he was planning, and with his approval and his help, Jason went at the work of repairing the house and redeeming the piece of land that Mahlon Spellman had thought so worthless that he had even forgotten to mention that he ever had purchased it.

CHAPTER XVI

"The Eyes of Elizabeth"

At a famous hotel in a summer resort where people of wealth gathered, in the bridal suite, pampered and indulged in every whim, Edith Moreland was supposed to be recovering from her illness. She had been greatly disturbed over the money matter. The more she thought of it, the more frequently she said to Junior: "You know, as I have time to study about it, I see that Mahala couldn't possibly have taken that money, even though she couldn't account for its disappearance. You see, if I had been calling there instead of being your wife, and if I had been arrested, I couldn't have proved that I didn't take it."

By unlimited and plausible lying, Junior managed to keep her reasonably satisfied. He kept her room filled with flowers. He gave her expensive pieces of jewellery. He spent the greater part of his time with her, but she only grew more irritable and felt worse. Junior could see that she really was ill and that, in spite of his best efforts, she was not regaining her health. He began to fear that she was thinking of Mahala and brooding over her when she was supposed to be talking and thinking of other things.

Junior had been distinctly surprised at himself concerning Edith. In a fit of angry disappointment at Mahala's rejection and her scathing arraignment of him, he had naturally turned to the girl, who all her life had taken pains to let him see that she highly approved of him. His one thought had been, that since he could not have Mahala it made no difference whom he married. But in courting Mahala, the thought of marriage had strongly entered his mind, and the night of Commencement had shown him that Edith was a woman of distinctive beauty. He worshipped beauty almost as deeply as he worshipped money. From the books in the bank he had been able to gather a very agreeable estimate of Edith's fortune which was so considerable, that once convinced that Mahala would never marry him, Junior proved the reckless trait in his character by immediately marrying Edith.

She was quite as handsome as he had thought her. He was surprised to find himself enjoying the demonstrations of affection that she lavished upon him. He was willing to wait upon her. His father and mother were consumed with wonder when they saw him fetching and carrying, but if they protested, Junior merely laughed at them and went on doing everything that Edith asked.

One evening, to escape the constant chattering of women on the upstairs veranda, in whose talk Edith was not interested, she arose. She stepped into her room, and picking up a Persian shawl, threw it over her shoulders and walked the length of the veranda. At the corner of the building she turned down a side porch and made her way past the windows of the other guests, pausing occasionally to look down to the grounds below.

Seeing that she appeared ill and pale, a woman sitting before the French doors opening into her room, shoved a chair in Edith's direction and asked if she did not wish to sit down and rest for a few minutes.

"Thank you," replied Edith, "you're very kind. I have been ill, but I am much better now."

She glanced at the woman, and seeing that her dress and manner indicated that she was not a babbling person who would tire her with senseless chatter, she took the chair and sitting down, leaned against the balcony railing and looked at the people moving through the grounds below. There were wide stretches of beautifully kept lawns, every kind of tree and shrub imaginable. There were fountains around which grew tropical water plants and in which goldfishes swam lazily. It was the first minute of quiet that Edith had experienced outside of her rooms. She enjoyed the night air. She watched big, velvet-winged moths fluttering toward the lights at the entrance to the grounds and to the building. A sense of peace and rest stole through her. The torment of doubt and uncertainty that had racked her ever since her marriage to Junior eased slightly.

She had cared for him so intensely that she found herself doing what he asked without stopping to look into his reasons, but after a few weeks of deliberation, she had reached the conclusion that while he was doing his best to be nice to her, to keep her pleased and happy, he did not love her and he never had. This had bred a bitterness in her heart surpassing anything she ever before had experienced. Undoubtedly, it had been the cause of her illness. Her one hope had been that in time Junior would come to care for her as she knew he always had cared for Mahala. When the real breakdown came, and the mystery of the lost pocket book refused to be solved, Edith was tried to the breaking point. She could not eat; she could not sleep; she could not keep from thinking, and occasionally in her thoughts there would be thrust into her consciousness ugly things that she always had heard said about the elder Moreland and Junior.

Hour by hour, she kept reviewing her whole life in reference to her relations with Mahala. With Junior she never had come in contact except through Mahala. She remembered how she had stood with her programme ready Commencement night and he had not even asked her for one dance as he stood laughingly sprawling his name all over Mahala's card. Even Henrick Schlotzensmelter had known that it was proper for each boy of the class to ask each girl for at least one dance. For a minute as she descended from the omnibus, Edith had thought that at last Junior had really seen her. His words had furnished her the spur that carried her through her first public appearance triumphantly, when she had started with every expectation that she would fail and be forced to resort to her written speech.

She had her hour of hope, but Junior had seen to it that it was promptly quenched; and then, in a short time, he had come to her urging the hasty marriage to which she had consented because she preferred whatever life might bring to her in his company to what it would bring without him.

To-night she was realizing more keenly than usual that it might be going to bring her a very sorry scheme of things. Leaning upon the railing, she forgot the woman sitting a few yards away, as she sat staring down into the rapidly deepening shadows.

Then her eyes widened. Her breath caught in a gasp. One hand crept up to her heart, as she leaned forward, peering down intently. She must be mistaken, yet certainly a man passing through the shadows from the back of the building, accompanied by one of the maids, was Junior. Gazing earnestly to convince herself that she must be mistaken, she saw them pause and look around them to assure themselves that no one was watching. As the man turned, she saw for a certainty that he was Junior. With her lips parted and her eyes incredulous, she sat an instant watching him indulge in familiarities with the maid. She saw him give her money. She saw him take her in his arms and kiss her.

Quite unconscious of what she was doing, possibly in order to make sure of what was really happening, Edith arose, leaning far over the balcony. As the maid started to go, Junior caught her back and kissed her repeatedly. A terrible cry broke from Edith's lips. The hand upon which she was leaning, slipped. Head first she plunged over the railing and down to the stone walk far below.

At the sound of her voice, Junior looked up. The next instant he saw her plunging fall. He stopped a second, cautioning the maid to disappear. He was the first to reach Edith. He gathered her in his arms and carried her down the walk, offering the plausible explanation that in leaning over the railing to speak to him as he was passing below, she had lost her balance and fallen.

He carried her to their room and physicians were summoned, but it was found that her neck was broken. So it was Junior's task to take her back to Ashwater, lay her away with every outward sign of mourning and lavish expenditure, and ingratiate himself as deeply as possible with her relatives by a clever semblance of heart-broken grief.

The morning after the funeral, Junior entered the president's room of the bank and closing the door behind him, went to the table and sat down, facing his father.

"Dad," he said, "you've looked so ghastly ever since I've been home that I've come to put you out of your misery. Cheer up! Things are not as bad as they might be. In the first place, you will be rejoiced to know that I've got complete control of all of Edith's finances. And in the second place, if I don't mistake my guess, for once you will be even more rejoiced to know that what happened really and truly was an accident. I was downstairs. Edith did lose her balance and fall. There was a woman on the veranda with her near enough to see what happened and there were people on the veranda below when she came smashing down. I got to her first because I was coming that way and it wasn't far. But it was an accident pure and simple."

Moreland Senior leaned back in his chair and breathed to the depth of his lungs.

"Well, Junior," he said. "I don't know that I ever heard anything in all my life with which I was better pleased. I may, or I may not, have a few things I regret on my own soul, but I'd hate to undertake the strain of carrying a burden like that concerning you. As a man grows older, he doesn't sleep so well as he did when he had the cast-iron constitution of youth, and there are times when the night gets pretty bad if a man's conscience is not altogether clean. Of course, I'm not intimating that I've got anybody's blood on my hands, but in the wild, hot-headed days of youth I may have done two or three things and been through a few experiences that I'd hate to see measured out to you. I want you to have a good time and get all you can out of my money—which is really your money—but be slightly careful. See to it that you don't get into anything that'll raise the hair on your head about three o'clock in the morning twenty years from now."

Junior laughed. "Sure!" he said. "Don't worry, Governor, I'll be careful. I've never done anything so terrible and I'm not planning to do anything except go on with the work I'd started before I went away. Has anything come up concerning Mahala?"

Mr. Moreland shook his head.

"That's one of the things, Junior," he said, "that I'm not quite easy about. It was a big sum to disappear and I was after the Spellmans and I didn't hesitate to give it to them as hard as I could, but to tell you the plain truth, I haven't an idea where that money went. I don't know how it got out of the house, or whether it was out of the house. Are you sure you put that pocket book on the table when Edith told you to?"

"I certainly am," said Junior. "I went into the room, laid it beside her coat, and stepped back. You'll remember that Mahala testified that it was there when she finished Edith's hat and laid it with the things she was going to wear."

Mr. Moreland slowly nodded his head.

"I remember," he said. "That piece of testimony of hers is about the only alleviation I've got when Elizabeth Spellman looks at me too hard, at three in the morning. Sometimes I'm tempted to send to Chicago for a real detective and put him on the case. I find that there are things that I can do with impunity, and then there are some that I can't. I'd rather see Mahala Spellman freed from that ugly charge against her than anything that could happen on earth right now. It's beginning to react against us, pretty strongly, my boy."

"In the present circumstances," said Junior, "so would I. But money is a material thing. The earth doesn't open and swallow it up. It's somewhere, and I cautioned you before I left to do the most thorough piece of searching of Mahala Spellman's *home* that could possibly be done. *I was sure you'd find the money there.* I don't see yet how it happens that you didn't."

Mr. Moreland drew another deep breath. He picked up a letter in one hand and a letter opener in the other. Junior suddenly realized that his face was drawn and haggard and that the eyes that were lifted to him had a hunted look.

"Well, it happens, no doubt, because it wasn't there," he said. "If it had been I'd have found it. I've worn myself out searching our house and when I haven't been at the job, your mother has. This thing has hurt her a great deal worse than it has either one of us. I strongly suspect, that among the old hens of this town, she's likely getting hers. Since people have had time to think things over, I get a hint once in a while that the thing I cautioned you would happen is slowly happening. As people have time to calm down and to study things, there's a kind of sentiment growing that Mahala never could have taken that money. After all, she didn't really need it. Jemima had furnished her shelter; she was honestly earning her daily bread, while that damned Rich dug up a forty-acre piece of land that doesn't need anything but cultivation to make it as fine river bottom as you ever laid your eyes on. She knew about it before this thing happened. She wasn't what you might call destitute or in extremes, and she had a kind of pride that made her meet the thing in a way that her mother couldn't have done. I've got a notion in my head that Elizabeth Spellman would have been prouder of her girl if she'd laid down beside her and died with her, instead of putting on an apron and beginning to sew for a living."

Junior arose and stood looking at his father.

"No doubt you're right, Dad," he said quietly. "You most generally are. But since you didn't have anything to do with this, since you are in no way to blame for it, don't you think you'd better stop worrying about it? Let it go for what it's worth."

"Well," said Mr. Moreland, "my dear friends and my devoted neighbours are beginning to make me feel that I'm none too popular in this community. That little ape of a Spellman, feeling and flecking and scraping, could make himself a commanding and respected figure, and I thought I'd done it, but I'm none too sure that I have. I'm none too sure that it wouldn't take only one more little slip on my part to have every dog in the county worrying at my throat. I understand that Albert Rich, Peter Potter, and Jason Peters, are pooling issues against us. They're doing everything in their power to find some hook or crook by which they can clear Mahala, and if the thing happens, and happens to our discredit——" The Senior Moreland paused and drew fine lines down the side of a blotter with a sharp pencil.

Junior stood waiting, studying him intently. At last the elder Moreland resumed: "If the thing happens, and happens to our *discredit*, I'm not any too sure that things won't go pretty rough with us."

Junior laughed outright, but it wasn't a hearty laugh, and not a mirthful one.

"Don't you think it!" he cried. "Don't you think it!"

Martin Moreland drew a line so deep that it cut through the blotter. "I don't think it," he said with a terse, cold incision that arrested Junior's deepest attention. "I don't think it. *I know it.*"

Junior stiffened slightly and stood studying him.

"There's just one thing that can save the situation," said the elder Moreland. "If you're ready to go to work, go to work now on the task of finding out where that pocket book went. Find it in such a way that it will be a credit to *us* to have found it. Find it in such a way that it will turn public opinion in our favour. Give me the chance to be the leader in doing anything that could be done to reinstate Mahala."

As he finished, Junior laughed again, this time more naturally. "That's something of a job that you've set for me, Pater," he said. "I haven't an idea in ten states where that pocket book is, but if that's the way you feel about it, I'll get on the job and see if I can resurrect it, or duplicate it, or do something. And in the meantime, is there anything you want me to do in connection with putting a small slice of the fear of God into the hearts of Albert Rich, and old Potter and Jason?"

The Senior Moreland thought intently a few minutes and then he said quietly: "Right there you had better stay your hand. They happen to be on the popular side right now. You had better just drop that and evade it, and get around it the best you can, and in the meantime, you had better spend some time and money on seeing how popular you can make yourself in this town right now."

"All right," said Junior, "at least one of the jobs you've set me is agreeable. I don't mind in the least seeing how popular I can make myself. As a matter of fact, I deeply enjoy it, and in about ten days I'll show you an altogether different atmosphere. It's evident to my young mind that this village has needed me, that I'm of importance on this job, and in the meantime, I think you had better take Mother and go on a vacation. If you'll allow me to say so confidentially, you're looking as if a keen blast of the wrath of Heaven had struck you."

Junior left the room. Martin Moreland went on decorating the blotter. No one kept any account of the length of time he spent or the intricacy of the designs that he drew. He heard the whistles blowing for noon before he arose and reached for his hat, and as he left the room he was saying softly to himself: "'The wrath of Heaven.' I wonder what the wrath of Heaven can do to me?"

CHAPTER XVII

"A Millstone and the Human Heart"

During the days that Mahala lay approaching the culmination of the final test as to whether her physical forces were strong enough to endure the ravages of the fever and leave her only sufficient strength to go on breathing, Jason worked frantically. For the first time in his life he found himself doing the thing that was popular. Every one was willing to help him. Carpenters would work over hours and on holidays; painters and paper hangers were equally accommodating. The neighbours on the farms surrounding Mahala's forty acres came to his rescue. Without being asked, they mowed weeds, burned brush heaps, trimmed the orchard, and rebuilt tottering fences. They made a day of straightening the leaning stable on its foundations and staying its framework, so that with new roof and sheathing, it would be a tenable building for many years to come.

Jason superintended everything, but he confined his personal work to the house. While the men were nailing shingles and laying flooring, he was peeling off rotten plastering, tearing away broken lathing, working wherever he could lend a hand in most swiftly furthering the task he had undertaken. Every morning he stood at the foot of Mahala's bed looking down at her a few moments before he went to work. All day her tortured face was the spur that drove him to accomplishments worthy of the best efforts of two men. Jemima kept assuring him that he need not be so terribly anxious. There would be a crisis, but she and Doctor Grayson and the nurse were watching for it; they would be prepared; they would save Mahala.

But there came a day when Jason staggered into the little house wearing a ghastly face. He paid no attention to the food Jemima set out for him. He made his way to Mahala's room, and clinging to the foot of the bed, he stood staring down at her, an agony of doubt, of fear, written over his face and figure. Finally, Jemima could endure it no longer. She put her arm around him and helped him from the room. He went out and sat down on the back steps, where Jemima followed him.

"Don't feel so badly, Jason," she said. "You're working so hard that your nerve is givin' way. All of us feel that Mahala is holdin' her own. She's goin' to come out of this. You needn't be so afraid. We won't let her die."

The face that Jason lifted to hers was so ghastly that Jemima never forgot it.

"You haven't stopped to consider," he said, "that death might be the best thing that could happen to her."

"No, I haven't," said Jemima stoutly, "because I don't think it. She's young, and she's strong, and she's innocent."

Jason sat so still that it occurred to Jemima that he had stopped breathing; and then he said quietly: "One man said she was innocent. Eleven say that she is guilty. That is a stain that is going to mark her the remainder of her life. I'm not sure that life is the best thing for her."

"The only thing of which I'm sure," said Jemima heartily, "is that you've worked to the breaking point, or you may have picked up this fever yourself. Doctor Grayson says people do get it from one another. Now you come and get some food, and go to bed and have a good sleep, and to-morrow you work just half as hard as you have to-day."

There were three anxious days at the time the fever ran its course, but Doctor Grayson was a skilled and a conscientious physician and he was dealing with a condition that he had handled many times in his life when he did not have the vitality of youth to aid him. The thing that he would have to combat in Mahala's case would be her lethargy, the indifference that he felt sure she would feel, when consciousness returned, as to whether she lived or died, and this proved to be the hardest battle that he had to fight. But she was young; she was physically strong. Jemima, the nurse, and Doctor Grayson never faltered in their unwavering work and faith. The result was, that a week after the crisis, they were beginning to whisper of mysterious things to Mahala. There was a journey that she was to make; there was a wonderful surprise in store for her; something delightful was going to happen.

Because she was very weak, because she was desperately tired, because her heart had been as nearly broken as human hearts ever come to that condition without ultimate completion, Mahala found the easiest way was to listen, to accept what was being said. Several times she had sat in her chair by the window for an hour; her feet had touched the floor; she had stood upon them and performed a few wavering journeys around the room.

Jemima had been dismantling and sending away everything in the house belonging to Mahala that she could spare. Her clothing was packed, and she was counting the days until the removal could be made, when there came to the faithful creature a telegram from her daughter-in-law, and this time the hand of fate had fallen heavily upon Jemima. In the prime of her son's life, in the full tide of his strength, with his wife and a house full of small children depending upon him, a piston had burst in a piece of machinery upon which he had been working in the factory that employed him, and the remainder of Jemima's life was taken out of her hands. She was asked to come and help to rear and to support seven children, all of them youngsters needing everything. She was asked to come immediately, so there was nothing to do but to tell Mahala that there was trouble in Jemima's family; that she had been called, and to leave Mahala to the care of the nurse.

So many things had happened to Mahala that one more did not matter. She wept a few weak tears of compassion for Jemima and pity for herself and went soundly to sleep at the hour of Jemima's departure. The nurse was a kindly woman, a judicious woman, and for the remainder of her stay she found herself adhering very rigidly to the rules that Jemima had explained to her. Backed by Jemima's reasons, they seemed very good rules. People who had failed Mahala in her hour of tribulation might stay away and attend to their own affairs; they might learn the lesson very thoroughly that the friend in need is the one who is the friend in deed; and that if people were not friends in need, there was every likelihood that they never would be friends again in any conditions that might obtain.

On the day that Jason announced that the house was ready, that he was very certain that he and the daughter of one of the neighbouring farmers who had been helping him to arrange the house, would be able to care for Mahala in the future, the nurse helped him to lay springs and a mattress in Peter Potter's delivery wagon and make up a comfortable bed. With a smile on her pale lips and that brand of hopelessness in her heart which amounts to passivity, Mahala walked between the nurse and Jason and was lifted to the bed. With closed eyes she lay quietly while she was driven through the streets of Ashwater, out country highways, and slowly down the River Road until they reached the house she once had visited.

As they had driven along in the warming sunshine she had felt that it made small difference to her whether she lived or died. When she saw the transformation that had taken place in her house and land, there came to her with a distinct shock the feeling that it would be ungracious of her to die. There was an expectant look about the face of the waiting house. It proclaimed itself with dignity and pride; it was alluring to look at—all fresh paint and lace-curtained windows. It was standing up straight upon its foundations. A veranda had been added across the front, and everything was a vision of peace and quiet beauty. It gave Mahala the feeling that she would not be doing the square thing not to live in it, not to love it, not to search for happiness there.

Sitting on the veranda was an attractive young girl. When she saw the covered wagon coming, she arose and came down to the gate, swinging it open. She was a slip of a thing with light hair, wide-open questioning young eyes, and a provoking red mouth. She was quite tall for a girl, slender, and neatly dressed. There was the vivid pink of fresh air, an outdoor flush on her cheeks.

Mahala looked at Jason; her lips formed the one word: "Who?"

Jason answered: "Her name is Ellen Ford. She's the daughter of your nearest neighbour. She's taken a lot of interest while I was fixing up the place. She's agreed to stay with you and take care of you until you feel well enough to manage by yourself. She's a real nice girl with sufficient sense to keep her mouth shut. She thinks you wonderful and she's crazy about having the chance to stay with you."

For a long time Mahala's eyes looked intently down the road in front of her. The sight of the little house, almost buried in green, of the neatly fenced fields, and the thought of searching for happiness again had brought rushing back to her brain the one thought that, since her day of direst disaster, had persisted with her. Suddenly the big tears began to brim from her eyes and slide down her cheeks. Then she lifted her head and looked into Jason's eyes.

"Jason," she cried, "you know that I never touched that money!"

Jason put his arms around her and muttered words of comfort. He was telling her to be brave, to be calm, to think of nothing but that she was coming to her very own home, that for the remainder of her life, if she chose, she was to do nothing but tend her flowers and her garden and do whatever she pleased there. When they stopped, Jason lifted her bodily, carrying her across the veranda and into her room where he laid her on the bed upon which she had slept as a child.

When she opened her tired eyes, she saw that the room was almost an exact reproduction of her old one. She swung her feet to the floor, and steadying herself by the furniture, made her way around the room in wonderment almost too great for words. At sight of her, the gold bird burst into song. She looked into the living room and she cried out in astonished delight when she saw upon the walls pictures that had belonged to her father and mother, the oil portrait of her mother hanging above the mantel—a whole room full of precious things that she had thought lost to her forever. There were several cases of the books they had loved like old friends waiting to greet her. She forgot her weakness. She voiced a cry of delight as she stood in the middle of the room gazing in an ecstasy at each precious thing she never had hoped to see again.

She made her way to the door of the next room, and there she found a guest chamber furnished with more of their home possessions, and another door led to the dining room—floor, side walls, furnishings—each object was familiar to her. Crossing it, she looked into the kitchen, furnished as were the other rooms, with her possessions. And there she saw Ellen Ford busy preparing supper for her. Through the back door she could see a roofed veranda having chairs and a small table, and on back to the old orchard from which she could hear the humming wings of bees, and the voices of the bluebirds. She could see the stable with white chickens busy around it and a cow and a calf in the lot beside it. Her quick eyes took in the upper part of the stable where she judged, from the arrangement of windows, that Jason had made a room for himself while he worked.

With the bravest effort at self-control of which she was capable, Mahala turned to Ellen Ford. "I want to thank you very much for your kindness in helping to make a home for me," she said.

"Oh, it's nothing," answered the girl, busy over the stove. "We join land, you know, and we always try to do what we can for any of our neighbours."

And then, in an effort to be friendly, to cover an embarrassing situation, she rattled a kettle lid and fussed with some things on the table as she remarked casually: "Of course, we'd expect you to do anything for us that I've tried to do here, in case we needed it."

Mahala looked at the girl quickly. She divined that the speech had been made to put her at ease, but she also divined something else. It was innocent, it was simple, it was honest. Here was some one who had faith in her, who had been willing to bolster that faith with works; some one who was proud to be with her, to help her till she should again be able to help herself. Before she thought what she was doing, she found herself standing face to face with Ellen Ford. She realized that her hands were reaching up to the shoulders of the girl, who was taller than she. She found herself crying out: "You know, don't you, that I never touched that money?"

Instantly the stout young arms closed around her. Mahala felt herself drawn to Ellen Ford and a work-coarsened young hand was stroking her hair. "Why, of course you didn't!" she said. "Every one with any sense knows you couldn't!"

Mahala turned suddenly and went back to her room where she was greeted with another gush of song from the throat of her bird. She was too weak to reach its cage. She dropped upon the side of the bed and sat staring through the window. When Ellen came presently, saying supper was ready, she went to the dining room and tried with all her might to force down her throat some of the very good food which the girl had deftly prepared. Then she sat for an hour in an arm chair on the veranda, looking at the flowers redeemed from the trespassing of overrunning weeds, fertilized, and cultivated. How they would bloom in the spring, how well the bushes looked, and the trees; how rank the grass! By and by, the moon came up and the night was filled with the soft sounds of fall. It was Jason who said to her: "I wish you would lie down now, Mahala. I think you're taxing yourself too far. You've got to take this slowly. In a few weeks you'll be surprised at what the air, and the food, and the work that you will find, will do for you."

Mahala arose and went to him. She laid her hands upon his arm. "Jason," she said in a shaking voice, "I had hopes about this land the minute I saw it. It will take all the rest of my life to tell you what a wonderful thing I think you have done in fixing up my house for me. I never, never can tell you what it means to me to have these things from my home back again. How does it happen?"

"Don't, Mahala," said Jason, taking her arm and trying to guide her toward the door. "Don't worry about these things now. Don't try to talk. There's a long time coming when you can tell me anything you want to."

Mahala stood looking up at him.

"Jason, are you going back to Ashwater to-night?" she asked.

"No," answered Jason, "I'm only going to Ashwater when business takes me there. I've still got my interest with Peter. I am going to help him with his books. I'm paying a good man that I trained myself to take my place. After I got your house started enough that I knew what it would cost, I had sufficient money left to buy forty more acres joining yours, so I went into partnership with you. As soon as you're able, you're going to do the house work and I'm going to do the farm work, and we're going to share and share alike. There's nothing the matter with your land. All it needs is work. The cost of the improvements on the house I have charged to you; I'll take that much out of your share. Now you go to bed and go to sleep. My room is over the carriage room in the stable, and Ellen's going to stay all night with you as long as you want her."

Then Mahala found herself standing beside her bed. Slowly, she slipped down on her knees. She leaned forward; she tried to pray. But she found there was nothing that she wanted to say to God except to beg of Him to take care of Jason, to reward his thoughtfulness and his kindness. Then she put out the light, laid her head on her pillow, and in spite of herself, began an intensive review of the day.

She recalled and dwelt upon each incident and suddenly, with the torture of memory, there came to her the thought that while Jason had overwhelmed her with kindness, had given her every assurance that she would be sheltered and cared for, he had not said the words that her heart had been hungering to hear him say. He had not gripped her hands tightly and looked straight into her eyes and said with the firmness of deliberate assurance: "Mahala, I know that you didn't touch that money."

The thought shocked and startled her. She recalled that she had expected it. She wondered how he could have forgotten to give her the assurance that he must have known her heart would crave. She found herself sitting up in bed, looking through the window at the moon-whitened world outside. The notes of a whippoorwill came sharply stressed through the night. Back in the orchard she could hear the wavering complainings of a hunting screech owl. She could hear the little creatures of night calling. With her hands gripped together and pressed hard against her heart, she heard her own voice repeating: "Oh, Jason, I didn't! I didn't!" Over and over she reached the moment of the question she had asked. Finally, she was able to comfort herself with the kindness of the things that he had said, with the manifestations of the thoughtfulness and the planning and the work that he had done in her behalf. She succeeded in making herself believe that Jason was so sorry, and his mind so filled with what he had been doing, that he had merely neglected to speak the words her heart so longed to hear.

She made a brave effort in the days that followed, to keep that thought from entering her mind. She was too proud to mention the matter again, but constantly she kept watching Jason. She found that she was waiting to hear him involuntarily say the words that she longed to hear. As she studied him and the situation, there came to her the realization that he was thinking for her, that he was planning for her, that he was working for her, but equally he was thinking, he was planning, he was working for himself. He was making the money that would insure her having a home again and freedom, but he was assuming nothing. Whatever he made, he divided equally. For the share of land that she furnished he was doing his equivalent in work. The division was fair enough. She did not know, until Jason told her, that he always had loved the country, that it had been a boyhood hope to own and to work upon land, that he had only done the thing that he was glad in his heart to do when he had escaped from the grocery through the arrangement he had made, and found himself free to devote most of his time to the development and cultivation of land. He pointed out to her the extent of the land he had purchased adjoining her nearest neighbour, James Ford, the father of Ellen who was still helping her about the house and in the garden.

Nothing could have given Mahala more comfort at that minute than the thought that Jason was not sacrificing himself; that he was doing the thing that he had hoped, and for a long time planned, to do; that he was happy with the wind in his hair and his feet in the freshly turned earth of a furrow. Watching him at his work, sometimes answering the chatter of Ellen, who was so full of the joy of living that she talked upon any occasion that she felt it proper that she might speak, milling these things over in her heart, there came to Mahala the realization that Ashwater stood to Jason Peters in some small degree in the same light as it now did to her. It had been a place where an unkind fate had bound him and he had suffered from taunt and from insult; he had suffered from unjust persecution; manhood had brought to him the power to fend for himself and the friend he needed in his hour of trial, but it had not taught him to love the place in which he lived or the people among whom he had endured humiliation and suffering.

The first wave of gladness that she had known since her earliest calamity had befallen her, washed up in Mahala's heart with a real comprehension of the fact that Jason was happy; that he wanted to live upon the land; that he enjoyed every foot of his environment. It pleased her when she discovered that he disliked that day upon which he was forced to go upon errands to Ashwater to repair implements or for food.

When she had watched him until she thoroughly convinced herself of these things, one degree of the bitterness in Mahala's heart was assuaged. Another thing that helped her on the road toward an approach to her normal condition was the attitude of Ellen Ford. Ellen was a charming girl. Mahala soon learned to love her. She was frank, unusually innocent. Mahala decided that her mother must have used a much greater degree of caution in speech before her daughter than she had understood was common with country women in general. Ellen came when she was wanted; with perfect cheerfulness went home when she was not. She chattered on every other subject on earth, but she never evinced the slightest curiosity concerning Mahala or what the future might have in store for her. If the task Mahala laid out for herself was so heavy she could not finish it, Jason went down the road and told Ellen. The girl came singing, did what was wanted efficiently, begged the privilege of brushing Mahala's hair or doing any possible personal service for her, and went back singing, Mahala thought, as spontaneously as the bluebirds and the fat robins of the garden and the orchard. For these reasons, Mahala found her heart running out to her; found herself praising her and loving her; listening for her song and her footstep; wishing that she might do for her some pleasing service in return for the many kind and practical things that Ellen could think of to do for her.

Imperceptibly each day, but surely in a total of days, Mahala's strength began to return, and with it came a high tide in her beauty. Washed in rain water and dried in the sun, the golden life came back to her hair; an adorable pink flush into her cheeks;

a deeper red than they ever had known stained her lips. The one place that the mark remained was in the depths of her eyes. In them dwelt a dread question, a pain that never left them. Looking deep into them at times, Jason felt that the one thing for which he could thank God was that he did not there find any semblance of fear. The horror that had hovered over his boyhood from a gnawing stomach, a beaten body, and a tormented brain, had left him in such a condition that at times he acknowledged a sickening surge of pure fear sweeping through him. Whenever this happened, he set himself to master it, to prove that he was not afraid. There had been a few times in his life when the obsession was heaviest upon him, that he had deliberately put himself in Martin Moreland's presence, in order to prove to himself that he could stand, in those days, at the height of the banker with his shoulders squared and his eyes able to meet those of any man straightly. He never had been afraid of Junior physically since the first day in which he had tested the high tide of his youth upon him. Knowing what Junior had been able to do to him, feeling in the depths of his heart that the troubles that had fallen upon Mahala were of Junior's devising, would breed and keep in Jason a nauseating nerve strain springing from mental suffering, so strong that it caused physical reaction.

Mahala spent much of her time in the house. She experienced such joy as she never had hoped for again merely in walking over the carpets, in touching the curtains, in handling the linens, the books, the needle work, and the silver that had been her father's and her mother's. By imperceptible degrees she had altered Jason's arrangement of the house until the place became a reproduction of the delicate colour, of alluring invitation, of nerve-soothing rest that she had homed among during her childhood. When she could find nothing further to prettify inside her house—the little house that was truly hers—she walked around it lavishing love upon the flowers and the bushes, the trees and the shrubs. She spent a great deal of time on her knees before the boxed bed running around the house, loosening and fertilizing the soil, picking out the sly weeds that tried to find a home under the shelter of the star flowers and the daffodils and the iris. She loved every foot of the old garden. On her writing desk there were catalogues from which she was selecting the seeds and bulbs she meant to order for fall planting so that the coming summer her garden should once more spread its tapestry of colour and wave its banners of beauty on the air.

She liked to cross the corner of the orchard and feed the chickens and the white pigeons that shared the barn loft with Jason. She liked to pet the calf and make friends with the cow. With the assistance of Ellen, and under the advice of Mrs. Ford, remembering what she could of Jemima's methods and following the instructions of several cook books, she began to prepare meals for Jason and herself which were nourishing and sustaining, and at the same time, appetizing and attractive. It was several months before the morning dawned upon which Mahala realized that the full tide of health was flowing in her veins; that strength had come back to her; that when she sent for Ellen, most frequently she was doing it because she wanted company, for the day had not yet arrived when Mahala would face Ashwater.

211

There was no one there whom she cared to see; nothing there that she cared to do. A written slip naming her necessities went in Jason's pocket on his trips to town on business connected with the grocery or conveniences necessary for his farm work. She found, after a few months of experience of living with the woman who was herself, that a mark had been set upon her, literally burned into her brain, her heart, and her soul,—a mark that never could be effaced. The other doors and windows of the house stood wide open. The front door was always closed, always locked. She found, too, that if, while she sat by an open window sewing or under the trees of the dooryard, she heard the rattle of wheels and saw a face she recognized, she arose and on winged feet put herself out of hearing in case any one should knock upon her door, so that she would not be forced to open it and face them.

There were times when she deliberately tried to determine what she thought and felt concerning Jason, but her brain was still in such tumult that she could not be definite even with herself. Life had narrowed her proposition to the one fact that he was everything that she had left of her old life. She could not look at any beloved possession that had belonged to her father and her mother without the knowledge that, save for him, she would have been denied even this poor consolation from life. She could not move through the small home that in her heart she soon grew almost to worship without the knowledge that she owed to him her joy in having it to live in so soon. As she tried to think things out, it appealed to Mahala that the time had passed in which she could spend even a thought on remembering the days of his youth. She herself had been stripped to the bone. She had lost everything but her respect for herself. Every material comfort she had, she owed to him. Slowly in her heart there began to take form the decision that whatever there was of her personality, of her life, belonged to Jason if he wanted it. If there was any way in which he cared to use it, it was for him to say what he desired.

During the winter Mahala found herself living passively. She found that she was allowing each day to provide its duties, and on land she learned that they were many. Whatever there was to do, she went about casually and determinedly. Slowly, through absorption in her work, through contact with the growing and the rejuvenating processes of nature, through the healing power of spontaneous life around her, the shadow began to lift. One day she stopped short in crossing the kitchen with a pan of odorous golden biscuit fresh from the oven in her hands, stunned by the realization that she was hearing her own voice lifted in a little murmuring song. There had been days in Mahala's life when she never expected that song could ever again return to her lips. After a while, she realized that she was laughing with Jason over things that occurred when he came in ravenous from work to food of her preparing. She found herself talking happy, nonsensical things to the calf and the chickens that she was feeding, and she had trained the pigeons until they came circling around her, settling over her head and shoulders like a white cloud when she entered the barnyard with her feed basket.

So spring came again.

To repay Ellen Ford for the many things that she had done for her for which she had refused to accept payment in money, Mahala had selected, from samples she had Jason bring her, a piece of attractive pink calico and a blue gingham and a finer piece of dainty white goods. From these she fashioned attractive dresses for Ellen. The white one she made foamy with lace and feathery with ruffles. Ellen was delighted. She made bold to throw her arms around Mahala and kiss her repeatedly in an effort to express her thankfulness for this gift. But when the Ford carriage passed the house on Sunday morning, taking the family to church, Mahala was surprised to see that Ellen was wearing the pink dress instead of the white one.

As she served Jason's plate at dinner that day she said to him: "I thought Ellen would wear the white dress I made for her to-day, but I noticed as they passed that she wore the pink one."

And Jason answered: "Perhaps she's saving the white one for some very special occasion."

"I suspect that is it," said Mahala. "Maybe there's going to be a picnic or a party."

A few days later, sitting on her front steps in the soft air of evening, Mahala saw Ellen slowly coming down the road in her direction, and then she saw Jason coming from one of his fields carrying a hoe over his shoulder. His lithe leap carried him over the fence as Ellen was passing. She saw them stop and begin talking, and then she saw Jason lean his hoe in the fence corner, turn, and slowly walk back down the road with Ellen. He stood for a long time at her gate talking with her before he came back, picked up his hoe, and came on to the house.

For a long time Mahala sat thinking. Then she got up and went to her room. She shut the door, and lighting a lamp, stood before her mirror and looked intently at the reflection of her face. It was a very white face that she saw and it was gazing at her with wide, questioning eyes. Then slowly she undressed and went to bed without saying good-night to Jason.

For a few days Mahala went about her work in a sort of stupefied fashion. Sometimes she lifted her head and ran her hands over her face as if it were a numb thing that needed, in some way, to be galvanized into expression by an outside agency. And then, a few days later, there were steps on the veranda, the door opened, and Jason and Ellen Ford came in together. Ellen's face was flushed, her eyes were dancing, and her red lips were laughing. The white dress was clothing her beautifully.

In a voice that was steady but slightly husky, Jason said: "Mahala, Ellen is my wife. We were married an hour ago. I am glad that you've learned already to love her."

There is large advantage in having been born a thoroughbred. Mahala kissed Ellen's pink cheeks. She patted down a white ruffle that was not quite in place. She said very quietly: "Indeed I have learned to love Ellen."

She offered Jason a steady hand and hearty congratulations, and then she sat down and said evenly: "Now tell me about your plans."

Their plans were extremely simple. Ellen's people were selling their farm and moving away. Jason meant to buy what he needed of their furniture and set up housekeeping in the home the Fords were abandoning. He told Mahala that the reason he had set up the bell in her back yard a few days before and stretched a cord to her room was so that she might ring any time during the day or night when she wanted either of them. One ring should be for him, two for Ellen. There was to be no change in anything except that Jason would not take his meals with her and instead of sleeping over the stable, he would be across the road and a few yards farther away. Otherwise they were expecting life to go on exactly as it always had.

Then Ellen kissed Mahala repeatedly, and with an arm around Jason's waist and his hand on her shoulder, they went down the road together. Mahala fled to her room and locked the door behind her, without realizing that there was no one against whom she need lock it. Once more she faced herself in her truthful mirror.

"Exactly the same," she said at last, "exactly the same." And then she cried out at her reflection: "Fool! Fool! You big fool! You've worried your brain, you've lain awake nights, trying to figure out whether Jason was good enough for you. He's settled your problem by letting you see that you're not good enough for him. Fool! Fool! You big fool!"

Her eyes turned inward and backward. Wildly she tried to understand how this thing could have happened. Then, suddenly, realization came to her. Her face was dead white, her lips stiff when she announced the ultimatum: "The reason he didn't say anything the day we got here was because he thinks I took it. He thinks I'm a thief. He wouldn't make me the mother of his children because in his heart he believes I'm guilty."

Then Mahala dropped over in merciful unconsciousness. Far in the night, a heavy moon ray, falling persistently on her face, aroused her. She drew herself up on her bed and lay as she was till she heard Jason's step on the back porch the next morning. Then she forced herself to her feet, unlocked the door, and went out to meet the day as if it were going to be exactly like any other day that had passed before it.

In the days that followed, Mahala learned that the extent to which the human heart can be tortured is practically without any limit. One may suffer and suffer for years, only to discover that there are still unplumbed depths of pain and degradation to which one may be forced. In these days she really was a primitive creature, stripped to the bone. She was seeing herself now, not as she always had seen herself, but as other people were seeing her, and slowly there was beginning to rise in her heart the feeling that if some one did not do something to reëstablish her before the world and in her own self-respect, she would be forced to do it herself. With every ounce of strength she had, she fought herself to keep Jason and Ellen from seeing that she was suffering, that once more the power to see beauty had left her eyes. Her ears no longer heard song; hourly they were tortured by the sound of her own voice muttering in dazed amazement: "He thinks I'm guilty!"

CHAPTER XVIII

"A Triumph in Millinery"

Just at the time when Nancy Bodkin felt that life might be taking on a happier aspect for Marcia, she heard the slam of the screen door and looking from her work down the long aisle of the store, she saw coming toward her what she thought was the handsomest man that she ever had seen. In her hasty summary she could note that he was tall, that he was dark, that he was tastefully and expensively clothed. Her eyes raced about the room searching for Marcia who was standing before a case in which she was arranging some finished hats. She saw Marcia start and cast a glance in her direction. She saw her hesitate before she moved forward to meet the stranger. Nancy laid down her work, crossed her hands on it, and sat watching intently. She saw the young man take an envelope from his pocket and with a few polite sentences he drew therefrom some old yellowed papers which he showed to Marcia but did not give into her keeping. She saw him hand Marcia some clean, new papers, and with a bow of exaggerated deference, she saw him turn and leave the store. She watched Marcia follow him, close the door and turn the key in the lock. It was mid-day; customers might come at any minute. In a daze she watched Marcia with a ghastly face come the length of the store toward her and draw the curtains behind her. She felt the papers thrust into her hands. Then she realized that Marcia was on her knees; she felt the weight of her head in her lap, the clinging grip of her arms around her.

The little milliner slowly straightened. She never had felt quite so important, quite so confident, quite so worth while in all her life. Suddenly, to herself she became a rock upon which a craft was being splintered. The hand she laid on Marcia's bent head was perfectly firm.

"Now you buck up," she said authoritatively. "You must. I don't know what this means till I've had time to look and to hear, but I can make a fairly good guess. Whatever it is, I can tell you without either looking or hearing that we're going to fight."

Marcia sat back on the floor. She exposed a pitiful face.

"Fight!" she cried passionately. "Fight? It's all very well for the innocent to fight, but how can the guilty wage battle?"

Nancy looked at the woman she loved—her efficient partner, the being upon whom she had come to depend for hope and help and human companionship when stiff bones and gray days and a sordid stomach and nerves that pulled and muscles that twitched were upon her. With a gesture that was truly regal, she shook open the papers and carefully went through them. Then she looked at the formidable sum total at the bottom. It would practically wipe out the savings of six years for Marcia and cut heavily into her own.

"Do you owe this?" she asked tersely.

Marcia shook her head.

"They're vultures," she said. "They prey equally on the quick and the dead."

Nancy stared at Marcia. The thumb and first finger of her right hand were busy working her lower lip into folds.

"Marcia," she said softly, "you've never told me anything, and I've never asked; but now we're at the place where I must know. So tell me. Were you the mother of a child born of Martin Moreland?"

Marcia promptly and emphatically shook her head.

"But there was a child?" insisted Nancy.

Marcia nodded. "Yes," she said, "there was a child, but I was not his mother. Martin Moreland brought him to me when he couldn't have been more than a few hours old."

"Check!" cried the little milliner in tones of triumph. Then she sprang up. She lifted Marcia to her feet. She kissed her and smoothed her hair. She shoved back the curtains, unlocked the front door and set it wide. Then she returned to her work table, pushed aside the soft feathers and the gay flowers, and taking a big sheet of paper and a tall pencil, she sat down and began asking Marcia searching questions and recording the answers. Inside of an hour she had completed a considerable bill for nursing Jason in infancy, caring for him for sixteen years, washing, mending, nursing, and boarding him.

When she had finished, she went over her work to verify it, and then she looked up at Marcia and said: "Now, then, let the Morelands come on! Let them undertake to collect a bill for the rent of that house for sixteen years! Unless I've lost all my art at figuring, I've got this bill strictly within reason and nearly three times the amount of theirs, which will allow it to be lopped considerably and still make you some profit."

Marcia picked up the sheet and studied it, but her hands shook so that she was forced to lay it upon the table and sit down in order to go over it accurately.

"It is all right," she said. "I haven't a doubt but that in law it will hold, but it spells ruin. I can't go into court with this thing and come out of it unscathed. It means that while I may make him pay it, I must turn over to you my share of the business; I must leave the only home and the people I know, and the only one on earth who loves me, and go somewhere else and start all over again among strangers."

Then Marcia began to cry, terrible sobs that racked and shook her. Again she stretched out helpless hands and again Nancy stood rock bound.

"Now stop!" she said firmly. "Stop it! We haven't got anything to do but send this to Martin Moreland. We must make him think that it was sent by a lawyer. We've got to let him know that we're able to fight, that we will fight. But you can bank on one thing that's certain and sure. He isn't going to explain to the public to whom the child he brought for your care, belonged. He isn't going to want the other deacons of the Presbyterian Church and the directors of the bank and the county officials to know where he got the boy he forced you to take care of. Certainly he isn't going to want to face the question, 'Who's his mother?' You needn't be the least bit afraid. Never in the world will he let that happen. He's just what you said he was—a vulture. He doesn't care whether the meat he lives on is fresh or rotten. He can thrive on either kind equally well."

Marcia sat a long time gazing into the kitchen. It was a strange thing that she could draw comfort from a cook stove and pots and pans. They are not particularly attractive to many people, but they were attractive to Marcia. There are souls in this world so stranded that they are fortunate if they have an animal upon which to lavish their affections; and there are others whose lives are so bleak that they must love mere things—the bed on which they sleep, the chairs on which they sit, the pots and pans in which they cook the food that they eat. And then, pots and pans are a symbol. They do not mean beauty, but they mean utility. They suggest nourishment, strength, and sustenance. They spell home, and home means sheltering walls and sometimes it means love. It meant love to Marcia. As she looked up at Nancy, still in her rock-bound attitude, she saw upon her face a thing that swept a wave of emotion through Marcia's sick soul such as it never before had known. She was not going to be forced to give up the accumulations of years against comfort for age and illness. That meant something. But it did not mean the highest thing. She was still young and strong. She knew that there were several ways in which she could assure bodily comfort. The thing of which she got assurance in that hour was the greatest thing in all this world. It was the assurance that the little milliner would stand by, that she was not going to desert a sinking ship. Whatever happened, her friendship was going to weather; whatever storm broke on her friend, she was going to be the anchor that would hold.

In that hour Marcia deliberately went down on her knees again. She put her arms around the waist of Nancy, she met her eyes frankly, and she purged her soul. Torn beyond control when she had finished the last word of self-condemnation she had to utter, when the last scalding tear she had to shed had burned its way down her cheeks, she pulled open the dress she was wearing, exposing her firm white breast to her friend. Her own eyes were upon it.

"Look," she said, "it looks soft and white, doesn't it, but the dreadful scarlet brand has scorched for years; it's burning there now. It always will. I can see that for your sake, for the sake of the business, I must go on hiding it until I die. Personally, it would be almost a relief to stand up outside our door or before the altar in the church, and tell every one what I have told you."

Nancy Bodkin was doing some crying for herself at that minute, but presently she wiped her eyes and surprised even herself with the joy of her inspiration.

"That isn't necessary," she said. "It wouldn't help in any way. The thing you must do is to go to God. Tell Him what you have told me. Ask His help. Your sin is against God. He will forgive a woman whose greatest fault is that she loved the wrong man; that she loved a man who betrayed her and used her for his purposes when he should have sheltered her and sustained her. God is great and He is merciful."

Nancy helped Marcia to her feet. She led her to the door of her room, and opening it, she shoved her through. "Go and make your peace with God," she said. "I have nothing to forgive you. If He has, He will know about it and He will let you feel His forgiveness and His love."

She shut the door, and going back to her work table, she sat down, and with steady hands, she sheared, twisted, and sewed, and by and by, when Marcia came from her room with peace in her heart and less pain in her eyes, the little milliner almost paralysed her. She held up a thing that was really a creation and she cried gayly: "Go wash and powder your nose and get ready to try this! I believe it's the damnedest best-looking hat that I've ever made!"

CHAPTER XIX

"Rebecca Pronounces Judgment"

The seasons run with swift feet. It was in February that Mahala answered a hasty knock at her door. She jumped into her coat and overshoes and hurried down the road through the snow and the storm of a wild night on the shaking arm of Jason. She could see that the house to which she was going was filled with light. When she entered it, she found Ellen's mother in charge and Doctor Grayson at work. An hour later, through one of those queer turns of fate which no one can explain, it became her part of the thing that was taking place there to carry a small, warm bundle, strongly suggestive of olive oil and castile, and lay it in the arms of Jason.

It seemed to Mahala as she carried Jason his son that the bitterness which at that minute surged up in her heart surpassed anything else she ever had known. She turned from him and went to lay her hand on the head of Ellen. There it was her mission to report that Jason thought his son was fine and wonderful.

By noon the next day she was back in her home. Everything had been done that was necessary. Ellen's mother and Jason could care for her. There was no reason why Mahala might not go back to her little house and again take up her life with her dead. Because that was what Mahala was doing in those days. She was living hourly with her father. At first it had been difficult to vision him in the country house, but now she could see him before the bookcase, at the hearth, in the dining room. Sometimes she dreamed of him, and with the awful reality of dreams, she again heard his voice, her nostrils were filled with the personal odours of his body, every familiar gesture was before her eyes.

Her mother came there, too. Hourly now she stepped down from the frame above the mantel and walked through the rooms, twitching a curtain into place, setting a picture at a different angle, drawing a finger across a polished surface to make sure that no particle of dust had settled there.

In those days when winter was the coldest and the storms raged outside, and the amount of physical exercise required to keep her in good health was difficult to obtain, Mahala paced the rooms of the little house, and beside her walked another of her dead. Jason was there—thoughtful, kind, always taking care of her, always watching that she should be sheltered, that she should be comfortable—but he was a dead Jason. There was no life in him. The living part of him belonged to Ellen. The mouthing little pink bundle lying on Ellen's breast very shortly would be on his feet, holding Jason's hands, making demands of him.

The one thing for which Mahala tried to be thankful in those days was the steady round of duties entailed by living. After Mrs. Ford had gone home, there were days when Ellen was feeling badly and the baby cried, that Mahala went down to Jason's home, and with light step and skilful fingers, straightened out problems that were too much for Ellen, taught her patience and forbearance and the love that ministers, that expends itself and demands little. Then she went back to her house and during the long nights she deliberately turned her pillow where she could look through the window at the storm-whipped arms of the old orchard and watch the elements having their way with the world, rolling on its age-old route around its orbit.

In these days Mahala found that, in her own home, life had simmered to the asking of one question. She did not ask it of God. She had stopped praying when she had been overwhelmed. She asked it of her mental vision of her father: "Why?" She faced the skilfully painted portrait of her mother, and with stiff lips cried to her: "Why?" She asked the walls of each room in the house. She asked the authors of the books she tried to read. She looked from the windows and asked the winds raging past. She asked the moon of night and the first red rays of morning. "Why?" Eternally, "Why?"

When spring had come again and all the world was busy with the old miracle of rejuvenation, when the apple orchard was sweetest and the lilacs were a benediction and the star flowers were shining, when the doors were opened and Nature was trying with all her might to rejuvenate the hearts of men as easily as she pushed welling sap into bud and bloom, one day when Mahala's lips had cried "Why?" to the white pigeons and the bluebirds of the orchard, her question was answered.

A livery conveyance from the village stopped at her door, and in wonderment she watched Albert Rich and the town sheriff, the Presbyterian minister and dear old Doctor Grayson alight from it. She took one swift look at the party as they were coming through the gate, and then, without stopping for thought, she flew to the back door and gave the bell one violent spang. A pause, and then another. It was her pre-arranged call for Jason to come with all speed.

Hearing, Jason said to Ellen: "Something has gone wrong with Mahala. She never rang like that before. I must go."

He dropped a rake that he was mending at the back door, raced across the yard, sprang over the fence, crossed the road, and leaping another fence, took a short cut toward Mahala's back door. As he ran, he could see the carriage, he could see the men going up the walk and crossing the porch, and without knowing why, a sick apprehension sprang in his heart.

He entered the back door and came through the kitchen. He reached the door of the living room as Mahala was offering her guests seats. His first glance was for her. He saw that her face lacked all natural colour and he noticed that she was perfectly controlled, that she was greeting her guests with the graciousness of the lady she had been born to be.

As she returned from laying aside their hats, Albert Rich went to meet her. He deliberately put his arm around her. Then he said: "Mahala, dear, Rebecca Sampson made trouble in the bank to-day. She may have slipped or they may have been rough in putting her out, at any rate, she fell and struck her head a severe blow. She's now lying on the couch in the directors' room and every one agrees that she's quite sane. Her first conscious words were to ask if you found the money that Junior Moreland told her to take from their parlour table and hide in your house for you when no one would see her."

"*Here?* Does she say that she put it *here?*" cried Mahala. Both hands were gripping her heart. She had seemed to shrink, to grow into a helpless, childish thing. The tremors that shook her body were visible through her clothing.

The men were eager in their acquiescence.

"She says," answered the sheriff, "that she put it through a hole in the plaster on the right-hand side of the front door. You're vindicated, Mahala, beyond a doubt in the mind of any one, but it would be better, it would be fine, if we could discover that pocket book."

Jason stood straight in the doorway. His eyes were travelling from the face of one man to another, but they avoided Mahala. Slowly his form tensed, his breathing began to come in short gasps. Albert Rich turned to him.

"Jason," he said, "get an axe. I'm going to break through the wall on the right-hand side of the front door and search the place where Becky says she put that pocket book."

Slowly Jason shook his head. His lips were very stiff, but he managed to speak.

"There's no use," he said. "You'll find nothing there. I mended that lath and plastered that broken place with my own hands."

Suddenly Mahala's head fell forward, and then she lifted it, and as people have done since the beginning of the world in the ultimate agony, she called on God. Her voice was torn and pitiful past endurance. She was calling on God, but she was reaching to Jason, stretching out her hands to him.

"Oh, God!" she cried. "Help me! Won't you please help me? Why couldn't it have been there? Why couldn't vindication have been complete? Oh, God, won't you help me?"

Big tears rolled down her cheeks.

She cried directly to Jason: "Oh, Jason! think! Think hard! Can't you think of any place that it might be?"

She appealed to Doctor Grayson: "You're sure Becky says she brought it *here?*"

"Yes," said Doctor Grayson, "she says you gave her food here, you told her that this was the only home you had, that this was your house."

Mahala slowly nodded her head.

"I did," she said. "I told her that this was the only home I had left."

Again she turned to Jason. "Oh, Jason!" she cried. "Do this much more for me! Find it! Oh, find that pocket book!"

Jason's face was that of a man in fierce physical torture. With one hand he was tearing at the neck of his shirt, trying to pull it open. Suddenly the attention of the entire party centred on him; it became patent to every one that he was on the rack. For a long second he hesitated, staring with wide eyes of anguish at Mahala, then slowly he ran a hand into his pocket. He drew from it a heavy pruning knife. He stepped across the room and lifted from its fastening above the fireplace the oil portrait of Elizabeth Spellman. Setting it to one side, he ran his fingers over the papered wall behind it, feeling for something. When he found it, he inserted the knife, and ran it around a small space that had been papered over. Prying off a light wooden cover, he stepped back. In the opening where a couple of bricks had been removed, lay a long, black bill book.

For one instant a wild light of rejoicing leaped into Mahala's eyes, and then a sick horror overwhelmed her as she looked at Jason. She opened her lips, but no words came. Suddenly she stepped back; both her hands clutched her heart tightly. Unable to endure her gaze further, Jason made a gesture toward the opening. His head fell forward on his breast, and, turning, he staggered from the room.

Mahala recovered herself only with the utmost effort. She stretched one hand toward the sheriff, but her eyes were upon the minister.

Her voice said: "You are the executor of the law. My hands never have touched that pocket book. They never shall. Lift it down, and in the presence of these witnesses, open it."

The sheriff obeyed her. He spread the money, the railroad tickets, and the contents of the pocket book upon the table. The minister, at the call of Mahala's eyes, went to her. He put his arm around her and drew her shivering little body to him with his strength. Looking into her eyes, he said: "Tell us, Mahala, why did Junior Moreland want to ruin you?"

Mahala drew a deep breath that steadied her. "You must ask him," she said, never so true to her best instincts as in that hour.

Albert Rich came to her other side and took hold of her also, because he was human and his heart ached intolerably. Across her, he said to the minister: "Ask me. They were classmates from childhood. She watched the development of his character, day by day. Fashioned as God made her, she could do nothing but loathe him. Repeatedly she refused to marry him. This is her punishment. This is a new demonstration to Ashwater of the power of riches directed by the Morelands."

Mahala thrust her hands wide spread before her. She drew away from the men, who were trying to reinforce her strength with theirs. She said to them: "If all of you are satisfied, will you please go?"

Albert Rich said to her: "Mahala, are you strong enough? Could you endure a trip to town with us? Becky feels that she can't die in peace until she has seen you. She is begging for you constantly."

Mahala assented. "Wait in the carriage," she said. "Give me a few minutes to think, to make myself presentable, and then I will try to go with you."

She hastily straightened her attire, then she went through the back of the house. She found Jason sitting in the kitchen, his face buried in his arms. In tones of cold formality as to a stranger, she said to him: "Becky is asking for me. Will you close and lock the house and then come to the bank after me? They say she is dying, that she feels she cannot go in peace until she has seen me. I am forced to go."

As they drove through the brilliancy of spring along the River Road, the men tried to say kindly things to Mahala. Presently, they realized that she was not hearing them, that they were wasting words.

The outskirts of the town of Ashwater showed that it had been shaken from centre to circumference. Women were running bareheaded across the streets. Men were hastening here and there, and it could be seen that their hands were shaking, that their faces were set, that the expressions upon them more clearly resembled ravenous animals than men. They were calling out to each other, they were breathing threats, they were uttering awful curses. Man was telling man what the hands of the Morelands had done to him. Here was a man whose land had gone delinquent, and before he was able to redeem it, Martin Moreland had taken it from him for a third of its value. Here was a seamstress who had not been able to pay the street taxes in front of her little home, and because she had borrowed from Martin Moreland she had lost her shelter.

Even from the country there were beginning to come teams driven by men whose faces were pictures of outrage. Conspicuous on the village streets was the form of Jimmy Price. He was rushing around with a sickle in one hand, telling every one who would listen what every one else had said. For once in his life he had forgotten to try to make himself ridiculous. In his excitement he became a pathetic thing. He who never had anything to lose was blustering, threatening, and wildly gesticulating over the wrongs of others. Men who had lost heavily, many of them the savings of a lifetime, were in a different mood. They were gathered in grim consultation. They were passing from house to house, in harsh tones they were making sure of their grievances: "Just what was the sum he skinned you out of, Robert?" "Did you say, John, your wife needn't have died if you hadn't been forced to move her in mid winter when she'd just had the baby?"

They were remembering, they were recalling, they were computing, they were sowing the germs of a mob spirit right and left, but their work was certain and methodical. Unmolested, the boys of Ashwater had been busy. As the carriage came down the street, Mahala could see great streaks of yellow paint smeared across the front of the bank. The bronze dogs, so proudly referred to by Martin Moreland as the "watch dogs of the Treasury," had been crudely muzzled with heavy wire, the yellow paint had been liberally used on them. Some one had broken off their tails and stuck them between their legs; the rough stumps were festooned with tin tomato and peach cans.

When the carriage stopped in front of the bank, the party could only force their way a step at a time to the door. At sight of Mahala pandemonium broke loose. Here was the most tangible thing upon which they could lay their hands. On her they might give their imaginations free rein, with justice. Nothing could be done that could ever, in any degree, atone for the misery through which she had passed.

She had thought that she was keeping her set white face straight ahead and pressing forward as swiftly as she could force her way, but as she neared the door she saw an arresting sight that caused her to pause and turn, looking the mob in the face. At first glance a spasm of fear shook her. She was forced to look penetrantly to recognize some of the faces she had known all her life. They were so distorted, so unrecognizable in the spasms of emotion now possessing them. Swift as memory flies, she recalled a few of the stories in the hearts of some of the men in the front of that circle, and yet, pressing nearest of all to the building, with disarranged clothing, disordered hair, and almost frothing at the mouth, pranced Jimmy Price. Encouraged by the growl behind him as Mahala paused, he was the first man to lift a hand and crash a brick he carried through the heavy plate glass of the bank window. Even as the glass cracked and broke there came to Mahala the realization that it was very likely that Jimmy Price never had deposited ten dollars in the First National at one time in his life. He never had owned real estate, and the thought came to her even in that crisis, that among the mob probably there were many others like Jimmy taking a vicarious revenge when no personal wrong had been done them. Her sense of justice and fair play came to life instantly.

She lifted her hand and cried out to the mob: "Wait! For the love of God, wait! Learn the truth and act sincerely. Nothing can right the past for some of us, but I beg that you will wait!"

The mob drew back slightly, but it did not disperse. In alternating waves of quiet and of flaming anger as some new recruit from the suburbs, or the country, arrived and began detailing his grievances, it surged back and forth before the bank. When the door was unlocked from the inside, Mahala entered and followed the men to the directors' room. As she stepped through the door, she saw Rebecca lying pillowed on a leather couch. All the look of childish unconcern had left her face. As she turned toward Mahala it could plainly be seen that she was in possession of her reason. She was a middle-aged woman, tried and hurt past endurance. Her breath was dragging heavily. One hand was fingering nervously at the edge of the leather, the other tightly gripped the osier, the white flag lying across her knees.

Swiftly Mahala knelt beside her. She tried to smile. She opened her lips and she was almost surprised to hear her own voice asking evenly: "You wanted me, Becky?"

"Yes, oh, yes!" cried Rebecca. "The cloud has lifted but it's a strange thing that there remains in my memory every least little thing that ever happened to me. I know

now what happened to the best friend I ever had in Ashwater, when I did what Junior Moreland told me would please you so."

"It's all right now, Becky. Don't try to talk," whispered Mahala, taking the straying hand in both of hers and holding it close against her breast. "We found the pocket book. It's all right now."

"But I must talk!" panted Rebecca. "I must hear you say that you forgive me. You had been kind to me, you had fed me, you told me that the little house on the River Road was your home. I thought I was repaying you for your promise to help me in my search. I thought I was doing a thing that would surprise and please you. Junior said you would be so surprised when you found the money in your home."

In bitterness Mahala bowed her head over Rebecca's hand. For an instant her mind worked over that thought. The sardonic humour of Junior saying that she would be surprised when the money was found in her home! Certainly she would have been if it had been found there. A chill shook her as she paused a moment concentrating on the quality of Junior's mind. He must have known that to have the money found in her home would kill Elizabeth Spellman as cruelly as death could be inflicted; that it would possibly fasten lasting disgrace on her; yet he had done his best to accomplish those things. Recalled by Rebecca's clinging hand, she tried to comfort her.

She said to her: "Since every one knows now that I never touched the pocket book, it's all right, Becky. Don't try to talk any more. Lie quiet so that you will soon be better."

But Rebecca shook her head.

"First I had to have your forgiveness," she said. "Now I must see Martin Moreland."

Mahala turned to Albert Rich. "Step to Mr. Moreland's private office and ask him to come here," she said.

Albert Rich assented, but he returned in a minute saying that Mr. Moreland refused to come. The wave of whiteness that swept Rebecca's face, and the spasm of pain that shook her body, both reacted upon Mahala. She lifted her head.

"Mr. Moreland has no option," she said steadily. "He is no longer the controlling factor in the life of this town."

She nodded to the sheriff and to Albert Rich. "Once he worked his will on me without authority. Now it is my turn. Bring him here."

Forced by a strong man on either side of him, Martin Moreland stood at the feet of Rebecca Sampson. For what seemed an endless time to the tensely silent people waiting in the room, Rebecca's eyes studied Martin Moreland.

Then she cried to him: "That my soul may pass from this foot-sore body in peace, tell me, Martin Moreland, was I a scarlet woman?"

Up to that time Martin Moreland had refused to look at Rebecca. He had kept his eyes turned toward the doorway, to the ceiling. At that appeal, in spite of his intentions, something in his inner consciousness forced him to meet her look. To Mahala, at that minute, Rebecca was appealingly beautiful. The mass of her waving fair hair had been loosened and spread over the pillow around her in the examination of her injury. The maturity that realization had brought to her face only gave to it greater appeal. No matter how widely she had journeyed, or how inclement the weather, she always had kept her person with the neat daintiness of any fine lady. It seemed to the onlookers that Moreland was moved to some degree of remorse. There seemed to be forced from him, in spite of the effort he was making for self-preservation, the cry: "No! No! You were my wife. The divorce was fraudulent, not the marriage."

The rigours of Rebecca's body eased. She sank back with a deep breath and two big tears trickled from her eyes. But almost immediately she roused again. She drew from Mahala's clasp the hand she was holding and stretched it to Martin Moreland.

"My baby!" she cried. "What did you do with my baby? I want him! Oh, Martin, I want to see him before I die!"

Martin Moreland drew back. Slowly he shook his head.

Rebecca appealed to Mahala. She began to cry in a pitiful, broken way, her body torn by physical emotion added to the difficulty in breathing that the concussion was making.

"Mahala," she begged, "you know the weary years that I've hunted and I've hunted. You're the only one I ever told that I ever had a little baby—a darling little baby—and Martin Moreland took him away, and I couldn't find him! You said you'd help me. Beg him, oh, beg him, to give me back my baby!"

Mahala arose. She took one step toward Martin Moreland and slightly extended a hand.

"Mr. Moreland," she said, "I'd die on the rack before I'd ask anything of you for myself. Because of my word to Becky, I'm asking you now to give her back her baby."

Mahala did not realize that the baby for which Rebecca was asking must be a man at that time. She was visioning a little pink bit of humanity bundled in white as it must have been when Rebecca had lost it. For an instant she stood thinking. She realized that some one had taken a place beside her, and looking up, she saw that Jason had been admitted to the room, and was standing near enough to reinforce her strength with his.

The dying woman saw him also, and instantly she stretched her hand toward him.

"You have always been my friend," she said. "Help me only this once more."

"What shall I do, Rebecca?" asked Jason.

"When he was a tiny thing, only just born, Martin Moreland took my baby," she said. "I only had him once for a minute. Make him give him back to me before I must die."

Jason stood looking in a dazed way from Martin Moreland to Rebecca. Then he looked at Mahala as she spoke: "For the love of God, Martin Moreland, tell Rebecca what you did with her baby!"

She dropped on her knees beside the couch and again gathered to her breast the hand that Rebecca was reaching to Martin Moreland.

Jason lifted his head. He shook it, and his shoulders twitched as he stepped forward, his face ashen and cut deep in lines of torture. Throwing out his arms, he pushed back the other men and closed on the old banker. With a powerful hand he gripped one of his arms and drew him nearer to Rebecca. There was something terrible in his voice, something final and ultimate, something discernibly deadly as he ground out the question: "Is this woman's child living or dead?"

Martin Moreland was pulling back. He had taken one look at Jason's face, and what he had seen appalled him. His lips were white and stiff; it was only a whisper, the answer he made: "Living."

Then Jason demanded: "Do you know where he is?"

The banker nodded.

Jason gripped him more firmly. He drew him closer and then he said in tones of finality: "You shall tell Becky where her child is."

Martin Moreland shook his head.

"You shall tell her," said Jason, "or I'll take you out and explain to the mob that is howling for your blood."

Again Martin Moreland shook his head.

Suddenly Jason swung him around; he shoved him in front of him across the room and into the hall from the back end of which there could be seen the big plate glass window, shattered at the top, and the glass door. Pressed against what remained of the broken glass of the window and the door, and reinforced by the width of the packed street behind them, there were faces topping the forms of men, yet one scarcely would have recognized them as the faces of men,—menacing faces by the hundred, upon the bodies of men who had been men of peace, men of patience, godly men. They were farmers and business men and day labourers. They had been outraged to a degree that had turned them into a compact mob of snarling, blood-thirsty beasts. In their hands could be seen revolvers, rifles, sickles; some of them carried axes, some of them bricks and stones, or clubs. At the sight of the banker a snarling cry broke from them and they surged forward until the front of the building shook with their impact.

Galvanized with terror, Moreland summoned strength to break from Jason's grasp and rush back toward the directors' room. But Jason was at his heels as he reached the door, he caught and whirled him around, once more forcing him to face Rebecca. She struggled to a sitting posture and stretched out both hands in a last appeal.

"My baby! Give me back my baby. Let me have him only one minute before I die!"

Martin Moreland shook his ghastly white head.

Then Jason gripped his other arm and brought his strength to bear until the old banker shrank and winced. Rebecca was rapidly losing strength. Great tears began running down her cheeks.

"Martin, I loved you so," she pleaded. "Don't you remember that I gave you everything? And you took all I had to give and you took my baby, too, and you threw me away and God punished me. He made me an outcast and a wanderer, while you had everything. It wasn't fair. I've spent my life searching for my baby, and I can't find him——"

Suddenly the beast broke in Doctor Grayson, in Albert Rich, in the sheriff, in the cashier. With black menace on their faces, they crowded up to reinforce Jason. The old banker looked around wildly for an avenue of escape; and there was none. He hesitated an instant longer and then he lifted a shaking hand as he said: "If you will have it, then, there is your baby." He indicated Jason.

Rebecca lifted herself free of all support. She stared at Martin Moreland and then she studied Jason. Her eyes seemed to leap to his face and to cling there. A desperate inquiry was running in waves over her tortured face. She began to see lines that she recognized, a likeness to herself in the colouring of the hair and the eyes, suggestions of the lean face of Moreland, reproduced in Jason. A look of wonder crept into her face, and then one of horror. She drew back from Martin Moreland, a look of repulsion on her face, on every line of her figure.

"You devil!" she cried to him. "You let me walk the roads of earth every day seeking my baby, every day seeing him; experiencing his kindness, and not knowing he was mine. That knowledge would have cured my sick brain, would have saved me——"

She paused from weakness, but an instant later she gathered her forces and raised her hand.

"The curse of God shall fall as heavily on you as it has on me," she cried. "It is His justice. He wills that you shall now take up the white flag that I have been forced to carry every day for the salvation of my soul, and for the salvation of yours you shall carry it for the remainder of your life! After all, you are the worse off of the two. I lost my baby; you have lost your soul. Now you shall go and seek it."

She thrust the white flag into his hands and said to the men: "Let him go free. This is the work of God. Start him on his journey."

The men stepped back. With bowed head, the flag in his hand, Martin Moreland turned and sought what safety was promised him in the shelter of his private room. There were men in his employ awaiting him there, and they watched him with repulsed eyes as he tottered into the room carrying the white emblem. Freed from the

228

torturing hands that had gripped him, he tried to think. He made an effort to recover the ground that their faces told him he had lost in their estimation. Mechanically, he made his way to his chair. The absurd flag was in his hands. What would he do with it? He glanced around and then he thrust the holder into an urn standing on a bookcase behind his chair. It was an unfortunate disposal to make of the flag, for when he dropped into his accustomed seat, it was hanging directly over his head, its snowy whiteness stained by contact with the street and with the blood of the woman who for many years had borne it, a self-imposed penance for the easement of her soul.

In the directors' room, Rebecca lifted her face to Jason. She stretched out her shaking arms.

"Jason!" she cried, "do you think this is the truth? Are you my baby? Oh, are you my baby? And if you are, will you come to me only a minute before I go?"

Jason came crashing to his knees beside her. He slid an arm under her body and caught her shoulders in a firm grip.

"Yes, I think it is the truth," he said. "I believe you, and I believe him. In my heart I feel that you are my mother."

He gathered her into his arms and kissed her face and her hands while she made her crossing.

CHAPTER XX

"The Decision Marcia Reached"

When Marcia and the little milliner finished compiling the bill for the length of time that Marcia had boarded and cared for Jason, they did not know what to do with it. They were in doubt as to whether they should present it at once or wait until the Morelands made their move and then use the bill to counteract it. They discussed every phase of the situation repeatedly. They waited what seemed to them a long time, and at last it was Marcia who reached a decision for both of them.

"I simply refuse to live in this uncertainty any longer," she said to Nancy. "I'm going to take this bill to Ashwater. Albert Rich is the best lawyer there. In the old days I did a great deal of work for Mrs. Rich. I believe that he is a considerate man. I know that he has no cause to love Martin Moreland. I'm going to tell him what I think is necessary. I'm going to ask his opinion. I'm tired shivering and shaking and being tortured with fear. I realize that Martin Moreland's hand is heavy, but after all, there are two things that are stronger than he—one is public opinion and the other is God. Both of them would be against him if the truth were known."

Nancy thought deeply.

"You are right," she said. "It isn't fair that he should keep us shivering and shaking and make our days unhappy and our nights a terror. Go to Ashwater. Tell this Albert Rich what you think is necessary. I can't see that you need to go into full detail. Make him understand only what is essential."

"All right," said Marcia, "I'm going."

Nancy put the kettle to boil and brewed a cup of strong tea while Marcia was dressing, for it could be seen that she was labouring under heavy mental strain. Nancy followed her to the corner where Marcia took the daily omnibus that ran between the two towns. She kissed her good-bye and clung to her hands with a reassuring grip. After she had gone back to the shop, she condemned herself that she had allowed Marcia to go alone. She felt niggardly. Why did people let their fear of losing a few pennies intervene when matters concerning their hearts and their souls were at stake? What was money that it should make such dreadful things of men and women? After all, men had made money; it was an emanation of their brain. It was not one of the things that God had made. It was an invention by which man, himself, had put upon his soul such shackles as the Almighty never would have imposed. She wondered why she had not locked the door and let people think what they would. Was there any woman in Bluffport who needed a hat so badly that she could not have waited one day while Nancy sat beside Marcia and gave her the comfort of the grip of her hand, the sound of her voice, the chance to say a word here and there that might have distracted her mind from its burden?

Nancy sat trying to think how she would feel if her soul were stained with the red secret that she realized never ceased to burn and to eat into the consciousness of her friend. And because she was her friend, and because she had learned to love Marcia as she loved no one else, the big tears rolled down her cheeks and several times that day she sewed their stains under deftly folded velvet.

When Marcia stepped from the omnibus at the courthouse corner in Ashwater, she realized that some disaster had overtaken the town. Here and there she saw women weeping and wringing their hands. Little children scuttled past with terrified faces. Half-grown boys went running in one direction, their faces small mirrors of their elders', their arms loaded with sticks, with bricks, with stones. Men hurried past, some of them carrying antiquated firearms on their shoulders, flintlocks, and old army muskets; some of them with guns of modern make, with revolvers; and there were men in that crowd who carried a grubbing hoe, the blade of a scythe, a hickory "knockmaul," or an axe.

She had difficulty in finding any one who would stop long enough to tell her about the brain-storm that was sweeping Ashwater, but soon she had the essentials of what had occurred from people with whom she talked upon the street. She struggled for self-control, but in spite of herself she grew terribly excited over the recitation of the tragedy that the Morelands had worked in the lives of Rebecca Sampson, of Mahala, of Jason, of hundreds of other people.

She had known Rebecca all the years of her residence in Ashwater. She at once understood that Martin Moreland had lured her, Marcia, from her home in an adjoining county to the little house in which she had lived for so many years, for the sole purpose of using her as his tool in taking care of Jason. He had made love to her in the most alluring manner possible to him, and hers had been a nature that gave without question and without fear. For him she had sacrificed relatives and friends and gone with him willingly. Both the questioning and the fear she now knew came later, and in an intensified form. What she realized was, that, through all the best years of her life, under cover of a menial task, she had been merely a servant for Martin Moreland. It was not true that he was bound in an unhappy marriage from which he was vainly striving to free himself, as he had told her in the beginning. He had never meant to free himself. He had never intended to offer her marriage and an honourable position. He had planned to take everything she had to give; to have her take care of the boy, for whom she had always struggled to keep from forming an attachment, because the threat had hung over her that any minute he chose Martin Moreland would take him away.

Her mind was milling over her own problem; there then came the problem of Rebecca Sampson, and she saw, that even before he had determined on the wreck of her life, Rebecca had gone down; yet these people were saying that he had admitted that he was legally married to her. Rebecca had been weak, a clinging thing, a tender, delicate girl; yet she had a spirit and a resistance that he could not break; so he had been forced to marry her. No one on the streets knew from where she had come or who her people were. They remembered that a young thing lacking mentality was sheltered by a little house in the outskirts. The few who had tried to make friends with her in the beginning had been repulsed with insane spasms so menacing that they had allowed her to go her way, as people in that day were permitted to go, even though it was known that they lacked balanced mentality.

Finally, in her mental milling, Marcia reached Mahala, and her soul sickened over the things that people on the street were saying. By the hour she had handled Mahala's little undergarments and wash dresses. She had mended the delicate laces and the embroideries that Elizabeth Spellman's fingers had fashioned. Through the papers and Bluffport gossip, she had heard of the tragedy that had overtaken her. She had talked it over with Nancy, and she had said to her: "To save my life, I cannot believe that Mahala Spellman ever laid her fingers upon anything that did not belong to her. There must have been some reason, there must have been some plan on the part of the Morelands to ruin her. If there was property they could get by doing it, the wreck of a woman's life would not stop them."

Now the motive was furnished. Albert Rich had not hesitated, when the crisis came, to tell people why Junior wanted to do anything that would hurt and humiliate Mahala.

Finally, she reached Jason. She found herself saying aloud: "Jason was a good boy. If I had been permitted, I could have made life different for him."

Not knowing what the outcome of the trouble in Ashwater would be, Marcia felt that since the Morelands had come into the open and were doing terrible things to other people, her time would soon come. They would crush her as they had crushed Rebecca, Mahala and her mother, Mr. Spellman and the other men who had fallen into their power in a financial way—these other men who were raging up and down before the courthouse block in the main business square of the town, like blood-thirsty hyenas.

It seemed to Marcia that in order to collect her thoughts, she must get away from people, she must go where her mind would not be diverted by what she was seeing and hearing on the streets. She had thought that she might find refuge in the office of Albert Rich, and she had gone there, but it was locked and when she inquired for him, she had been told that he was in the bank. No one knew what was happening there or when he could be seen. Then Marcia followed an impulse she could not define, did not realize that she was following. Her face turned to a familiar direction; her feet carried her on a well-known path. She went straight to the house in the outskirts where she and Jason had spent so many years together. The whole place had been changed. It was now comfortable. It was gay with paint; there was grass in the dooryard; there were flowers blooming in small round and square beds and lining the inside of the new fence. There was a carefully tended garden, but she could see no one and hear no one as she paced up and down before it. She thought that the people, who evidently were living happily there, must have been drawn down town by the excitement.

Being very tired, Marcia went slowly up the walk. She sat on a chair on the veranda shaded by the big, widely branching maple tree, and there she tried to think. It was quiet and a robin was singing in the branches, but she found that her brain, her heart and her blood, were in such turmoil that she was unable to sit still. So she left the veranda, and following the street to where it reached the country, she took up a foot path across a meadow and at last she entered the wood behind the house where Jason had taken refuge as a child.

Tired out at last, she sat on a log in the stillness of the deep wood, and there she tried again to think. But she found that instead of thinking, she was seeing things. As she looked at the dark floor of the forest with the great trees, the thickness of the bushes, she began to see a vision of the night of horror that a terrified boy must have spent there when he fled before the wrath of Martin Moreland. As if she really had shared that night with him she saw the things that had tortured him. She visioned his return to the deserted house and his grief and loneliness when he had found himself abandoned. She remembered what she had been told of the success that he had made of life, of how he had prospered in partnership with Peter Potter, and how his love of land had culminated in his efforts for Mahala and himself.

Into her vision there came the pathetic figure of Rebecca, hiding the bloom and the beauty of her young face, proclaiming herself everywhere she went with her self-imposed emblem of purity, trying to convey to others the belief that possessed her that her soul was white even as she suffered torments in the fear that it was scarlet. Marcia thought of the long path over which Rebecca had journeyed. She even tried a mental estimate of the hundreds of miles that one woman's feet had travelled, driven in insane unrest from point to point. She recalled having been told that in three different states the white flag had been seen, a voice had been bravely lifted exhorting every one to acknowledge the love of the Saviour, His power to heal. Marcia, in imagination, saw Rebecca's waving banner gleaming in the light, her tireless eyes always searching from side to side, looking at the arms of every person carrying a child, peering into the little buggies in which women dragged after them the babies they had brought into life through love, and were permitted to keep. She thought of Rebecca a long time and wondered who her people might have been and where her home might be; she thought of the price that she had paid to protect her honour, and very slowly a resolve began forming in Marcia's heart.

Into her vision Mahala came flying down the village street, her feet scattering the gold and red leaves of the maples of autumn, her broad hat hanging across her throat by its ties, her pretty, wide skirts blown around her, as she dexterously rolled a gay hoop before her. She thought of the girl's youth and her beauty, and of how she had been stripped of her parents, her home, her friends, and worse than all that, of her honour.

Then Marcia saw a woman coming toward her through the forest, a woman of her own height and form, a woman of her own face, but she wore a long, trailing robe of scarlet, and she was lost. Her outstretched hands seemed to be feeling their way, her eyes were not efficient; they were looking up, but they were not helping her feet to find the path. Sometimes as Marcia saw her in a shaft of sunlight, there was the hope in her heart that the stumbling creature might find the way; sometimes she saw her standing lost in deep darkness, but always one hand was covering her heart, and always she was stumbling over the scarlet robe that trailed around her and seemed to creep up to her arms and her shoulders like the hot scorching of a flame.

Finally, the figures of the two Morelands came through the forest. They were like giants that had broken into the wood. They did not seem to be made of flesh and blood; they did not seem to be men like Mahlon Spellman and Albert Rich and Doctor Grayson and the Presbyterian minister; they seemed to be made of bronze or iron, while their hands were huge, without hesitation crushing little children, frail women, and weaker men; they reached out and wrested from people their homes, their most precious possessions, and with heavy feet they trampled upon everything that came in their path.

Then she saw the son leave the father and advance toward her, his unsparing hands outstretched, his feet ready to trample, on his face the sneer that had been there when he had entered her place of business and found enjoyment in dealing the blow that had struck the light from her eyes and hope from her heart.

Suddenly, Marcia arose and slipped through the wood in the dark, inconspicuous dress she had selected to wear. When she came to the open, she was amazed to find that it was night. Fully half the day she had struggled alone in the forest. She came from it with one determination fixed in her mind. She went to the business part of the town, being unnoticed among the throngs that still crowded the streets, until she reached the bank. She was familiar with the back part of it. She watched her chance, slipped down the alley, climbed the back stairs, and tried the door. It was locked, but she easily climbed through the open window into the room that bore Junior's name above the side stairs.

The flares of light on the street lit the office intermittently. She walked around the room. She went to Junior's big desk; she sat down in his chair in front of it. She looked over the books and the litter of papers that were piled on it. She moved slowly and deliberately. Then she began opening the drawers in front of her. In the top right-hand one lay a big revolver. It seemed to fascinate her. She picked it up and fitted it to her hand. She laid her fingers upon the trigger. Then she heard a rush of footsteps coming up the inside stairway from the private room of Martin Moreland. Snatching up the revolver, she shoved the drawer shut, and running across the room, entered a closet the door of which was standing slightly ajar.

234

CHAPTER XXI

"Whatsoever a Man Sows"

Jason remained with Mahala and Rebecca in the directors' room of the bank as long as there was life in Rebecca's body. After that he spent some time in consultation as to what was to be done. With his own hands he carried Rebecca from the bank to the rooms of the undertaker. When he had finished the things that required immediate attention, he went back to the bank and demanded admittance to the private room of the president; but the door was locked. Then he inquired for Junior and found that no one knew where he was. Suspecting that he might be in hiding in his room above the bank, Jason went around the block and down the alley. He crept up the back stairway and going to the window which looked into Junior's room, he saw him sitting before his table. He seemed to be leaning forward, and was so still that Jason fancied that he might be completely exhausted or even asleep.

He stepped through the window, and walking around the desk, placed himself in front of Junior. He saw that Junior was crouched in his chair; that there was a ghastly expression on his face. A revolver was lying on the table in front of him. His left hand was gripping his clothing that he was pressing hard over the region of his heart. In the air two predominant taints were mingling. Either of them was sickening. About the combination there was a nausea that shook Jason on his feet, but he braced his hands on the table, and leaning forward, he tried to stare deep into Junior's eyes.

Junior smiled at him in a stiff, set way that was disarming. The first time his lips moved, Jason could not catch what he was saying. He leaned closer, and then he heard distinctly: "You have come to settle with me?"

Jason nodded grimly. He studied Junior an instant longer and then he said quietly: "With my naked hands I'm going to tear you limb from limb!"

To his surprise, Junior nodded in agreement.

Jason continued: "And when I have finished with you, I am going to do the same thing to your horrible father."

Surprise arrested Jason as he saw Junior's lips draw back over his teeth in a stiff smile, a stiff, set smile, and yet there was something about him, about the wave of the hair around his white face, about the light in his eyes, that was bonny. He must have been a beautiful baby. His mother might have been excused for loving him to idolatry.

Junior's voice was hoarse, scarcely understandable: "You're too late," he said. "A woman got ahead of you."

Jason rounded the corner of the table. He seized the coat which Junior was holding to his side. Then both of them heard a battering on the outer door. Both of them recognized the voice of Mahala crying: "Jason! For God's sake let me in!"

Jason withdrew his hands from Junior and stared down at him, and then he looked at the door. But Junior met his eyes, and gathering his forces, he said quietly: "Let her in. It is her right to be present at the finish of the Morelands."

Slowly Jason crossed the room and unlocked the door. Mahala rushed inside and Jason slammed shut the door after her, relocking it. He could almost feel the steps rocking from the weight of the men crowded upon them. Mahala's eyes raced over Jason from head to foot and a breath of relief escaped her. Then she turned to Junior. She saw his ghastly face; she saw a slow red spread over the hand that was gripping his side. She saw the revolver on the table before him, and she cried out in horror: "Oh, Jason! Am I too late to keep you from blackening your soul?"

Junior gathered his remaining forces. He made a brave struggle to straighten in his chair. The smile that he meant to be attractive was ghastly. There was something beyond description in his tones: "Mahala, you've been a long time coming," he said to the terrified girl. "Pardon my bad manners, I would stand to welcome you if I could."

Mahala watched him in fascinated wonder and again that awful smile flashed across his face.

"Don't look so horrified," he said to her. "This is not fratricide."

He lifted his right hand and grasping the revolver, drew it toward him. "I have the honour to inform you," he said, "that at the eleventh hour I have had the decency to remove myself from the world for the express purpose of saving a lady and my dear brother the disagreeable task. In about three minutes, Mahala, I'm going to be a very dead man."

A door near the closet opened and Martin Moreland hurried into the room. In a panic of terror, he rushed to Junior, calling in a high, strained voice: "Up, boy, up! This is no time to sleep! The mob is hot after our blood! The mob! They mean business, I tell you! They're going to beat us and strangle us like dogs!"

He rushed to Junior, seized him by the shoulder and dragged him to a sitting posture. "Wake up, Junior!" he cried. "Wake up!"

There was still life in Junior. With a gasp and a rattle, he answered his father: "Too late, Dad, I've finished this in my own way. They can't get me, because I'm not here."

Then he relaxed, and what might have been a beautiful and a gallant spirit took its flight.

Seeing the revolver clasped in Junior's hand, and realizing what he had said and what the blood-soaked side and hand meant, Martin Moreland stood still. The room was filled with the roar of angry voices. The door was shivering under the blows that were being trained against it. He raced across the room to take refuge in the closet. He jerked open the door and stood facing Marcia looking at him with cold, relentless eyes. In his fear and agony, he did not realize that she was a living woman; it never occurred to him that she could be standing there in flesh and blood. He thought what he was seeing was an avenging spirit. He drew back, overcome with horror, and then suddenly he dropped on his knees and reaching up his hands to her, he began to pray as he should have prayed to the Mother of God. He begged her to forgive him, to have mercy; he implored her to restore to him the life of his beloved son.

Looking down at him, in a tone of utter finality, Marcia suddenly began to quote: "'Whatsoever a man soweth, that shall he also reap. For he that soweth to his flesh shall of the flesh reap corruption.'"

Under the lash of her pointing finger and her white face of accusation, the last trace of reason fled the brain of the old banker. He shrank back from her, and cowering on the floor, began jabbering incoherently.

Marcia stepped from the closet and faced Jason and Mahala. Instantly, they recognized each other. Jason left Mahala's side and went to Marcia.

"You?" he cried in bewilderment. "Did Junior shoot himself to save you from having blood on your soul?"

"Yes, Jason," answered Marcia. "Junior knew that I already had enough sin on my soul."

Jason cried out in protest: "No! No! Your soul always has been white."

Marcia held out her hands. She bowed her head, but presently she lifted her face and made her confession.

"No, Jason," she said deliberately, "I gave myself to the man I had learned to love in defiance of everything. God knows that I have had, and shall continue to have through all the days of my life, my punishment. Maybe He will forgive me some day. But, Jason, will you forgive me now for your unloved childhood? I never dared teach you to love me, but I do feel that my chance with God would be better, if you would say that you forgive me before I make my appeal to Him."

Jason took her in his arms. He ran his hand under her chin and lifted her face. He laid his lips on her forehead.

"Don't cry, Marcia, it's all right," he said quietly.

There was no time to say more. The outer door would give way any minute. Martin Moreland crept to the feet of Mahala, whimpering like a frightened dog. He kept working her body between him and Jason.

Mahala looked at him in sick dismay. "We must get him out of here," she said to Jason.

"Let them have him!" cried Jason. "His blood belongs to a hundred men in that crowd, only God knows to how many women."

Mahala looked down at Martin Moreland, crouching, fawning. "Stand up!" she cried suddenly; and he obeyed. "Did you come here by an inside stairway?" she asked.

Martin Moreland drew a ring from his pocket, but his shaking fingers could only indicate the key. He turned to the door by which he had entered. Mahala opened it and said to Jason: "You and Marcia take him down to his private office. I'll come in a minute."

When the door closed after them, Mahala drew the lock and opened the outside door so that the sheriff and the men crowding the stairs could come into the room. She indicated Junior. "There is one of the men you want," she said, "but he is out of your reach."

She pointed to the revolver lying near his right hand. "He admitted to three of us and his father that he took his own life," she said, "which is his way of acknowledging his guilt and showing that he was too big a coward to endure himself, what he put upon me—— But let that go, the debt is paid now."

As she talked, Mahala backed toward the door to the inner stairway. When she reached it she added: "I was here when Martin Moreland heard Junior say he had shot himself and then he saw a ghost, and his brain gave way. The father is as far past your vengeance as the son. He is a cringing maniac. You people must go home quietly. Your work is finished for you."

She swiftly stepped through the door and hurriedly locked it after her, running down the stairs. At the door to the private office she stood dazed. Martin Moreland, with shaking hands and babbling voice, was exhorting Jason and Marcia to pass under the white flag in the exact words of Rebecca, but there was no light of reason in his eyes.

Mahala looked at him a long time. Then she said to Jason: "Both of them have escaped you, and for your sake, it is best. Come on, we will take him home. No mob will attack an insane man, and once we have taken him to his home, our share of this is finished. Bring him along."

"Wait a minute," said Jason. He turned to Marcia. "There is no necessity for you to face the mob and be connected with this," he said. He stretched his hand toward Mahala. "Give me those keys until I find the one that fits the back door. As soon as I let Marcia out, I will come back and do what you wish."

As soon as Jason returned, Mahala went through the directors' room and down the hall where she was in sight of the mob. As soon as they saw her, quiet fell upon them. She advanced to the front door, and unlocking it, she threw it wide. Then she stepped out, lifting her hands for silence. Before she had time to speak, the sheriff came down the outer stairway and took up his place beside her. At sight of him, a babel of cries broke from the mob and they surged forward, shouting: "Where are they?"

Mahala began to speak. When they heard her voice, silence again fell on the mob.

"Men and women of Ashwater, I have this to tell you," she said in a clear, cold voice. "I admit the justice of your anger, but none of you has so great cause against the Morelands as I have. I admit that they have escaped me, and I am here to tell you that they have escaped you. The sheriff and the men accompanying him found Junior lying in his room. He has made the great crossing by his own hand. He admitted to three of us, and in the presence of his father, that he had taken his own life. That was his admission of guilt. When his father realized this and turned from it to see a ghostly spectre of his past standing before him, a strain that must have been of long duration, gave way. Dying, Rebecca Sampson cursed him and declared that the punishment God had meted out to him was to spend the remainder of his life carrying the white flag and preaching the doctrine of purity as her conscience has forced her to do all these years among us. Coming from the sight of Junior's ghastly face, his father saw the flag that Becky had decreed that he should carry. He had brain enough to recognize the justice of the obligation. He is standing in the directors' room with it now. I beg that you will agree with me that this is finished. I beg that you will stand back quietly and let him pass; let us lead him to his home and turn him over to another woman who does not deserve punishment, yet who will be bitterly punished by the sins of the Morelands. Men of Ashwater, will you let an insane man pass?"

Slowly the faces of the mob changed. The snarling anger, the hatred, began to fade. A few in the immediate foreground stepped back. Others held their places. Suddenly, Mahala leaned forward. "If you will let him pass unmolested," she said, "I will promise you this. A committee shall be appointed, headed by Albert Rich, and the claims of each one of you and your papers shall be carefully investigated, and where wrongs have been committed you shall have back your property. I know that Mrs. Moreland will agree to this, and I know that the courts of the county will compel it. Now, will you let us pass?"

Slowly the mob fell back. Mahala turned and beckoned to the doorway. A minute later there appeared in it the shaking form of Martin Moreland. His clothing was in disorder, his white hair disarranged; his face was ghastly. With his left hand he was clinging to Jason, who could scarcely support him; in the right he was clutching the osier that bore the white flag, at that minute stained with the blood from Rebecca Sampson's broken head. The sheriff stepped to his side and assisted Jason. Between them he advanced to the steps leading to the sidewalk. Fear had fled the face of Martin Moreland with the going of his reason. In still amazement the mob saw him swing over them the blood-stained banner and heard his voice, flat and toneless, begin a sort of chant in the exact words with which Rebecca had familiarized them through many long years: "Behold the emblem of purity! Clean hearts may pass under with God's blessing. Come, ye workers of darkness, wash your hearts clean by passing under the white flag!"

Slowly the look of hate and of anger faded from the faces of the people. There is in the average mob at bottom a sense of justice. They are moved to the course they take by indignation over a great wrong, but there is always the possibility of their being swayed quickly, as they were swayed at that minute by the fact that Martin Moreland was insane. Had he stood there, clothed in his right mind, they would have fallen upon him and torn him like beasts. Bereft of his reason, he was a helpless, childish thing. Not one of them cared to touch his soiled, repulsive body. Silently they drew back; they allowed him to go down the steps and to make his way toward his home unmolested. There was a look more of pity than of anger upon their faces as they saw his shaking hands, his tottering step, and heard the high, strained quality of the voice that besought every one he met to pass under the white flag.

CHAPTER XXII

"Behind the Lilac Wall"

As soon as it was possible for Mahala to escape from the Moreland residence, she left Ashwater and was driven back to her home. She sought it instinctively as a shelter. It seemed to her that the River Road was unending, that she never again would see the light of her house; and because there was no light when she reached it, she was surprised at last to find that she was there. As a haven she plunged into it and closed the door behind her to shut out the horrors she had witnessed. Predominant in her mind at that minute was the thought that there was nothing in the whole world so dreadful as the power of riches wrongly used. When she thought back to the peace, the happiness, the sheer beauty of her childhood and her home life, it seemed to her quite impossible that such disaster as had overtaken her had been made possible by the unscrupulous power of one man holding his position through the right of riches dishonestly accumulated. After the passing of her father, after the testing of her own strength, she had found that she was sufficient; that she could take care of herself and of her mother as well. There was the possibility that she might find a confident sort of happiness in facing life and making it clothe and provision her that she never would have found had she gone ahead under her father's sheltering care. She had come dimly to realize that the sheltered life is rather a dull affair. It lacks the spirit, the development, the fraternity that can be found in an equal battle with other men and women for food and shelter.

Then had come the final blow. The Morelands had heaped dishonour upon her. From that hour she had felt that to be vindicated was the only thing that life held in store for her. Now the thing had happened. A thousand people had rushed around her. They had almost crushed her in their desire to touch her, to weep with her, to tell her that they always had known that she never could have been guilty. And there had been an impulse hot in her soul to cry out at them: "Why, then, was I deserted? Why, then, was I left alone? Why, then, did you not rise up and make the thing that happened to me impossible as you have made it impossible for the work of the Morelands upon their fellow men to continue?"

The thing that dazed her, that kept sleep from her eyes, the knowledge of how weary she was from her brain, and sent her wandering from one room to another all through the night, and at the break of day, to the little gold bird that still sang in her window, to the garden, and from the garden to the pigeons, and from the pigeons to the calves, and back again to the cases of her father's books and to the pictured faces of Mahlon and Elizabeth—the one thing that she found predominant out of the whole matter, the one thing that in the end mounted above everything else, was the fact that

Jason had doubted her, that because he doubted her, he had made another woman his wife, the mother of the child that should have been hers.

All the morning Mahala struggled to understand him. She tried to tell her heart that it was because of the scorching humiliations he had endured in his youth, the worst of which she now understood she had never realized. It was the taunts that had been flung at him, the loneliness of his unloved childhood, that had influenced him in his decision not to make any woman concerning whom there was a shadow of doubt, the mother of his child. It was not in the power of a woman like Mahala to gauge the depth of physical passion, to understand the force that drove Jason, in addition to the knowledge that he had found the money where he supposed she had, in some way, managed to have it placed.

Throughout the day, Mahala found her heart crying out achingly and unceasingly over Jason's lack of confidence in her. She had learned that she could spare the rest of the world. They might think what they pleased. It was Jason alone who mattered. In living over the previous day in her tortured wanderings about the house, through the orchard, in the dead stillness that always precedes a summer storm, she found herself speaking aloud at times. She cried to the walls of her room: "Oh, Jason, I would not have doubted you, if I had seen you take the money myself!"

To the trees of the old orchard she stretched out her arms. She said to them: "If it had been Jason, I'd have known that there had to be some explanation. I'd have felt that anything else might have happened except that he could have been guilty."

Across the road and down a few rods farther, Jason had reached his home and Ellen in a condition that alarmed her. He had tried to tell her what had happened. He had tried to explain to her, but she had felt that he was speaking as if there were a weight upon his heart and brain that was almost more than he could endure. She had felt that he scarcely realized what he was saying to her. She had tried to feed him; she had wept over him; she had rejoiced with him that there could be no stain upon his name and upon his birthright, and through it all she had seen that he did not hear her, that he did not care for anything she might say or anything she might do. Then she watched him stagger across the road and start toward Mahala's house.

She stood awhile meditating. She decided that probably there were things that she might do. She ought to go herself and prepare some food. She might give Mahala the comfort of playing with the baby while she worked. She was half in doubt as to whether she should go, and yet she could think of many reasonable excuses. She realized that it was on slow feet that she walked down the road carrying the baby that every day was growing a heavier burden for her slight young shoulders. She was thinking a queer thing as she went along. He was heavier to carry when he was asleep than when he was awake. Asleep, he lay a dead weight on her arms; awake he clung around her neck, he scattered his weight over her chest and shoulders. She was surprised that she had thought this out for herself.

As she reached the gate, she was saying to herself: "He's a dead weight asleep. He's not near so heavy when he's awake!"

Seeing that the front door was closed, she followed the narrow path of hard-beaten earth running around the house. As she came to the big clump of lilacs at the corner, she heard Mahala's voice cry, "Jason!"

Through the lilac bushes she saw that Jason had fallen at Mahala's back door. He was lying face down upon the ground, either exhausted or unconscious. She stood one instant in paralysed apprehension. The thing that kept her from movement was the look that was upon Mahala's face as she crossed the back porch and went to him. Ellen saw that Mahala's skirts were drawn back and there was a look of scorn and repulsion on her face. It was quite out of the girl's power to move. She merely stood and stared at them. As she watched, she saw a slow change pass over Mahala. She saw her clenched hands relax; she saw her face soften and break up; she saw a quiver come to her lips and big tears squeeze from her eyes; she saw her fall on her knees beside Jason, and with unsuspected strength, lift and turn his body. She saw Mahala take Jason's head on her lap and lean over him; she saw her hands slip under his vest and down to the region of his heart. She caught the torn note of agony in Mahala's voice as she cried to him: "Jason, have the Morelands killed you, too?"

Then Ellen saw Mahala lose her self-control. She stood watching her as she took Jason's head in her arms and kissed him from brow to lips.

"Jason! Oh, Jason! I understand you now! I know that you've always loved me. But you couldn't, you simply couldn't, make me the mother of your child when you thought it would be born through me to the suffering you have known. Oh, Jason, it wasn't fair of you! Your love always has been mine! Your very body is mine! Your child should have been mine!"

As Mahala talked she smoothed his hair, she beat his hands, she tried with her fingers to make his eyes open. Ellen stood and watched. When Jason came to his senses and realized where he was, she saw him look up at Mahala, and then she saw him cover his face with his hands. She watched with a kind of dumb indifference while his body was torn and racked with the deep sobbing that seemed to rend him through and through.

She saw Mahala kneeling before him, looking at him. She heard her saying to him: "I understand now, Jason. I understand you now!"

She watched him struggle to a rising posture. She saw him reach out his hands and help Mahala to her feet. She heard a voice that she did not know crying: "Great God! What have I done? If I had not been a common thing, a vile thing, myself, I might have known!"

Then Mahala laid her hands on his arm. She looked up at him and said quietly: "Square your shoulders, Jason. You've got to adjust them to the burden they must carry for the rest of your life. We both know now, but we must finish our lives as if we didn't."

Then Ellen saw Jason lean forward. She saw his strong hands reach out. She heard him cry: "Mahala, you know, you always have known, how I love you. If there had been in me the manhood to wait for this hour, would you have been mine?"

She watched Mahala lay both her hands in his. She saw her look at Jason for a long time. She saw the smile of ecstasy that broke over her face. She heard a sweetness she never before had heard in the tones of a human voice as Mahala said: "Why, Jason, when I think it all out, I can't remember the time when my heart was not fighting your battles for you—when I didn't love you."

Standing there, Ellen saw Jason gather Mahala in his arms, lift her clear of the ground, and kiss her face, her hair, her shoulders, even, in a passion of utter despair.

Then Ellen came in for her share of the Moreland tragedy. She turned softly. Lightly she picked her steps around the house. She flashed through the gate; with flying feet she ran back down the road to her home. She had forgotten how heavy the baby was. There seemed to be wings on her feet. When she reached home, she laid him in his cradle because that was the thing she was accustomed to doing when he was asleep. Then she dropped on her knees beside him and caught his little hands, and without caring whether she awoke him or not, she laid them against her face, on her throat, on her eyes, on her hair. At last she found her voice.

She told him: "Your father does not love me. He loves Mahala. He always has loved her. He is really hers and you should be hers. Oh, Baby, tell me what I must do!"

She was kneeling there in a sort of dull lethargy when Jason staggered back home, bowed by the weight of the crucifying revelation that Mahala always had loved him; that he had sacrificed her love; that he had thrown away the beauty of her soul and her body through his doubt of her.

As he stepped inside his door and saw Ellen kneeling beside the cradle, her unheeding head being rumpled and battered by the uncertain hands of the baby, he wondered for a moment. Then he stepped over to her and lifted her to her feet, and then he saw her distorted, pain-tortured face, and there he learned, that in some way, she knew. There was only one way in which she could know. Even then he revealed an inherent fineness. He made no accusation.

He said to her gently: "You felt that you would be needed? You followed me?"

Ellen assented. Then he was speaking again.

"You saw us? You heard what we said?"

She bowed her head in acquiescence.

Jason released her and dropped into the nearest chair, and Ellen sank down again beside the cradle and buried her face in the baby's clothing. Finally, Jason could endure no more. He went over to Ellen and lifted her up; he helped her to a chair.

With a halting voice and stricken eyes of misery she said to him: "Because you found that pocket book when you were fixing up the house, you thought that in some way she'd had it put there?"

Jason nodded.

In the passion of her agony, she cried at him: "How could you? Any one so delicate, so beautiful—why, I have always known she never could have done it! I couldn't have loved her if I had thought her a common thief."

Before the storm of her wrath Jason stood bowed and helpless. She seemed a long way from him, and yet he could hear her voice crying at him: "You loved her. You would work for her, you would take care of her, but you had not the manhood to wait for her hour of vindication!"

Then Jason spoke: "When I found the money hidden in her house, I thought there never could be such a thing as vindication. With my own hands I hid it where it never would have been discovered, waiting for the hour when she should come to me and tell me herself that she had taken it."

Ellen cried to him: "And now, what are you going to do?"

He looked at her helplessly. The finger she was pointing toward the cradle was shaking but her voice was clear: "You are giving her your love. You have given me your child. What are you going to do?"

So these two souls battled in agony during an evening of that tense stillness which almost always presages heavy storm in the Central States. The elements outside seemed in keeping with the inside strain when a sudden wind sprang up and boiling yellow clouds were driven before it, and heavy black ones took their place. In a short time their world was enveloped in thick darkness, broken by the flash of lightning, the jarring of thunder and dangerous winds.

Worn out at last with nerve strain, Ellen stood up. She faced Jason, crying: "You haven't been fair. You had no right to make me the mother of your child when you knew in your heart that you didn't love me. It isn't truly mine. Martin Moreland robbed Mahala of her people, her home, her wealth. He would have taken her honour if he could. And how much better are you? You have robbed her heart of the love of a lifetime. I heard her say it. And, at the same time, you robbed her of motherhood. Your child belongs to her, not to me! You may take it to her!"

Jason had endured nerve strain almost to the limit. He was at that dumb place where the brain ceases to function for itself. He realized that he might have had Mahala in his home and in his arms if he had kept firm rein on his physical nature and had had Ellen's faith in her. The foundations of his life had been shaken. It seemed to him that nothing further could happen. He was past thinking clearly for himself. The first thought that came to his muddled brain was one of protest.

"No, Ellen, no!" he said. "That can't be done! You're insane to think of it!"

Nerve strain works one way with some people; it works differently with others. First Ellen had cried until she was exhausted. Then she had argued until she could think no further. When she reached her decision, at that time she had meant what she said. She proved the courage of her convictions by lifting the baby from its cradle, wrapping the blanket around it, and thrusting it into Jason's arms.

She opened the door, and with apparent calmness and deliberation, she said to him: "I have told you until I'm tired. That child does not belong to me. You may take it to its real mother."

Jason took the baby because he did not know what else to do. But he stood shaking his head.

"You can't do this, Ellen," he said to her pleadingly. "For God's sake, try to understand that you can't give away your baby!"

Ellen caught up the words. "Give away my baby?" she repeated after him. "It is not I who give it away. It is you. You gave it to me when it belonged to Mahala. I tell you to take it to her!"

She pushed him into the night and closed the door behind him, regardless of the storm into which she was thrusting him. Then Jason's soul knew fear. He was worn to the marrow with as keen suffering as any man can experience. Every nerve in his body was strained to the breaking point and a ghastly nausea possessed him inside. There was only one rational thought in his head. He must get the baby out of that storm. He must do what he had been told.

He was reeling like an intoxicated man as he staggered blindly down the road through the wildly gathering storm which broke in a torrent as he reached Mahala's door. He realized that he might have been unable to find her door if her house had not been filled with light. Evidently, she was nervous and afraid. He could see light in every room of the house, and as he stumbled toward it, he could see Mahala's figure passing from room to room, and he knew that she was alone and that she was afraid.

There was in his heart a fear that his knock might frighten her further, so he called at the same time. He heard her footsteps flying across the floor, and she swung the door wide. He stepped through it, already drenched, with the face and eyes of a stranger, huddling the baby against his breast.

As Mahala closed the door, she stepped back to the centre of the room. Jason held out the bundle to her. He was past the point of trying to screen her. He was past anything except a parrot-like utterance of what he had been told.

With no preliminaries, he said to Mahala: "Ellen saw us this afternoon. She won't have her baby any longer, because she knows now that I never really loved her. She made me bring it to you. She says, because I love you, my child is yours."

Mahala held out her palms before her as if to keep back an enemy. Every trace of colour faded from her face. Her eyes stretched their widest in amazement. She had been trying to think, trying to plan, trying to reason, all the afternoon, and the conclusion she had reached was, that to the end of their days, she and Jason must travel different roads, each carrying a burden upon their tortured shoulders, the weight of which they must learn to endure. But here was the climax. This was the worst of all. They might not even be permitted to suffer together. All afternoon she had been thinking: "Ellen has had nothing to do with this. She is perfectly innocent. She must never know."

And now, smashing as the crash of the lightning outside, she was facing the terrible knowledge that Ellen did know, and that she had practically lost her reason through that knowledge. Her heart was primitive like the heart of every other woman. She had seen her man, she had loved him, she had taken his head on her breast, she had given him all she had to give. And through youth and inexperience, through willingness to believe, she had believed that she was having all that he had to give in return. Now she knew that she had had nothing. She had merely been an instrument. This knowledge had driven her to frenzy.

And this was the thing that Mahala now had to face. Through the months of torture that she had experienced, striking her first in the heart, then in the brain, and then physically, she had learned what this must mean to Ellen.

She could only cry: "Impossible! Quite impossible!"

Jason advanced toward her, holding out the baby. It had awakened with the flashes of lightning and the jarring of the thunder. Throwing up its little arms, it pushed the blanket back, revealing its face, the soft, curling brown hair, the pink cheeks, the delicately veined temples. The little fellow knew Mahala. She was his beloved playmate. He reached his hands toward her, crowing and laughing and begging to be taken for one of the romps he was accustomed to indulging in with her. He liked spatting her cheeks with his hands. He liked to tousle her hair. He liked her kisses on his hands and his feet and the back of his neck and all over his little head.

Mahala retreated until she was pressed flat against the wall. Even her hands, as they stretched out at her sides, were hard pressed, palm to the wall, behind her. She could go no farther. She was a tortured thing brought to bay. Jason advanced.

"You've got to take him," he said in a voice torn with suffering. "You've got to take him!"

Then Mahala began to cry. She looked at Jason imploringly.

"What does my heart know of the heart of a child beating beneath it?" she said to him. "How are my dry breasts to furnish life for another woman's baby?"

Jason still pressed the child toward her. Mahala became primitive. The strength of temper that had always characterized her swept through her. She lifted her head shamelessly. She used the lids of her eyes to squeeze the tears from them. Her voice was stern and relentless as she said to Jason: "You big fool! Ellen can't give away her baby. Haven't you got the sense to see it? It's bone of her bone and flesh of her flesh. Take it back to her and make her listen to reason! Make her see that a real woman couldn't possibly give up her baby. You would drive her as insane as your father did Rebecca."

"You're right," said Jason.

He wrapped the blanket around the child, turned its face to his breast, and started toward the door. As he opened it, there was a horrible crash. He was blinded with running streaks of lightning till he staggered back. There was the ripping sound of a bolt that had struck something solid so close that it rocked the house. He turned appealingly to Mahala. She darted past him and pushed shut the door.

"Wait!" she said. "Wait till I get the lantern, I'll go to Ellen with you. I can make her understand better than you can."

Jason looked down at the small bundle struggling in his arms. "I ought not take the boy out in this," he said. "We might be struck."

Mahala shook her head. "Ellen can't be left alone. We've got to go. Some terrible thing will happen."

Mahala hurried to the kitchen to find and light the lantern. For one second she stood at the window, her hands cupped around her face, trying to peer through the darkness, to see if the lights were burning in Jason's house. She would not have been surprised to see great tongues of flame leaping from it, but the rain was beating in sheets against the window, small branches and wet leaves were plastered on it and a black bird, blown from its shelter among the bushes, struck the glass and slid down, white lights streaming from its green eyes, its wings outspread, its breast bleeding.

As the door closed behind Jason, Ellen had turned and fallen across the empty cradle. As she raised herself, her hands struck the warm sheets and the little pillow where the baby's head had lain. On her knees staring into it, there came the first realization of what she had done. She had sent her baby to be mothered by another woman. Dazed at the tragedy that had befallen her, she caught up the little pillow and held it warm against her face and then her empty arms folded around it.

Suddenly she was on her feet. She threw the pillow back into the cradle and sprang to the door. She opened it wide and screamed into the night: "Jason! Jason! Bring back my baby!"

She bent her head and tried to hear his voice in answer. But the wind howled past her. Flying leaves and branches and a dust storm from the road almost blinded her as she tried to raise her voice, to scream with all her might: "Jason! Jason!"

She realized that she could not make him hear her above the fury of the storm. She realized that she had only a minute. The rain would come in torrents very soon. With her arms extended before her to protect her face and breast, she rushed into the night. She found the gate and started down the road. With every flare of lightning she could see a few yards in advance of her. Until the next flare, she was in darkness. The wind blew her wide skirts so tightly around her that she could scarcely step. She realized that she could not have found her way had it not been for the light in

Mahala's house. That she could see, and she tried to go straight toward it. The difficulty in running told her that she had lost the road, but so long as she could see the light, she knew that she must reach the house. Once she had a fight to extricate herself from a thicket of bushes and then she ran into a big tree, and the tree told her where she was. She was very near the house now. This was a friendly tree in whose shelter she liked to walk whenever she went to Mahala's house. She had stopped beneath it to pick up shining acorns for the baby to play with. She had seen the squirrels racing up and down it. She had seen great, horned owls spread their wings and sail from their day-time shelter among its heavy, gnarled branches. It was almost like meeting a friend in a time of extremity.

She threw her arms around it and laid her face against it and waited for the next flare of lightning to show her how to find the road again, but following that flash there came a dreadful bolt that struck the oak tree, rending it from top to base.

Through the most terrific storm she ever had experienced, holding the lantern high above her, Mahala stumbled down the foot path beside the fence trying to light the way for Jason who kept as close behind her as he could with the baby's face buried in his breast. Trying to see her way ahead of her, Mahala stumbled over the body of Ellen lying in a crumpled heap at the foot of the oak tree. The flickering glare of the rain-dripping lantern showed her still face and the splintered tree beside her.

Wordless, Mahala set down the lantern and held out her arms for the child. Jason gave the baby to her and lifted Ellen. Mahala picked up the lantern, and they carried Ellen home and laid her on her bed. The baby had fallen asleep and they put him in his cradle and covered him. Then they knelt, one on each side of Ellen, and sobbed out the pain, the grief, and the torture that had torn their hearts to the limit of endurance.

CHAPTER XXIII

"The Flag on Its Journey"

Stumblingly Marcia made her way from the alley, and finding the nearest livery stable, she had some difficulty in persuading a man to drive her to Bluffport. During that ride she realized only one thing. The hand of God had intervened and she was forever freed from the power of either of the Morelands. Never again need she fear the Martin Moreland whom she had last seen clutching the white flag and babbling over Rebecca's speech. Never again need she fear the sardonic smile, the merciless cruelty of the beautiful boy, who, with the utmost politeness, had taken the revolver from her shaking hands with a deep bow and a gay, "Permit me," and with no instant of hesitation had discharged it into his own breast. He must have known that no escape was left him and that the wrath of Jason would be as inexorable as Fate itself. He had preferred escaping all of them in his own way. Abominable as he had been, Marcia was almost stunned at herself as she rode through the night thinking things over, to find that she had been unable, either when she stood before him alone, or as she watched from the closet during the appearance of Jason and Mahala, to keep from admiring Junior. She found herself saying to the darkness: "What a wonderful man he might have been! How lovable, how brave!"

It comforted her heart as they came down the main street of Bluffport, to see a light in the back of the Bodkin Millinery, to know that there was food and a warm welcome awaiting her. In a few minutes more she was sobbing in utter abandonment on the narrow breast of Nancy. After she had regained her composure and Nancy had done everything to comfort and to console her, they sat until almost daybreak talking things over.

When she had rehearsed every detail of the day, Marcia lifted her head: "I think," she said, "that I am as safe at last as I ever can be. Jason will never do anything to harm me. All the mentality Martin Moreland has left will be occupied from now on with fulfilling the curse set upon him by Rebecca. I truly believe that I have nothing further to fear."

Nancy sat thinking for a long time. Then she looked at Marcia and said softly: "And now, Marcia, will you listen to the minister?"

Marcia sat a long time in deep thought, and then she said quietly: "To have the love of a good man, to have the home and the security that he would give me if he did not know, might be a wonderful thing. But I could not marry him without telling him, because, so surely as I did not, some way, some of my graves would open and the dead would confront me; and there is the child that I would not be considered suitable to mother. The only way I can see out of it is for you and me to go on together making the best that we can of life."

It hurt Nancy Bodkin sorely to see Marcia suffer. She had a pang, too, for the minister, but deep in her heart she was ashamed of herself for the little throb of rejoicing that sprang up at Marcia's words. She might dismiss her remotest fear. Nothing ever could sever their partnership or spoil their friendship; until one or the other of them lay down in the final sleep, the Bodkin Millinery would go on doing business and each of the partners would give to the other the undivided devotion of a sincere heart.

When another winter had run its course, under the old apple trees of May, Jason sat on a bench in the orchard with young Jason on his lap. Kneeling in front of them, Mahala was playing a game almost as old as babies. Holding up one pink, bare toe for every line, she chanted:

"This is a fat king, out for a ride,
This is a fair queen, close by his side.
This a tall soldier on guard with his gun;
This a fine lady who walks in the sun.
This is a baby curled up in his bed,
Here go all of them over your head!"

Jason and Mahala laughed together with gleeful shouts from the baby.

As she lifted her head to push back her hair, Mahala glanced down the road and a flicker of white slowly coming beside the river caught her attention. She said nothing, but she kept watching, and after a time she recognized a tottering figure, bowed and stumbling along slowly.

The penetrant sun of spring was beating mercilessly upon Martin Moreland's old white head. When Jason realized who the traveller was, he drew back repulsed, but Mahala arose, and as Martin Moreland came past the odorous lilacs and across the grass toward them, she motioned him to a seat. He refused to be seated, but he drew himself together the best he could and made her a courtly bow.

In a wavering voice he said to her: "Beautiful little lady, you seem strangely familiar to me, yet I do not recall your name."

Fearing that her name might awaken unpleasant memories that would produce such an attack as in her childhood she had seen Rebecca suffer from, Mahala merely smiled at him and said: "Names do not matter. Was there something you wanted?"

Martin Moreland tried to stand straight. He struggled till the pain of the effort to think was visible on his face; but at last he gave up.

"There was a reason for my coming," he said, "but I regret to say that I cannot at the present minute recall it."

In a low voice at her side Jason said to Mahala: "Send him away. I can't endure the sight of him."

Mahala lifted her hand to silence Jason. Patiently she said to the old man: "Maybe I can help you to remember what it is that you have forgotten. Did you want to tell me something, or was it Jason?"

At that name Martin Moreland lifted his head. A flash of memory came back to him.

"I want Jason," he said. "I wanted my son, Jason. He is the only friend that I have left in all the world. I am old, I am tired, I am tortured, I lack food. I have come to beg of him only a crust of bread."

Mahala went into the house. She brought food and drink. She helped Martin Moreland to seat himself securely upon the chair she brought. She tried to relieve him of the white flag, but he would not allow it to be taken from his fingers. With one hand he clutched it tightly. With the other he took the glass of milk Mahala offered him, but he was shaking so that he could only lift it to his lips with her help. The food he did not touch at all.

He rested a few minutes and then he arose and extended the white flag. He lifted his face to the skies and with more strength and sureness in his voice, he cried: "Behold the emblem of purity. Clean hearts may pass under with God's blessing. Come, ye workers of darkness, wash your hearts clean by passing under the white flag!"

Mahala gently turned Martin Moreland's face toward the road again. She led him to the gate and pointed in the direction of Ashwater. "I think," she said, "that there are a number of sinful people coming along the highway. No doubt many of them will be glad to pass under your flag."

"Thank you, little lady," said Martin Moreland. "Thank you. Now that you suggest it, I believe that is the case. I will go forward in my work of upholding the white emblem of purity. I wish you a very happy good day!"

Mahala went back and once more dropped on her knees beside Jason. She put one arm around him and the other around the baby, and buried a face of compassion against the hearts of both of them. Until it faded from sight, they watched the bowed, lean figure trudging the River Road, the flag flashing white in the sunlight.

THE END